PIRATES OF THE
NARROW SEAS 4

Heart of Oak

M. KEI

KEIBOOKS
PERRYVILLE, MARYLAND, USA
2011

ISBN 978-0615513638

Printed in the United States of America, 2011.

KEIBOOKS
P O Box 516
Perryville, MD 21903

PIRATES OF THE NARROW SEAS

BOOK ONE: THE SALLEE ROVERS
BOOK TWO: MEN OF HONOR
BOOK THREE: IRON MEN
BOOK FOUR: HEART OF OAK

The ebook versions of the series are published by Bristlecone Pine Press, Portland, Maine

POETRY BY M. KEI

Slow Motion: The Log of a Chesapeake Bay Skipjack
Heron Sea: Short Poems of the Chesapeake Bay
Catzilla: Tanka, Kyoka and Gogyoshi about Cats (editor)
Take Five: Best Contemporary Tanka. (editor-in-chief)
Fire Pearls: Short Masterpieces of the Human Heart (editor)
Atlas Poetica: A Journal of Poetry of Place in Contemporary Tanka (editor)

TABLE OF CONTENTS

CHAPTER 1: CHRISTMAS EVE

The *Amphitrite* turned her head into Algeciras Bay as the sun sank in the west. Long shadows of Spanish mountains reached across the grey waters to lap at the foot of the Rock whose silhouette they had come to know well over the course of the autumn. They had run messages back and forth between Britain and the Mediterranean, alternating the cold, damp days in England with the cool, dry days of southern Spain. Third lieutenant Peter Thorton had more reason than anyone else on the quarterdeck to look forward to shore leave: his lover was waiting for him in Gibraltar. No one but he knew it. If the Service ever found out, it would be the noose for him. Article Twenty-Eight of the *Articles of War* prescribed death for any man guilty of the abominable crime of sodomy or buggery.

"Mr. Thorton, a word with you." Captain Horner was a tall, thin man with pale blue eyes and a dour face. He was standing to windward where he watched the winter sea and sky in the lonely splendor of a captain's right.

"Aye, sir." Thorton presented himself and stood to attention.

Horner spoke meditatively. "'Tis Christmas Eve. Tomorrow we celebrate the birth of our Savior."

Thorton grew cold. "Aye, sir."

Horner studied him. "For a follower of the Prophet Mohammed, 'tis just another day."

"That is true, sir."

"I am giving all my officers shore leave so that we may attend midnight services at the chapel. Will you come with us?"

Thorton said quietly, "By your leave, I'd rather not, sir."

Horner nodded. "I thought as much, but I wanted to offer you the choice."

Thorton's tenor voice was so soft that only Horner could hear it, "There is no God worthy of worship but Allah and Mohammed is His prophet."

Horner acknowledged Thorton's words with a slight tip of his chin. "I hope you will not mind it very much if I ask you to keep the ship so that Master Blakesley may have shore leave."

In the months since Thorton had converted to Islam he had made it through many cold and awkward moments, but this was the coldest and most awkward of them all. He glanced over at the lee side where the other officers were gathered to gaze with impatient anticipation

7

towards the lights of Gibraltar. He longed to go with them, to experience the fellowship of a religious service with his brother officers, and to lift his voice in songs known by heart since he was a child. The reassuring glimmer of candlelight on stained glass, the incense in the air, the warmth of a luminous and crowded church . . . These things were barred forever to Peter Thorton. After the service he could have called upon Master and Commander Alan Abby in his snug suite of rooms. He could have spent the night in warm comfort with a fire on the grate and his arms around his lover as they snuggled deep into a feather bed.

No one knew that Thorton had a lover waiting for him. No one could know. He wanted very much to spend his night ashore in the safe haven of Abby's arms, but he schooled himself to show no reaction. Blakesley, as ship's master, was part of the standing crew and rarely granted shore leave. He and the other warrant officers stayed on board when the lieutenants and midshipmen were roistering in the town. Blakesley was a hardworking Christian man who would be deeply grateful to his captain for a favor so unexpected.

"I shall be happy to stay with the ship, sir," Thorton replied. "I had planned to call upon Commander Abby when I went ashore. Will you convey my felicitations of the season to him, please?"

"I will be delighted to do so."

"I have a present for him. Will you deliver that also?"

Horner peered at him from beneath shaggy blond brows. "Of course."

Horner and Thorton were of equal height, both blond and blue-eyed, wearing navy blue frock coats and matching breeches, but there the resemblance ended. Horner had a thin build while Thorton was solid. The captain was ten years older and his hair was thinning while Thorton had a thick braid of blond hair bound with a black ribbon. Horner was also a widower with children. He knew exactly how he differed from his most junior lieutenant in that regard.

Thoughtfully he said, "You may slaughter the lamb for Christmas dinner tomorrow. Please make a few remarks on my behalf to the men obliged to stay aboard. Something about their sacrifice in parting from those they love would be appropriate."

With those words Thorton knew that Horner had guessed. "Aye aye, sir." He dared say nothing more, and fortunately, naval protocol did not require him to. "Happy Christmas, sir. I hope you enjoy your run ashore."

Horner was even giving himself shore leave; he had already told them that he planned to grant leave to every man possible. Those left behind would clean and fumigate the ship with vinegar, air out the bilges, careen her boots and tops, take on water, wood, and victuals, replace her worn out sails, and other routine chores. It would be physically demanding work, but not difficult. Meanwhile, the commissioned officers were free to spend the holidays drinking themselves stupid, to return hungover and broke on the second of January.

"I'll send you a relief on the twenty-seventh," Horner replied.

"That's not necessary, sir."

"The lieutenants will rotate in turn on board. I'll be back within the week myself. You need your shore leave as much as the rest of us."

"Thank you, sir."

"Mr. Blakesley!"

"Aye aye, sir." The man presented himself. He was shorter than either of the two blond officers, stout, greying, solid, and dependable.

"Mr. Thorton has agreed to remain with the ship so you may go ashore. A week of shore leave for you, sir."

Blakesley's jaw dropped. He grabbed his captain's hand and kissed it, then turned to Thorton to shake his hand. He was nearly overcome with emotion. "You are very kind, sir. I am in your debt."

Thorton smiled wanly as he squeezed his hand. "Not at all."

"Your mates will be granted two days each in turn until we have finished fitting out. I'll leave orders." Each man would get three or four turns ashore that way, but hopefully would not drink themselves into a stupor or go broke, knowing that they had to return to the ship in short order.

"Thank you, sir! They will be most grateful!"

"That will be all."

The quarterdeck hands had naturally eavesdropped and began to sing at their work. Horner snapped, "Silence! You aren't ashore yet!"

The men grinned and worked silently, but their good spirits were bubbling over nonetheless. Just after dark the men lined up on deck with their kits over their shoulders, impatiently waiting their turn to be ferried ashore. The men working the oars made trip after trip back and forth between the ship and the shore. Once their feet hit shore, the sailors started singing—and they weren't Christmas carols. The rest of the town was in much the same condition. Various vessels had let their crews go ashore for Christmas Eve services. Some of them had been there for days and were already soused—and likely to remain so despite the religious nature of the holiday. Nothing could dissuade a British seaman that Christmas was his day to get roaring, stinking drunk.

After Horner and the other officers were ashore, Thorton climbed the ladder to the nearly deserted quarterdeck. It was eerie to have so few people aboard. They seemed lost, like a handful of farthings rattling around the bottom of what had once been a treasure chest brimming with gold. They stood at the rail gazing toward the lights of Gibraltar. The whole town was lit up with candles in the windows and carriages rattling along the streets for Christmas Eve services, but it was a silent scene. The ships at their anchors were too far away to hear the hymns sung for the glory of God, or the thankful prayers of men who had been delivered from the sea one more time. The ship's lanterns were surrounded by halos of light as snowflakes began to drift down from above. Snow was uncommon in Gibraltar, but by God, it was snowing for Christmas.

Thorton was despondent in the extreme, but he was now, however briefly, in command of a fifth-rate British warship. The ranking officer remaining was the bluff-faced Scottish boatswain. "MacDonald!"

"Aye, sir?"

"Set a picket to row round the ship tonight."

"D'ye think the Spanish will get up to mischief, sir?"

Thorton glanced over to where the lights of Algeciras could be seen on the opposite shore. "I doubt it. Barcelona is keeping them busy. However, that doesn't mean some of our own men won't try to grant themselves a little extra shore leave, or harlots come aboard."

"Aye aye, sir. I hae fended off a rum-seller already, but nae harlots. They've got an easy touch in town tonight. They'll be making money even if they're besom ugly and stane drunk."

Thorton sighed. "You're probably right, MacDonald."

"A wee bit like the auld days, don't you think, sir?" MacDonald had been one of the men stranded on a sinking galley with Thorton the previous April.

"Chilly and foul weather? Yes, I think so." Thorton looked involuntarily south towards Africa.

"What do the Mohammedans do for Christmas, sir?"

"Nothing, MacDonald. They honor Jesus as a prophet like Moses and Abraham, nothing more."

MacDonald nodded. "Ah weel, there's tae much popery in Christmas onieway. Did ye hear? They say the king hae set up an evergreen tree inside o' the palace like the Germans do." He tsked at the thought of such foreign customs.

"Dear God. I'm going to have to read the Christmas service!" Thorton suddenly realized.

"George Plumm was a Quaker preacher afore he was pressed. Ye could ask him to read the service."

"Pass the word for Plumm."

"Aye aye, sir." MacDonald turned and bellowed, "George Plumm to the quarterdeck!"

With the matter of the divine service safely in the hands of a putative minister, Thorton retired below for the evening. He had been in charge for only an hour on the quietest night of the year and his nerves were already shot. He would have found it easier to fight a pair of Spanish frigates with damp powder.

CHAPTER 2: CUTTING OUT PARTY

Thorton huddled in his hammock and felt sorry for himself. The night was cold and it penetrated the oaken hull of the *Amphitrite*. He missed Abby. Even with wool socks his feet were still cold. Had his lover been curled up next to him the winter night would have been bearable.

"Ahoy the ship!" someone called. The sound was muffled by the hull, but the sleepless lieutenant heard it clearly in the silence of the night.

"What boat?" the watch called back.

The exchange that followed was quieter and Thorton could not make it out. Still, a boat coming in the middle of the night required his attention. Dispatches, perhaps? He put his legs into his breeches and his feet into his shoes. He donned his coat over his nightshirt. Nightcap still on his head, he went on deck.

"Officer on deck!" the watch called.

The men startled to attention.

"As you were," Thorton replied.

They relaxed and went back to watching the boat. Thorton looked over the side. "Who is it?" he asked MacDonald.

MacDonald grinned at him and said, "Abenfysverchlefan."

"Speak English, man!"

"Peter!" called out a new voice. Somebody was standing up in the boat, taking off his hat, and showing the smoked glasses he wore balanced on his nose. He wore a dark grey cloak over his civilian suit.

"Alan Abby!" Thorton shouted. He laughed. "Why aren't you in church?"

"I was! The service is over. I thought I'd pay a call on you and wish you good cheer, if I may, Mister Thorton."

"Of course! Come up!"

The boat bumped against the ship's side and the sailors hooked onto the chains. The blind commander groped, found the battens, and climbed up. He came through the entry port with MacDonald piping the call for a commander. Men hastily lined up to present arms. They had only a dozen marines left on board and they were all in their smocks or peacoats. Their scarlet coats were neatly stowed until needed. The late hours of Christmas Eve was not a time any of them expected to be called to duty.

"Let me give you a kiss of Christian fellowship," Abby said mischievously. So Thorton let Abby peck him on the cheek, then returned the favor. He couldn't help grinning from ear to ear. Abby tucked his hand into Thorton's elbow. "I've brought a valise. I thought I might stay a day or two. If you'd like company."

"Of course I do! We're delighted to have you. You'll make the days brighter," Thorton assured him. The valise was passed up and Thorton snagged it with his free hand. They went down the companionway together.

"Is there anyone in the wardroom?" Abby asked.

The wardroom of the *Amphitrite* was a comfortably club-like space. The arched doorways between the wardroom and the rest of the gundeck had green baize drapes to close them off. The mizzenmast was forward of the bulkhead, so they had a long oak table for their mess with benches on either side. Louvered doors shut each officers' cabin, and carved scallop shells ornamented the woodwork around the windows. The walls and doors were painted white, but the woodwork was light green.

"Not a soul. Horner gave every one of them shore leave."

"Good!" Abby threw his arms around Thorton's neck and kissed him passionately.

Thorton groaned softly and kissed him back. The smaller man was slim and firm and warm in his arms, and the blood coursed more hotly in his veins. Abby hugged his shoulders tightly and whispered fiercely, "I missed you! It was cruel of Horner to deny you shore leave."

"I'll have a few days after Christmas. I'll come to you then. Did he give you my present?"

"He did. When he left, I opened it immediately. The shawl is lovely. He'd be scandalized if he knew."

"I think he guessed," Thorton replied.

Abby made a face. "He did it to spite us, the bastard."

Thorton shook his head. "No, he didn't. But never mind that. You're here. Come to bed. 'Tis cold tonight!"

They proceeded to make themselves very warm in Thorton's berth, so it was well that there were no neighbors in the wardroom.

Much later they snuggled together in the hammock. With the blankets tucked tight around them and wool socks on their feet, they were cozy warm. The ship was very quiet around them. Only the watch and picket boat were awake. The rest of the minimal crew was sound asleep in their hammocks. Half of them were snoring drunk, having managed to get their hands on liquor only God knew how—nothing beat a British sailor for ingenuity when it came to liquor.

Thorton was falling asleep when Abby whispered, "What was that?"

"I don't know," Thorton replied, opening his eyes. He listened carefully. Knowing the ship as well as he did, he could tell that something had changed.

They both listened intently. The sounds came again: muffled curses and the soft scrape of shoes at the stern of the vessel.

Thorton was instantly awake. "My God. We're being boarded!"

The two hastily tumbled out of the hammock. Thorton peered through the louvers but could see nothing, so he opened the door a crack. Dark shapes were going past the wardroom windows. Behind him Abby was putting on his breeches and shoes in the dark. Hasty footsteps and thumps overhead told him that the boarders had already gained the quarterdeck.

"*Amphitrite*, awake!" he bellowed. "Tritons, repel boarders! Rise up, ye sea dogs!"

Somebody fired a pistol and the sternlight glass shattered. The ball buried itself in the oak table top. Thorton was blinded by the muzzle flash and fell back into his cabin. Abby darted past him.

"*Amphitrite*, awake! Repel boarders!" the Welsh commander shouted as he ran along the gundeck. Shorter than Thorton, he could duck easily under the beams. He slapped at hammocks and shouted to rouse the sleeping men.

The invaders had no further need for silence. More glass shattered and the thud of a man landing heavily on the wardroom deck sounded near at hand. Thorton leaped forward and tackled the figure. The man had a cutlass, but he lost it when Thorton slammed into him. More glass shattered and more figures leaped through the broken windows.

Spanish was hissed from somewhere close by. An upraised cutlass aimed for Thorton's head, but it didn't fall. Instead he was punched in the stomach. More men piled on him, beat him, and dragged him down. He bit, punched, clawed, kicked, twisted, and rolled, but it was a heap of men against one.

The ship's bell clanged in sudden alarm. The sound carried clearly across the water and woke the other sleeping ships. It carried even to the town. Bell after bell began to ring.

Thorton was held down and his hands bound behind his back by men who worked by feel in the dimness of the wardroom. His mouth was bloody and his head rang from the blows he suffered. Where Abby was he had no idea. He no longer heard his lover's voice calling to the men. The boarders called their signals to each other and rushed the gundeck. Pistols spoke, and British blood spilled on the deck. The anchor cable was cut.

The sails bloomed overhead and the *Amphitrite* gained way as Spanish hands worked her lines. Thorton groaned in despair. The ship had been left in his care, and he had lost her to a Spanish cutting out action. Christmas Eve, with the British lulled, gulled, drunk, asleep, on leave, with hardly any hands to defend themselves . . . Folly, folly. No one had expected a Spanish attack, nor had they thought that the Spanish would choose such a minor target as a fifth rate frigate. A cutting out action might have seized an entire battleship on a night like this.

His captors spit on him. "*¡Renegado! ¡Sódomita!*"

They dragged him out into the cold and trundled him to the quarterdeck. He staggered up the steps, tripped on his nightshirt, and was clubbed across the back of the head for good measure. Stars meandered through his vision as rough hands dragged him to the Spanish lieutenant in charge of the expedition. Thorton blinked and peered, but the man's red breeches and waistcoat might as well have been black in the darkness. A single bull's-eye lantern was unshuttered to light up the captive and permit him to be examined. The captive squinted his eyes and turned his head away. He couldn't see anything in the glare.

"Peter Thorton, heretic and sodomite." The perfect Castilian voice dripped contempt. "I take great pleasure in ruining you as you ruined me. I was busted back to lieutenant and made a laughingstock because of you!"

Thorton couldn't see, but he could hear. He recognized that voice. "Renaldo!" he exclaimed. The man had been the captain of the *San Bartolomeo*, and that had been the beginning of Thorton's highly variegated career. "'Twasn't my fault you were incompetent and a coward. If you had stood your post as I did, none of this would have happened," he retorted.

The man slapped him so hard across the face his head rang. "You're going to pay."

Thorton was instantly immersed in the stink, the filth, and the misery of the *San Bartolomeo*. His vision was filled by the image of naked, filthy, battered slaves, chained like the vilest of beasts, left to drown while Renaldo—*this man*—saved his own skin. Among the galleyslaves was one man abused more than the others, his back a lacerated and infected mess. He was so emaciated and ill he had kept his feet by sheer force of will. The man known to the English as 'Captain Tangle' had been beaten, whipped, starved and humiliated for the crime of being a corsair, and this man, Alonso Renaldo y Villanueva, had been the lord and master of it all.

His revulsion must have showed because Renaldo's gloved hand smashed across his face again. His head snapped and his legs buckled. Even as he crashed to the floor he could not help comparing the two. "Tangle has more honor in his little finger than you do in your entire body."

They beat him for his impudence.

CHAPTER 3: SPANISH VENGEANCE

The sound of pistols came from the fo'c's'le. The man with the bull's-eye lantern swung forward to illuminate a small part of the waist of the ship.

"Order your men to surrender," Lieutenant Renaldo said.

"No," Thorton replied. He spoke Spanish as well as Renaldo did.

"I can't see a damn thing. Go ahead and light the lanthorn," the Spanish lieutenant told his subordinates. The hinge creaked and a moment later the great lamp bathed the quarterdeck in a golden glow.

The Spanish aristocrat was a man of medium height and build with black hair and a small black goatee and mustache. His cloak was thrown back over one arm to reveal the blue uniform coat with a long red waistcoat.

"You cost me my command, my honor, and my reputation. Now I will have my revenge. If you have any decency, which I doubt, you will spare your men."

"Go ahead and kill me. I will never surrender and neither will my men." Thorton's head was ringing, but he didn't care. Everything that had happened to him over the past eight months had been set in motion because this man had not known how to handle the galley he had commanded.

"You'll be tried and hanged as the piratical sodomite you are," Renaldo said. "Then my honor and rank will be restored."

Thorton laughed a breathless laugh. "That won't change the fact I beat a pair of Spanish frigates right here in Algeciras Bay! Were you aboard, *Teniente?* Did I whip you twice?"

Renaldo backhanded Thorton so hard he hurt his own hand. He massaged it and snarled, "Shut him up! Tie him to the mizzenmast!"

They threw Thorton against mast and his legs buckled. He fell down in a heap. They tied him like that with his legs splayed out on the deck and his back pressed to the foot of the mast. The Spanish marines kicked him in the stomach a couple of times for good measure. He doubled over and couldn't talk. The blaze of pain in his middle blotted out the freezing cold seeping through his socks and the cool breeze that cut through his nightshirt like paper.

Somewhere in the winter night a British gun boomed a challenge.

"Hoist the flag of Spain," Renaldo ordered. He looked over his shoulder and added, "Pile on all sail." To the helm he snapped, "Keep her full and by. I don't care which way you go, just go!"

17

Thorton's eyes narrowed as he assessed the *Amphitrite's* position, the wind, and the sails. The helm obliged Renaldo by turning further south. The wind blew over the *Amphitrite's* starboard quarter and she gained speed. The crew the Spaniard had brought with him went aloft to make more sail. Down below a small body kept the remains of the English crew pinned in the forecastle, but the Britons would not surrender.

Thorton closed his eyes. *Dear Allah. Let Abby be safe,* he prayed silently.

Something cold touched his cheek. He opened his eyes to see a thin veil of snowflakes drifting through the light of the lanthorn. He laughed through gritted teeth—Renaldo should have not have lit it. The British could follow him easily. If they followed. Surely they would. A gun boomed close by; it must belong to the *Valiant*; she had been anchored nearby. She would not abandon the chase before it was even started. His hands were pulled behind the mast and tied together by a length of rope, so he was able to struggle to his feet by sliding his arms up the mizzenmast. Standing, he could see over the taffrail. He grinned to see a pair of British frigates tearing after them. Twisting his aching head around, he saw a dot of light out in the bay that was probably the Spanish ship that had launched the cutting out party. It was much further ahead than the British were behind.

The bow chase guns on the British frigates roared and spat tongues of fire. Four pound balls went humming through the air around him. One tore through the lateen mizzensail while the others passed harmlessly to either side. He began to count the seconds. After he counted to two hundred and fifty, the next volley roared. A cannonball smashed into the stern and shattered glass. He heard it slam into the bulkhead beneath his feet and go caroming into the coach. No one was hurt, but it left a trail of debris.

Thorton shivered. When he had stood the quarterdeck in battle he had not been afraid of the shot flying around him; he had been too busy to worry about it. Now he was a helpless prisoner incapable of doing anything else. That he might be killed by friendly fire struck him as grossly unfair, but there was nothing he could do about it. Even if the frigates had known, they would have fired anyhow. One lieutenant was not worth losing an entire frigate.

Standing was cold and drafty, so he slid carefully down in such a way that the nightshirt covered his lower legs as he doubled up on the cold deck. The flannel garment might as well have been lace for all the protection it gave him. He huddled against the mast and prayed silently in Arabic.

A pistol fired belowdecks: the Spanish had still not breached the forecastle. The besiegers were in no hurry; once they joined up with their consort they would receive reinforcements and could force the issue. More cannonballs tore through the rigging and a chunk of wood dropped to the weather deck with a wild clatter. Thorton gritted his teeth and looked up. The lateen sail over his head had a hole in it, but the spars and rigging were all sound. Should it fall, it would break his arms and shoulders, if not kill him. He added a short plea to his regular prayers: *Please, Allah, let them hit the rudder and not the jeers!*

The minutes ticked by. Cannonballs screamed overhead or smacked into the stern. One stove in the taffrail and went bounding along the quarterdeck, tore out one of the balusters in the forward railing, and pitched onto the weather deck along with a fire bucket. It had passed within three feet of him. He caught his breath and felt his heart stop for a moment, but he was unharmed.

Renaldo issued orders and a crew of men mounted the quarterdeck to load one of the sternchasers and answer the British harassment. The *Amphitrite's* gun roared out, but he could tell by the gun crew's behavior that they didn't hit. They reloaded and he counted out the seconds—more than three hundred. Five minutes to reload. God they were bad. Meanwhile the British guns were breaking up into a series of independent shots as the gun crews worked at different speeds. Every fifty seconds or so a ball whizzed past, tore through the rigging, or crashed into the stern. Thorton spared a minute to feel sorry for Captain Horner as his furniture and books were torn to pieces by British shot. Needless to say, the Spanish had not bothered to clear for action and didn't care about their enemies' personal possessions. Sudden laughter beneath the deck informed him that looting was in progress—they had found Horner's supply of brandy. Renaldo barked orders to his ensign who ran down and tried to restore order in the cabin beneath them.

Thorton's shoulders ached from being pulled back into such an unnatural position for so long. The ache grew into a pain, and the pain became a fire. He was miserably cold in every other part of his body, but his hands were numb. His head and stomach ached from the beating he'd received. He was so cold he stopped shivering and simply huddled against the mast. The snow fell thicker and no longer melted when it landed on his nose or nightshirt.

A clatter of footsteps came running up to the quarterdeck and a panicked sailor cried, "The helm is free! She doesn't answer at all, and there's no weight on the wheel!"

"What?" demanded Renaldo.

The *Amphitrite* fell off the wind and drifted aimlessly. She lost her way and turned her starboard side to the wind. The waves and wind were breezy and not dangerous—but the shoals of Gibraltar were to her lee. Renaldo ran down the ladder and swore at the helm, but the man told the truth. The wheel could be cranked back and forth and it made not one bit of difference to the ship's course.

Renaldo called some of his small crew to go below to inspect the tiller. They went, but fetched up against the barricaded door of the gunroom. They pounded on it, but it would not give way. Inside the gunroom MacDonald began to sing a lusty Scots song nobody could understand. "Hame came our goodman and hame came he and spied a saddle-horse where nae horse should be! Whit's this now, my goodwife, whit's this now I see? How came this horse here wi'out the leave o' me?" He burst out laughing.

Renaldo ran down to shout, "Break it open, you fools! We must be able to steer! The English dogs have sabotaged us!" Then he shouted up to the quarterdeck, "Send down the marines to break it open!" The two marines who had been left to guard the quarterdeck made haste below in answer to his summons.

Thorton raised his head and listened with interest in spite of his frozen body. If MacDonald was in the gunroom, where were Abby and the rest? What were they doing? He was cheered by MacDonald's sabotage of the tiller ropes, but his aching head could not puzzle out the rest of it. He began to hope for a rescue. Just then a cannonball smashed into one of the sternchasers, dismounted the gun, and sent debris hurtling along the deck. He twisted violently to the side, wrenched his shoulders, and cried out in pain. Shrapnel peppered his lower leg and blood stained his wool sock. He could feel warmth spreading, then stiffness as it cooled and coagulated in the winter air. He gave a groan.

The gun crew scampered away but some of them were hurt. A short man with a black jacket and cap cradled his broken wrist against his chest and swore some choice Spanish oaths. The others looked at the debris, then at the man with the broken wrist, but the mate and ensign gave it only a glance. They were too busy worrying about the helm. They didn't see the first hand appear in the breached taffrail. Thorton didn't realize he saw it, either. The hand was joined by a second, then a pale face beneath a Monmouth cap. By sheer brute strength the man clambered up the sculpture and window sills of the stern, then hauled himself over the edge. Down below MacDonald was shouting in Scots and beating something against the woodwork to make as much racket as possible to cover the sound of Tritons clambering up the stern.

The first man onto the quarterdeck pulled a pistol out of his waistband. Taking shelter behind the skylight cover, he knelt, aimed his pistol carefully and waited. The second man slithered over the edge and onto the quarter deck. Thorton was happier than he had ever been to see boarders swarming over his stern.

Renaldo stormed back up the ladder to the quarterdeck and swore at the men gawking there. They jumped back with guilty looks and turned back to their duty. They froze as they found themselves staring into a pair of British pistols. A Spanish seaman with more valor than sense tried to use his rammer as a club. A pistol barked and he spun around and dropped to the deck with a ball in his shoulder. Renaldo flew up the last step and found himself staring at the remaining pistol.

"Drop your weapons," the sailor ordered in English. Thorton translated.

Renaldo reached for the pistol butt in his belt and the sailor fired. He missed entirely, and Renaldo got his gun out and shot him dead. Another Spanish sailor snatched up a handspike, but Thorton swung his leg over and kicked him in the side of the knee. The Spaniard staggered off balance and the handspike clattered harmlessly to the deck. The British sailor threw himself at the Spaniard and they rolled on the deck together. Two more men came over the taffrail when the shooting started, and another as quick as he could after them. The Spanish ensign, a boy of not more than sixteen, drew his dirk and charged, but Thorton scissored his legs and tripped him up.

Renaldo drew his rapier and ran toward the mizzenmast. "Die, you godless heathen!" he shouted.

Thorton twisted desperately to scramble to the other side of the mizzenmast, but with his arms bound he could not elude the enraged Spaniard.

A shot rang out. Renaldo staggered and his sword drooped. He put his hand to his stomach, but the blood welled around his fingers and stained his pale hand. He staggered, but lifted his sword manfully as he turned to meet the new attack.

Abby finished scrambling over the stern. He stumbled over an abandoned cutlass, scooped it up, and ran forward. As Renaldo faced him, he shoved the blade into the man's belly and twisted it up. Renaldo gurgled and fell dead on the deck. His useless sword flopped down inches from Thorton's hip.

Abby peered at the prisoner. "Peter? It is you, isn't it?"

"Yes!" Thorton gasped in relief.

"Thank God! Are you hurt?" Abby stepped forward and groped. His hand found Thorton's arm, walked up it to his shoulder, then down to the rope that tied his hands behind the mizzenmast. "You're bound!"

"Thank God you're here! Is the ship secure?"

Abby shouted, "*Amphitrite,* report!" as his fingers traced Thorton's arms to the bindings and worked them loose. The rescued lieutenant's arms flopped free and he groaned as sensation began to return. Abby chafed his wrists as he listened to the reports coming in.

"Quarterdeck secure, sir."

"Weather deck secure, sir."

A message was relayed from below. "Gundeck secure."

"Lock the prisoners in the hold," Abby commanded.

A round shot smashed into the frigate's quarter, and three more peppered her stern.

"Strike the Spanish colors!" Thorton shouted. He was so cold he was numb. He grabbed onto the knighthead to haul himself to his feet.

A man in a short blue jacket hauled down the Spanish colors and raised the British flag instead. More shot smacked into the stern and went bowling along the quarterdeck before the British ensign was in place.

"Make the private signal!" Thorton bellowed. Voices echoed the calls through the ship and shortly thereafter a pair of small guns barked out a one-two cadence and two red lights were hoisted to the mizzen peak.

The *Amphitrite* continued drifting helplessly as the two British frigates bore down on her, one passing to either side to double her. Their broadsides ran out as they passed close by, but they did not fire.

"Pass the word for MacDonald! Splice the steering cable!" Thorton called.

No more shot came through the rigging, but the two British frigates lay right alongside him, grappled, and boarded. A red-coated officer swarmed up the ladder at the head of a body of marines. He pointed his pistol this way and that, but the quarterdeck was already secure. It was Lieutenant Barnes, the *Amphitrite's* own marine lieutenant.

He scowled. "'Tis the bugger-boys. Why am I not surprised?"

Thorton replied crossly, "Stop waving that pistol around, Lieutenant. What in the hell are you doing here?"

"Rescuing you," Barnes replied with a sneer. "I was visiting the *Valiant.* What in the hell are you doing?"

"You're drunk, Mister Barnes."

Barnes waved his pistol again. "Sober enough to board a ship, damn you."

"Lieutenant, stand down," Abby snapped. "The ship is secure. If you want to do something useful, you can take off our Spanish prisoners."

Barnes snarled, "Aye aye, Miss Allen." He turned his back on the lovers and stormed down the ladder. "Transfer those Spanish dogs to the *Valiant!*"

CHAPTER 4: A BLIND MAN'S VALOR

Thorton and Abby (both properly dressed) faced Captain Horner before breakfast on Christmas morning. Early light streamed through half the glass windows of the cabin. The other half had been replaced with deadlights on account of the broken glass. The cabin itself was neatly arranged, although the captain's desk was missing, and so was a chair from the dining table. The dining table had a splinted leg, so it resembled Thorton whose wounded ankle was stitched and wrapped in a bandage. Various other holes punched by British gunnery had been repaired, but a four pound cannonball was still wedged in the wall beneath the sideboard. Horner was looking more dour than usual as he listened to their reports. Going bald on top, the remains of his thin blond hair were pulled back into a ponytail and tied with a black velvet ribbon at the nape of his neck. He clasped his hands behind his back.

Being a civilian, Abby was dressed in a light grey suit and white stockings, although it had a naval flair with cuffs *a la marinère*. Retirement was not sitting well with the twenty-five year old commander.

Abby continued his recitation. "They left a few men to keep us pinned under the fo'c's'le, but they were not keen to press the fight. We fired a pistol occasionally to keep them at bay. After a while we heard merriment among the Spaniards, and the fellows laying siege to us grew envious when they heard their mates had found the captain's brandy."

Horner did not react to the news that his personal stash had been looted. His blue eyes continued to bore into Abby's, but the smoked glasses perched upon the blind officer's nose shielded him from the intensity of the captain's gaze.

"So I called out to them, saying I had the key to the spirit locker and would give it to them if they would let us go over the side in a boat. They agreed, and we came out. We spoke friendly to them, then knocked them on their heads and tied them up. MacDonald barricaded himself in the gunroom and cut the tiller rope while the rest of us crawled out the wardroom windows and climbed up the carved works to the quarterdeck. Speaking of which, the sculpture on the stern is very ornate, but what is it?" He had never actually seen the sculpture.

"Amphitrite and Poseidon with the fruits of the sea," Horner replied. "How did you manage to find your way?"

"I am not entirely blind. I can tell a hawk from a handsaw," Abby reminded him. He pulled the dark glasses down his nose and looked over them at Horner to demonstrate. "And a good thing, too, because when I came over the taffrail, somebody was menacing Peter. All the blue coats looked alike to me, but that one had a red middle, so I knew it was a Spaniard. 'Twas uncivilized of me to shoot him in the stomach, but it was the only way I was certain to hit my target." He sounded apologetic about that.

"Then you gutted him with a cutlass," Thorton put in.

"He didn't fall when I shot him, so I thought I'd missed."

"You couldn't see the blood on his red waistcoat," Thorton guessed.

"Aye, that's so. You I would know anywhere, even if you weren't the only man on the quarterdeck in his nightshirt."

Thorton smiled at him. "I was very glad to see you!"

"I salute your resourcefulness, Commander," Horner said. "I am very pleased the Spanish raid did not succeed, although I am disturbed they even got aboard. We found your picket. They surrendered quietly when the Spanish surprised them. The Spanish clubbed them insensible, tied them up, and left them adrift. They should have sounded the alarm, even if it cost them their lives. I'll flog them. I'll need the names of the men on deck watch, too."

"Aye aye, sir," Thorton replied, standing to strict attention again. Abby's story had put him at ease, but the matter of punishment reminded him that he had been the officer in charge of what had very nearly been a loss. "I'm very sorry, sir."

"I'm sorry the *Amphitrite* didn't put up a better fight. I am aware that you personally sounded the alarm, Mister Thorton. And Commander Abby, your behavior is to be commended, but there was a general breakdown in discipline in my absence that displeases me." His steely gaze fixed on Thorton. "How did the men get liquor?"

Thorton wilted. "I don't know, sir. I let them have an extra ration because it was Christmas Eve, but it wasn't enough for them to be drunk in their hammocks."

"The sobriety of the crew is your responsibility, Lieutenant. Had it been a few men, I would have held them accountable, but by the accounts received so far, it was half the men. You did not secure the ship against spirits when you knew they would be wonderfully tempted. Was the watch drunk as well?"

"I don't know, sir." Thorton was sagging.

"Send MacDonald. I'll decide your fate after I have gathered all the facts. Dismissed."

"Aye aye, sir." Thorton made a speedy departure.

Abby lingered. Being a civilian now and the son of an earl with an interest in the Service, he felt that certain orders did not apply to him.

"Yes, Commander?"

"Peter didn't do anything wrong. He set the picket and the watch, and he fought the Spanish with his bare hands."

"*I* wasn't even here, but the Admiralty will hold me accountable because I am the captain," Horner replied icily. "Rank grants responsibility, Commander, and 'bad luck' is never an acceptable excuse."

"Aye, sir. But I hope you'll lenient."

Horner's eyes bored into Abby's glasses. "I will not. I have been extremely kind to Mister Thorton over the last few months, which is why I felt I could trust him with the ship. I am disappointed. I cannot help but wonder if you distracted him from his duties."

"Peter was already in bed when I came aboard. I woke him with my visit. Had I not, he would have been sound asleep and never heard the boarders, and then your precious ship would be in Algeciras! I have been good luck for you, Captain, and I pray you will remember it."

Horner was a silent a moment, then said, "I am cognizant of your valor. Your conduct will be mentioned in my dispatch."

"Very gratifying, I'm sure. I will write my father about it."

Horner's face hardened. "I have made my way thus far without the benefit of noble patronage. Do not think I will be unduly influenced by you or your father."

"I was forced into retirement against my will, but I still care about what happens aboard this ship," Abby retorted.

"You are fortunate to be retired, Commander. Were you still under my authority, such remarks would be considered insubordination. Dismissed!"

Whether Abby was in Service or not, Horner was still captain, and that made him lord and master aboard his ship. Abby flounced out in a fury, but since he had not been directly ordered off the ship, he didn't leave. He went looking for Thorton.

CHAPTER 5: EXILE ASHORE

The news that the *Amphitrite* had been the target of a Spanish cutting out raid brought her officers back from shore leave. Some of her ratings returned as well, but most of the men on leave were dead drunk on Christmas Day and continued so through Boxing Day. They sobered up in time for New Year's Eve but promptly made themselves useless for another three days. The blind commander remained aboard as a guest of the wardroom.

Thorton and Abby kept each other warm at night, so much so that Perry banged on the partition that separated their cabin from his. They froze in mid-gallop.

Thorton turned bright red. "He heard!"

"What of it?" Abby said petulantly. "He's just sorry it isn't him. Carry on!"

Thorton couldn't. He eased off and quickly righted his breeches.

Abby glared at him. "You're not going to leave me like this, are you?"

"Alan, be reasonable. And button your breeches!"

Abby pulled up his drawers and scowled. "I don't see why you care what Roger thinks. He was going to hang you!"

"It was only because Walters put him in an impossible position. Besides, he didn't. He warned me."

"If that's what you call it. How about him offering to shoot you?"

"It was all a misunderstanding. We have smoothed it over."

Abby tucked his shirt into his breeches and buttoned his waistcoat. "You are simple, Peter, if you think you can trust that one."

Thorton cast an anxious eye towards the thin deal boards that separated the berths, but he couldn't guess what the other lieutenant might be thinking. The door to Perry's cabin opened and shut, then his footsteps went past their door as he went on deck. Thorton heaved a sigh. He made certain his clothes were in order. "Let's go take the air, Alan."

"I don't want to."

Thorton didn't want to stay in a cabin with a sulky lover. "Please?"

"No." Abby crossed his arms over his chest. "You need to finish what you started."

"I can't!"

"Fine. You go take the air with Roger Perry, if that's what you want."

"Now you're being stubborn."

Abby put his nose in the air and turned away from Thorton.

"All right. I'll go without you." He went.

Abby had not expected that. When Thorton's footsteps died away on the companionway, he checked himself with his hands to make certain he was in order, then ran up to the quarterdeck.

Horner was pacing the windward side of the quarterdeck with an intense frown on his face and his hands tightly clasped behind his back. His subordinate officers steered well clear and gathered in a knot to brood next to the leeward pinrail.

Thorton knew better than to disturb the captain in his walk. He joined the others. "What's the matter with Horner?" he asked in a low voice.

Barnes snorted at him. "Don't play stupid. You know what's wrong."

Thorton gave the redcoat a glare.

"He's come back from Admiral Leggott," Forsythe whispered softly. "He hasn't said a word."

"Has he had anything to drink?" Thorton asked the first lieutenant quietly.

"No, he's sober."

Abby was in a contrary mood. He perched on one of the quarterdeck guns and said, "You'd think he'd be happy he still has his ship." He did not bother to lower his voice.

Horner's eyes narrowed as they fixed on Abby, but he said, "Mister Thorton, a word with you."

Thorton hastily skirted the skylight and presented himself.

Today the captain was wearing a modest blond wig beneath his cocked hat. He had adopted the habit of wearing a wig socially or when a dress uniform was required because it looked better than his own thinning hair. By contrast the lieutenant's blond hair made a thick queue down his back wrapped with black ribbon. Crow's feet marked the corners of Horner's eyes when they narrowed, and they narrowed now. Thorton felt his bowel turn icy.

"Mister Abbewyvern has worn out his welcome. See that he gets a boat and whatever help he needs to get his things ashore."

"'Tis pronounced Abbleverfan," Thorton replied as politely as he could.

"I don't care how the Welshman pronounces his name. See that he goes ashore immediately."

Thorton swallowed hard, but said, "Aye aye, sir."

"Dismissed."

Thorton went back to the leeward side and said softly, "Alan, let's get your things."

Abby jumped off the gun and the two went below to the wardroom. Alone belowdecks, he burst out, "He can't treat me like that!" But they both knew he could. Horner was the captain and Abby was present solely on his sufferance.

"Let it go," said Thorton.

"He's a fool! How does he expect to get ahead in the Service if he offends men who could do him some good?"

"I don't know," Thorton replied. Looking around hastily to make certain they were alone, he lifted Abby's hands and kissed them. "If I get shore leave, I'll visit you."

Abby tilted his chin down so that he could look over the dark glasses at Thorton. "I miss you. You keep my bed warm. 'Tis cold without you."

Thorton smiled a little. "You're not angry with me anymore?"

Abby tossed his head and stomped his foot. "I *am* angry!"

"Will you forgive me?" Thorton gave him a winning smile.

"I suppose I must," Abby conceded. "But not yet. I am going to be cross with you until you bring me a present."

Thorton laughed. "I will. As soon as I get shore leave. Now let's get your boat." They collected his things and went on deck.

Thorton watched the boat rowing away with Abby and his valise. Abby turned to watch the ship receding and waved in his general direction. The ship was a dark blur and Thorton a blue smudge in the entry port.

Thorton raised his hand in farewell.

Perry stepped up next to Thorton. "We need to talk."

Thorton colored a little to remember what Perry had overheard. "I'm sorry if we disturbed you. We were trying to be quiet." He stepped back from the entry way so it could be closed.

Perry gave him an exasperated look. "Get below, you blockhead!"

Thorton followed him down the companionway. "Why am I a blockhead this time?" he wanted to know as soon as they stepped into the wardroom.

Perry turned and faced him. "Because you shouldn't discuss such things with men at hand!"

"You brought it up!"

"No, I said I needed to speak to you, you idiot!"

"Don't call me names. I don't like it."

Perry reached up and grabbed him by the ears. Thorton's cocked hat knocked against Perry's as the shorter man pulled his face down so that he could speak directly into it. "Discretion, Peter! Discretion! Have you learned nothing? You're lucky Barnes wasn't in his cabin and that he snores when he sleeps!" The marine lieutenant had the cabin forward of Thorton's.

"He was on deck."

Perry shook Thorton's head. "Peter, Peter, Peter. What am I going to do with you?"

"I don't know," Thorton replied with complete honestly.

The moment of exasperation stretched out and transformed. They both felt it. Perry tilted his head so that their hats would fit together and kissed Thorton full on the mouth. Thorton closed his eyes and let him. His own feelings welled up in a bewildering admixture. Once upon a time he had been infatuated with Roger Perry and been rejected. He never thought Perry would kiss him—not after Thorton had been court-martialed and Perry had helped to lay the trap. If Captain Tangle hadn't fatally wounded Admiral Walters in a duel, the admiral would have hanged him.

So many things had happened! They filled him with intense feelings. He kissed Perry, wrapped his arms around his body, and bore him back against the bulkhead. Perry gasped as his back collided with the wall and cut off his escape. He grabbed Thorton's shoulders as his knees went weak. He kissed the other lieutenant harder until a groan of despair escaped him. Thorton heard it and knew what it meant. He kept the brunet lieutenant pinned against the wall and felt the heat coursing through his veins. He still wanted Perry. Wanted to make love to him, wanted to punish him, wanted to tell him everything, wanted to fuck him like an animal, wanted to slap him silly. There were no words to describe how he felt; only direct action could assuage the sensations that had been building for eight months.

Perry squirmed in misery. He was a passionate man who had not had a lover in months. He wanted surcease from the torments of his body and mind, but his flesh and thoughts were whirling in opposite directions. "Stop! Please, Peter. No more!"

Thorton gazed into Perry's brown eyes. The scar that ran across his face from above the left eye, over the bridge of his nose, and onto his right cheek did not diminish his male beauty in Thorton's eyes. He felt the way Perry clung to him, the way he pressed himself full length against his body, the way his chest heaved with the extremity of his feelings, and the way his own body responded in kind.

"You like it." He pressed close against him so that their groins ground together.

"No, I don't!" Perry struggled to push him away, but Thorton didn't move. "Let me go!"

"No." Thorton tried to kiss him again.

"For God's sake! Think what you're doing! Anyone could walk in!"

Thorton was instantly contrite. He let go and stepped back. "I'm sorry, Roger. I was carried away."

Perry ran into his cabin, slammed the door, and set the hook. Then he dragged his sea chest across the floor to barricade the door.

Thorton sighed a long heavy sigh. He went into his own cabin, wrapped up in his blanket, and climbed into his hammock fully dressed. He didn't bother to remove his shoes or hat. He felt sorry for himself because he didn't understand Perry at all. He didn't understand men, not even himself.

Chapter 6: Condign Punishment

Thorton entered the great cabin and stood at attention. The milky light of winter shone through the windows and cast a grey light over everything. It made Horner look older and the cabin colder. The captain was staring out the stern window with his hands clasped behind his back. He had doffed his wig, and it lay on the crude wooden desk the ship's carpenter had built to replace the one destroyed in the raid. His stance was erect and tense. He brooded at the window for a long time before he finally turned to acknowledge Thorton.

"I have delivered my report to Admiral Leggott," was his preamble. His mouth was turned down and his blue eyes were narrow and cold like a brace of dueling pistols. The lines that ran from the corners of his nose to the corners of him mouth were deep.

Thorton stood stiffly and fixed his eyes on the beam by the captain's head. "Sir," he replied.

"The admiral is displeased. He reminded me of the great favor he has done you and I and all the officers by giving us assignments when there were few to be had. He does not consider our current conduct to have lived up to his expectations." Horner's voice was cold.

"Aye, sir." A trickle of dread worked down Thorton's spine. He kept staring at the beam while his stomach rolled over and played dead. If the *Sea Leopard* had come alongside just then, he would have run for it and damn the consequences. "The blame is mine alone. I was the officer in charge. This should not reflect on you, sir. I beg leave to go to Admiral Leggott about it."

"I have already informed him of the details. Fortunately, you were in command of the *Amphitrite* before she was boarded by the *Valiant*. You and I have escaped court martial by the narrowest of margins."

"I'm glad for you, sir."

He didn't care to think about what would have happened to him; he had already survived one court martial and didn't think he would be so lucky a second time. Alan Abby was a civilian and couldn't be court-martialed, but he doubted Abby's father would bestir himself on behalf of a man like Thorton.

Horner was speaking again and he glued his eyes to the man's face. "The pickets and watch are to be turned over for court martial, and so is the cockswain of the boat. The men who were drunk and the men who knew anything about sneaking liquor aboard are to be flogged immediately."

"Aye aye, sir. I think we may need to flog them in relays. 'Tis a lot of floggings, but only a few of the marines have returned from leave."

"I will address them first and see if I can persuade them to take their medicine. If they have any love at for me, they will not disgrace me by rioting."

"They do love you, sir, but they love liquor more."

"That they do, Mister Thorton. That they do. You must remember it, or you will never control them."

"I'm sorry, sir. You depended on me and I let you down." Disappointing Horner hurt him more than any sentence a court martial could have meted out.

Horner brooded in silence with his steely blue eyes fixed on the younger man's. Thorton's stricken expression and ashen complexion told him that the junior lieutenant felt the weight of events very keenly.

The captain sighed. "'Twas mine own fault. I left you with too little support, so they were able to sneak the gin aboard. Did you find out how?" Horner had, but he wondered if Thorton had figured it out.

"No, sir. MacDonald ran off a rum-seller before he got alongside. I'm positive they didn't get anything from the bumboat."

"They made a pact. One of them on shore leave brought it back to the boat. The cockswain hid it, and the men in the boat connived to get it aboard. A simple ploy, really. Every time the boat went back and forth, it brought more liquor."

Thorton's shoulders sagged when he saw how easily he had been duped. "I never thought they would do such a thing."

"A mistake born of inexperience. I tend to forget that you have been a lieutenant only a little while. You are the very devil in combat, Mister Thorton, but you do not understand the management of a vessel and her men."

"I have been a lieutenant more than a year, sir."

"Just so. But not long enough to make a proper lieutenant of you."

Thorton hung his head. "I'm sorry, sir."

Horner let his anger go. "My judgment was in error. I did not take the correct measure of my men and officers. I left the wrong man in charge. Still, I think it might have gone equally badly had it been Forsythe or Perry. I left the ship short-handed. With the holiday and the peace talks proceeding well, I didn't think the Spanish would get up to mischief." He turned away. "I want brandy."

Thorton licked dry lips. "We have some in the wardroom, if you'd like it, sir."

"We have discussed brandy before." Horner didn't look at him. He stared out into the grey December morning. Somewhere ashore people were singing glad songs, eating good food, and putting coins in the charity box at church. Somewhere men were celebrating the mild and merciful Savior who forgave them their sins and shielded them from their enemies. Jesus had never served with the British navy.

"Aye, sir."

"You urged me to rely on my friends instead of the bottle."

"Aye, sir. I did." He watched the captain uncertainly.

Horner turned his head to study Thorton. "Each of us takes our comfort where we find it. I don't blame you for wanting Alan's company on a cold night."

"If you say so, sir." It hurt Thorton to be forgiven more than it would have hurt him to be punished. He felt he deserved to be punished. If it hadn't been for Abby, he would have lost the *Amphitrite* and destroyed Horner's career.

Horner knew it as well as he did. He stood with his hands clasped behind his back as he stared out the window. "We owe Alan a great deal."

"He was very gallant. I'm grateful to him."

Horner's clasped hands tightened on each other. "He's been insufferable about it ever since. He lacks modesty."

"Alan is very full of himself right now, but what of it? He did something grand. He saved us both."

Horner did not speak for a long time. Finally he said, "I have not been gracious. I have been thinking too much of myself. I must make amends."

"Shall I give him a message, sir?" Thorton asked hopefully.

Horner turned around with a flash of blue eyes. "You're not going ashore. Do you think that when men are to be court-martialed and flogged left and right, you're going to disport yourself? No. You personally are going to clap the men in irons, then rig the gratings for the floggings."

It was a dismal job, but who else should do it? It was Thorton's fault and he would have to do the dirty work. "Aye aye, sir. I'll get started immediately."

"See that you do. Dismissed."

The sailors gathered in ranks to witness the grating rigged at the break of the quarterdeck and the guilty men lined up in a long ragged line. They all shivered in the cold. The snow had not lasted, but the day was as chilly as any in England.

"All hands to witness punishment," Thorton announced.

Twenty men to flog. When MacDonald and his mates got tired, Thorton took up the cat and laid it against the miscreants' bare backs himself. The men on deck shuffled their feet and blew on their hands, but the exercise kept the boatswain and lieutenant warm. Those who were merely drunk got a dozen stripes, but those who were drunk on duty received two dozen. The coldness of their bare skin exposed to the winter air made it hurt even worse. Neither Thorton nor MacDonald showed them any mercy. They flogged them until the blood ran. Being accustomed to delivering such punishments, MacDonald had removed his coat and rolled up his sleeves, but Thorton's cuffs were speckled by blood before it was over.

Horner stood at the quarterdeck rail to address the crew, "Let this be a lesson to you. Never let yourselves be incapacitated by drink. The Spanish are right there, waiting to pounce." He pointed across the bay to the Spanish xebec on patrol. "Every one of you owes a debt of gratitude to Commander Abby and your sober shipmates. If it were not for them, you would all be languishing in a Spanish prison. If any man among you feels that the cat is too harsh a punishment for mere drunkenness, speak up, and I will happily turn you over to the Spanish."

No one spoke.

"Dismissed."

Thorton handed the cat to MacDonald and he put it away in a green baize bag. The sailors shuffled away and those off duty went belowdecks to buzz about the punishments and help their mates with their bloody backs. Thorton went below and curled up in his hammock. He was miserable. It was all his fault. The Spanish had raided the *Amphitrite* because they wanted revenge on him, and he had been a fool and fallen right into their hands. His own sailors had outwitted him with their scheme to obtain liquor. Previously he had thought highly of himself because of his successes in combat, but there was more to being an officer than being good with gunnery. He was keenly aware of his deficits now, deficits he had not even known he had until they were exposed for all to see. He sank into a gloom.

Chapter 7: The Bawdy Boat

On New Year's Day a new provocation appeared: a trim little felucca loaded with women and wine. She had a parrot green hull, sharp bow, and two large lateen sails. She was slim and flirty with her pintail lazyboard and petticoats for flags. To top it all off, she had feminine eyes painted on either side of her bow. The custom of painting eyes was common on the smaller vessels of the Mediterranean, but these were dark sloe eyes lined with kohl and long lashes. This extraordinary vessel was denied permission to dock, but nothing could prevent her from dropping anchor down the shore.

"We have to go," Perry told Thorton. "While they're still fresh and almost virgin."

"I don't want to go," Thorton replied.

"Nonsense. You're only saying that because you never have."

"Roger, you know me. Why on earth would I want to visit such a place?"

Perry's brown eyes were sparkling with delight as his head spun all kinds of fantasies about what might be aboard that vessel, as if a whore afloat were somehow different and better than a whore ashore. "Look here. You've never had a woman, have you?"

"No, I haven't. I don't want one."

"That's your problem. Once you've had a woman you'll be cured of your affliction and can live a normal life. You only like men because you don't know any better."

His argument threw Thorton into confusion. Was it really that simple? He didn't think so, yet it made sense. "My first experience with a man was very bad. You'd think that would put me off men entirely," he said doubtfully.

"Tangle is a Turk. They are a violent, lascivious people."

"It wasn't Tangle," Thorton glared at him. "It was the bosun's mate on the *Marigold,* damn him to hell. He forced me."

This was a story Perry didn't know. "You never told me."

"It was a long time ago. Before I ever met you, and before I was captured by the Spanish. Years and years ago. I was a boy." He crossed his arms uncomfortably over his chest.

Perry absorbed this news. "A bad experience at an impressionable age will cause troubles until it is corrected. You have to go, Peter. You should have gone a long time ago. Damme, if I'd known, I'd have made sure you took the cure! You ought not keep things so close to yourself. Secrets will only cause you trouble."

Thorton had had a great deal of trouble from his secret, the worst being that it had not stayed secret. He sighed. "I'll go with you, since you want to go, but I don't want a whore."

"You can buy one for each of us. You have plenty of prize money. I'll tell you everything you need to know and you'll be fine."

Thorton was anxious. What if Perry was right? What if his strange proclivity was all a horrible mistake? He would feel a fool. Worse, he didn't think he would know himself. His allegiance to men had seemed so much a part of himself he could not imagine who he would be without it. Peter Thorton, mooning over cleavage and shapely ankles? Impossible.

"I don't have leave, Roger. Horner will be furious."

"Shush. We shall row round the ship on the way back and you can say we were making an inspection." He pushed Thorton into the boat with the other men.

Thorton looked at them as he climbed in. Lieutenant Barnes in his scarlet uniform was back from leave; Wiggins, the master's mate, was wearing his good blue frock coat; and Doctor Ferncastle in his wig and green coat was there as well. He thought they were handsome in their finery while their deep voices made a pleasing music to his ear. Would he feel the same tomorrow? A knot of dread was growing in his belly.

Perry climbed in and the sailors pushed off and began to row. Thorton looked up in fear as the parrot green hull of the floating bordello drew near. He remained seated as the sailors hooked onto the chains and the rest of the officers scampered up the accommodation ladder and over the gunwale. Perry had to tug his arm to make him go. The brunet lieutenant came close behind to make certain Thorton did not turn tail and drop back into the boat.

A yellow and white striped awning hung over the deck. Tripod braziers provided heat and lanterns were hung beneath the canvas. The weather deck was thus transformed into a barroom. Barrels served as tables and crude benches provided seating. A bar was set up forward to serve beer and wine and gin. A tall, swarthy fellow dressed in green was greeting the guests as they arrived. He had a yellow kerchief tied over his hair.

"Jack Murada, what are you doing here?" Thorton asked him in surprise. He knew the man a little.

"Making money," Murada replied. "Peter Rais?" he asked.

"Lieutenant Thorton, if you please. This is Lieutenant Roger Perry. We serve with the *Amphitrite* frigate now." To Perry he explained, "Captain Jack is one of the masters the Sallee rovers hired to take the xebecs back to Africa last fall." Turning back to the tall man, he asked, "How did you escape the Spanish?"

Murada grinned, "Pretty women." He was an extremely good-looking man in his thirties, rangy and muscular, with a lively, caramel-colored countenance. Brown eyes sparkled with mischief and he had an easy grin. His eye ranged appraisingly over Thorton and Perry. "I regret I don't have any comely boys, but I think I can take care of you, gentlemen."

Perry glared at him. "I want a pretty girl! None of your bugger-boys for me!"

Thorton turned bright red and wished that he could fall through the deck and vanish. On second thought, that would probably land him in some whore's crib on the lower deck. "Time to go!" he said and turned back to the gunwale.

Perry grabbed him by the arm. "You're not going until you've had a woman! He's shy," he explained to Murada.

Murada had a hard time not laughing. His mouth quirked in a grin. "Have you ever had a woman, rais?"

"No, he hasn't. 'Tis high time he did," Perry retorted.

"Roger!" Thorton protested.

"I see. That's going to require something special. Wait here." Murada departed.

Immediately thereafter a pretty girl dressed in petticoats and corset approached bearing a tray with a bottle of Madeira and two cups. "On the house," she said with a curtsy. "Compliments of Cap'n Jack."

Perry was quick to pour the wine and press a cup into Thorton's hands. "Drink up! 'Twill fortify you for the ordeal ahead. How do you know Captain Jack? I can't imagine you keeping company with rogues and pimps."

Thorton didn't answer. He was too busy drinking deep. Although he was not one to imbibe to excess, he thought now might be a good time. If he was falling down drunk they would have to pour him into the boat and send him home.

A few minutes later a berry brown woman almost as tall as a short man approached. She had a red corset cinched in so tight it plumped up her breasts into round mounds that looked as if they might burst their bounds at any moment. A black velvet cord went around her neck and supported a small red jewel. Her waves of lustrous brunette hair were piled on her head and trailed artfully down to caress her neck and bare shoulders. She wore no chemise, no, not even a camisole. White petticoats frothed around her legs, but were so short her calves could sometimes be seen. She wore low, flat, red dancing slippers on her feet.

"Miss Brandy!" Perry exclaimed in surprise as he recognized their former barmaid. "What are you doing here?"

She smiled at him and her nose crinkled. Her full rosy lips needed no cosmetics to enhance their sensual color. "England is very cold in winter. When Jack told me his plan to make some money, I was eager to come. I may not go back!"

Perry smiled at the caramel bosom so freely displayed. "I'm very happy to see you again," he told her breasts.

She smiled warmly at him and patted his cheek "I'm very happy to see you again, too, Mister Perry." Then she turned to Thorton and gave him a peck on the cheek. "How are you, dear? We never got the chance to chat back in England. Come and sit with me." She took his hand and led him under the quarterdeck.

When Thorton realized where they were going and why, he protested, "I don't know anything about women."

She gave him a sunny smile. "That's all right. I know quite a bit about men." She pulled him into the cabin.

Barnes came over with his beer. "How in the hell does Thorton get the mistress? I was after her all the time in England and never caught her."

"You and me both. She's a nimble lass. Thorton will either humiliate himself or she'll make a man of him," Perry replied.

Barnes snorted at that. "I'm betting on the former. He won't know what to do when she hikes her skirts."

Perry ought to stick up for his friend, but he was pretty sure Barnes had the right of it. He drank wine instead and looked around for a tart of his own. Sadly, the green and yellow vessel was doing a lively business and all the girls were occupied. He'd have to wait his turn. At least he had a free bottle of wine while waiting.

Eventually Thorton emerged from the great cabin. He strolled towards them with the languid pace of a well-satisfied man.

"Well?" Perry demanded.

Thorton grinned giddily. "We did it."

Perry laughed and slapped his back. "I told you needed it!"

Thorton blushed and cleared his throat self-consciously, "She's a very knowledgeable woman."

Perry handed him a pewter wine cup and clinked with him. "If that doesn't improve your opinion of the female species, nothing will. Now you owe me a turn. How much did it cost?"

"Not a penny. She never asked for any money. She told me I was handsome and that she likes bashful men who don't chase after her." Thorton drank his wine unaware that he had scored points against each of them.

Barnes glared at him. "I thought you and Alan Abby were bosom friends."

Thorton stiffened. "You've no cause to slander us just because we don't share your low taste in women."

"You don't share anyone's taste in women! I think you paid the whore to lie for you!" Barnes snarled.

"Joshua! There's no call for that!" Perry remonstrated with him.

Captain Jack was already bearing down on the three of them. "Is there a problem?"

Barnes was still raging at Thorton. "You're a damned sodomite! Don't think any of us believe this little charade of yours!"

"If you don't cool your red head, I'll pitch you into the sea," Murada warned him.

Barnes was six foot. He did not often meet men taller than himself, but Murada had two inches on him. That did not deter him. "Butt out."

Thorton plucked Perry's sleeve. "Let's go."

Murada still confronted Barnes. "Off the boat. Captain's orders." He hooked his thumb over the side.

"No."

Murada shook his head sadly, said, "Tsk tsk," then kneed him in the balls. The marine crumpled and lay moaning on the deck, cupping his abused anatomy. "An order's an order, mister," the felucca's master told him. To Perry he said, "Get him off my boat, or so help me, I'll drop him overboard."

Perry sighed. "Give me a hand, Peter. We'll put him in the boat."

"Let him find his own way home! I'm not going to help him, not after what he said!" Thorton retorted.

"Fine. You stay here. I'll take him back."

Thorton hesitated, looked around at the debauchery in progress, and said, "I'll help." They each took an arm and dragged the marine to the gunwale.

Barnes scowled as he staggered to his feet, but Murada stared him down. Two beefy sailors, one black and one white, came to stand beside the brown captain. The wall of men was a sufficient deterrent to the angry marine. He gingerly clambered over gunwale. Perry scrambled after him, then Thorton dropped into the boat and they rowed away.

CHAPTER 8: PRISONER EXCHANGE

On a cold brisk morning, Thorton, Horner, and Barnes mounted up in the streets of Gibraltar. The city was wreathed in a faint drizzle that made the lanterns glow with halos. Clouds of steam puffed from the horses' nostrils and the mouths of men. The Spanish prisoners shuffled into a loose group under the wary eyes of British marines. The clatter of wagons echoed hollowly and the teamsters swore at their charges.

Thorton had never ridden a horse in his life. He needed a boost from one of the marines to crawl into the saddle. The stirrups were too long and the orderly had to adjust them for him. He clung to the pommel and reins together because he was afraid of falling off. Barnes rode like a centaur and was highly amused. A stony truce had prevailed between the two until now.

"You can't hang onto the pommel forever. Hold your hands like this." Barnes demonstrated with the reins in his left hand, leaving his right free for the crop.

Studying the redcoat, Thorton shifted his grip to try to manipulate the reins with one hand. It was awkward and he kept fiddling with them.

"Keep your hands quiet! Every wiggle says something to the horse."

"What are my hands saying?" Thorton asked.

"I'm an idiot," Barnes replied. The gelding tossed his head in agreement.

Thorton scowled at him. Barnes grinned at him.

Horner mounted up with dignity. It helped that no one was watching him; the marines and teamsters were highly amused by Thorton's novice antics. "If we are ready to get under way, Lieutenant Barnes," Horner said pointedly.

"Teamsters! Line up!" Barnes shouted.

They rolled through the No Man's Land between the massive embattlements of the Spanish and British fortifications. Ice cracked beneath hooves and sere grasses crunched beneath the boots of the marines. They passed a tumbled heap of stones that had once been a chapel, then drew up before the mighty brown fortress of San Felipe. The faint glow of dawn lightened the eastern sky, but that made the dark bulk of the fortress appear even more menacing. The great gate opened with a dolorous clanking, then a party of Spanish officers in long grey coats with red breeches and high black boots rode out to meet them. They reined up just short of the British party.

"I am Major Ruiz y Romero. In the name of His Most Catholic Majesty, I bid you welcome," the Spanish officer called out in decent English.

Horner replied in serviceable Spanish, "Captain Ebenezer Horner of His Britannic Majesty's frigate *Amphitrite,* reporting with prisoners. Do you have our passports?"

"I do." He handed them to his assistant.

Thorton dismounted awkwardly, stumbled on legs already aching from the saddle, and walked forward to receive them. The Spanish aide dismounted with a flourish of long legs and strode forward with the easy strides of an equestrian. "Show off," Thorton muttered. He accepted the packet and they saluted each other. Conscious of the Spanish watching him, he marched back to Horner with a ramrod straight spine.

Horner opened the packet and inspected the papers. "Thank you. The papers appear to be in order. Mister Barnes, you may transfer the prisoners."

Barnes bawled, "Marines, fall out! Prisoners, advance!"

The ragged prisoners hesitated a moment, then started to run towards the other side. Spanish soldiers came forward. They wore long dove grey coats, red breeches, and red stockings. White baldrics supported the musicians' drums. They struck up a Spanish tune and escorted the freed men inside the gate of San Felipe. The wounded were transferred to a Spanish ambulance. It wheeled slowly away.

"If you will follow me, gentlemen. I can offer you the hospitality of Fortress San Felipe," Ruiz said.

"Thank you kindly for the offer, but we need to push on. We hope to reach Santos Nunilo and Alodia by nightfall," Horner replied.

"As you wish. I will provide you with an escort."

The British fife and drum struck up a marching cadence as they followed the Spaniards into the canyon between the towers of Fort San Felipe. It was dark as the River Styx within the walls and the rumble of wagon wheels echoed loudly in the confined space. Murderholes seen dimly in the light of the lanterns warned them how difficult it would be to force an entrance; without Spanish sufferance, the British could not have advanced an inch.

In the courtyard of the fortress they received their Spanish escort: a party of marines and a mounted officer to command them. The red and gold flag of Spain hung limply on its staff, but it glowed in the lantern light. They pushed on. Morning became a watery sort of daylight and they paused to break their fast, then forded a small, icy river. By mid-afternoon they reached the Río Guadarranque, but mercifully didn't

have to ford it in the freezing cold. They followed a rutted road along
its banks, climbing into the hills above Algerciras Bay.

It was full dark by the time the British party reached the foot of the
hill upon which sat the convent of the child martyrs Nunilo and Alodia.
A Spanish officer in a splendid white coat came down from the convent
to greet them. He wore tall black boots over his knees and his coat had
black cuffs. He spoke such rapid Spanish they missed his name, but
they caught the gist of the message. "His Excellency Major Álvar Soto
y Espinoza, commander of Santos Niños, welcomes you and invites
you to join him for dinner."

That sounded marvelous to the officers, except Barnes, who knew
he would have to make camp while Horner and Thorton dined.

"Thank you. We are happy to accept," Horner replied. "Mister
Thorton, come along."

Inside the walls of the convent, a low rambling chapter house
fronted on the courtyard, two sides of which were lined with cells that
had formerly housed nuns but now contained British sailors. They were
all locked in for the night and the courtyard was in deep shadow except
for a few lanterns. The thick adobe walls that had protected the nuns
from the material world did an admirable job of confining the
prisoners.

They were escorted into a salon where several Spanish officers and
a pair of priests were already ensconced. Their host came to greet them.
He was about thirty, short, fit, with a lively yet graceful way of moving.
His long auburn hair hung over his shoulders in waves and he wore a
long white coat, red breeches, and black thigh boots.

He greeted them in Spanish. "*Caballeros*. Welcome to my humble
home. My house is your house. I beg your forgiveness for not being
able to speak English."

Horner made a leg and bowed politely to his host. He had had the
benefit of a French dancing master in his youth and conducted himself
well. Thorton had had Perry and Abby to drill him in manners and
conducted himself adequately.

Horner replied in Spanish. "*Teniente* Thorton and I are both fluent
in Spanish. We are quite comfortable in your language and appreciate
your kind hospitality."

The room had a beamed ceiling and fireplaces at either end.
Leather sofas and wall sconces with plenty of candles gave the room a
golden glow. Other Spanish officers wore the same uniform as Soto.
They were a sullen lot, either old or drunk or pockmarked. Two priests
were with them, and one of them in particular caught their attention. He
was a plump, ruddy man in black.

"Father Sánchez, the local Inquisitor," Soto said pleasantly.

The priest inclined his head politely as he looked down his nose at the pair of English heretics.

Soto introduced the rest of them, but the names went by in a blur. Then he said something they understood perfectly well and hastened to obey. "Come, warm yourself by the fire. We have mulled wine. It will revive you."

"Thank you, *Señor,*" Horner replied. He accepted a cup and drank a deep draught of the warm, fragrant liquid. Thorton made a beeline for the fire and hitched up the tails of his coat so that he could warm his aching backside.

"Are you the celebrated Peter Thorton we have heard so much about?" a small dark officer asked him.

Thorton was never comfortable with attention or praise, and even less comfortable to be caught with his tails in his hands like a callow midshipman. "I am sure I have not done anything worthy of your notice, gentlemen." He hastily smoothed down the skirts of his coat.

"Nonsense. *Teniente* Morrida tells me you have been capturing our ships left and right!" Soto replied.

"I have had a bit of luck in that regard," Thorton replied cautiously.

"Come, you are too modest. We want to hear about it!" Soto encouraged him.

"Captain Horner has had a much more illustrious career than I," Thorton replied. "I am only a junior lieutenant."

The Spaniards transferred their attention to Horner.

Put on the spot like that, Horner said, "I have been the captain of the *Amphitrite* only a short time. Naturally I look forward to any opportunity to serve my king, on land or at sea.

Their host spoke, "Modesty is an overrated virtue. But my apologies. We are pestering you when you are cold and hungry. If you are feeling warmer, let us go in to dinner. You can tell us your stories in comfort. We are hungry for news. Algeciras is only a few miles away, but it might as well be America."

The table was set with fine black and white china and a crystal chandelier hung overhead. The linens were lustrous white and the chairs covered in watered black silk. A roasted pheasant, various fruits, vegetables, and sauces were served. Horner and Thorton stuffed themselves; it was a very fine table. Excellent red wine went around and Thorton found himself getting tipsy and sleepy. Conversation flowed around the table as the officers talked about the war and the negotiations with Portugal. They all agreed that the end of the war between Britain and Spain was approaching.

Horner was mindful of their mission. "I am hoping you will be kind enough to allow us to interview Admiral Wolfe."

43

"Of course. He is ill, but you are welcome to visit him tomorrow. I regret to say I have not received any directions regarding his release."

"No. We didn't capture any prisoners of high enough rank to exchange for an admiral," Horner admitted. "Just Captain Cathcart and forty common sailors. How many do you have here in total?"

"Two hundred and eleven. Disease has carried off eighteen. We did what we could, but it is a prison." Soto shrugged apologetically.

"We have brought supplies for the prisoners' care."

"Of course. You may distribute them. You understand that we will need to inspect them first."

"Of course, *Señor.*"

"We would prefer you take away the sick and troublesome prisoners."

"I will take them if they are well enough to move."

"Certainly."

"If you could see your way clear to release any other prisoners for humanitarian reasons, we would be most grateful."

Soto smiled. "There may be one or two I can send for compassionate reasons, but you understand I cannot exceed my instructions."

"Yes, of course. But instructions always have provisions that require interpretation."

Soto gave a self-deprecating smile. "I am not popular with my superiors right now, so I am doing my utmost to discern their intentions and abide by them." He noticed Thorton nodding off. "*Teniente* Thorton, you look like you could use some fresh air."

Thorton jerked his head up at the sound of his name. "'Tis very warm in the room, *Señor.*"

"So it is. *Capitán* Horner, if you and the other gentlemen will withdraw to the salon, I will take *Teniente* Thorton for a walk to revive him."

"I'm awake!" Thorton protested, but everybody was rising and heading to the other room.

Soto came around and took his arm. He opened the door to the patio and the cold air hit Thorton like a shock. He woke up quickly as the Spanish officer walked him around the cloister. Lanterns hanging at intervals provided a soft glow.

"I admire your reticence and good sense in not showing up your superior officer, but now that we are alone, you must tell me about your adventures. I am all ears." Soto's arm was hooked companionably in Thorton's.

"'Tis impolite to talk about Spanish misfortunes while enjoying your hospitality, *Señor.*"

Soto laughed at that. "You and I are men of action. Those fellows down at Algeciras won't get off their butts until every detail is arranged for their convenience. I am not offended if you tell me that you whipped them. In fact, I will enjoy it."

"I had the good luck to catch a couple of wounded frigates by surprise. Anyone could have done what I did."

They passed doors and windows until they came to another door. Soto opened it and stepped into the dim interior. Thorton followed him inside. A low fire glowed on the hearth and the shadowy pillars of a four-poster bed loomed in the dimness.

"I want to hear about all of your adventures, Peter. Don't be shy. Talk to me." His voice was warm and inviting.

Thorton licked suddenly dry lips. "I don't think I understand you."

Soto stepped up close to him. "I've heard a lot of stories about you. I enjoy tales of adventurous men." He reached up to stroke Thorton's hair.

Thorton replied nervously, "You should not trust rumors, my lord."

"Call me Álvar." He rose on his toes so that he could kiss Thorton's mouth.

The lieutenant turned his face away.

Soto slipped his arm around Thorton's neck. "You're bashful. I didn't expect that. I thought you'd be brash and rude. They paint you as the very Devil, those old prudes in Algeciras."

Thorton's tanned face turned copper as the blush infused it. "I have a lover, *Señor*."

"But he isn't here, is he?"

"Fidelity is a virtue I strive for."

Soto laughed again. "Strive for, but never achieve, I hope!" He began to unbutton Thorton's waistcoat.

Thorton stepped back in panic. He grabbed his waistcoat and held it shut. "You misunderstand me, my lord!"

"I don't think so. We both know why you're in my bedroom."

"I didn't know when I entered!"

"But you know now and haven't left," Soto replied in amusement. He sat on the side of the bed and said, "Sit with me and talk." He patted the bed next to him.

Unwillingly Thorton sat down about two feet away from him.

Soto moved closer. "You're very handsome."

Thorton wouldn't look at him.

Soto slipped his arm around his waist again and caught his chin. He tried to kiss him again, but Thorton turned his head aside. "Don't be coy. I have been looking forward to meeting the bold adventurer," Soto breathed in his ear.

Thorton's heart thudded in his chest. "I need to go, *Señor*," he whispered.

Soto's patience began to wear. "You should be kind to me, Peter. I can do you favors."

"What sort of favors?"

Soto hooked a finger into the waistband of his breeches. "That depends on what sort of favors you do for me."

Thorton pushed his hand away. "I do not deal in that sort of 'favor,' *Señor*."

"Don't make me angry, *Teniente*. My walls are very thick and my gates are very strong. I don't have to give you anything."

Thorton froze as he realized the spot he was in. If the British mission to retrieve the prisoners failed, it would be his fault for refusing to humor the corrupt Spaniard. He couldn't tell that to the Admiralty, though. Not when Thorton's own reputation was slowly eroding under rumors of the unmentionable vice.

"If I give you what you want, will you give me what I want?" Thorton asked him.

"If it is within my power and honorable to perform, yes."

"You speak of honor a little late, my lord," Thorton replied bitterly.

"Now you're angry with me, pretty boy." Soto sounded amused. "Is it so horrible to kiss a man like me?"

"You are a fine looking man, *Señor*, but I don't trust you."

"Very well. I give you my word as a Spanish gentleman."

"No thank you. I've known too many Spaniards."

Soto cocked his head and said wryly, "You've just insulted the entire manhood of Spain."

"I know whereof I speak, *Señor*. I was four years in the Armada."

"You don't speak Spanish like a sailor. I would have thought you were raised an *hidalgo* if I didn't know better."

"I had a friend. He was the son of a Spanish professor. He said that if I was going to learn Spanish, I should learn it properly."

"Then we are not all ogres, are we?"

Thorton's face fell. "No, sir. I apologize for speaking too freely."

The rake's face softened a little. "You aren't what I expected."

Thorton searched his face. "Will you release Wolfe?"

"Yes."

"Just like that?"

"Either you take me at my word or you don't. There is nothing I can say to persuade you if you are unwilling to be persuaded."

Thorton was not reassured. "I must go. My captain will wonder where I am." He jumped up from the bed.

Soto remained seated. "Then leave. You're free to go."

Thorton didn't believe him, but hurried to the door and opened it. He paused with the door ajar and looked back over his shoulder. "Would you really let him go?"

"Yes."

"Why?"

"I don't give a damn what happens to Wolfe. If it makes you happy, why not? My superiors are already angry with me. They put me here as a punishment. I am as much a prisoner as your Wolfe. Maybe more so. He has hopes of being traded. I do not."

"You could have given him to Horner when he asked."

"Horner isn't young and handsome. Besides, he asked me in front of the Inquisitor."

Thorton stared at him in consternation. "You would really give up Wolfe for such a petty reason?"

"Is it petty to you?"

Thorton hesitated, then answered, "No."

"Nor me."

Thorton shut the door and took two steps back towards the man. "What do you mean, *Señor*?"

"I'm a blasphemer who would rather bugger pretty men than kiss the Pope's ring. In the eyes of my superiors that makes me unfit, so I am wasting in away in a goddamn monastery that's been turned into a prison while they, those gloriously moral bastards, sit on their fat butts and do absolutely nothing."

Thorton came forward. "Will you write a letter for Wolfe's release?"

"Yes. I'll do you even better than that." He got up, took a taper from the fire, and lit a candle on the bedside table. He rummaged in the drawer, produced ink, quill, and paper. Using the nightstand as his table, he wrote out the letter. He pressed his signet ring into the wax and handed it to Thorton.

Thorton read it, then folded it in thirds and put it in his breast pocket. Steeling his nerve, he removed his coat and hung it over the back of the brocade chair. Taking a deeper breath, he removed his waistcoat and draped it over the arm of the chair. He untied his stock and laid it on top.

Soto rose and came to him. This time when he kissed Thorton, the lieutenant returned the kiss.

CHAPTER 9: BARGAINS IN THE DARK

Thorton returned to the salon in the company of Major Soto. The officers rose and Horner asked, "Are you all right, Lieutenant?" when he saw the lieutenant's flushed face. "I hope you're not falling ill."

"I'm all right, sir. But the hour is late. We should let our host go to bed."

Horner knew Thorton well enough to know something was up. The Spanish didn't know him at all and surmised nothing. They took their leave and a junior officer escorted them to the gate. The two British officers ducked their heads and stepped through the pedestrian door, then it clanked shut behind them and the bar dropped into place with a clatter. They were met by a British sergeant and two marines. The marines fell in obediently behind the officers.

Once clear of the gate, Horner asked, "What happened?"

Thorton glanced around quickly to make sure they were not overheard. Keeping his voice low, he replied, "I beg your pardon for not consulting you, sir, but Major Soto was in a mood to take action."

"What sort of action?"

"He's defecting to Portugal. Tonight. He's bringing all the prisoners out by the postern gate. We must abandon our camp quietly. We can't take the wagons or tents and must leave the fires burning so our Spanish escorts think we are still in camp. If we're successful, we can steal a march on them. We must send a courier to Leggott tonight and ask him to send boats to pick us up at dawn at the mouth of the Río Guadarranque."

Horner stopped dead in his tracks. "What? Are you mad? Why would Soto do such a thing?"

"He's in ill favor with his superiors."

"He should have spoken to me!"

"He couldn't. Not with the Inquisitor there. I'm sorry, sir. I did remonstrate with him, but he had an excuse to walk privately with me and not you. I thought I ought to do anything I could to retrieve Admiral Wolfe." Thorton gave him a worried look. "Was I wrong?"

Horner pinched the bridge of his nose and took a deep breath. "Wrong, no. Impetuous and ill-considered, yes."

Thorton watched him anxiously. "I asked for Admiral Wolfe, but he gave me all the prisoners. I thought it would be wrong to refuse when I had the chance to save them."

Horner walked slowly along the road to the camp as he weighed the matter in his mind. "You are not political, Mister Thorton. The end of the war is near. The Spanish raid on the *Amphitrite* not withstanding, I expect Portuguese independence will be settled and the blockade of Gibraltar lifted. The prisoners will be going home soon enough, I think. There is no need for this adventure."

Thorton's face fell. "Wolfe is ill, sir. He may be dead by the time the war is over. Maybe the others as well."

"Mister Thorton, you are an officer of considerable tactical skill, but you are a blundering fool where politics are concerned. You obligate me and Admiral Leggott to things for which would rather not bear responsibility! You did not have the right to strike such a bargain."

Thorton shriveled. "I'm sorry, sir. Shall I go back to Soto and tell him so?"

"No. We'll meet him at the postern gate. You must carry Wolfe safely back to Leggott while I bring the rest of the prisoners. If Leggott doesn't send boats to meet us, I shall endeavor to bring them out via San Felipe. Soto shall have to write us a pass."

"Aye aye, sir." After a day in the saddle Thorton was weary and his legs and butt were sore, but he couldn't rest yet.

At midnight Horner met Soto at the postern gate. While they spoke, a carriage with no lights rolled up. The gate opened and several dark figures staggered or shuffled to the coach and climbed in as best they could. Thorton hastily dismounted to give a hand to the bundled figures. Once they were all inside, he folded up the carriage step and shut the door. A leather curtain was lifted at the carriage window and a pale hand beckoned to Thorton.

"Sir?" he asked, raising his hat. He could tell from the cuff it was an officer, even if it was filthy.

The curtain drew aside and Thorton was face to face with the drawn face and sunken eyes of Admiral Wolfe. "Major Soto told me I have you to thank for our rescue."

"I did what I could, sir."

"You have my gratitude, Lieutenant."

"Do you know who I am?"

"I do, Mister Thorton. The irony is not lost on me."

Wolfe was the friend and second-in-command of Admiral Jonathan Walters. Had Captain Tangle not shot Walters in a duel, Wolfe would have presided at Thorton's court martial. Thorton didn't know the man well enough to guess whether he would have decided the case on its merits or would have hanged him for sodomy as Walters intended. The lieutenant had not actually been guilty at the time of his arrest, but he was most certainly guilty now. As it was, Wolfe had taken up the admiral's duties, so the blame fell on him for the British losses in the Balearic Islands. He had been a prisoner of the Spanish since the Battle of Majorca.

Thorton's tone was respectful as he said, "I'd like to ask a favor, if I may, sir."

"What favor, Lieutenant?"

"Please restore Lieutenant Roger Perry's seniority, sir."

Wolfe seemed surprised. "He testified against you, you know."

"I know, sir, but we have made up our quarrel. Even if we hadn't, the blame is mine alone. It isn't right that he should be punished for what I did."

Wolfe's hollow eyes gazed at him for a long time. Finally he said, "I doubt I will be in a position to aid anyone, not even myself, but I will do what I can."

"Thank you, sir." Thorton touched his hat respectfully.

At that moment Horner came up. He raised his hat to Wolfe and said, "Admiral. Mister Thorton will be your escort. Your release is irregular; you shall have to go in secret. Can you ride?"

"I can do anything that will take me away from this hellhole, Captain."

Half an hour later Wolfe was dressed as a common sailor in a wool smock and bumfreezer jacket, a woolen Monmouth cap tight over his head, striped trousers on his legs, darned wool stockings and a worn out pair of shoes on his feet. The clothes were patched and dirty. Thorton donated his own black ribbon to bind up the man's pigtail; a proper seaman would have had a long queue of tarred hair, but it was impossible to tar the admiral's hair in the middle of a Spanish night. Wolfe required help to get into the saddle. Thorton worried about him, but there was nothing to do about it. Too much tenderness to his 'servant' would give away the game.

Before they could leave, Soto came flashing up on his white horse. He wore tall black boots over his knees that were dark against the flanks of his horse.

"Captain Horner! I have a remount for your messenger."

Horner replied, "Thank you, Major. Mister Thorton is the messenger. He was about to leave."

Thorton dismounted the tired English steed with a thud, groaned, then heaved himself into the Spanish saddle. The Spanish horse was small and lively and the saddle was slighter than the English saddle. A Spanish orderly adjusted the stirrups for him. Thorton inspected the equipment: he had saddlebags with food, water, and a brace of pistols with powder and shot. Horner tucked his flask into Thorton's pocket.

Soto handed Thorton a pass. "This will help you through the Spanish lines. *Vaya con Díos.*" They had not seen fit to share the details of their ruse with Soto.

"*Muchas gracias, vuestra merced,*" Thorton replied.

As the disguised admiral took his place at the lieutenant's side, Soto asked, "Are you taking a man with you? The pass is only for one."

"I am only one man. That is a servant," Thorton replied.

The matter settled, Horner said, "Ride, Peter. Godspeed and God bless. I hope to see you with boats at the Guadarranque at dawn."

"And you, sir. Farewell." Turning to his companion, he said, "Come along, man. Time's a-wasting!" He wheeled away and kicked the horse's flanks. The lively beast sprang forward and he nearly lost his seat. He cursed and reined up sharp.

Wolfe came up beside him at a gentler pace. He put a hand out to touch Thorton's reins. "A ship and a horse have something in common, Lieutenant. They must be eased into doing what you want them to do. Only when you are thoroughly familiar with their ways can you give a sharp command and expect to have it obeyed."

"Thank you, s— Stirling," Thorton said. The habit of calling his superior 'sir' was a deeply ingrained one.

The faux seaman knuckled his forehead. "Forgive me for speaking out of turn, sir." He was sick and grey, but there was a quirk at the corner of his mouth as he played his part.

"Not at all, Stirling. I never rode a horse before today. I value your advice."

"Aye aye, sir," the man replied with a glint of good humor.

The two horsemen started on their way.

CHAPTER 10: WOLFE'S RESCUE

Thorton wanted to set a brisk pace but had to go slowly because of the badness of the road. The dirt track was well rutted and icy and pocked with rocks and holes. His good eye was sharp enough to find the way, but his left eye had poor night vision. Frustrated, he removed his blue and white checked kerchief from his pocket, folded it into a blindfold, and tied it at an angle over his left eye. He had to swivel his head to see to the left, but his right eye by itself was sharper than the two of them together.

He had to wait for Wolfe. The admiral slouched in the saddle and clung to the pommel. He was grey and drawn and sweat ran down his face in spite of the winter cold. He groaned and his eyes were out of focus. He was barely sensible.

"We must keep moving, Stirling. I do not care to trust your disguise to daylight and wide-awake Spaniards."

"Aye aye, sir," came the cadaverous voice.

Wolfe was spent already and they had twenty miles before them. Thorton did not dare let the man dismount to rest; he was afraid he would never get him back in the saddle. He transferred to the same mount and rode double behind him. He wrapped his arms around the fever-hot body and Wolfe huddled against him and shivered. Thorton kicked the horse's flanks and they trotted until Wolfe slumped and would have fallen if Thorton were not holding him. Wolfe had once been a goodly figure of a man, but he had lost at least two stone during his captivity. He seemed as hollow as a skeleton whose marrow has run dry.

It was hours later when they arrived at a fishermen's hamlet at the head of Algeciras Bay. Thorton got down and caught Wolfe as he pitched out of the saddle. He laid him on the ground and let him rest. Kneeling beside him, the blond lieutenant took a shot of brandy from the flask Horner had slipped into his pocket.

Wolfe croaked, "The horse, Mister Thorton. Tend the horse first, then yourself. Give him water from your skin. The river's not fit to drink, even for an animal."

"Tend the horse, aye," Thorton replied automatically.

He poured water from his skin into his bare hand and offered it to the horse. The warm tongue lapped at his fingers and the water vanished in an instant. Thorton poured some more. When half the skin was gone, he knelt beside the stricken admiral again. "Drink, sir."

Wolfe stared at the night with glassy eyes. Thorton helped him to sit up. He leaned heavily against the kneeling lieutenant and drank slowly from the skin. Thorton capped the water, then pulled out the flask. He administered a good jolt to the sick man who coughed violently. After a moment Wolfe said, "Thank you. That warms me, Lieutenant. I'm grateful for your help. I know I'm a burden to you."

"Just doing my duty, sir." He continued to cradle the sick man against the warmth of his chest. He kept his back to the wind to give the man what shelter he could.

"You're a decent man, Peter Thorton."

"Thank you, sir."

"I mean it. Not many men would have the grace to do as you have done."

Thorton was uncomfortable with the praise. "'Tis nothing, sir." It was a strange twist of fate that had led him to do his duty in another man's bed, but that was a matter he could not discuss with Wolfe.

"I want to go home, Mister Thorton. Even if it is to disgrace. I want to see my wife and children. I want to see my house and the green park around it. I want sit in my library and read my books with a cup of tea at my elbow and my dog at my feet. The country will blame me for our losses; I know they will, but I can bear it if only I am home again."

"It sounds like you have a lovely home, sir." Thorton had no home; the sea, the ship, whatever room he might rent when he was on the beach; those were his home. For a moment he envied Wolfe.

The man coughed, spit in the weeds, then rubbed his mouth with his filthy sleeve. "You can count on my favor for whatever good it may do you, Lieutenant."

"Thank you sir, but we've got to get you home first."

Wolfe leaned heavily against him. His fever-hot brow rested against the lieutenant's muffler and Thorton could feel the heat through the wool.

Thorton thought about boats. Wolfe was unfit; the admiral would not make it all the way to Gibraltar on horseback. Making up his mind, Thorton eased Wolfe down, then unsaddled the horses and removed their bridles. He left them grazing with their gear on the ground nearby. Picking the boat that seemed in best repair, he dragged it to the water's edge. He went back, pulled Wolfe's arm over his shoulders, and half carried, half dragged, the man over the gunwale and settled him in the bottom. Wolfe's head lolled and he moaned, but he offered neither help nor resistance. Thorton wrapped the saddle blankets around the sick man for what warmth they could offer, then put the saddlebags, waterskins, and pistols in the boat.

The wooden hull made a grinding noise as Thorton pushed it across the sand. He waded quietly into the icy water, climbed aboard, and glanced back at the dark hovels. No one stirred, not even a dog. The cold wind blew down from the hills above Algeciras Bay. He tied the tiller to steady it as he set the single lateen sail. The boat began to drift southward. He took a seat in the stern, unbound the tiller, and skimmed quietly over the bay. His weary butt and aching legs were glad to be quit of the horse. The cold hard wood of the sternsheets felt delicious by comparison.

He plotted his course by the lights of San Felipe in the distance on his left, trimmed his sails a little looser, and in half an hour the first British warship loomed up out of the dark before him. He kept well abreast to avoid the pickets rowing round the ships, but they saw him. He had no lantern or he would have made a signal. The picket rowed to pace him.

What a wonderful year it had been, full of adventure, excitement, mayhem, and novelty. In that moment Thorton was the happiest he had ever been in his life. He regretted nothing. His tenor rang out loud and clear, "Heart of oak are our ships, heart of oak are our men; We always are ready, steady, boys, steady! We'll fight and we'll conquer again and again!"

"Be off wit' ye, ye damned drunk!" the cockswain of the boat bellowed. Thorton sheered off a little and left the picket behind.

The *Duke of York* appeared before him. A lofty first-rate battleship with a hundred guns, she had watch lights lit. The state room was dark. Thorton turned his helm in and skimmed up to her starboard side. The watch was not sleeping; they saw him and shouted, "Ahoy there! What boat?"

He spilled his wind and stood up so they could see him better. "Admiral Marcus Wolfe of the *Triumph!*" he called back.

"What the hell? You're not Wolfe!"

The slumped figure of the admiral righted himself, removed the Monmouth cap, and said, "No, but I am."

A swift scramble brought them both aboard; Wolfe in a boatswain's chair, and Thorton climbing the battens with numb hands and cold feet. They were escorted to Leggott's cabin. It was aglow with lamplight and warming rapidly thanks to a small iron stove. The admiral's steward was fixing breakfast on a china plate with eggs sunny side up, toast with jam, and bacon. The savory aroma wafted through the room. Leggott came out of his sleeping cabin buttoning up his waistcoat.

"Thorton! What on earth are you doing here? What's this about Wolfe?"

Wolfe detached himself from Thorton's support and wobbled forward. "Hello, Charles. 'Tis good to see you again."

Leggott stared at Wolfe in astonishment. "My God. Marcus. It *is* you."

"So it is." Wolfe's legs buckled and he fell to the deck. Thorton knelt beside him.

"However did you get him?" Leggott demanded.

"Soto struck a bargain. He's defecting to the Portuguese."

"What?"

"The dispatches, sir." Thorton handed over the leather pouch. "But the real dispatch is in my head. The paper was for the Spanish in case I was stopped." He remained kneeling by the prostrate admiral.

Leggot's eyebrows shot up to his hairline. "The real dispatch?" He untied the red tape, scanned the paper quickly, then dropped it on his desk. It was a handsome cherry piece in the Queen Anne style. The entire cabin was furnished in a way that would have done St James Square proud. He snapped at the steward, "Pass the word for Doctor Rollins."

When the steward left, Leggott demanded, "What's this about Soto and private dispatches?"

"Major Soto, commander of the prison at Santos Nunilo and Alodia, is defecting to Portugal. He has released all the prisoners in exchange for an introduction to Duke Henrique of Coimbra. We require transports to pick up the prisoners at dawn."

"You *require*, do you? No man may *require* anything of the Royal Navy! Do you have any idea what sort of chaos this will cause? The Spanish will be furious! What in the hell was Horner thinking? He has overstepped his orders!" he roared.

Thorton rose up ramrod straight. He fixed his eyes on the furious admiral's. "Begging your pardon, sir, it wasn't Horner."

Leggott's pale blue eyes narrowed as he fixed them upon Thorton. "Speak up."

Thorton swallowed hard. "Captain Horner did ask for Admiral Wolfe, but Major Soto turned him down. The Inquisitor and some other officers were present. A little later I was unwell, so Major Soto escorted me outside for fresh air. He made overtures to me, so I dared to ask for Wolfe again. He said yes and gave us all the prisoners. I thought I should accept, sir."

"You thought! A mere lieutenant does not *think*. He obeys orders! You have embroiled us in a terrible situation. The Spanish will be outraged. We have overstepped the terms of the prisoner exchange. The war was nearly at an end, and you have provoked them!"

Thorton quailed under the verbal assault, then his temper flared. "They provoked *me* by attempting to cut out the *Amphitrite* during the truce! If you trust them, you're a fool!"

Leggott was startled to have a mere lieutenant shout at him. "You're insubordinate, Mister," he barked.

"Good God, Charles. Don't shout. I'm not dead yet," Wolfe said from the floor.

They both looked down at the supine admiral. Before they could do anything, a knock sounded on the door.

"Let the doctor in, Lieutenant," Leggott snapped.

Thorton sprang to the door.

"Belay that," said Wolfe.

Thorton froze with his hand on the latch.

Wolfe said, "Help me up."

Thorton hesitated a moment, gave Leggott a wary look, then returned to Wolfe's side and eased him into a sitting position. Wolfe did not have sufficient strength to rise, so he gathered as much dignity as he could muster while sitting on the floor wearing an ordinary seaman's smock. His voice was weary but determined. "Lieutenant Thorton acted at my direction. No blame is to attach to him or any officer involved in my rescue. I'm still the Rear Admiral of the White, and by God, you'll treat me like it."

The two admirals stared at each other. "It pains me to acquaint you with the facts under these circumstances, but you were relieved of your post in absentia. You are an admiral without distinction of color, sir, while I am the Vice Admiral of the White, and your superior."

What little fire Wolfe had went out. His voice was ashen as he spoke, "I thought they'd at least wait until I was dead or court-martialed. Very well, I submit to your authority. I regret I have no sword to surrender, sir."

Leggott relented. "I do not require your sword, Marcus." A long silence fell as he contemplated the ruined man before him. "The traitor Soto shall bear the blame. Our official position is that we believed the commander of the prison was fully authorized to make such a decision. Naturally we accepted his gracious offer. That's the best face we can put on it."

"Use him tenderly, Charles. Thanks to him I will die in England instead of a Spanish prison. I'm grateful for that."

Leggott grunted noncommittally, then barked, "Thorton, get something to eat. You're going to be taking the boats to the rendezvous. Not a word of anything you've seen or heard: this is privy business."

"Aye aye, sir."

"Let the doctor in on your way out. Dismissed."

CHAPTER ELEVEN: MAL ODEUR

The Spanish broke off negotiations. Portuguese independence and British peace were left dangling. The Spanish renewed their blockade of the Strait of Gibraltar. Publicly, the British denied all knowledge of irregularity and blamed Soto. Privately, Leggott let Horner and Thorton feel his wrath. Thorton was assigned to clean the *Amphitrite's* bilge. Personally.

First he and his crew pumped the bilge dry. Next they moved ballast: slimy granite bricks that made their arms ache to lift and feet hurt when they dropped them on their toes. When they had moved enough ballast to get at the bottom planks, they crawled through the cold narrow space with brushes to scrub the sludge from her timbers and disinfect them with vinegar. Thorton was leading by example. As ordered.

He was wearing old clothes. A blue and white checked kerchief covered his blond hair and a tarred canvas jacket covered an old knitted smock. His worst blue breeches were patched with a mismatched button on the left thigh where a missing Tudor rose had been replaced by a whittled bit of wood. The crotch had been mended, but was in danger of tearing out again. The knees were patched. His feet were bound in rags because shoes and stockings were too expensive to subject to such treatment.

He'd been down there two and a half days already. His knees and ankles and feet and hands and elbows were rough and red and sore. He had bruises and splinters from crawling among the timbers. Every part of him was cold and damp and smelled bad. He and his crew were into the really messy part of the bilge: midships. Everything foul and undesirable coagulated in the lowest part of the hull.

Up above somebody shouted, "Pass the word for Mister Thorton! Cap'n wants 'im!"

Thorton sighed and said, "Mister Bettancourt, keep them at it."

Bettancourt was a brown-haired midshipman in his mid-teens. The midshipmen and their divisions were taking turns at the nasty chore, but Thorton was condemned to the duty until it was done.

"Aye aye, sir," the youth replied.

Thorton climbed out of the hold. He smelled of bilge and vinegar and looked like a common laborer, but he knew Horner wouldn't mind. The man knew where he was and what he was doing. And why. He left murky footprints on the deck, so pulled the rags off his feet and went barefoot to the great cabin. The sentry at the captain's door caught a whiff of him and gagged. The redcoat stepped as far away as he could in the narrow confines of the coach. Thorton ignored him and knocked.

"Enter!"

Thorton opened the door, ducked under the lintel and entered the great cabin.

Lounging indolently upon the cushioned locker was His Grace Henrique, Duke of Coimbra, claimant to the throne of Portugal. The duke was the ugliest man Thorton had ever laid eyes upon. Time had not improved his looks. He wore a long blond wig with many curls and both of his eyes were crossed. He couldn't see Thorton very well, but he could smell him.

"What the hell have you been doing, Peter?" he demanded in Spanish. "You smell like the douche water from a Spanish twat!"

Thorton straightened abruptly and banged his head on a beam. He staggered at the blow and said "ow" instead of "sir." He rubbed his aching crown instead of saluting.

Horner looked as dour as a Quaker as he stood next to the gaudy uniform of the Portuguese admiral. "I believe I mentioned that Mister Thorton has been cleaning the bilge," he replied.

Henrique's uniform was sky blue with primrose yellow lapels and a lemon yellow waistcoat. The coat was laden with gold braid around the skirts, up the front, and on the arms. It had epaulettes to top it off. Should he ever fall overboard, the weight of gold bullion in his lace would drown him. Sitting with his legs akimbo the fact he was lame in one leg was not obvious, but the personal endowment contained by the tight breeches was. He had pristine white stockings of the finest silk and real gold buckles on his stylishly high-heeled black shoes. In a case of gilding the lily, his heels were gilded, too. He was a tall man with a large body, both in frame and flesh, although he was not fat. He was lightly tanned thanks to his employment as an admiral, but that had caused freckles to appear. His nose managed to be both bulbous and hawkish at the same time. He could focus his watery blue eyes only with great effort. He stared at Thorton and took in his shabby, wretched appearance.

"Bathing in winter is bad for the health, but by God, Peter, you need a dunking!"

"Aye aye, sir," Thorton replied, which was the only thing that could be said to a duke who was an admiral with a claim to the throne of Portugal.

"If you prefer, I'll hold Mister Thorton's mail until he is in a fit condition to receive it," Horner suggested.

Thorton's eyes instantly fixed on Horner with an eager light. Who would write to him? He had not written to his mother in years. He didn't know if she was even alive. He had no other kin. Maybe it was from Shakil or Captain Tangle. The hope that it might be from either of his former lovers made his heart leap.

Henrique made a moue at Horner. He reached into his breast pocket and pulled out a creamy envelope of the finest linen paper. He held it out to Thorton. Delicate lace fell around his big hand and diamonds sparkled on his fingers. Thorton's eyes darted to Horner, who nodded.

Thorton removed the fingerless gloves he had been wearing and stuffed them into the pockets of his jacket. He blew on cold fingers to warm them up, then took the envelope with a bow. It was addressed to "Peter Rais Thorton" in very elegant calligraphy. He broke the seal and opened it up. Inside was a formal invitation written in Portuguese. He was fluent in Spanish, so was able to make out that he was invited to the wedding of His Grace, Henrique, Duke of Coimbra, and Her Highness, the Princess Antónia of Portugal.

Henry explained, "'Tis João's way of buying off my claim to the throne. He has the better claim, but he doesn't have any sons. He's too fat and old to beget any more heirs. That undermines the Church's support since they want a firm and uncontested succession. God knows the Church will never support *me* for king, even if I am male and potent. Without the Church's support I'll never be anointed, even if I do take the throne. João's giving me everything I want, with the exception of a beautiful wife."

"The princess is not beautiful?" Horner inquired.

"She's my second cousin. Imagine me as an old hag. You've seen me in a dress."

Horner contemplated the hunchbacked popinjay. "She sounds like the perfect mate."

Henrique laughed at that. "Pity our children. They'll be hideous."

"Beauty is overrated. Intelligence is more useful than looks."

"For a man, perhaps, but for a woman to be ugly is a sin. She's twenty-six and unmarried. They say she's bookish, pious, proper, chaste and destined for a nunnery if no man will have her. 'Tis a lot to ask a man to sleep with a horse, even if she is a princess."

"So it is. Then again, many a woman has been obliged to sleep with a horse's ass for lesser reasons," replied Horner.

Henrique narrowed his eyes at Horner. He couldn't tell if the captain was making a jest at his expense or not. Horner's expression remained placid.

The duke turned to an easier target. "Of course you'll come, Peter." His jeweled hands rested on the golden head of his cane.

"I'm not at liberty to accept, sir. I must apply to my superior officer for leave," Thorton explained.

"Feh. You're all invited. I shall be very put out if you don't come. Even you, Horny." He flicked his wrist at Horner and gave him a cross-eyed glare that was meant to be firm.

"I shall inform Admiral Leggott of your gracious invitation, but it will be up to him to grant or deny leave," Horner replied smoothly.

The future son-in-law of the apparent King of Portugal snorted. "He'd better, or I shall be vexed. I came to deliver the invitations in person because I anticipated difficulties, although not so many as I was given! How dare that oaf Soto disrupt negotiations! Spain was about to recognize Portuguese independence! He ruined it! They think I had something to do with it, which I don't, and I resent the insinuation that I do! I know nothing about the lunatic and I have informed them as much. The first I knew was when he came flying up Algeciras Bay in a commandeered fishboat to demand refuge with my squadron. The ass had the temerity to expect a reward for ruining Portuguese independence! Can you believe it? What on earth possessed you to write a letter of introduction for him?" The last was directed at Thorton.

Thorton was never any good at dissembling. Put on the spot like that, all he could do was blurt out the truth. "He said he'd release Admiral Wolfe if I did, sir."

"Bah. What good is a half dead British admiral to me?"

"Soto is handsome," Thorton ventured. "I thought you might like him."

Henrique snorted. "I am besieged by men who think their looks are sufficient reason for me to grant them rank and preference. But here's the thing: I am utterly incompetent when it comes to anything useful like the government or the navy, so it is essential that I select officers who are actually useful. God knows if we are obliged to depend upon my good looks and expertise, Portugal is doomed."

"Your Grace shows unusual wisdom by insisting upon qualified officers," Horner remarked. "The defects in the Spanish system are largely due to patronage at the expense of skill."

"Soto is a thorn in my side. I can't hand him over to the Spanish because if I do, nobody else will defect to me. But I don't want the fool, either." The gold head of the cane suddenly rapped Horner's desk and made the captain and lieutenant jump. "Enough of that. You're coming to my wedding. Leggott owes me something after inflicting Soto on me."

"I am not in a position to dictate to Admiral Leggott," Horner replied. "You must make your case yourself."

"I will call on him, but I want to be certain that you *will* come. I'm not going to put myself out for you if you're going to snub me."

"Your Grace, we are flattered and gratified that you remember us so well. We are honored to be invited to your wedding, and should Admiral Leggott grant his permission, we would be delighted to attend. I did not mean to sound reluctant, only practical." Horner gave a small bow.

Henrique allowed himself to be mollified. "I will count on it. I know you are a man of your word. When you say something, you stand by it. Very well, I shall call on Admiral Leggott."

"I know Sir Charles will be most interested to meet you," Horner replied.

What the gruff, short-tempered Leggott would think of the diamond-studded peacock was easily conjectured, even by Peter Thorton, who was not clever when it came to estimating the cogitations of other men. 'Interested' was the diplomatic way to put it.

Henrique rose and used his cane for support. He had to crouch under the low deckhead, but he did so with hunchbacked grace as if he were not even aware of the wooden beam that skimmed his wig. "There'll be a dinner invitation, of course. I'll want all the officers from the *Ajax* there."

"I believe we can accommodate you for dinner, Your Grace," Horner replied.

Henrique smiled warmly at him. "I'll send word at the last minute as I always do. I'm sure it will inconvenience you, but that's an admiral's prerogative, is it not?"

"We will hold ourselves in readiness for your command, sir," Horner replied. He kept a bland countenance.

The steward came forward with the duke's hat and cloak. Thorton put the cloak around the uneven shoulders and Horner handed him the hat laden with ostrich feathers.

"I'm going ashore for some refreshment. Where do you recommend for pretty harlots and good wine?" Henrique asked as he accepted his hat.

"Our shore leave was cut short by a Spanish raid, so I have not had the opportunity to become familiar with the local establishments. However, if you are inclined to the picturesque, there's a green and yellow boat at anchor that may entertain," Horner replied.

"I saw it. The one with the striped awning, no?"

"The same."

"Captain Jack is a friend of Commodore Tangueli," Thorton dared to put in.

That caught Henrique's attention. "Is he? I shall definitely investigate. Now gentlemen, I bid you adieu."

He ducked under the lintel and lurched out the door with his exaggerated mincing gait. They accompanied him on deck. Marines presented arms and the boatswain's call shrilled. The drums ruffled. They assisted him through the entry port and watched with trepidation as the ungainly figure clambered down the battens. With the Portuguese admiral safely in his boat, Horner stood the men down.

Turning to Thorton, the captain remarked, "I feel like I've been henpecked by a parrot."

Thorton laughed in spite of himself. "His Grace has a large personality," he agreed.

"I suspect His Grace is going to keep us busy with social obligations and minor political storms. That being the case, I am going ashore this afternoon to tend my errands. I shall be back after supper. Pass the word for Mister Forsythe."

"Aye aye, sir."

CHAPTER 13: THE CAPTAIN'S AFFAIR

Lieutenant Roger Perry was at the wardroom table reviewing a list of needed supplies when Thorton sidled up to him. The brunet officer looked up. "I can smell you coming, Peter, so there's no use sneaking up on me."

Thorton was crestfallen. "I need your help, Roger. I haven't had any shore leave."

"You want me to slip you ashore while Horner's gone?"

"Aye."

Perry looked around, but they were alone in the wardroom. Nobody had cared to follow the aromatic lieutenant. A weak sun shone through the stern windows. It qualified as 'warm' by English standards: they could not see their breaths.

"I suppose I must. God knows you've helped me sneak a little unofficial shore leave often enough. But first you must bathe. You can't go anywhere smelling like that."

Thorton smiled warmly at him and nodded. "I will. I want to see Alan."

Perry's mouth turned down. He looked away for a moment, then said, "All right. If you must."

"Thank you, Roger!" He darted off, calling for Ra'uf. In a matter of minutes he was scrubbing in cold salt water and harsh soap.

Meanwhile, Perry approached Forsythe on the quarterdeck. "Sir, I wonder if I might borrow Mister Thorton this afternoon. He's never been responsible for requisitioning supplies and I think he ought to learn. All is quiet and in good order; the ship can spare him."

Forsythe hesitated. "Is the bilge done?"

"Nearly so," Perry lied smoothly. "No reason Bettancourt can't finish it up. God knows Thorton's been working hard down there. Besides, Horner had him up to chat with the duke, so he's out of durance vile."

"I'm not sure," Forsythe replied.

"Mister Thorton has been vigorous in combat, but you and I both know the ship runs on her belly. He really ought to learn about supplies." He smiled warmly at the first lieutenant.

Forsythe caved under Perry's charm. "Very well. But make sure you get him back before Horner returns!"

A squeaky clean Thorton changed into his good frock coat, put some money in his purse, clapped on his hat, and joined Perry in the boat. The sailors rowed them to shore.

Perry laughed as they walked along the quay. "This is like the old days, except now it is I who am reluctantly helping you go absent without leave instead of the other way around!"

Thorton ducked his head and blushed. "I miss Alan."

"Damme, but there's too many men in Gibraltar. I haven't even been able to knock down a barmaid," Perry replied. He touched the scar that ran across his face. "It isn't as easy as it used to be," he complained.

They reached the main street and turned left toward the Admiralty warehouses. The street was paved and well-trafficked. Suddenly Perry grabbed Thorton's arm and dragged him into a doorway. "Horner! Stay behind me."

Perry peered out into the street. He was supposed to be ashore and was traveling in the correct direction to be doing his duty, so there was no harm in him being seen, but Thorton was supposed to be in the bilge. "Hey, Alan's with him!"

Thorton stuck his head out. "What?"

Perry shoved him back into the doorway. A marine officer came out of the shop just then, so Thorton got whacked in the back by the door as it opened. It knocked his hat off. He caught it.

"I beg your pardon!" the marine said.

"'Twas my fault," Thorton replied. Then "Barnes!" as he recognized the man.

"Thorton!" Barnes' green eyes narrowed at him. He held the door open. "You need it worse than I do," he remarked cryptically.

Thorton eyed him askance, but he thought it better to step inside than make a scene. Perry followed him. The redheaded marine gave a mocking laugh and shut the door behind them. The glass in the door was smoked so he couldn't see what they were doing, but it didn't matter. He knew what sort of shop it was. He sniggered as he walked in the opposite direction.

Thorton made a beeline for the window that looked into the side street and paid no attention to the contents of the shop. Perry looked around, took note of the nature of the establishment, and coughed.

The shopkeeper came forward with a smile. "How may I help you, gentlemen?"

"I think we're in the wrong shop," Perry replied.

The shopkeeper smiled knowingly. "Of course, sir. Our services are entirely discreet, so it is easy to make a mistake. However, it is your good fortune to have stumbled over us by accident. I was just showing our latest device to a previous customer. 'Tis straight from Italy where it has proven effective in the prevention of the pox. The Italians are experts upon the pox," he said with a bit of humor. The referenced article was a linen sheath designed to fit over the male member. It lay openly on the wooden counter.

Thorton was too busy looking out the window to pay any attention. As he watched, Abby and Horner went arm and arm around the corner. Abby wore his dark glasses and carried his cane. The two were chatting as they walked. A pang of jealousy clenched his heart. He told himself that Horner was merely being kind to assist the retired commander; Gibraltar was not easy for a blind man to find his way around. The commander's servant boy was prone to wandering off.

The commander and captain disappeared from his view, so he turned around. When he saw what was on display, his jaw dropped.

Perry couldn't resist twitting him. "What do you think, Peter? Will it protect your peter from the Italian disease?"

"I-I-I don't know," Thorton stammered and blushed.

"We also have sheepskins for the prevention of pregnancy. I have never yet met a young naval officer who felt he was ready to be a father," the clerk informed them. He was a man in his thirties with a neat brown wig, tidy cravat, and modest brown coat. He looked like an apothecary, which was what he was, albeit in a highly specialized field.

"I imagine your services are much in demand here," Perry replied, "given the number of men who pass through Gibraltar each year."

The clerk smiled and gave a small bow. "I like to think my profession is a patriotic one. I support the health and happiness of His Majesty's soldiers and sailors."

"I don't need anything like that," replied a red-faced Thorton.

"You will," the apothecary replied complacently. "Remember where to find us when you become concerned about the health of your virile member, or when your mistress is crying over a delay in her monthly curse."

Thorton stammered something unintelligible and hauled Perry bodily out of the shop. On the street he stopped to mop his face with his handkerchief.

Perry burst out laughing. "You're such a ninny, Peter. You have to admit, it was a useful discovery. I have never been clapped up yet, but I have had a close call. I feel more at ease knowing where to find discreet treatment. I don't care to expose my pillicock to Ferncastle, or anyone else I eat dinner with."

"Will you stop!" Thorton whirled away and turned the corner. He hid behind a tree and watched Abby and Horner walking far down the street.

Perry laughed at him again. "Are you going to follow them? Are you that jealous?"

Thorton glared at him. "Yes!"

Perry was amused all over again. "Now I can pretend I'm you and lecture you. 'He's not worth your time, Peter. If he's cheating on you, you're better off without him. Why are you wasting your time on someone like that? Peter, you're making a fool of yourself. Show some sense!'" He wagged his finger in mock dudgeon.

Thorton got even redder. "I take it all back. I've never been jealous before! What am I going to do?"

"Give into it. Follow them. Prove to yourself that you're a knob-headed fool with oakum for brains. Next time you'll remember what an ass you made of yourself and behave better."

Thorton wasn't sure it was good advice, but it agreed very much with his own desire to spy upon his lover and captain. "All right. Come with me."

Perry strolled along the street as Thorton darted from tree to tree. A few passersby gave Thorton strange looks, but Perry told them cheerfully, "Don't mind him, he's having a jealous fit and following his lover."

A carter in patched jacket laughed and showed his broken teeth. "Good luck to 'im, sir." He went on his way.

"You do realize you're making a spectacle of yourself, don't you, Peter?" Perry asked cheerfully as he came up to where Thorton hiding behind a hedge. Thorton was completely oblivious. He was too busy spying. Perry looked past him to watch Horner wrap an arm around Abby's waist and lift him carefully over muddy ruts at the next intersection. Abby's white gloved hands held onto Horner's shoulders.

"Right. If that had been my girl, I would have felt a pang just then, but Horner is a good Christian. You know Abby can't see very well."

Thorton whimpered. The two lieutenants watched covertly as Horner set the slim commander down. Abby's hands stayed on the taller man's shoulders a moment longer than strictly necessary. He smiled up at the captain and spoke to him.

"Alan is flirting with him! Don't you think so?" Thorton was sure of it, yet terribly uncertain.

Perry muttered, "Alan likes to flirt with everyone. He thinks he's too clever for us, but we're on to him. He's going to get a poke in the nose someday."

Abby hooked his hand in Horner's elbow. The two of them ambled along the street talking. They turned onto a residential street and disappeared from view.

"I thought they didn't like each other!" Thorton wailed.

"They appear to be getting on famously," Perry replied. "But don't worry. You know Horner's not that kind of man."

"But he is." Two spots of color appeared on Thorton's cheeks.

Perry laughed. "Him? Old Horny? He's a widower with children. He's so damned upright and proper I think he swallowed a ramrod." After a pause he said, "You don't really think Alan is trying to seduce him, do you? That would be too much, even for him. Horner will be angry if he figures it out."

"I think he knows perfectly well what Alan is up to. I have a right to be jealous, don't you think?"

Perry started walking towards the side street where the naval couple had disappeared. "I think you have reason to be piqued by Alan's behavior, the minx. Has he ever cozened you before?"

Thorton walked quickly along the street with Perry. "I don't know. However, I haven't been strictly faithful to him, either. Maybe he's giving me a dose of my own medicine."

Perry gave him a startled look, then said, "Oh, you mean Miss Brandy. He shouldn't hold that against you. It was medical treatment."

"Not just her." He walked fast enough to leave Perry behind.

Perry ran to catch up to him. "I hope you're not counting me in that."

"Ah, no. Someone else."

"Who else? Tell me! You know all about my affairs; I never kept them from you. Who was it?"

Thorton paused at the corner of the street and peeked around. Halfway down the block Horner and Abby were standing on the porch of neat two story brick house with white trim. They were talking, then Horner bent to place a kiss on Abby's cheek. Abby gave him a warm smile, then returned it with a peck on the cheek as he went into the house. Horner waited for the door to shut, then came down the walk with a bounce in his step. Thorton hastily ducked back around the corner and collided with Perry.

"My God. You were right!" Perry said as they both pressed up against the wall of the corner house.

Thorton grabbed his arm and pulled him into the narrow space between two houses. The side yard was so narrow they could extend their arms and touch the walls on either side. They retreated deep into the shadows until Horner passed by. Uncharacteristically for him, he was swinging his arms and whistling a jaunty tune.

They stood in the cold, dark shadow between the houses without speaking for a long time. Finally Thorton said, "What am I going to do, Roger? If he weren't my commanding officer I'd challenge him to duel, but I can't shoot my superior officer. After all this time I finally have a good captain, and he steals my lover!"

Perry removed his hat and ran his fingers through his hair. "Who would have thought it? Horner! I'm starting to think every man is bed with every other one."

"It does seem more common than I had originally supposed," Thorton agreed. "But in Horner's case . . . I think he's lonely."

Perry snorted. "I think he's got the horn like any other man."

"Well, yes. It happens to all of us, doesn't it?"

"It certainly does."

Thorton took off his hat and worried the brim. "Maybe I should tell Alan what I saw and ask him to explain himself."

"You may not like the answer."

"Will you come with me?"

"Of course. I have to see how this penny opera ends."

An hour later the two were nursing beers in a tavern. Thorton stared morosely into his tankard. Perry said, "I hate to say 'I told you so,' but I told you so."

Thorton lifted his mug and drank deep. He slammed it down on the scarred wooden table top. "Why did he pick Horner instead of me?"

Perry immediately replied, "Because Horner is a gentleman of a certain class, and you're not. You don't have the breeding to keep up with someone like Alan. He's the son of an earl. Your father was a halfbreed Indian. I won't mention your mother."

Thorton winced. "He didn't mind before. Besides, my stepfather was a minister. That's respectable."

Perry leaped to his feet. "Sir."

Thorton looked up, stared in shock at Horner, then jumped hastily to his feet. The captain gave the two lieutenants a long hard look. "I am not surprised to see Mister Perry ashore, but I wonder what Mister Thorton is doing here."

"Lieutenant Forsythe thought Mister Thorton ought to learn about the supply process, sir, since he has never done so before."

"Did he think that up on his own or did you suggest it to him, Mister Perry?"

Perry stood at attention. "I had the privilege of drawing his attention to the opportunity, sir."

Horner snorted. He knew his lieutenants well enough to know exactly what had happened. "Very well. I do not question Mister Forsythe's judgment. He has the right and duty to act in my absence. Mister Perry, you need to need finish your errands. Mister Thorton, Commander Abbelefan was asking for you. You may call on him, but make certain you're back by the end of the second dog watch."

Thorton choked out, "I have already called upon him, sir."

Horner stared at him with steely blue eyes. "I see. Then there will be nothing to delay your return to the ship." He turned back to Perry. "Bring him back before he ruins himself with drink."

"Aye aye, sir," Perry replied.

"That will be all." Horner turned on his heel and walked away.

Thorton slumped into his chair again. Perry sat down next to him and pushed his beer in front of him. "Have another drink."

"What am I going to do?"

"You're going to drink until you forget about it. Then I'm going to take you back to the ship and pour you into your hammock to sleep it off."

Thorton drank.

CHAPTER 13: BOMBARDMENT

Thorton woke up in bed next to Perry. They were in an actual bed, not a hammock, and although it seemed the room was swimming, the bed was behaving with perfect propriety. In other words, it did nothing at all, which was exactly what a respectable piece of furniture ought to do.

Hazily he recalled the previous few hours. Perry had gotten him drunk then hired a bed for him to sleep it off. Bamboozled by beer, Thorton had completely forgotten they were supposed to go back to the ship. Now that his head was aching as he sobered up, he remembered quite clearly and wondered how very late they were, or was it so late as to count as the next day? Horner was going to be furious.

That brought him to a fuzzier series of recollections. He could not decide if they were the yearnings of his beer addled brain, or if they had actually happened. He turned his aching head—there was Perry asleep next to him. Long black lashes lay against the tanned cheeks and made him look angelic in the faint moonlight in spite of the scar. Yet what Thorton thought he remembered was decidedly devilish. Gingerly he lifted the bedclothes to take a look. They were both naked. He gently lowered the sheet. He wiggled his bum experimentally and felt a certain twinge. He let out a groan.

Perry yawned and opened his eyes. He wrapped an arm around Thorton's waist and kissed his cheek, then made a face. "Ugh. You need a shave."

"I don't remember last night."

Perry laughed. "You were drunker than I've ever seen you."

"You took advantage of me!" Thorton accused.

"You were very willing," Perry replied.

Thorton blushed. "I don't remember."

Perry's arm tightened on him. He murmured against Thorton's shoulder, "I do."

"Why, Roger? Why did you do it?"

Perry rose on his elbow to stare into his face. "Because I wanted to. You've had me mixed up inside for months. I had my chance, so I took it. Go ahead and be angry if you want. 'Tis done."

"I can't remember!"

"You enjoyed it."

"Bah. How would I know? I was drunk." He was aggrieved to finally get Perry in bed but not remember it. He was doubly aggrieved that Perry had taken by foul means what he could have had by fair, if only he had asked.

"If you don't believe me, ask the neighbors. They pounded on the wall," Perry grinned at him.

Thorton turned bright red and pulled the coverlet over his face.

Perry pulled it down again. He looked at Thorton very earnestly. "I want you for my lover, Peter. God help me, I do."

Once upon a time they had been best friends. Thorton had been secretly, hopelessly in love with him. Then Perry had done him wrong. His Sallee friends had warned him, but they had made up and become friends again. Now Perry had gotten him drunk and taken advantage of him. Thorton was feeling peeved about that. But Perry was giving him an earnest look with those big brown puppy dog eyes. He melted.

Who knew him better than Roger Perry? Who had gotten into and out of countless scrapes with him? Whose life had he saved back on the *Dauntless?* Who had he lived with, worked with, slept with? Roger Perry wasn't perfect, but nobody was.

He wrapped his arms around the brunet lieutenant. "Yes."

Perry kissed him passionately. Thorton surrendered to the giddy delight of love. The decision was made; he had no regrets. This time when Perry made love to him he remembered every detail of it.

They were dozing in the aftermath when the roar of artillery thundered them awake. They bolted out of bed, stumbled in the darkness of the strange room, then groped frantically for their clothes. Orange light from rockets flickered like lightning beyond the curtains. Their inn was only a few blocks from the naval yard where the shells rained down.

Other doors were opening in the hallway outside and men called questions. The answer was always the same, "The Spanish are attacking!"

The wayward lieutenants got dressed by the glow of the rockets. It flickered, went out, then flashed again. The rumble of Spanish battleships was continuous.

"They haven't answered yet," Thorton moaned. "Why don't they answer?"

"They were in their beds and taken by surprise, just like us. They have to get the powder up."

They finished dressing and ran out of the inn without paying their bill. They quite forgot about it in the excitement. Sailors, some still drunk and others hungover, ran toward the waterfront. Marine officers on horseback raced to the quay. Clouds of steam issued from the mouths of men and beasts. Thorton and Perry ran along the street with the rest of the desperate men, Thorton's head pounding at every step.

Reaching the waterfront they tried to find a boat. Those that were for hire were rapidly being taken up. Suddenly Thorton saw a forlorn figure: Alan Abby. He was clutching his cane and his grey cloak was around his shoulders. "A boat!" he called. "I want to hire a boat!"

Thorton and Perry ran over to him. "Alan! Where's your servant?"

"Peter, thank God! He ran off at the first gun, damn him! I found my way to the waterfront, but I can't find a boat. Do you have one?"

"Not yet," Perry answered.

Abby gave Thorton a desperate look. "Take me with you. Don't leave me alone in a siege. Take me to the *Amphitrite*."

"All right," said Thorton. He grabbed Abby's hand and pulled him along.

Perry spotted some men he knew piling into a boat further along the quay. "Hey, *Pegasus!* Can we ride with you?"

"Get in," the officers replied.

Perry, Thorton, and Abby squeezed into the overloaded boat. The sailors at the oars swore as they hit somebody on every stroke. Thorton pulled Abby into his lap to try to give the man beside him more room. The boat rode dangerously low as they made their way over the shimmering waters toward the line of battleships at anchor. The rockets continued popping over head, accompanied by the throatier roar of the artillery. Fire reared up amber and awful, but they couldn't tell what building. Everywhere along the waterfront boats were launching to take men on leave back to their ships.

The *Duke of York* roared her defiance. Being to leeward they could not see ten foot long tongues of flames leaping from her guns' mouths, but they could see the orange flash that momentarily limned the masts, then died away as precious seconds ticked by as Leggott's flagship reloaded for another cannonade. More British ships replied until the thunder of gunnery became continuous. It reverberated against the Rock and rolled back from the hills above San Felipe.

"They're raising anchor," Perry reported when he could make out the *Amphitrite*. "We're almost there!"

The lookouts on the frigate were called out, "What boat?" as the overcrowded launch approached.

"Officers from the *Amphitrite!*" the cockswain called back. "Permission to hook on? We've got three of your boys."

"Permission granted."

The entry way opened as Perry, Abby, and Thorton crawled up the accommodation ladder. Thorton could hear the trill of the boatswain's pipe governing the capstan. "Wait in my cabin," he told Abby.

Abby nodded and hurried to the companionway. He knew every inch of the vessel and needed no cowardly servant to show him around. Thorton and Perry ran up to the quarterdeck to report.

Horner was on deck in his slippers and nightshirt with his dressing gown over them. He still wore his nightcap and his dentures were out; he spoke with a lisp through the hole in his front teeth.

"Misher Perry! Misher Thorshon! You're lathe."

"We're very sorry, sir." They showed contrite faces.

"The *Duge of Yorg* shignaled us tho shand by for dispashes. God'th blood, I wanth my theeth! Thage shashions. Shend Forshythe up. He'z doing both your duthiez."

Perry couldn't make him out at all, but Thorton had spent time around him with his teeth out before. "Take battle stations and send Forsythe up, sir?"

"Yesh! Go."

"Aye aye, sir."

They fled.

"Thank God he didn't have his teeth in or he would have bawled us out until our ears bled," Perry said as they raced belowdecks.

On the gundeck Forsythe was trying to get the anchors in and prepare the guns, both of which were Perry and Thorton's duties. He had breeches and wool socks under his nightshirt and coat. He had no hat. His blond hair gleamed dully in the lantern light.

"Peter! Roger! I'm glad to see you!"

"We relieve you, sir. Horner wants you on the quarterdeck."

"Save the anchor if you can, but cut it in an instant if you get the word."

"Aye aye, sir," they both replied. Perry grabbed an axe. Supervising the cable was part of his duty.

Marines in their jerseys and drawers had tumbled out of their hammocks to work the capstan. It could take as much forty-five minutes to get the anchor up even if there were no complications. Sailors and powder monkeys were at work passing cartridges and shot along the deck to ready the guns.

Thorton passed quickly along the port side to inspect. He heard a man say, "Cor, look at 'im! Silk stockings day and night for that one."

Thorton and his aching head were in no mood to be criticized. He whirled on the man and snapped, "You're out of order, sailor! Shut your mouth and keep your mind on your duty." Then he helped himself to a ladle of beer from the bucket to quench his thirst and cure his hangover. He couldn't tell if it was the drum or his brain that throbbed so.

"Aye aye, sir," the man replied, knuckling his forehead sullenly.

A few minutes later word was passed, "Double shot! Round and chain! Captain's orders!"

"Double shot! Round and chain, aye!" Perry and Thorton sang out in turn. They supervised their guns and left the capstan in the capable hands of MacDonald, the Scottish boatswain. Either they would get it up in time, or they wouldn't.

CHAPTER 14: THE DEVIL'S COACHMAN

A boat came along the port side and several men climbed the accommodation ladder without ceremony. Some of the hands on shore had managed to make it back to the ship and every one of them was wanted.

A few minutes later orders came. "Let slip the anchor! Captain's orders!" Midshipman Sinclair ran down the ladder with a shout.

"Damme. I thought we were going to get it," said Perry. "You heard him. Pawl the capstan." The pawl thunked into position. "Is the cable buoyed?"

"Cable is buoyed," came the reply.

"Release the buoy!"

"Release the buoy, aye." A moment later, "Buoy away and fair."

MacDonald put his knife to the line and swung the back of the axe against it. It required several hard blows to sever the hemp that was as thick as a man's arm. When the cable parted, the severed end went whizzing across the deck and disappeared out the hawse hole. The buoy tied to the cable would mark the spot so it could be fished up later.

The gun crews continued to prepare the guns. They didn't have half the men they needed.

"Careful!" Thorton shouted. "Make the first shot count and you may not need a second!"

Overhead men swarmed aloft to make sail. Soon the *Amphitrite* was under way. She clawed close-hauled along a lee shore. Thorton cocked his head to listen. Another set of guns was pounding away southwest of them. The throaty roar announced a battleship. He shivered. They'd have to run a gauntlet of big ships to make their escape; he didn't fancy it. Small guns were answering from the same quarter: a frigate.

"Roger! Can you see anything?"

Perry opened a gun port and looked out. He scanned the bay, then pulled his head in. "Line of Spanish battleships about a mile out. They're pounding the navy yard. One of our ships is on fire. We'll be coming out from behind the screen of battleships shortly. There's action southwest of us."

"Can you see it?"

"No, just the flash of their guns."

"Sounds big."

The noise rumbled in through the open port.

"Aye," Perry replied. "Line of battle ship." He squatted with one foot out flung to sight along the barrel. "Mount the muzzle a little."

Two men on each side put handspikes into the carriage and heaved with all their might to raise the gun. Perry scooted the quoin back an inch. "Down easy." He took another sight.

"How big?" Thorton asked.

"Not sure, maybe a sixty-four or seventy." A single broadside from such a vessel threw more weight of metal than the entire armament of the *Amphitrite*.

Word was passed from above, "Aim the for the sails and rigging." Normally the British preferred to hull their enemy, but it was highly unlikely that a mere frigate could sink a battleship. The best they could hope for was to disable her sails so she could not maneuver.

"Christ. You don't think Horner will really take on a battleship, do you?" Perry asked.

"He has before," Thorton replied.

"Damme. We're on the low road to Hell tonight."

Midshipman Jackson spoke up. "We've whipped the dons before. We'll do it again. Mister Thorton's whipped them a deuce at a time."

Perry glared at the young officer who promptly piped down.

Thorton, being on the lee side, would have little to do; it was the starboard that was exposed to the Spanish line. He paced with his shoulders bowed under the low beams and rubbed his aching head. Chambers and Jackson were pale and quiet as they stood their posts. Jackson, being the elder, had hopes of making lieutenant in the not too distant future—if fortune favored him. The *Amphitrite* heeled further as she gained speed.

"Godspeed," Thorton said suddenly.

"Godspeed indeed. We'll need a clean pair of heels tonight, begging your pardon, sir," the captain of the nearby gun replied.

"The *Tritie's* fast," somebody replied.

"None faster," another man agreed.

Thorton smiled. The *Amphitrite* could indeed fly, but he had been a Sallee rover for a few brief months. He had served under a man who knew how to wring the utmost speed from a vessel: Isam Rais Tangueli. His *Sea Leopard* could make fourteen knots. She was sleeker, leaner, sharper, and shallower than the *Amphitrite*, and her lofty lateen rig was severely overhatted by British standards. He said nothing about it. He listened to the men hearten each other as they bragged about the *Amphitrite's* speed, her captain, and her guns. Their officers had drilled them mercilessly at sail evolution and gunnery and now they were glad, although they had caviled at the time.

Minutes ticked by. "Hurry up and wait," remarked Thorton.

"Aye aye, sir," the nearest hands replied.

The command came at last, "Run out the guns."

"Two, six, heave!" Thorton called.

The men put their backs into it and the decks vibrated with the growl of iron shod wheels as the guns inched out. Cold wind swirled through the close air of the gundeck. The sound of the Spanish battleship came louder to them even as the bombardment of Gibraltar lessened. Not that the Spanish had eased up; no, it was only that the *Amphitrite* was running further away from the iron hail that pummeled Gibraltar.

"Glad we're going," somebody remarked.

"Silence!" Perry barked. "Stand your posts! It will be soon!"

Thorton stuck his head out the forward port. He could see a burning hulk southeast of them: the Spaniard's victim. Guns were still firing; the victim had a consort. He peered into the night. The vessels were low and sleek and there were four. "The Portuguese squadron! I guess Henrique didn't have enough diamonds."

More men stuck their heads out to survey the scene. "Look! The bawdy boat!" Somebody pointed east and a little north. Thorton flipped one of the lenses up on his spyglass and looked through the night glass. The two triangular sails of the floating whorehouse could be seen among the shoals. She was hugging the shore as she slipped south towards the mouth of the bay while the Portuguese and Spanish fought.

"Hope she makes it," somebody said.

"Aye," came the general agreement.

Word was passed from above, "Wait for the captain's command to fire."

"Soon now," somebody said.

"Damn, that wind is cold." Their sea chests were stowed in the hold where they couldn't get any warmer clothes.

"Silence!" Thorton roared. Sweat trickled under his hair in spite of the chill.

They heard a whistling high over head.

"Greetings to you, too," Perry replied. "They've seen us, but they haven't got the range."

"Ready, lads, steady," Thorton crooned to them.

A shot plunged into the sea half a cable off their starboard. Men closed their eyes and prayed the Spanish never did find the range. Suddenly the *Amphitrite* swung as close to the wind as she could claw. Her sails shuddered and thundered, then she fell off a point and held it.

"We're going to cross her wake! Thorton, be ready!" Perry shouted.

Thorton thrust his head out a gun port, then jerked it back in. "Mount the muzzles!" he shouted. The greater heel depressed his guns and he did not want to spend his first precious broadside in the sea. The men heaved the handspikes and the gun captains pulled the quoins back several inches. The barrels thumped down again. Thorton went along them and checked each one.

"Too high! Down a bit." He ran to the next one. "Good!" Then the next, "Up a bit!"

"Fire!" came the word from above.

Thorton ran forward. He crouched down behind the gun, sighted, and stepped aside. "Gun two, fire!"

The even numbered guns were all on the port side. The gun roared and a spout of fiery orange sparks erupted from the vent to char the deckhead above. Acrid smoke swirled through the confined space. Thorton stuck his head out the port to try to get clear of the smoke to watch. "Through her mizzen topsail!"

A cheer went up.

One by one he ran to each gun, checked their aim, and timed their shot. Every few seconds another gun roared as the *Amphitrite* crossed the stern the Spanish battleship. In that position only the Spaniard's sternchasers could answer at them. He saw the tongues of flame six feet long leaping from their barrels before the sound of the shot came to him. Overhead something cracked and fell heavily deck.

His crews were working frantically to worm, sponge, load, and run out again. The Spanish guns began a rolling broadside as the *Amphitrite* came far enough forward to be in their traverse. Shot whistled through their rigging and smashed into the hull. Splinters flew and men cried out in pain and fear.

"Sand!" Thorton shouted as blood spilled. A boy ran forward to toss handfuls of sand on the blood.

"Number four loaded and ready, sir!" one of the gun captains called.

"Fire at will" Thorton shouted.

The gun thundered. The other guns were all ready a few seconds later than their neighbors, but still posed an impressive volley. Impressive for a mere frigate. The battleship shrugged them off.

Sinclair ran down the ladder. "Damage report!"

"Two wounded, no damage," Thorton replied crisply.

Perry added, "No damage here."

"Two wounded, no damage, aye," the youth said, and ran back up again.

Thorton watched the men work. Each leeward gun was restrained by a tackle hooked to the carriage and secured to a ringbolt amidships to prevent it from rolling down the sloping deck and running itself out before it was loaded. The gun captain put his leather-clad thumb over the vent to prevent a rush of air through the vent from firing any smoldering materials as it was sponged. The rammer sponged, making certain to turn and twist the sponge to drench any 'honeycombs'—pits of corrosion within the barrel. He worked it vigorously back and forth in the barrel four or five times, then drew it out. He banged it on the side of the carriage to shake off any fouling. Bits of black stuff flaked to the deck.

The loader took a cartridge from the boy who held it, inserted it into the muzzle with his left hand, and shoved it as deep into the gun as he could. If the sponger had not done his job properly, the embers would light the cartridge and blow his hand off. No such accident occurred, although it happened often enough. The rammer reversed the sponge and used the rope-wrapped end to ram the cartridge home. To Thorton it seemed to take an eternity, but the men worked quickly and carefully as they had been taught. They had great respect for the 'Devil's Coachman' that had carried so many men to Hell.

The gun captain inserted his priming prick into the vent to make certain the cartridge was seated properly and to open a path for the priming powder. Next came a wad, the round shot, another wad, then the canister, and yet another wad. When that was done, the gun captain filled the vent with powder and poured some behind it as well. He crushed the powder with his horn so it would catch more easily, then handed off the horn to another man who kept it well clear of the gun. The tackle was released and the gun ran itself out across the slanting deck. The carriage slammed against the hull and Thorton winced.

"Tighten that tackle! Don't let it slam into the side like that!" Thorton directed.

A shattering screech of wood above decks told them the Spanish had the range. Thorton was grateful the Spanish were firing at the rigging. He might live through the night. Not so the poor sods on deck. He rubbed his aching head, waved his hand to try to clear lingering gunsmoke from his face, then walked along the line of guns, squatting down to check their aim. On the other side, Perry waited tense and ready, knowing that his turn would come.

CHAPTER 15: A RESCUE

Thorton peered out a gun port as they passed beyond the Spaniard's range of traverse. The Spanish continued firing on the Portuguese vessels. The Portuguese swarmed in a long line, taking advantage of their greater maneuverability to thump her bow and stern. They were pummeled in turn when they passed amidships and that was a heavy toll to bear. The Spaniard had springs on her anchor cables so she could twist to bring her guns to bear better, but the agile xebecs darted around her like dogs around a bear.

Perry came over to stick his head out next to Thorton's. "Damme, do you think they can take the Spaniard? They have the advantage of numbers."

Thorton shook his head. "I don't see any gaps in her guns. She's not holed, and she doesn't need her sails. The Portuguese xebecs only carry nine pounders. I don't think they can hurt her. She'll pound them to pieces unless they run."

"You'd think they'd know that."

"I imagine they do."

"So why stay? They could escape."

Thorton could think of only one explanation. "They're defending their burning flagship. They've got to get Henrique off her."

"Prepare to wear ship!" came down from above.

Perry jerked his head back and ran to the starboard side. The *Amphitrite* came around and began to run back the way she had come: to the windward of the Spanish battleship. Now it was Perry's turn to sweat and swear and make certain his guns were well-pointed.

The Spaniard thumped them as they came into range, and the ship shuddered in her timbers. Each of the *Amphitrite's* starboard guns roared in turn as they unloaded a rolling broadside at the much larger ship. Perry took it upon himself to adjust the aim lower: deck level. They had not been able to see the Spanish springs when the order to fire at her rigging had come, so attacking her rigging to immobilize her had made sense. Now it was a waste of ammunition.

A ball crashed through the bulwark overhead and they heard it carom across the deck to smash through the opposite bulwark and into the sea. A little lower and the cannonball would have shot through the starboard hull, crossed the gun deck, and opened a hole in the opposite side.

They tacked again and Thorton steeled his nerve and pointed his guns a little lower. "Aim for the quarterdeck," he told his men. "Let's see if we can disrupt their command. Guns two, four, and six, fire together. Wait for my command."

A Spanish cannonball smashed into the bow, blew through the galley, and shattered the chimney. Thankfully, the galley fires were always put out before battle. The sound of shattering crockery added to the din. A minute later came the sound of the carpenter's mallet thumping a plug into place.

"Two, four, six, fire!" Thorton said, watching through the number eight gun port. They belched flame with a fiery roar. On the deck above a cheer went up. Thorton waved gunsmoke away from his face. "Did we hit?" but nobody on the gundeck see well enough to tell him.

"Numbers eight, ten, and twelve, fire!"

The three guns roared and leaped against their tackles. The lines caught them up, then one snapped. The gun went plunging across the deck to crash into the mainmast and make the big timber shudder.

"Jackson, secure that gun!" Thorton bawled.

"Aye aye, sir."

A moment later a messenger was shooting down the ladder with the same order. "Captain Horner says secure that gun!" Even with the din of battle Horner on the quarterdeck could recognize the sound of a loose cannon.

"Aye aye, already doing it," Thorton replied to the messenger.

Under Jackson's supervision a new rope was reeved through the carriage and secured to the ringbolt in the deck. They timed it so the roll of the ship would help them move the three thousand pound monster back into place. Thorton did not have time or attention to spare for them. He was busy gauging the next shot.

"Numbers fourteen, sixteen, and eighteen, fire!" he barked. Once more the volley thundered out. He was nearly deaf and thought his aching skull would split. He paid no attention to the wounded being carried down the companionway at his back. They disappeared into the orlop deck and the surgeon's care.

Coming out the other end of the Spaniard's broadside, Perry was on pins and needles to see if they would turn again, but they didn't. The *Amphitrite* continued south along Algeciras Bay. They all heaved sighs of relief.

"Damage report!" both lieutenants sang out.

"Number twelve gun secure, sir."

Thorton and Perry began to get the gundeck cleaned up. Boys swabbed the floor to clean up blood and threw down sand on the wet places. The guns were run in and very thoroughly sponged out. The gun ports were closed. The men began to chatter as they worked.

Thorton paused to pay attention to the minute changes in his world. The *Amphitrite* was heeling less; the angle between his feet on deck was not so acute. Her rigging was not humming as loudly. He worried. Why was she losing speed? He shot a concerned glance at Perry. Perry gave him a puzzled look, then paused to look around. He motioned Thorton over. "Are we holed?" he asked very quietly.

"I don't hear the pumps running," Thorton replied.

An order came from above, "Triple shot: bar, chain, and canister. Aim for the rigging."

"Triple shot: bar, chain, and canister, aye!" Thorton bawled out.

The men leaped into action and shoved cartridges into the guns. The requisite ammunition flowed up from the shot locker.

"Mount your muzzles!" Thorton shouted. Pulling back on the wedge-shaped quoins allowed the breech to settle lower. That let the gun pivot on its trunnions to raise the muzzle. Thorton hunched along the line checking the guns. The *Amphitrite* heeled as she came around on a new heading. Thorton stuck his head out and froze.

The Spanish battleship had slipped her anchor and was under sail in pursuit of a Portuguese xebec. A frothing white mustache of a bow wave creamed along her sides. The *Amphitrite's* course would put them between the battleship and the xebec. The xebec had piled on every scrap of canvas and was running down the bay, but she was badly shot up and it was not certain she was outrunning the battleship. The *Amphitrite* had slowed to let her pass and was now gathering way to charge the much larger battleship.

A moan of dismay passed through the crew.

"Courage, men! We're only going to cross her hawse," Thorton exhorted them. "It won't be nearly as bad as the other passes."

The Spanish bowchasers spat fire at them and smashed into their leeward bow. They heard planks cracking at the blow.

"Fire as she bears!" came the command from above.

"Run 'em out! Rolling broadside! Mind your aim! Make it count! Take her heads'ls!" Thorton shouted.

One by one the *Amphitrite's* triple-shotted guns bellowed like demons in torment. A massive cloud of brimstone gathered under the deckhead. Thorton coughed and held his kerchief to his mouth. The stink of sulphur made it seem the Gate of Hell itself had opened up. He couldn't breathe, but the men did their duty and fired their guns in neat order. The sound made him deaf and he couldn't hear anything, not even when number fourteen gun blew up and overturned on the deck. Only the strange contortions of the men around him drew his attention to the barrel lying amid wailing and writhing men.

"Stretcher! Move that man!" he bawled. "Get that gun remounted!"

"She's blown her breeching, sir!" someone shouted in his ear.

"Dammit all to hell. Clear the wreckage. Secure the barrel." The *Amphitrite* was swinging around to run back across the battleship's path, coming even closer the second time. The starboard battery made ready for their turn in the fire.

"Ready, men, steady!" Perry was calling to them. "Wait for my command!"

The starboard crew crouched beside their guns and paid no further attention as loblollies hauled men with shattered legs aft.

The trunnions prevented the dismounted barrel from rolling, but it slid a few inches in the blood and sand. Rope went around the muzzle and the breeching line was caught. The lines were secured to ringbolts and the big black barrel lay pinned to the floor, but it was in the way of the number twelve gun.

"She's foul," Thorton said, clambering among the wreckage. "Straighten her so she lies athwart. Jackson, make it so."

The gun barrel weighed almost three thousand pounds. They reeved tackle and dragged the muzzle end around to put her perpendicular to the hull. They had to step over the barrel to pass powder and shot to the other guns, but number twelve could roll freely again.

Splinters flew and something that whined like a gigantic wasp buzzed past Thorton's head so close he could feel its breath. The cannonball smashed through the hull on the starboard side and disappeared into the sea. He noticed several other new holes.

"Roger! Are you all right?"

Perry picked himself up and plucked splinters from his sleeve. "Fine. You?"

"That was close!"

A headless man lay at Perry's feet. "Move that corpse," the second lieutenant directed. It was in the way of the number five gun. Two men grabbed the body by the legs and dragged it aft. Unlike some ships, they did not throw the dead overboard. Horner gave them all decent burials. Thorton hoped they would never get into a bloody enough situation where such formalities would be disregarded.

He shook himself. "Don't just stand there, you stupid curs! Load! Triple shot!"

Horner did not challenge the battleship again. He ran south and received several shots peppering his tail, one of which shattered the skylight. Down below, Perry and Thorton once again cleaned up the gun deck. They left the ports open to let the gunsmoke dissipate, but the air was still thick and warm when the *Amphitrite* slowed again.

Perry groaned, but did his duty. He went along the guns and checked them all, steeling himself for another rush at the Spaniard.

Thorton stuck his head out, then pulled it in. "We're picking up a Portuguese boat!"

Wood thumped wood as the boat clashed against the larboard hull. The boatswain's chair dropped into the boat even before they hooked onto the chains. A heavy figure swathed in white bandages was strapped into the boatswain's chair and hauled up. At the same time a figure in a soiled white uniform with red cuffs grabbed onto the edge of a gun port and attempted to drag himself onto the gundeck.

"Dago!" somebody exclaimed and grabbed an axe to deal with him.

Thorton shouted, "Belay that! Get him aboard!" He grabbed the man's collar and hauled him in.

More hands grabbed the Spanish uniform and dragged the boarder the rest of the way through the gun port. Because he was a Spaniard, they dropped him unceremoniously on the deck while men stood guard over him with axes and handspikes.

Álvar Soto stood up and said, "*Teniente* Thorton. How good to see you again."

CHAPTER 16: THE DOG OF PORTUGAL

The *Amphitrite* escaped into the Strait of Gibraltar and left the Portuguese squadron to its fate. It was no surprise that the sound of the bombardment attracted the attention of Salletine cruisers on patrol, so they fell in with a squadron of five Sallee xebecs. The lead vessel was a large, heavily canvassed xebec that flew the broad purple pennant of a Salletine commodore. Thorton was called to the quarterdeck to translate.

Thorton wiped his grimy face with a blue and white checked cloth, then peered through his spyglass in the early morning light. "'Tis the *Sea Leopard*, Isam Rais Tangueli in command. I'd recognize that tall Turk on the quarterdeck anywhere. They're asking us for news."

Horner looked back at the Rock of Gibraltar and the mouth of Algeciras Bay. The strait was under Spanish blockade and he had to run it. He swiftly decided the Sallee commodore could provide material assistance in accomplishing his mission.

"Invite the commodore aboard, Mister Thorton."

"Aye aye, sir."

Thorton made the necessary signals, transliterating Arabic with English flags. It was a time-consuming job but was made simpler by Arabic omitting vowels.

"He accepts, sir. He directs us to take station one cable off his starboard."

"Make it so, Mister Blakesley."

The sailing master replied, "Aye aye, sir." He in turn gave instruction to the helm. The *Amphitrite* was an old-style frigate; her wheel was housed in the coach under their feet. It was not ideal for communication, but it did protect the helm from enemy fire.

"Mister Forsythe, you have the conn. Gentlemen, I am going below. Mister Thorton, please greet our guests and escort them to my cabin. Mister Perry, fetch Major Soto and bring him to the great cabin."

"Aye aye, sir," they all said.

The *Leopard's Whelp* launched and a pair of purple uniforms climbed into it. The boat with her single lateen sail skimmed over the waters and tied up alongside the *Amphitrite's* port. Boarding by the port meant the formalities were omitted, but still, an officer had to meet them. Thorton smiled warmly as the rangy Turk hauled himself up the accommodations ladder and came in through the entry port.

"Peace be upon you, Peter Rais," Captain Tangle said in his mellow baritone. He spoke good English, albeit with a Turkish accent. The letters 'b' and 'p' were indistinguishable in his pronunciation.

Thorton responded in Arabic, "And also upon you." He stepped up and kissed the man on each cheek in the French fashion. Tangle smiled warmly and kissed him back with the perfunctory but affectionate kisses of a Mediterranean friend. Then he stepped aside so that the second uniform could come aboard.

"Shakil!" Thorton exclaimed.

Shakil was a slim man of average height with hazel eyes and a lightly tanned face. He had a fringe of beard along his jawline and an impeccably white turban on his head, the tail trailing down to his purple clad shoulder. Where Tangle wore a coat laddered with heavy gold lace, Shakil's coat was as plain and severe as a purple coat could be. It was a shade darker and a line of plain brass buttons marched down the front.

"Peace be upon you, Peter Rais," he replied gravely.

"And also upon you," Thorton answered. He gave Shakil a chaste and slightly self-conscious kiss on each cheek.

Shakil smiled crookedly and gave him the lightest peck in return. "I hope you've been well," he said pleasantly. He gave no sign that he had jilted Thorton some months ago.

"Very well. I've had another adventure."

Tangle's white grin flashed in the grizzled beard. "We want to hear about it!"

Thorton didn't want to share the details with either of his two former lovers. He brushed that aside by focussing on the business at hand. "Captain Horner is waiting in his cabin. Please come with me, gentlemen." He lead the way under the break of the quarterdeck.

Thorton was astonished to discover the Duke of Coimbra sitting on Horner's locker with his arm in a sling and a bandage around his head. His sky blue and yellow uniform was torn, sooty, bloody, and wet. He had Commander Abby sitting next to him in a dove grey suit with white waistcoat and stockings. Soto stood in silent solitude in a corner of the cabin. His gunsmoke stained white coat was splattered with somebody else's blood. Perry, smelling of gunsmoke but otherwise tidy, stood next to him. Horner was completely imperturbable in his second best uniform and white silk stockings. His wig was in good order and he'd put his dentures in at some point. In no way did Horner's appearance show that thirty-two pound shot had been tearing up the quarterdeck around him. He was as neat and calm as if he had been promenading a tree-lined square in London.

After presenting the guests, Thorton slunk aside and listened quietly. It wasn't actually eavesdropping, but it was an oversight on Horner's part. Tangle was keeping him occupied with a discussion in Spanish—he forgot to dismiss the lieutenants. With a shock Thorton realized he had bedded every man in the room except for Henrique. He was pretty sure that if he didn't move fast enough the lame duke would have him too. His color heightened; he wanted to turn tail and run. Unfortunately, it was too late. He couldn't sneak out of the great cabin when he hadn't been given permission to leave.

'Peter Thorton,' he told himself, 'You've been a horrible slut and you're going to get into trouble. Please Allah, don't let them figure out what I've done! I shall be chaste as the snow from now on.'

Sailing orders and signals were being discussed. Henrique, although he was an admiral, grew bored and flirted with Abby in Latin. It was their mutually intelligible language.

The real naval men drew a little apart. Whenever they consulted the duke out of respect for his rank, he waved his fingers airily and said, "I trust the judgment of my officers," which explained how a man with no naval training (aside from a few short days pretending to be a British midshipman) could manage the affairs of the infant Portuguese navy. His only asset as a naval officer was immunity to sea sickness.

Perry's curiosity naturally gravitated to where Horner and Tangle were deep in discussion, but Thorton wanted to stay far away. He wound up lurking in the corner with the grim-faced Soto. Feeling sorry for the man, he sidled up to him.

"How are you getting along with Henrique?" he asked in soft Spanish.

"Poorly. He blames me for antagonizing the Spanish against Portuguese independence." Soto's baritone betrayed his bitterness.

"I'm sorry, Major."

Soto threw him a despairing glance. "There is no place in the world for men like us, *Teniente*."

"You're very handsome. I thought Henrique would like that."

They two of them watched Henrique flirting with Commander Abby. Abby, being blind, could pretend he did not understand the duke's insinuations, but he smiled all the same.

"Many men have deserted their Spanish masters and pledged him their lives and fortunes because they believe in a free and independent Portugal. Some of them, like Souza, his flag captain, are ardent supporters of his claim to the throne. They are willing to give their lives in service to a cause they believe in. I was bought with a single night of lust. He finds it an insufficient foundation on which to place his trust. I can't say I blame him. I don't give a damn who is King of Portugal."

"Then why did you go?"

"I believed you. Until I met him, I thought I could shelter under him and love where I pleased. But he's a buffoon and a madman and a wastrel."

"Then go somewhere else."

"No. I've turned my coat and made my pledge, even if Henrique doesn't want it. I shall follow him like a dog and do whatever service I can until I drink myself into an early grave."

Thorton eyed the man askance. "That doesn't sound feasible."

Soto gave him a morose look. "Why do you think I went into the boat with him? And dragged myself aboard your ship even though he doesn't want me? I will do what I can or die trying. I may have been bought cheap, but I will give good service for my fee."

Thorton had traded the favors of his body to rescue Admiral Wolfe. Although he felt distaste for the transaction, he also felt he had accomplished something worthwhile. He did not reproach himself. Soto, on the other hand, had made a bargain that ruined his name and would forfeit all his lands and titles for it. Thorton wished he could do something for the man. Putting his hand into his pocket, he realized that he could.

He approached the lame duke and waited to be noticed. Henrique looked up from petting the blind commander, "Yes?"

"Your Grace, once you gave me this as a token of your esteem." He held up the diamond ring that Henrique had given him months ago. "Now I have come to beg a boon."

Henrique turned and faced him with the gravity suited to a king. "Ask, and if it be a thing that is within my power and can be done with honor, I will do it."

Thorton went down on one knee as if Henrique were in fact the King of Portugal as he had once claimed. "I beg you to receive Major Soto as you have received other Spanish gentlemen who have risked their lives, their fortunes, and their sacred honor for you."

Henrique stared into Thorton's blue and guileless eyes. His crossed eyes soon tired and slid out of focus. He gave a soft sigh. He shut one eye so that he could look at Soto standing hunched and dejected in the corner. Horner, Perry, Tangle, and Shakil fell silent as they watched the little tableau. Henrique's lower lip jutted out; he did not like Soto. The major watched without hope.

Henrique returned his gaze to Thorton. Reaching out, he reclaimed the ring. "What you ask shall be granted."

Thorton released the breath he didn't know he was holding. "Thank you, Your Grace." He took Henrique's hand in both of his and pressed the back of it to his lips. "I don't need your protection, sir, but other men do." His eyes strayed to Abby. "You can do more for them than I can."

Henrique tossed his blond curls and the insouciant aristocrat was back again. "If I surround myself with enough handsome men, maybe it will rub off on me," he quipped. "Very well. Major Soto, I have a commission for you in the marines."

Stunned, Soto hurried forward. He went down on one knee before Henrique and kissed the back of his hand fervently. "Thank you, Your Grace! You won't regret it. I shall be loyal to you and only you until I die."

"It will be quite sufficient if you are loyal until *I* die. I don't fancy having you moping around my tomb. Now then. We really must do something about the uniforms for the marines. They clash terribly with the naval officers."

Shortly thereafter the meeting broke up. They put the injured duke into a boatswain's chair and sent him over the side. Soto hurried down the accommodation ladder to receive the duke and help him into the *Leopard's Whelp*; the Portuguese party was transferring to the *Sea Leopard*. Next Commander Abby stepped out the entry port and climbed down the battens into the waiting boat.

Horner watched as the man who had briefly entertained his affections deserted him for an admiral. Deep lines ran from his nose to the downturned corners of his mouth.

"Now you know how I felt, sir," Thorton couldn't help saying.

Horner winced. "Your dart strikes true, Mister Thorton. Say no more."

Tangle and the Salletines went over the side into the boat. Shakil paused to murmur, "Go with God, Peter Rais," then he too settled into the boat.

Thorton stared down at them and watched as his lovers and his freedom rowed away. He was left on the deck of the *Amphitrite* with two men, either of whom would be the death of him if he pursued them. Knowing Horner, he was positive that should it come to a choice between Peter Thorton and duty, the man would choose duty; whereas with Roger Perry, should it come to a choice between whatever suited Perry's convenience and Peter Thorton, he was sure Perry would choose himself. Neither prospect comforted him. He was jealous then; he could have asked Henrique for a position and the duke would have given it to him. He could have been a captain in the Portuguese navy. With Henrique as his admiral he need not fear punishment for his amours. If not, he could have, should have, run away with Tangle long ago and been safe beneath his aegis with a commission in the Salletine navy. There would be prize money and fame for him there, and no official censure of his love affairs.

Until now Thorton had let the tide of events carry him. He was so accustomed to thinking of himself as a person of no importance that it had never occurred to him that he might be the master his own destiny. He had always put his own wishes aside in favor of doing what he thought was right, but when would it be time to do what was right for Peter Thorton? He was a man of nine and twenty years and the spring would see him turning thirty. He was not a boy any longer. Brooding, he went below.

CHAPTER 17: ARTICLE TWENTY-EIGHT

The convoy of Salletine warships ran dark and silent through the night. They showed a single lantern in the stern cabins, a light that could be seen only by the vessel directly astern of them. The light was purple, a sure signal of their identity. No other navy in the world carried purple lights. The *Amphitrite* had no such light and followed in complete darkness in the train of the Sallee rovers. A third man was added to the bow watch to be sure of keeping track of that purple light as well watching the sea for enemy ships.

It was a bitingly cold January night, and Thorton was grateful when Forsythe relieved him at last and he was able to go below. Creeping quietly into the wardroom so as to not disturb the other sleepers, he heard snores coming from Barnes' cabin, and also from Ferncastle's and Blakesley's. The wardroom was dark, but bars of light streamed through the louvers of Roger Perry's door. Thorton was cold and the light was warm; it drew him as lamp draws a moth. He hesitated outside the door. His relationship with Roger Perry caused confusion in his mind and made his heart uneasy. Finally he scratched lightly at the door to avoid disturbing the other sleepers.

"Who is it?" Perry asked in a low voice.

"Peter. Maybe I come in?"

"Yes."

Thorton let himself in, shut and hooked the door behind him. The lamp hanging from the deckhead cast a warm light and he couldn't see his breath in the room. It was what passed for 'warm' on a wooden ship in the middle of a winter sea. Perry was wrapped in his blanket with his night cap on his head as he perched upon his sea chest. The white collar of his nightshirt showed above the grey blanket and he had a book in his lap. Fingerless gloves let him turn the pages and almost keep his hands warm. One slippered foot protruded from the blankets to brace against the rolling of the ship and keep him from toppling off the sea chest. Brown eyes gave Thorton a quizzical look.

The blond lieutenant took a seat on the gun that shared Perry's cabin. Hooking his heel on the iron tire of the gun carriage, he gazed across at the other man and felt a yearning to be in his arms. Quite aside from any consideration of safety or morality, he wanted to be warm. In fact, he wanted to be warm almost more than he wanted company, but both desires were strong within him. He had no idea how to broach it though. "You're up late," he finally said.

"I couldn't sleep, so I'm reading." Perry lifted the book by way of indication. The grey blanket gapped open and showed the front of his nightshirt. Brown hair escaped his nightcap to curl along side his neck and spill over the collar. His expression was relaxed and open.

Thorton yearned to twine his fingers in those curls, to press cold lips against that warm throat, and to press tight against a firm body within the blankets. "'Tis cold and I don't want to sleep alone, Roger."

Perry's look changed to one of alarm. He edged along the sea chest to be further away from Thorton.

Thorton glared at him and said, "You're fickle, Roger Perry. Yestereve you said you wanted me for a lover. Now you're acting like you don't know me."

"For God's sake, keep your voice down!" Perry hissed.

Thorton moved to sit next to him on the sea chest and lowered his voice. He put his arm around the brunet lieutenant's shoulders. "I want to kiss you, Roger."

"I don't want to kiss you!" Perry retorted.

Thorton grabbed his head and pressed his mouth against Perry's lips. Perry held still and let him. What had begun as a forced kiss swiftly melted into something else. The reluctant lieutenant gave a soft moan and closed his eyes. His lips pressed back, then the book dropped to the floor as his arms went around Thorton's neck. His fingers played over the rough wool of Thorton's coat, then dug in. Thorton was surprised but pleased by the change. He pulled Perry into his lap, which helped to warm him in more than one way. He didn't try to move to the hammock; he wasn't sure Perry would go. He kept kissing the brunet man's face and neck while bracing himself with one arm and leg to keep from falling off the sea chest as the ship rocked over the swells.

Perry held him hard and tight. His flesh was burning hot and he was miserable. "I don't want you," he whispered, but nobody believed him, not even himself.

"You do too!" Thorton insisted. He burrowed his hand into the blanket. "I can feel it."

Perry turned scarlet and blustered, "I don't want to want you. I like women. I want a woman right now."

Thorton's hand stroked and squeezed the warm thing he found. "You like kissing me," he accused.

"God help me, I do."

Their mouths met and they kissed long and hard. Perry squirmed in his lap and he moaned in misery, but he didn't flee. Still, the precarious perch precluded Thorton making as much progress as he would have liked. To follow up on his advances he would have to let go of Perry or stop bracing himself, which would either result in them falling off the sea chest, or Perry's escape, and he was not willing to risk either development. He tried persuasion.

"I want to make love to you. I want to show you how it's done. I want to give you pleasure. I want you to feel what I felt!" Thorton told him earnestly.

Perry gave him a hard shove and jumped up. "No!" At that moment the ship rolled down a particularly large swell and water whooshed past the hull. Thorton flailed but there was nothing to grab except Perry, and Perry was not cooperating. He lost his balance and toppled off the sea chest. He landed on the floor with a thud, knocking into Perry who fell on top of him.

"Ow!" exclaimed Thorton.

"Oof," said Perry. He propped on his elbow and flipped the tail of his nightcap out of his face. He quipped, "Why is it whenever you're around, something bad happens to me? I've been shot, cut, my seniority docked, and lost a sea chest full of everything I own!"

"I'm sorry about that, Roger. I never meant any harm."

Perry sighed. "I know. You're not clever; you can't foresee the consequences of what you do. It makes me angry, but I can't blame you because there's no malice in you. Still I remember Midshipman Peter Thorton who would hang on my every word and do anything I asked. You were eager to help, back when you were the new middy on the *Dauntless*. You had a bad case of hero worship, and I liked you for it."

Thorton colored a brilliant shade of pink. "I was in love with you then. Nobody else was nice to me. They told me I was stupid and played pranks on me."

Perry smiled crookedly. "You were an easy target. You didn't know how to stand up for yourself. I remember when you lost your temper and punched Willy Ballantree in the face. You got your arse tanned for that." His fingers toyed with Thorton's lapel.

Thorton remembered that caning. It was one of several before he learned to keep his temper when Ballantree baited him. "He got under my skin, he did."

Brown eyes were gazing at him with nostalgic affection. "I miss you, Peter. You used to stick with me through thick and thin. You were my best friend. Back then I could always count on you, but not anymore. You ran off with your Sallee friends and you haven't been the same since." His smile faded.

Thorton gazed earnestly up at him as he lay there on the floor. "I thought you hated me. That when everyone found out what I was, you were ashamed of me. So I went away. I was afraid of ruin if I stayed." He choked out the last words.

"It was hard to get used to. Especially when I got in trouble for what you did! That wasn't fair. You have dukes and commodores for friends now, and your last lover was the son of an earl with an interest in the Admiralty! Even Horner likes you, but he doesn't like me. He lets you get away with things, but he shouldn't. 'Tisn't right."

"I'm grateful for Captain Horner's protection. I am well aware of what would happen to me on some other ship."

"Your fancy friends won't let you come to any harm, but nobody is watching out for Roger Perry. Not even you." Perry was bitter.

"I want to, Roger. I want to be friends again. I wish you would talk to me like you used to."

"Ha. You never listened. You'd roll over in bed and be cross with me."

"That's because you were talking about women, and I was jealous!" Thorton was getting pink again.

"You really have been in love with me all this time, haven't you?" The corner of Perry's mouth quirked up in a smile.

Thorton squirmed and turned redder. He didn't answer.

"Tell the truth, you are, aren't you?" Perry poked him in the chest.

"Maybe," Thorton replied. He avoided looking at Perry.

Perry reached out and drew his face around to look him in the eyes. "Do you still want to be my lover?"

Blue eyes met brown. A desperate hope flared in Thorton. "Yes," he whispered.

A spark leaped between them and they both felt it. Slowly Perry bent his head. Thorton held his breath. Until it actually happened, he wasn't sure Perry was really going to kiss him. He closed his eyes and lay still, only lips responding to the other man. His entire body was tense as he tried to control himself and not reveal just how much he wanted him. Perry shut his eyes as he savored the taste of that kiss: heat and desire and the sweet piquancy of forbidden fruit. He was vain enough to enjoy the effect he had on the man beneath him. With a slight grin he flicked the wet tip of his tongue again Thorton's lips. His eyes opened to watch the results of his tease.

Thorton's eyes popped open and his lips parted. He sucked Perry's tongue into his mouth, then a groan came from deep inside him like an ice dam breaking in spring. He gripped the other lieutenant and swiftly rolled him over in a wrestling move that took him completely by surprise. Perry whimpered but did not let go. His legs went around Thorton's lower body and held on tight as the bigger man pinned him against the floor. Thorton's weight was hot and heavy against his body.

"I want to do everything, Roger. I want to show you how good it can feel. I want to be the best you ever had."

Perry's legs tightened around him. "Show me."

A while later and the brunet lieutenant had to bite his sleeve to keep from crying out. Thorton held him tightly and groaned as Perry's pleasure became his own. He kissed Perry's nape and nuzzled his neck.

When it was all done, Perry collapsed. Thorton stroked the brown curls gently, but Perry grew cross. He elbowed Thorton. "Get off. If they catch us like this, they'll hang us."

Thorton eased off. "We have to desert. 'Tis the only way," he said.

Perry pulled his nightshirt down and huddled in a heap on the cold floor. "I'm an orphan. The navy is the only family I ever had. I can't run off with your rovers; they don't even like me. Tangle hates me."

Thorton pulled up his breeches and pulled the blanket around the two of them. He handed Perry his nightcap. "The Portuguese, then. Henrique will take us in."

"I don't speak the language."

"Somewhere. Anywhere but here."

"Don't leave me again, Peter. I don't have any friend but you. It doesn't matter if I love you or hate you. My fate is bound up with yours."

Thorton didn't know what to say to that, but he felt the burden settling on his heart. He wrapped his arms around the other man. "I'll look out for you, Roger."

Perry sighed and laid his head on Thorton's shoulder. The two cuddled together in the blanket.

Thorton whispered, "The deck is cold. We should go to bed."

"Not together. The stewards will find us."

"All right."

They picked themselves off the floor and Thorton crept stealthily into his own cabin. Changing into his nightclothes, he crawled into his hammock and lay staring at the thin lines of light that leaked through the deal planks from Perry's cabin. Then the light was blown out and he was left in darkness.

CHAPTER 18: STRIPED SAILS

Hours later Midshipman Chambers banged on Thorton's door, then stuck his head in. "Your watch."

"I'm awake. What's the weather?"

"Cold and damp."

"Thank you."

Thorton felt cold and couldn't shake a sense of foreboding. Last night weighed in his mind. He ought to feel happy about having a lover again, but he didn't. He had a knot in his stomach and it made him queasy. He sighed and rolled out of his hammock. Ra'uf brought him salt water to wash in, so he shaved carefully and washed himself, then knelt to pray in silence. Ra'uf joined him. Thorton didn't bother with a turban or to divine the direction of Mecca; there was no time for Muslim proprieties. He was stiff and his back ached. He was late for breakfast and had to bolt his food. As soon as he had shoveled the oatmeal down, he got his cloak and muffler and went on deck to relieve Perry. Forsythe's watch had come and gone while he slept.

The watch going below mustered aft while the watch coming on deck waited. The only light came from the binnacle. The two helmsmen were ghostly figures wreathed in a shimmering mist that was the breath from their mouths. Thorton checked the compass. "What heading?" he asked in a low voice.

"West northwest, sir."

"West northwest, aye," Thorton acknowledged.

Midshipman Bettancourt reported in his cloak and muffler. "The watch has been relieved, sir."

"Very good. Stand by."

The ladder to the quarterdeck was slippery with frost. Dark scrapes indicated where a few feet had gone up and down during the night. He climbed carefully, glancing up at Perry who stood at the rail watching. He couldn't help think of the warmth they had shared a few hours ago. He ventured a smile when he arrived, but Perry was hunched and brooding in his sleeved cloak. Wind as cold and sharp as a knife cut through their clothes.

"I relieve you, sir."

"Very good. We're running on a course west northwest. Spain's over there. We'll see it when the sun comes up. Horner's not happy, but the rovers aren't clawing off. Stay alert. The Spanish will know we're here come daylight."

"Aye."

"You have the deck, Lieutenant." Perry went below.

"I have the deck, sir."

Perry descended the slippery ladder and looked over the men of his division. Pale anxious faces stared at him and willed him to hurry up and say the words they wanted to hear. "Watch below, go below!" he barked softly.

They broke ranks with a buzz of conversation and complaint. "About fucking time." "I'm frozen!" "Damn, I want my bed!"

"Silence!" he said sharply. "A Spaniard could be right there in the dark and how would we know?"

"Sorry, sir," came the mumbled apologies. They slipped quietly down the companionway to the berth deck. Perry started for the companionway, then paused "Good morning, sir." He kept his voice low.

"Good morning, Mister Perry. Report, please," Captain Horner replied in an equally soft voice.

"All's quiet and the watch was just relieved. No change since you were last on deck, sir."

"That's well. Go below and try to get warm."

"Thank you, sir."

Horner inspected the binnacle then climbed the ladder to the quarterdeck.

"Captain on deck!" the marine guard announced. Thorton stood to attention.

"Quietly, Sergeant. Good morning, Mister Thorton."

"Good morning, sir. All's well."

"Thank you. Cold, isn't it?"

"Aye, sir. Very."

Thorton withdrew to the port side of the quarterdeck and left the windward side to Horner. The captain walked a stately walk back and forth along the deck. He glanced periodically to the north as if he could feel the invisible bulk of Spain bearing down on them. He was not in the habit of addressing his subordinates while taking his exercise, so Thorton stayed well clear. It was a cold bright dawn with a northeast wind blowing and he was cold in spite of his cloak and muffler. He hunched his chin into his collar and shivered. He paced to try and keep warm, but it didn't help.

Midshipman Bettancourt cast the log and Horner paused to hear the report. "Nine and a quarter knots." Horner grunted an acknowledgement. The *Amphitrite* was clipping along smartly and keeping pace with the rovers, even though the great lateen sails bellied out, pregnant with wind.

"Beat to quarters quietly, no drums, please."

Every ship in the Royal navy beat to quarters every morning. The men went to their guns and stood quietly while Horner and Thorton made the inspection. "We'll stay at quarters, Mister Thorton. Spain is too near for my liking. The men shall break their fast by divisions. See that the ladders are holystoned to remove the frost. Other than that, do what work you can manage. Keep us in fighting trim."

"Aye aye, sir."

Inspection completed, they returned to the quarterdeck. The sun rose higher and the coast appeared in a low brown haze to the north. They were alone in the sea except for the rovers. "Mister Blakesley! Let's have the charts of the Spanish coastline."

"Spanish coastline, aye." The master turned to his mate who ran down to the chartroom and brought them up. Using the slanting roof of the repaired skylight as their desk, he unrolled one of the charts. The master's mate and Thorton were commandeered to hold down the edges to keep them from curling.

"Mister Blakesley, what do you make our position?"

"I believe that is the Puerto de Conil we are passing now, sir." Not a Spanish speaker, he pronounced it Port-o dee Conn-ill.

"Are you sure?"

"No."

"Why not?"

Blakesley pointed to places on the chart. "Both the Conil and Saneti Petri have small islands in their mouths, and in each case, the coast runs at an angle to the northwest. I'm not familiar with this coast. I don't know how to tell them apart."

"Mister Thorton," Horner said.

"Sir?"

"Do you know where we are?"

Thorton shook his aching head. "I'm sorry, sir. I don't know the Spanish coast. The corsairs usually avoid it."

Horner consulted the chart. "Hills along the coast, that's not very distinctive, but there's a cut here, about three miles up from Saneti Petri. If we see it, we're nearly to Cádiz."

Blakesley said, "We ought to stand off, Captain. The Arsenal of Spain is in Cádiz harbor."

Horner looked up to watch the Salletine line. "We'll keep our position. Commodore Tangueli knows these waters far better than we do. We are better with his company than without."

"Aye aye, sir," the master replied unhappily. "You don't think he's lunatic enough to raid Cádiz, do you?"

Horner turned to Thorton. "What do you think? Is Commodore Tangueli going to beard the Spanish lion in his den?"

Thorton hesitated. "I don't think so, sir. I expect he's trying to pick up the cabotage coming out of Cádiz harbor. There should be traffic there, even in winter. He needs to take prizes to keep himself funded."

Horner grunted and folded up the chart. Then he gave Thorton a hard look. "Are you all right, Mister Thorton?"

"I didn't sleep well last night. I'm tired, that's all." The burden of his affair with Perry was disturbing his body and soul. He hoped the guilt didn't show in his face.

"Stay alert. We don't want any Spanish surprises."

"Aye aye, sir."

Horner resumed his pacing. The wind blew. The sun shone. The canvas was very white and the brass work gleamed. The *Amphitrite* threw up spray as she rolled over the waves. It was exactly the sort of golden day that made them all glad they had gone to sea, even if it was bitter cold.

The lookout shouted, "Deck! Signal from the rovers!"

Horner stopped his pacing, drew out his spyglass, and studied the rover ahead of them. Thorton stepped up next to him and drew out his own spyglass.

"What do you make of it?" Horner asked.

"Relay from the flagship. 'Three enemy sail northwest.' They are chasing."

"Very well. Follow where they lead," Horner replied.

"Aye aye, sir," Blakesley replied.

The rovers began to pull away from them.

"Studding sails," Horner ordered.

Blakesley bawled his orders and the men went aloft. Everything was cold and slick with frost, but they worked carefully and the starboard studding sails unfolded like wings. They swooped over the sea like an osprey hunting prey. Sheets of icy spray splattered the forecastle and sometimes reached as far as the coach.

"Toss the log," Horner said conversationally.

"Eleven and a half, sir," Midshipman Bettancourt reported.

Horner pursed his lips and stared at the *Amphitrite*. "Let's ease the sheets a trifle, Mister Blakesley."

Their course began to diverge slightly from the rovers. All the officers watched through their glasses.

"Log again," Horner ordered.

"Twelve less a quarter, sir."

"Mister Thorton, you have the conn. I am going to trim the load. MacDonald!" he bellowed for the boatswain.

Soon came a rumbling of things being moved down in the hold. It went on a for a long while.

"Deck! Striped sails!"

"My God," Thorton said. "The Spanish royal yacht!"

The middies and mates all looked at him in surprise. "Are you sure?" Blakesley asked.

"The Maltese *capitana* has a striped sail, but she wouldn't be this far west. Whatever it is, 'tis a high-ranking Christian vessel. The rovers will never quit the chase now. Not with a prize like that." Thorton picked up the speaking trumpet and shouted, "Masthead! What color?"

"Blue and white," came the answer.

"The *Tagus* for sure," Thorton said. "She's the tender to His Most Catholic Majesty's yacht *Gitano*. The Maltese carry red and white stripes."

They were all keen to see it.

"What sort of vessels are they?" Forsythe asked.

"Xebecs," Thorton replied. "Mister Jones, take a message to Captain Horner. Tell him the Salletines are in pursuit of the Spanish royal yacht."

"Aye aye, sir." The boy ran off.

"They may outrun the rovers," Perry said.

"I doubt it. The *Sea Leopard* is big and fast for a xebec," Thorton replied. "The question is whether the Spanish can make safe haven before the rovers come up. Cádiz is somewhere along this coast." Thorton longed to go to the masthead and look, but he had the conn.

Word ran through the ship. Thorton was not the only man who knew what the Spanish royal yacht looked like. Sailors crowded along the starboard gunwale to take a look while officers, mates, and middies crowded the starboard rail of the quarterdeck.

Thorton cleared his throat. "Gentlemen! The leeward rail is your prerogative."

Looking chagrined, they sheepishly moved away. The officer on duty had the windward rail by custom. Thorton claimed it and used his spyglass to watch. His head ached and so did his joints; he had not been getting enough sleep lately. He rebuked himself for his debauchery, but remorse did not improve his aching head.

Horner mounted the quarterdeck with dignified haste. He pulled out his spyglass and stood next to Thorton. "You're sure?"

"Positive. The French bend blue-checked sails on the gigs for admirals and commodores, but only the Spanish yacht tender *Tagus* carries blue striped sails. If the *Tagus* is out there, that means the *Gitano* is too, and probably a frigate for escort. That would account for the three sails the rovers reported."

"Toss the log."

"Just shy twelve," Bettancourt reported.

Horner grunted. They all waited for him to speak. He looked over toward the Salletines and Spanish. "It isn't our fight, but I'd like to break thirteen knots if we could."

"Thirteen!" Forsythe exclaimed in amazement.

"Thirteen," Perry said as if it were the name of lover. The chase had brought everyone on deck.

"I think you've wrung every bit of speed from her conditions will allow, sir," Thorton said.

The rigging thrummed and the timbers creaked. Great cascades of spray flew up and soaked the forecastle. Rivulets ran aft along the decks and into the scuppers.

Blakesley said, "She's working hard, sir. You're beating her unnecessarily. Ease off a bit. You'll catch up to the rovers when they make their strike."

Forsythe said, "She's Dutch built, sir. She can't take the pounding like an English ship."

"Silence!" Horner snapped in a tone that brooked no disobedience. He stared over the sea towards the rovers and their prey. The Spanish headland was hazy in the distance. He clasped his hands behind his back. He made up his mind. "Hold your course and speed. Sound the well every half hour and pump when it reaches two feet." Not 'if,' 'when.'

Thorton had been a captain. He had not been a captain long, but long enough for him to feel the ship was an extension of his body. He felt her sinews flexing and knew she was leaking as her seams worked; her masts strained their stays and her sails were taut with power. He wondered what her breaking point was.

Few of the English sailors had experienced such speed; it exhilarated them. They hung in the rigging and lined the gunwale to watch the chase. The blue and white striped vessel was falling behind her consorts, but the first four of the Sallee rovers swept past her without stopping. The last vessel in line claimed her as a prize.

They could see the red and white striped sails of the *Gitano* now, and also the big frigate-rigged xebec that was her escort. The xebec tore back towards the rovers and put herself between the royal yacht and the Salletines. She was biggest xebec Thorton had ever seen, bigger than either the *Amphitrite* or the *Sea Leopard*, and better armed, too.

The Spanish made no attempt to save the *Tagus*. The smallest of the three, she couldn't keep up. A tender only, it was a bother to lose her, but the royal *Gitano* mattered more than anything.

The *Amphitrite* came up on the rover and the *Tagus*: the Spanish colors were trailing in the water behind her stern and a faded purple Sallee ensign flew from her flagstaff. This close they could see the blue-painted hull and the bright work of the prize. The bulwark around her quarterdeck was painted in white, red, and yellow with lions and castles. Her transom was carved and gilded with more lions and the arms of Spain. She was fine and graceful, but she was not large. She had not been able to keep up with her consorts.

Meanwhile the red and white striped sail turned and darted between two headlands. Her escort followed her. A fortress on one of the headlands covered their escape.

Blakesley consulted his chart. "I am certain that is Saneti Petri River," he announced. "Cádiz is five miles north. The river bends in a curve around the Isla de Leon and joins with the harbor. The Arsenal of Spain is located there. They're taking the back door to safety."

The British saw the puff of smoke from the fortress' battery before they heard the boom. The rovers did not break off. They endured the fire of the fortress as they chased their quarry into the river mouth and disappeared. The thunder of gunnery echoed from the hills and a pall of gunsmoke began to fill the debouchment.

"The Turk has stones, I'll give him that," Perry remarked.

Horner spoke. "Clear for action. Prepare to tack, new course, due south."

He was not going to follow the rovers into the river. The *Amphitrite* had a few sweeps for maneuvering in harbor, but she was not a galley who could row her way out the confines of a river. The xebecs had their sweeps as well as sails and crews big enough to use them. They all watched over the taffrail, but the pall of gunsmoke filling the river mouth made it difficult to see anything. They could hear the reverberations of gunnery and sometimes see muzzle flashes in the smoke.

"Reduce sail," Horner said. The *Amphitrite* slowed. "Toss the log."

"Eight knots, sir," Bettancourt reported.

"Thank you. Maintain speed and course."

Suddenly the *Sea Leopard* emerged from the pall of smoke. Her bow was pointed right at them and they could see the white spume she threw up. Her purple pennant rippled in the wind. She had the wind over her quarter and flew on her best point of sail; she charged straight at them with a rapidity that made their hearts skip. Many a lesser vessel had seen that coming and simply given up. No ordinary vessel could escape from a cruiser with that kind of speed.

Thorton's heart froze. Then he remembered that she was a friend and breathed again. Although it seemed she charged them, in truth they were simply occupying the sea where she happened to be heading. He shivered in the cold and felt a tendril of dread working through his bowel all the same.

The *Amphitrite's* course was not the same as the *Sea Leopard's*. Slowly their ways diverged and the angle between them became obvious. They saw the red and white sails of the captured *Gitano* following her wake. The fortress roared all its fury against the captive to destroy her and so deny her to the enemy, but she kept coming. The other rovers ran out one by one and received fire in their turn.

"Course two points to starboard," Horner said. "Run parallel with her for now, Mister Blakesley."

"Aye aye, sir. Helm two points to starboard!"

Thorton leaned over the forward rail to make certain the helm below heard him. He felt queasy doing it and clung to the rail for support. He was not ordinarily given to sea sickness and attributed his malady to the excesses of recent days.

Cruising about four cables off the *Sea Leopard's* port beam, they saw that she was shot up and so were her consorts. The rovers had not come through unscathed, but by God, they had come through victorious.

"Let's give them a cheer, lads," Horner said.

"Hip, hip, huzzah!" they bellowed.

"One cheer more!"

Again they bellowed. Thorton dropped to the deck in a faint.

CHAPTER 19: RUN FOR AFRICA

Thorton woke to the pungent scent of smelling salts being waved under his nose. "Where am I? What happened?"

Dr. Ferncastle's green coat loomed over him. "You fainted. You're running a fever."

"Where are the Spanish? Are we under attack?" Thorton struggled to a sitting position.

"Deck ho! A sail! Frigate coming!" the masthead lookout shouted.

All heads snapped around and the glasses came up. A Spanish frigate was charging out in pursuit of the rovers.

"Make a signal. 'Enemy sail north, course southwest.' Fire a gun to draw attention to it," Horner said crisply.

"Aye aye, sir," replied Midshipman Bettancourt. He opened up the sail locker and collected the necessary flags. Up they went. The little black balls broke open and one of the quarterdeck guns boomed to draw attention to it.

Thorton got onto his hands and knees and wobbled to his feet. Not knowing what was going on or how long he has been in a swoon, he asked, "What's happening?"

"At ease, Mister Thorton. You are relieved of duty," Horner said.

"No, sir! 'Tis my watch!" Thorton's head swiveled as he attempted to take in the scene, but his eyes were hurting. He shaded them with his hands, but he could not make out the other ships in the sea.

The *Sea Leopard* acknowledged their signal and raised an English one of her own. "Take position two cables to port," Bettancourt reported.

"Acknowledge. Make it so," Horner replied.

"We have the advantage, but it could be interesting," Perry observed.

"She's bending west, captain," Blakesley said. "Lord, those xebecs can claw close to the wind."

"Match her," Horner replied.

"Aye aye, sir."

Thorton's legs buckled. He staggered and Ferncastle grabbed his arm, but he still went to his knees with a thud.

Horner returned his attention to the sick lieutenant. "Go below, Mister Thorton. Do as Doctor Ferncastle says. That's an order."

"I'm all right!"

"No, you're not. Pass the word for the loblollies," Ferncastle said.

Meanwhile, the rovers clawed up as close to the wind as they could go. The *Amphitrite*—and the Spanish—could not keep up with them. The *Tagus* and her captor were well ahead, but the Sallee line was closing on them. The *Tagus,* who could not outrun the rovers, was now a liability that could not keep up as they ran. They must abandon her or fight for her.

"Deck ho! Two sail coming out of the cut!"

Spyglasses came up. Further along the coast frigates were issuing from another location; Blakesley consulted the chart. "The Cortadura de Arrecife. 'Tis a small channel that separates the Isla de León from Cádiz proper. It reaches directly into one of the major basins."

"How deep?"

"No soundings on this chart, sir."

The frigates came on. They ran close-hauled to intercept the corsairs.

"Pardon me, but the Turks are signaling in Arabic, sir," curly haired Bettancourt reported.

"Doctor Ferncastle, I need to borrow Mister Thorton a moment. Prop him up, lads. Jackson, Chambers, help him up."

Thorton peered, "General signal, 'Form line of battle.'"

The *Sea Leopard* wore ship and swept back towards the Spanish frigates. Her squadron all wore ship and neatly fell into line after her. Her prizes continued running towards Africa.

"Take position two cables aft the *Gitano,*" Horner said. The *Tagus* and *Gitano* were splitting up; it would be much harder for the Spanish to recapture them if they ran separate ways.

The five Salletine xebecs charged the two Spanish frigates. The Spanish frigates were stouter vessels than the corsairs, but they were still outnumbered. They wore ship and fled back the way they came.

The rovers pursued. The frigates ran hard and fast for the shelter of the channel, but that could not seem a haven, not when the rovers had pursued the *Gitano* under the guns of a fortress and cut her out. Still, when the frigates reached the Cortadura, the rovers broke off and swept back to pick up their prizes.

The frigates came out again and pursued the rovers. They were joined by three more: now five frigates followed after the rovers. It was even odds—and getting worse.

Ferncastle spoke to Horner. "May I have a word in private with you, sir?"

"Not now, Doctor."

"Please, sir. It is important."

"Your boys are here. Take Mister Thorton below." It was an order.

The loblolly 'boys' were grown men unfit for any other work. One was a drunk and the other was old. They laid the stretcher on the deck. The drunk said, "Sir, your carriage awaits." He gave Thorton a little bow.

"I'm not going below," Thorton said. "I'm on watch."

The loblollies looked at Ferncastle.

"No, you're not. You're relieved of duty. Captain's orders. Make him go, lads," the doctor snapped. He turned back to Horner. "I beg your attention as soon as possible, Captain."

"Noted. Carry on."

The doctor's assistants advanced on Thorton. The stout one with a red nose said, "C'mon now, sir. You've been relieved of duty. You're going to get a nice nap down below where 'tis warm."

The word 'warm' nearly undid Thorton's resolve. He was bitterly cold, so cold he wasn't even shivering anymore. He huddled in his cloak. The loblollies scooted the stretcher up behind him, then the old man coaxed him, "Just you lay down, sir. You'll be more comfortable." The middies who were holding him up put him on the stretcher.

"Deck! Sails coming out of Cádiz!" Thorton started up again, but the drunk gave him a push. He flopped down onto the stretcher against his will and was taken below.

A total of eight Spanish xebecs, frigates and a battleship spilled out of the Cortadura. Like wolfhounds of the sea, they surged in pursuit of the Sallee squadron. Thorton was not on deck to see it. He was bundled into his hammock with extra blankets, given portable soup, and made to stay below. Ra'uf attended him, but Thorton ran him ragged sending him up to find out what was happening every few minutes.

"What speed are we making now?" Thorton demanded when Ra'uf reappeared.

"Ten knots, rais."

"At that speed we can outrun the battleship, but the frigates will overhaul us. Where are we? What's our course?"

"Due south. We're running for Africa, rais. We'll make Tanguel by nightfall at this speed."

The *Tagus* was not able to make the same speed as the rovers, but the Salletines weren't willing to give her up. Not yet. They ran as close to the wind as the captured xebecs would press, but it was not enough, The Spanish xebecs could sail that close to the wind, too. If the rovers abandoned their prizes they could trim another point closer to the wind and the Spanish would never catch them. The rovers bent every scrap of canvas they had to the *Tagus'* yards, even going so far as to improvise studding sails on the square topsail over the lateen mizzen.

They rigged a jib and a staysail. The *Tagus'* small suite of guns, water casks, firewood and everything else went overboard.

The wind began to back slightly towards the west. The rovers ran hard, but the *Amphitrite* kept pace. At noon the midshipmen and master took their sights and calculated their latitude. There was nothing to do but run, run, run.

Perry stopped by on his way to dinner. He reported, "The weather is very fair and cold with not a cloud in the sky. No rain or fog to cover the rovers' escape, and the moon will rise an hour after sunset. What do you think the rovers are going to do?"

Thorton huddled in his blankets. Even with two he was still cold. His mind was wandering, but he pulled his thoughts together with an effort. "They're running for Tanguel. They can get over the sandbar at the entrance and hole up under the guns of the fortress, but Tanguel can't withstand a Spanish assault. Once the battleship comes up, they'll be trapped."

"Us with them. The Spanish are not more than five miles behind us now. They'll catch us before dark."

"They'll kill Tangle if they catch him," Thorton replied.

"You, too, Peter." Perry's voice was soft. "They hate you both."

Thorton was too ill to muster any response.

Midshipman Jackson appeared in his doorway after dinner. "Captain Horner inquires after your health and asks if you know this shore. We have no charts for this part of Africa."

"I do." Thorton's eyes were glazed with fever.

"He regrets the necessity, but he needs you to come up." Jackson's voice was apologetic.

"I'll come."

Ra'uf and Jackson helped him out of the hammock. Thorton had been put into his nightshirt and flannel drawers, but they weren't warm enough for the wintry deck, so they helped him into heavy wool breeches, two pairs of woolen socks, and shoes. He insisted on his shirt and coat. He was not in his right mind, but they were not commissioned officers and had to obey him when he insisted on getting properly dressed. They put two jerseys on him, then his shirt, a long-sleeved white waistcoat, his frock coat, and sleeved cloak. They omitted the stock, but Thorton was not alert enough to realize it, especially after they wrapped the muffler around his neck. They put his hat on his head, and with one on either side to prop him up, half carried him to the quarterdeck.

A bright gale roared through the *Amphitrite's* rigging and filled every sail taut and pregnant like a beast that has devoured her foes. The ship rolled hard as heavy swells rocked her beneath a brilliant but cold winter sun. She groaned and complained as each heave of the waves caused something to rub, creak, and thrum in an endless wail of tormented wood. Down below the pumps clanked and water gushed from her side.

The scattered line of Spanish ships trailed across the blue waters of the Western Sea, each making as much speed as she could in a desperate bid to overtake the rovers. That the royal yacht and her tender had been stolen out from under their noses was too much to bear. Even worse was the affront of the escaped galleyslave, Captain Isam bin Hamet al-Tangueli, now *kapitan pasha* of the Sallee Republic, who had caused such havoc among them.

Tangle, true to form, had not reduced sail. The rovers were heeled over with their leeward guns plowing the sea while their windward guns pointed to the sky. The advantage was to them; if the Spanish took the weather gauge, they ran the risk of swamping their gun decks if they opened their ports. If they took the lee, they'd be hard on a lee shore with a gale blowing and the rovers to windward.

Smoke began to curl up from the *Tagus*.

"They're burning her," Forsythe said.

Smoke rose from the bow and stern, then her boats put off. The rovers paused to pick them up, then the line of Salletines gained speed.

Thorton's head rolled on his neck as he looked up. He squinted into the bright blue sky and made out the studding sails on the yardarms.

Horner replied. "Mister Thorton, I'm sorry to disturb you when you're ill, but the Spaniards are gaining. Do you know this coast?"

"I do, sir."

"Any good anchorages?"

"No, sir. Not until Tanguel."

"What sort of defenses there?"

"An old stone fortress with two hundred men. The Bey can probably call up the same number to reinforce it. The town is about ten thousand souls. There's a sand bar at the entrance the *Amphitrite* probably can't get over. The *Sea Leopard* went aground on it the last time I was there. However, they had started dredging before I left, so if they have finished, the channel ought to be clear."

"By any chance would you have a chart?"

"I do."

"I'd like to see it."

"Aye aye, sir. Ra'uf, fetch my chart of the Tangueli coast." Thorton couldn't hold himself upright as the ship rolled; they sat him down against the bulwark. Jackson sat beside him with an arm around him to keep him from toppling over. Weary and ill, he laid his head on

Jackson's shoulder. The younger man patted his shoulder and murmured something soothing to him.

Ra'uf returned with an oiled leather case and extracted the correct chart. The wind crumpled it, so Horner knelt on the deck and spread it near Thorton's side. Thorton leaned over and braced himself on his hand. His heart lurched; the chart was drawn in Captain Tangle's bold and angular hand. Thorton's first lover. The man who had carried him off and set him on his course of adventure and disaster.

Horner made a frustrated sound. "Arabic. I can't read it."

Thorton could. His Arabic was limited but sound on nautical subjects. He could not order dinner in Zokhara, but he could read the chart.

Blakesley knelt down beside Horner. He peered at the print. "Where are we?"

"We're at thirty-six degrees of latitude, which puts us a little south of Tanger," Horner replied.

"How many knots are we making?" Thorton asked.

"Eleven," the captain replied.

"Damn. We won't make Tanguel by nightfall. 'Tis at thirty-four thirty," Thorton said.

"Mind your language, Mister Thorton. How many ships at Tanguel? Is there any possibility of reinforcement?"

"Sorry, sir. There were several galleys there last summer, maybe more if the harbor has improved."

"What's the next harbor?"

"Salé, but 'tis ruined. After that, Fezakh, in Morocco."

"Too far," Horner grunted.

"It was a bold deed, but no good if he can't elude the Spanish, and a bad bargain if they bombard Tanguel," Perry opined. He was part of the cluster of junior officers hanging over the chart.

Horner ignored him. "Is there anything else you can tell us, Mister Thorton?"

Thorton leaned heavily against Bettancourt. "Watch the shoals at Tanguel," he said faintly.

"Anything else?"

"No, sir."

"Take him below."

Ra'uf collected his master's chart, then helped Jackson heave Thorton up. They maneuvered him down the stairs and put him back into his hammock. Thorton was too sick to object.

CHAPTER 20: MIDNIGHT TRAP

Thorton slept through the afternoon, but they woke him after sunset. Some hot soup and a piece of hardtack soaking in it fortified him. He arrived on the quarterdeck with his head clear although he was still cold and unwell. This time they had a hammock chair rigged to receive him. He eased into it gratefully. Horner already had Thorton's chart. Round-headed Chambers stood by with a lantern to light it.

The captain spoke. "I'm sorry to trouble you, Mister Thorton. Do you know where we are? I think we are here." He pointed to a spot on the chart. He had learned to read the Arabic soundings but could not make out place names. Still, he could equate the features of the coast with the marks on the chart. Tangle's chart was a good one.

"Shepherd's Rock. We're close to Tanguel. There are shoals here. Mind the channel, sir. You'll go aground if you miss it." The wind wasn't blowing as hard and the Sallee convoy had reduced sail. The Spanish were a mile in their wake and still running with heavy canvas. They were determined to catch the corsairs before they slipped into Tanguel.

"Does your man know the channel, Lieutenant?"

Thorton consulted with Ra'uf. "He does, sir."

"Good, he'll be our pilot. Get the lead out."

The little Arab took his place at the rail. He watched the land and water carefully, watched the ship ahead of him, and glanced back sometimes at the Spanish. He had learned a great deal of English in the last six months and spoke it badly but clearly. He sang out, "Helm touch left."

"Touch left, aye," the helm replied.

"Helm, steady up."

"Steady up, course due south."

Meanwhile the carpenter's mates were in the chains, flinging the heavy leads and singing out, "Quarter less four" and then on the other side, "Half three!"

Horner said, "Extinguish galley fires. Battle stations. No drum, pass the word quietly." The rovers must be at battle stations too, but no sound came from them.

"Aye aye, sir." Forsythe sent a messenger to the galley and the midshipmen on duty went below to inform their divisions. There were complaints, of course, but the men knew perfectly well why their meal was being cut short. They bolted the rest of their food as the trenchers and tables were cleared away. Next came the rumble of the guns being run in enough to work them and the clatter of powder monkeys running up and down the ladders.

The sun went down in the west leaving a lavender sky of dying light. The coast of Africa was already dark and the lights of cottages were pinpoints of light. The bulk of the fortress that guarded the Tangueli harbor entrance was a shadowy mountain.

"Arabic signals, sir," Midshipman Bettancourt reported.

They helped Thorton up so he could study them. "General orders, sir. 'Close up, half cable length. Ready sweeps.'" He could barely make out the signal in the gloaming.

"Make it so. Get our boats ready to tow if need be. Relay the message." Bettancourt hoisted the proper English signals and made a note of it in the log book. Whether the rovers behind her could understand them or not, the signal was relayed and the log would show it. The *Amphitrite* was behind the *Sea Leopard* and must play her part.

"Another signal, sir. 'Douse lights. Silent running.'"

The *Sea Leopard's* great stern lanthorn was lit. It formed a column of gold in the night that stood out vividly as the dusk darkened. The wind continued to drop. The *Sea Leopard* slowed as the wind decreased. The *Amphitrite* ghosted along under topsails only. The dark bulk of the fortress guarding Tanguel loomed on the approaching hill.

"Entrance to the harbor soon! Helm, stand by to make a hard left!" Ra'uf called.

One gun boomed from the *Sea Leopard*. Looking back, Thorton saw no lights from the Sallee squadron behind them.

The Spanish vanguard had to slow down to sound the shoals. The Tangueli fortress fired on them, but the Spanish did not sheer off. Once in the channel they were committed. The fortress raked them as they crawled slowly toward the harbor entrance. The Spanish frigates spat fire at the fortress. The thunder of the guns rolled back from the hills above Tangueli, reverberating and rattling the windows in the streets. The Sallee squadron did not fire; the Spanish were behind them and only the aftmost vessel could have fired her stern guns. It was no use. They had to get into the safety of the harbor and arrange themselves to resist a Spanish intrusion.

In the dark the *Sea Leopard* overshot the entrance to the harbor. Her light drifted toward the shore, then came to a stop. "She's aground!" Thorton cried, aghast.

"Come up on her, Mister Blakesley," Horner ordered.

When they drew closer Thorton frowned as he huddled in his cloak. "That's not the *Sea Leopard*."

Horner laughed softly. "Indeed, it is not."

They passed the tub with its set of lanterns mounted vertically on a shaft in imitation of a tall stern lanthorn. The wind had blown the false light onto one the mudflats south of the harbor entrance.

Thorton strained his eyes. "There she is!"

The *Sea Leopard* had shed all canvas and was rowing due west. Her spars were a faint spiderweb against the stars. If he had not been looking for her, he wouldn't have seen her. The *Gitano,* being a yacht, had only a few oars and was laboriously turning to follow in her wake. She kept her lateen mizzen set to help her turn.

"Get the boats out and tow us," Horner ordered. "Take in all sail."

Men rushed to do as they were bid. They had caught onto the rover's trick: when they disappeared from view, the Spanish would think they had turned behind the headland that guarded the harbor entrance. With luck the Spanish would go aground as they attempted to close with what they thought was the rovers' flagship.

Horner glanced at the east. "The moon will rise soon. We must get out of these shoals before it does."

They touched bottom more than once as they tried to follow the *Sea Leopard* through the black water. Thorton looked back and could see a faint gleaming of white where the oars of the other rovers followed behind them. Chills shook him and he collapsed into the hammock chair with a groan. His muscles ached and his stomach was queasy.

After a nerve wracking forty-five minutes of picking their way through shoals and mud, they reached open water. The *Sea Leopard* continued sweeping straight into the eye of the wind. Looking back they could see stationary lights where two of the Spanish frigates were aground. At least one of the Spanish vessels made it into the harbor as they could tell from the orange flashes behind the fortress. The glare of the guns flashed repeatedly and the Spanish ships were limned in amber light, then vanished in the darkness before their dazzled eyes. The fortress worked its guns as fast and hot as it could, even going so far as to sent red hot shot amongst the wooden ships that assailed it. More guns sounded in the harbor; maybe a corsair or two in the harbor was resisting the Spanish incursion. Through it all the Sallee squadron remained dark and silent.

Suddenly the *Gitano* darted south and raised canvas. At the same moment, the *Sea Leopard* wheeled north and her line followed her. The Sallee vessels bloomed into ghostly clouds of moon white sail as they paralleled the Spanish line outside the shoals. Thorton counted six Spanish vessels in the channel.

"Mister Blakesley, pick up the boats and make fighting sail," Horner said.

The topsails bloomed and the *Amphitrite* began to sail under her own power. Her boatmen scrambled aboard. The men who had been towing her were drenched in sweat in spite of the cold; they were given beer to refresh themselves, then sent below to the gun deck.

The horn of the moon rose above the horizon and the *Sea Leopard* revealed her claws. Her guns thundered out, and instantly the rest of the rovers opened fire in a crashing broadside that shattered the vessel at the head of the Spanish line. The wreck drifted helplessly upon the shoals and blocked the channel into the harbor. The Spanish had not even known the rovers were there until they received the Salletine shot.

"Fire," Horner said conversationally.

"Fire!" Forsythe roared.

The *Amphitrite's* guns spoke.

The Spanish found themselves caught in a strait place between the guns of the fortress and the free running rovers. They hastily plied their seaward guns, but they did not have a good idea of the range or location of their foes. Worse, they could not maneuver in the narrow channel. Most of their shots fell harmlessly in the sea. Passing the end of the Spanish line, the *Sea Leopard* pummeled the rearmost vessel as she attempted to get out of the channel and into the sea; Tangle wanted to bottle up the Spanish with a wreck at either end. The *Sea Leopard's* consorts followed her in neat order, the *Amphitrite* among them. The British delivered a broadside to the Spanish xebec they found there, but the rest of the Sallee fleet was not as swift to reload and could give only half their guns as they passed. The *Sea Leopard* wheeled and paced the Spanish line a second time, receiving their fire, and pounding them again. Her consorts delivered a ragged cannonade in her wake.

Horner looked over his shoulder. More Spanish ships were out there in the darkness; the battleship was far behind the much faster frigates and xebecs, but even those vessels had spread out depending on their sailing qualities. Half a dozen might be trapped in the channel, but their friends would come to their aid. The question was how soon they would arrive. No doubt they could hear the sound of gunnery and were making all haste to come up.

The evening wind was dying; the Salletines put out their sweeps and rowed to supplement their high-pointed lateen sails. Thorton didn't envy them; the rowers must stand between the fiery guns to work the oars on the weather deck of a xebec.

The *Amphitrite's* sails fluttered. Horner said, "Drop out, Mister Blakesley. We cannot maintain our place."

"Aye aye, sir. Prepare to tack," Blakesley said.

The *Amphitrite* wheeled slowly to the west.

"Steer clear of the shoals and stand north. We shall patrol." Horner ordered. That was all the less agile *Amphitrite* could do.

"Deck ho! A sail!" the lookout sang out.

"Where away?" Horner called through his speaking trumpet.

"Due north, on course due south."

Horner set down his speaking trumpet and took up his night glass. Moonlight revealed an upside down pyramid of canvas standing straight for Tanguel. He didn't need a correcting lens to tell him the first of the Spanish reinforcements had arrived. "Let sheets fly and sound a gun."

The rovers were not slack; they were expecting the rest of the Spanish line to come up, too. They left off mauling their victims in the channel and stood for the newcomer. Seeing her danger, the stranger tacked and fled back north. When they were sure that she was gone, the rovers returned to the sport of shooting fish in a barrel. Switching tactics, they dropped their line ahead formation and instead swarmed the rear Spaniard with a wolf pack: all force concentrated on one victim. Their shallow drafts and oars let them surround the helpless frigate and deliver more than a thousand armed men to her deck; the Spanish struck without further resistance. One by one the Salletines clawed their way up the channel using their shallowest draft vessels to come over the shoals at the deep-bellied frigates. Trapped in the confines of the channel, the frigates were not able to traverse their guns far enough nor work as a unit; it was a series of mismatched battles in which the Salletines were victorious. They took every single Spanish ship.

The Salletines towed the stranded frigates off the sandbars and shifted crews so that they could fight the prizes. Their force doubled, they cruised north with false colors flying. What happened next Thorton didn't know. His fever flared up again, and he was carried below to his hammock.

Sometime during the night Horner and Ferncastle came to check on him. They stood in his doorway and did not approach.

Ferncastle gave his report. "Small pox, Captain. The first vesicles have appeared in his mouth. The prisoners at Alodia and Nunilo were ill with it and some of them died. Admiral Wolfe is rumored to have it. You and Thorton were both in close proximity to the exchanged prisoners."

"I see. Institute a quarantine. Anyone who has been in close contact with the prisoners or Thorton is to wear a yellow cockade in his hat. They will mess separately and sleep separately. It is the most we can do. I hope to God you are wrong, Doctor."

"You will need a yellow cockade yourself, sir."

"I know, Doctor. Fortunately, I survived small pox as a child. I pray God I am immune. We will have a general muster at dawn and implement the quarantine then. We'll raise the yellow jack. Draw up a list of men who are to be quarantined and bring it to me immediately. Not a word to anyone until then."

"Aye aye, sir."

Thorton remained inert in his hammock. He had heard, but he was insensible. He was too ill for the danger to register.

CHAPTER 21: THE YELLOW JACK

The rovers picked off two more prizes during the night, but in the darkest hour before the dawn, they encountered the battleship. She was a second rate, the *La Santa María Magdalena*, of eighty-eight guns, and a complement in excess of eight hundred men. The *Sea Leopard* was a petty nuisance by comparison, but the rovers had eleven vessels and close to two thousand men aboard them. The conclusion was by no means foregone. Tangle resorted to guile; five of the captured vessels flew the Spanish ensign and formed a squadron flying north with the Salletines in hot pursuit. The decoys dove under the guns of the battleship and by this ruse were able to close with her and give her their broadsides before boarding. The rest of the Sallee wolf pack came up and surrounded her. With the maneuverability of their oars, they were able to keep under her stern and bow. The ululating battle cries of the sea ghazis drifted across the waters as they swarmed aboard the battleship.

Guns and muskets barked. Later came muffled blasts as the hatches were pried open and grenades were thrown down by the half dozen. The quarterdeck held out, but more grenades looted from the powder rooms of the captured frigates were lobbed up. It required a steely nerve to hold the round grenade until its fuse had burned down so that only a few seconds remained. Some of the grenades burst in the air, and that was just as effective as when they dropped to the deck and rolled amid the defenders.

As the aurora lightened the eastern sky, black gore sluiced from the battleship's scuppers and stained the vessel's crimson paint with a darker hue. The shattered bulwarks let the blood run from the quarterdeck and the ladders were slippery with human gore. Bodies were heaved through the breaches to clear the footing and the blue and red uniforms of Spain plunged into the sea. Marksmen in the Sallee vessels peppered the Spanish quarterdeck until the entire officer corp was a bloody shambles. Only then did the Spanish ensign flutter down.

A young Spanish midshipman, determined to save his flag from dishonor, wrapped it around his body, climbed into the breach of the rail, put his pistol to his temple, and pulled the trigger. Middy and flag vanished over the side. In his wake he left a dark and empty silence. No man spoke, not a Spaniard nor a Muslim. The sun continued to rise in a dawn as red and bloody as the carnage on deck. The only sound was the clatter of Spanish swords as the survivors threw down their weapons. Next the purple flag of the Sallee Republic rose on the flagstaff and fluttered out as clean and unsullied as the dreams of boys before they go to sea.

Thorton didn't see it; he was miserable in his hammock as the pox broke out on his face and neck, then his chest, the palms of his hands and his arms. He shivered and sweated for hours while Ra'uf bathed his flesh and sang softly in Arabic to soothe him. Ra'uf told him the story of the Salletine victory, but it was garbled in his dreams with Perry, Tangle, other men he had known, and the ghosts of the dead. He moaned and twisted in his hammock, fighting weakly against the blankets the steward tucked tight around him. He slept only in fits. Indistinguishable hours crawled by for the pox-ridden patient.

Late that afternoon the lieutenant roused enough to ask, "Have you ever had small pox, Ra'uf? You must not endanger yourself to attend me."

Ra'uf smiled. "I was *ingrafted* when I was young." He had to use the Arabic word.

"Ingrafted?" Thorton asked. "What is that?"

"When I was a boy, our clan hired an old woman to come with her scabs. She scratched us with a needle on the forehead, each arm, and each leg, then put some powdered scabs into the wounds and sealed them with a bit of shell she bound in place. After a week we were ill with a mild case of small pox, which we suffered for a few days. A week later we were well again. Now we're immune to the small pox."

Thorton marveled. "But the scabs could kill you! They are pure disease!"

"No, they are weak at the end of the illness when they fall off by themselves. Causing a mild case protects against the full power of the disease. When the small pox broke out in my village, only one of us died. A neighboring clan had not ingrafted their children, so five died and the rest were very ill. Those of us who were ingrafted were not scarred, either."

"No scars? So many who suffer the small pox and are disfigured by it. If they live." Thorton touched the bumps that covered his own face. "Mine own father was a halfbreed Shawnah Indian, and the Indians suffer greatly from the small pox. It is almost always fatal with them," he said in a worried voice.

"I will take care of you, rais," Ra'uf said in a soothing voice. "I will not let you die, *inshallah*."

A knock sounded at the door. Ra'uf opened it, then exclaimed in surprise, "Shakil Effendi!" He stepped aside to admit Shakil bin Nakih and Doctor Ferncastle.

Thorton stared at his former lover and said, "I must be delirious."

Shakil smiled at him and stepped up beside the hammock. "Not yet. When we saw your yellow jack flying, we asked what disease. When we learned it was small pox, Isam Rais sent me over to help. I am sorry to find you ill, Peter." They spoke Spanish as their common language.

Ferncastle stepped to the other side of the hammock and gestured to Thorton's mottled face. "It will be a bad case. The pox broke out about dawn, and he already has fifty on his face." He spoke English with Ra'uf to translate.

Thorton huddled in his hammock as he listened to the prognosis. "I feel better today than yesterday," he protested. "My stomach is upset, but the rest of me feels better."

Ferncastle replied, "There is generally relief when the pox break out, but it won't last."

Shakil asked in Spanish, "Do you have orange marmalade?"

'Marmalade' was not in Ra'uf's English vocabulary, so Thorton had to help with the translation. After a bit of discussion, everyone understood what was wanted.

Ferncastle shook his head. "I doubt anyone aboard the *Tritie* has marmalade. I have never seen it at the captain's nor the officers' mess. Wherefore do you want marmalade?"

"It will settle the stomach when nothing else will. We export a great deal of it to England," Shakil replied.

"We have portable soup for that. I thought perhaps you were going to tell me you made a poultice of it. I heard Commodore Tangueli sets great store by cinnamon."

"Cinnamon will help if you have enough of it," Shakil replied, "but it is so dear I doubt you can afford to bathe him in it."

"We can apply oatmeal topically. 'Tis too cold to soak him in an oatmeal bath, but we can make poultices of it. He's likely to be scarred even so," Ferncastle replied.

"No scars!" exclaimed Thorton. It didn't bother him to be scarred by a wound; that was a badge of honor he could carry with pride, but small pox was a disfigurement with no redemption.

Shakil was skeptical; he regarded British medicine as inferior to the Arab. "I suppose it can't hurt, but you must be sure he doesn't chill," he replied. "I will send some things from the *Sea Leopard*. I am sure Isam Rais will be generous when he knows who it is."

Tangle had been Thorton's first lover and Shakil his second. Since that time he had acquired a great deal more experience between the sheets, but Shakil's presence at such a moment brought back vivid memories. He clutched the purple sleeve. "Stay with me," he croaked through painfully spotted lips.

Shakil gave him a pitying look, then spoke Arabic to Ra'uf. Satisfied that the steward was immune, he shook his head. "Ra'uf will attend you. There is nothing I can do for you that he cannot."

Thorton continued clinging to his sleeve. "Don't go."

Shakil gently removed the sick man's fingers from his coat. He turned the hand over to inspect the vesicles on the palm. "Trust in God, Peter. He is the best friend any man could have."

"Pray with me."

Shakil was a pious man and a true believer. It was a request he could not refuse. He gently laid Thorton's diseased hand on his breast and pulled the blanket up over it. He began to recite the opening verses of the Qu'ran in slow and melodious Arabic.

"In the name of Allah, the Gracious, the Merciful. All praise belongs to Allah, Lord of all the worlds, the Gracious, the Merciful, Master of the Day of Judgment. Thee alone do we worship, and Thee alone do we implore for help. Guide us in the right path, the path of those on whom Thou hast bestowed Thy blessings, those who have not incurred Thy displeasure, and those who have not gone astray."

Ferncastle crept out and left the renegade lieutenant to the comfort of his alien faith. Shakil continued reciting until Thorton slept, then slipped out. Later a dozen loaves of soft white bread that were only a little bit stale, a tin of orange marmalade, a sack of oranges, a bag of couscous, a bag of garlic, and a gallon of goat's milk arrived for the care of the invalid.

Thorton's fever came on hard that night, and he threw up everything but toast with marmalade. Ra'uf held the basin and murmured soft words of Arabic to comfort him, then gently washed his face. He gave him water mixed with vinegar (because the water was beginning to turn) and juice of the orange (to disguise the flavor) to drink. Thorton was so ill that he didn't object to the unpleasant taste. He huddled in his hammock and shivered. Ra'uf brought his own blanket to wrap around him, then strung his hammock next to his master's. Wearing all the clothes he owned because he had given his blanket to the sick man, he kept his master company through the long night.

CHAPTER 22: AN EMBARRASSMENT OF RICHES

The rovers had a problem: not one of their officers had ever commanded a battleship. Neither had any of the Portuguese in Henrique's suite. She fell to Commodore Tangueli as the senior Salletine officer. He moved into the admiral's suite and found himself lost in the immensity of a great cabin loaded with Spanish luxuries. The bedchamber alone was the size of the great cabin aboard the *Sea Leopard*. Not only that, but his turban was in no danger from the ceiling beams, although he did need to dodge the crystal chandeliers.

Quite apart from her furnishings, *La Santa Maria Magdalena* was a handsome vessel with a halfdeck and quarterdeck, twenty-four pounders on her upper gundeck and eighteen pounders on her lower. She had a shebeck yard to carry a loose-footed gaff sail, a pair of triangular headsails above her watersail, and topgallants above her topsails and courses. She required a crew of eight hundred to work her, including marines, officers, and specialists. The rovers had taken so many prizes that by providing adequate crews for the frigates they had nothing left for the battleship. Only by stripping the crews of the smaller vessels of men who knew something about square sails could they hope to sail her, but doing so would leave all the vessels woefully undermanned and unable to work their guns. The rovers were like a python that had swallowed a camel, unable to digest it, but unwilling to regurgitate it either. They couldn't get the battleship into Tanguel by any means, and most of the frigates couldn't make it either, even with pilots to guide them through the shoals. The worst problem was that there wasn't enough money in all of Tanguel to buy their prizes.

On the other hand, Henrique assured the rovers Portugal would buy the prizes if they brought them to Lisbon. Thanks to the terms of the agreement between Portugal and the Sallee Republic, the rovers could use the Portuguese prize courts to adjudicate their prizes. The governmental ten percent would be split between the two nations, with seven percent going to the Sallee Republic, and seven percent going to Portugal, which added up to fourteen percent, much to the rovers' annoyance. Nonetheless, they were sure to get better prices in Portugal than in any Sallee port, with the exception of the xebecs, which would find ready buyers among the Muslims. Along with the other vessels, the rovers had taken a naval xebec of medium size as well as the royal yacht. Much to the rovers' disappointment no notable personage had been aboard the yacht; she had been on a shakedown cruise after maintenance. She was a fine vessel in her own right, made of Spanish oak, gleaming with brass, and richly furnished with rugs, tapestries, mirrors, paintings, plate, jewel-encrusted objects, and four comely Negresses whose duties consisted of keeping the vessel's furnishings in sparkling condition. Henrique was absolutely enamored of her and appointed himself her prizemaster.

Thorton knew none of this. He ached in all his muscles but especially his back and stomach. He vomited repeatedly, his eyes hurt, and some of the pocks were infected and added their pain to his suffering. Even his scalp was covered in pox and made his hair filthy. Ferncastle recommended cutting it off, but Thorton refused. He was not in his right mind, but he understood well enough when the scissors were brought. Ra'uf, ever loyal to his master, turned the scissors around and threatened to stab the doctor if he insisted on cutting Thorton's hair. Thereafter Ra'uf had the labor of washing Thorton's hair; no easy thing with a sick man, a rolling sea, and the great mass of waist-length hair thick enough to make an Indian proud.

Ra'uf made a bed of Thorton's sea chest, wrapped Thorton in his blankets as tight as swaddling clothes, then nailed the blankets to the sea chest. By this means Thorton was prevented from falling off. His head hung over the end with his long blond hair trailing in a bucket of salt water. Ra'uf was combing through it carefully and scrubbing it with soap to get the mess out when a knock sounded on the door.

"Enter!" the little Arab called, and the door opened to admit Shakil bin Nakih.

"Peace be upon you," Shakil said as he stepped into the dim room. He pulled out his handkerchief and held it against his face on account of the smell.

Thorton groaned, "Shakil?" He opened his eyes, but the visitor was upside down and swaying. Ra'uf picked up his head and supported it so that Thorton could look at the Moor right side up.

Shakil came and knelt beside him. "I'm sorry to bother you when you're sick, Peter, but it is an awful mess. They are arguing endlessly about whether to send the prizes into Tanguel or Portugal. Isam wants to take the prizes into Portugal because they will bring more money, even if we do have to pay both the Portuguese and the Sallee prize courts. He has proxies for Jamila and Nakih, but that's not enough to win the shareholders' vote. He needs your vote, so I have come to ask for your proxy."

Thorton was dizzy from his head hanging upside down while Ra'uf washed his hair; the rush of blood draining from his head now that it was supported in the correct position did not improve his ability to think. "Didn't I give you a proxy?"

"Only for the purchase of the share. Which you actually gave to Jamila. You left directions to vote for Isam for captain when the occasion arose, but you did not grant a proxy in full to any of us. You have exercised your rights by letters in the past, which has been sufficient, but it isn't really convenient. I hate to press you when you are ill, but we need your full and formal proxy."

"No." Thorton struggled to sit up, but he was a captive of his bedclothes.

"Rest, rais," Ra'uf murmured to him in a soothing voice.

"Please, Peter. I know you will agree to whatever Isam suggests, but for the sake of the other investors we need it in writing. Ali is being stubborn. I have taken the liberty of preparing it for you and translating it into Spanish." He unbuttoned the top buttons of his purple coat so that he could reach into the breast pocket and pull out the document. He unfolded it and showed Thorton the Arabic and Spanish.

"Let me up!" Thorton demanded.

Ra'uf got the hammer and pulled out the nails that were securing the blanket around his shoulders and chest. Thorton was so weak he couldn't sit up by himself, but Ra'uf put a shoulder under him and propped him up.

Thorton pushed the document away. "I will vote my own share. I am not Isam's puppet that will agree to anything he says." His head was wobbling on his neck in spite of his strong words. He picked at the grey wool binding his legs. "Let me up!" he said querulously.

Shakil privately thought that a man who couldn't even escape his bedclothes was in no condition to be doing anything at all, let alone attempting to argue with the great corsair. "You aren't well, Peter. I'm sorry to bother you. But the argument is at an impasse. We can't stay here; the Spanish will rally and we don't have enough men to work the guns." He offered the paper to Thorton again.

"I'll go to the meeting myself."

"Peter, you can't! Be reasonable. If you are doing this to spite me because I jilted you, please reconsider. I beg you."

"I'm a shareholder. I have a right to go to the meeting."

"You're sick with the small pox. You have no right to bring contagion aboard the other ships!"

Thorton grew stubborn. "I will vote my own vote! I am not Isam's shadow!"

"You're sick, and I forgive you. I know that if you were in your right mind, you would see reason."

"I am in my right mind! I want to hear the merits of the case myself!"

Shakil grew exasperated. "I have already told you! It is obvious that the vessels must go to Lisbon; money, safety, convenience, they all demand it."

"I'm going to throw up." Thorton fell half way off the sea chest and vomited on the floor. Ra'uf tried to put a basin under him, but too late.

Shakil sighed and clenched his fists. "I'm going to leave the proxy with you. Ra'uf, make him see reason!" He left the cabin.

Next the great corsair himself called on the sick man. Thorton woke to find Commodore Isam bin Hamet al-Tangueli, known to the English as 'Captain Tangle,' standing next to his hammock. He was not alone. A man dressed in blue and white stood next to him. The stranger had a curly full beard and brown eyes set above a hooked nose. He came up to Tangle's chin but no higher. Shakil accompanied them. Thorton blinked at them.

Tangle opened without preamble. Spanish was once again the mutually intelligible language. "This is Ali bin Hasan, purser for the *Sea Leopard*, and a shareholder. He holds proxies for several of the other investors. We disagree on the disposition of the prizes. At the moment he holds the majority by one vote. If you agree with him, I shall have to submit to the will of the investors and take the prizes into Tanguel, bringing us less money. If you vote with me, then there is a tie, and as the captain, I have the right to break that tie. I will take the prizes into Portugal."

Ali started talking. "Taking the prizes into Portugal will give both governments a claim in the amount of seven percent each, for a total of fourteen percent. This is a gross violation of the ancient and traditional ten percent that the corsairs have always paid. It is a very bad precedent to set. Having fleeced us once, they will try it again. Besides, there is no guarantee the Portuguese will pay—"

"Henrique has offered us twenty-five thousand sequins each for the frigates," Tangle interrupted. "The Portuguese are desperate for ships. 'Tis a guaranteed sale and a good price, even if we do have to pay fees to both Portugal and Sallee."

"Ha! How will they pay? Letters of credit that must be exchanged, for a fee, quite aside from the fact that the Portuguese debts are already being discounted thirty percent on the international exchanges!"

"They will make peace with Spain soon. I admit there is a risk, but now is not the time to be timid. Portugal will make good on her debts."

"The Turks will buy the ships in Zokhara. Their credit is good."

"That means running the blockade of Gibraltar with woefully undermanned ships! We can't even work the guns!" Tangle exclaimed.

The two argued in Arabic after that. Thorton's head was spinning and he deeply regretted insisting on making his own vote. He did not understand all the ins and outs of international finance, taxation, and political credibility. In fact, he did not understand one jot of it. "How much have the Portuguese offered in total?" he asked.

Tangle replied, "Four hundred and fifty thousand sequins. The *Sea Leopard's* owner share is nine thousand sequins, which means your share is worth seven hundred and fifty sequins, if we go into Lisbon."

"No, it isn't. If we go into Lisbon, we must take fourteen percent off the top," Ali pointed out.

"You're calculating it wrong! The owner's share is ten percent of the gross, not the net!"

"Then the men will be paid less," Thorton said. "Because only seventy-six percent shall be paid to them, not eighty."

"No, Peter. Forty percent goes for the maintenance of the ship, and forty percent to the men. In this case, that means the ship and men will each receive thirty-eight percent, which is not much of a loss, especially when you consider that the ships are unlikely to bring so much in Zokhara. If we submit to the Tangueli prize court, there is no way we will be able to sell all the prizes in Tanguel and must send them east. Through the blockade. Paying wages and the agent's fee. 'Tis a false economy. We know for certain what we shall get from the Portuguese."

Ali protested, "If we sell in Zokhara all the money stays in Sallee hands. The greater benefit is to the Muslims, even if we do not bring home as much individually. It is unacceptable that Christians should handle any part of our corsairing trade."

"I don't see how you can say that. Do not Jews and Christians buy our prize goods all the time? The merchants of Leghorn are our greatest customers. If you will accept Christian money for shoes and wine, why not for the ships themselves?"

Ali opened his mouth then shut it. He spluttered, "But it isn't right to give up more than ten percent to the government! Think what will happen! The Janissaries will be able to raise our taxes and refuse us letters of marque if we won't pay. Every corsair in Zokhara will despise you if you yield to this erosion of their ancient privileges. You won't be *kapitan pasha* after that."

It was Tangle's turn to fall into a brown study.

Thorton had heard enough. "I vote to bring the prizes into Tanguel. If the Portuguese want to buy the ships, let them bring the money here."

"Well said!" Ali crowed. "Tanguel it is."

Tangle contradicted him. "I refuse. We cannot guarantee the security of the vessels in Tanguel. We can't even get the battleship into harbor."

Thorton was dizzy, but he was certain they were missing something important. He rubbed his forehead and tried to think what it was. "You promised your home town that the corsairs would come if the channel was dredged, Isam. They dredged on your assurance. Will you cheat them now?"

Tangle sighed and muttered, "Damn you for a righteous man, Peter Thorton."

"Adjudicate the prizes in Tanguel, then sell them in Lisbon with your agent. You get the Portuguese price without paying a cut to the Portuguese government," Thorton suggested.

Tangle and Ali both furrowed their brows as they weighed the merits of Thorton's proposal. It answered Ali's complaint about the time-honored ten percent and kept the money in Muslim hands, but exposed the vessels to the risk of capture and Portuguese insolvency.

"The Portuguese still owe you for Eel Buff," Ali pointed out.

Tangle tugged the white streak in his beard. "With so many vessels under our control, we will be able to press the matter of payment."

"You would extract payment with the muzzle of a gun?" Ali asked skeptically.

"I never bluff. If they don't pay, I'll sell it back to the Spanish."

Thorton huddled in his blankets. He was sick and cross and hurting. "I don't care how you do it. Just go away and leave me in peace. You know my vote."

CHAPTER 23: THE AMBASSADOR TO PORTUGAL

Many days later Thorton opened his eyes on a sunny morning with light streaming through the louvered door of his berth. It was a glorious day of early spring that promised winter would not last forever. It was even warm. Not balmy, but very fresh. The hatches and ports had all been opened up to air out the ship except for his sickroom.

Perry propped the door open and waved his hand. "Fresh air, Peter! Do you feel it? Spring is coming and the sap is rising!" With a glance to make certain no one was around, he came over, bent into Thorton's hammock, and gave him a kiss on the tip of his nose, that being the only location where he could avoid dried out scabs of small pox. "How are you feeling?"

"I think I'm getting better," Thorton replied. "In fact, I'd like to get up." He had been sick for weeks and insensible to the ship's travel. He was vaguely aware that they had touched at Portsmouth, but currently he had no idea where they were or even what day it was.

Perry helped him out of the hammock. He tottered through the wardroom to the roundhouse and relieved himself, then tottered back. The wardroom was deserted; nobody was below decks on such a sunny day. Walking tired him out, so he sat down on his sea chest.

"I want a bath and a clean shirt." He had been so long a hermit in his cabin that he was in no fit state for human company.

Perry frowned out him. "You'll catch your death of cold if you bathe now, Peter. The weather is not that warm."

Thorton put a hand up to feel his greasy hair and grimaced. "I want a bath all the same."

"I'll boil some water for you, rais," Ra'uf told him. He slipped out of the cabin.

"Will you help me find a clean shirt?" Thorton asked.

"All right. I must admit you smell bad."

Thorton would have been offended by that remark, but he was afraid it was true. He moved off the sea chest and crawled back into his hammock. His back ached from spending weeks bent in the hammock and he rubbed it. Perry rooted through the sea chest and laid a clean nightshirt, nightcap, and wool socks on it. Thorton showed a leg and Perry gingerly peeled the woolen sock from it. He held the stinking sock with the tips of his fingers, grimaced horribly, and threw it in a corner.

Ra'uf returned with a pail of hot water. Fresh water. Salt water was supposed to be used for everything but drinking and cooking, but Ra'uf had his ways. He glared at Perry who gave way before him. The ferret-faced Arab took Thorton's foot, inspected it, then tucked it back into the hammock. He began at Thorton's face, gently daubing and wiping. The scabs came off and he saved them in a vial.

"You are fortunate, rais, only one scar on your face," he told Thorton.

"Where?" Thorton asked.

Ra'uf put his finger on Thorton's cheekbone near the corner of his left eye.

Perry came over to have a look and said jovially, "You can paint it black and pretend it is a beauty mark. Everyone will think you have a fashionable case of syphilis."

Thorton made a grumpy noise. Ra'uf gave the brunet lieutenant a reproachful look.

"He'll look like a duke," Perry replied.

"I am not a duke," Thorton replied crossly. "Besides, the only duke I know is a macaroni."

"If his taste were a little more up-to-date, methinks Henrique would cut quite the figure, even if he is hideous. As it is, he is too much the buffoon."

Once his body was washed Thorton knelt on the floor and bent over the bucket. "Help me with my hair, Roger."

Perry knelt beside him, scooped up the greasy hair, and put it in the water. He lathered up his hands with soap, then ran them through the blond locks. He rubbed the hair and massaged the scalp. Thorton let him. It felt quite good.

Perry sighed with pleasure as he rinsed the stands of dark blond hair. "A woman would envy you, Peter. Your hair is very thick and straight and long."

"I have never cut it since I went to sea," Thorton replied, his voice muffled in the bucket.

"I used to think you ought to cut it so that you would appear more like a gentleman, but it would be a shame to cut such glorious hair. Did your mother have such hair?"

"No, it was my father. He was a halfbreed, but he was fair all the same."

A rap sounded at the door. It opened to admit Midshipman Lemuel Jackson. "Begging your pardon, Lieutenant Thorton, but Captain Horner says the quarantine is lifted. He asks to know if you are able to attend him for an errand ashore."

Thorton raised his head with Perry wrapping the long wet hair in a towel. "Aye, I can. When?"

"Immediately, if you're able."

"I'll get dressed and shaved. I can be ready in fifteen minutes," Thorton replied. It took him a good deal longer, but that was because Ra'uf and Perry were helping him.

Eventually he arrived on the quarterdeck and gazed in wonder at the sight of a strange city to the north and a port filled with commerce all around him. The dun colored hills and occasional palm trees persuaded him he must be somewhere in Iberia, but beyond that he had no guess. He saluted crisply. "Lieutenant Peter Thorton reporting for duty, sir."

"I'm pleased to see you better, Lieutenant. I hate to call you to duty so soon, but we are required ashore."

"Aye aye, sir. I'm pleased to be out of bed."

The two went ashore in the captain's gig. Thorton looked around him in amazement. The river was broad and lined by whitewashed buildings with tile roofs. A number of tall new stone buildings could be seen on the north shore; it was a thriving metropolis. Trees and other plants were leafing out with bright green leaves. Turning to Horner he asked, "Where are we?"

"Lisbon," the captain replied. He was wearing his good frock coat, hat, and a neat blond wig. It looked like his own hair, except his hair was thin and he had cut it short to fit more readily under the wig. "We have been summoned by Baron Chippenham, His Majesty's Ambassador to Portugal."

They found a coach waiting for them at the quay. The feather springs rocked as they entered, then the footman folded up the step and shut the door. The interior was plushly upholstered in brown velvet. A warming pan in the middle of the floor and wool rugs kept them warm, but Thorton put his nose to the glass and watched the streets of Lisbon go by. He had never been to Portugal and marveled to see how like, yet unlike Spain it was. Since the earthquake a great deal of rebuilding had been done, and it was done in the lofty modern style with rococo features set on broad boulevards. The effect was very clean and elegant, interspersed here and there with Moorish galleries and heavy Romanesque churches that had survived the disaster. The waterfront was dominated by a new royal palace with a sweeping lawn that lead down to the quay and was planted with young trees. They rolled past it and into the city proper.

Horner spoke. "Sir Harlan White, Baron of Chippenham, is the brother of the Earl of Waverly, First Lord of the Admiralty. Rear Admiral Zeus White is their nephew. I don't need to impress upon you the importance of making a good impression."

Thorton sat bolt upright. "What does he want? I'm no good at talking to peers! What shall I say?"

"As little as possible. Answer the questions put to you and nothing more. He wants to question us about the Portuguese navy. We are more intimately acquainted with its leadership than anyone else in England. We know Henrique."

The carriage arrived at a townhouse on a hilly side street. It was not especially large by the standards of the nobility, but it dwarfed the ordinary residences with which Thorton was familiar. It was three stories tall and five bays wide with narrow windows in each section of the facade. The carriage drew up, the footman opened the door, and they ascended stone steps to the first floor. A housekeeper in a severely plain brown dress with a white mob cap and apron admitted them. The entrance hall was a large space with a fireplace of its own, tall wide doors opening into rooms to either side, and a square arch that lead to the back. Racks of antique weapons lined the walls from the top of the wainscot all the way to the ceiling. The weapons were sufficient to equip a troop of Caballeros and had done so a hundred years ago. The officers removed their hats and tucked them under their elbows.

The housekeeper lead them deeper into the house. A square stairway rose up to the left and was lit by stained glass windows depicting a battle scene from Portuguese history. Turbaned warriors were falling before an onslaught of Christian knights. She stopped before a massive wooden door. A voice called, "Enter!" and she pushed the heavy door open. Horner and Thorton stepped into the room.

The study was trimmed in dark wood and bookcases lined a portion of two walls. There must have been five hundred books in the room—a prodigious library. The shutters were folded back so that the room was flooded with light, and one of the windows was open to admit the fresh spring air. A broad oak desk from the last century dominated the room. Leather chairs sat on a woolen rug that depicted a woodland thicket. It was green, interspersed with flowers and small animals such as hares and squirrels. A heavy stone fireplace topped with an oak mantelpiece carved with oak leaves and acorns completed the room's furnishings.

The man at the desk was of average height. He wore a brunet peruke with two rolls of hair on either side of his face. He was in the prime of life, a bit thick in the body, but with a vigorous expression. He wore a brown suit with a fawn colored waistcoat under it. A gold watch chain ran across the front of his waistcoat. His secretary, an older man whose grey eyebrows contrasted with a neat black cap wig, sat at the end of the desk.

The housekeeper curtsied. "My lord, Captain Horner and Lieutenant Thorton of the *Amphitrite* frigate to see you."

"Thank you, Alder. That will be all."

The housekeeper withdrew.

When the door thumped closed, the man said, "I am Harlan White, Baron of Chippenham and Ambassador to Portugal. This is my secretary, Albert Robbins. Please be seated, gentlemen."

"We're delighted to meet you, sir," Horner answered for both of them. They bowed, then sank into the chairs. The leather upholstery creaked while the room smelled of cigars, leather, and money. They rested their hats in their laps.

Girlish laughter bubbled in through the window, then a young woman ran past with grey ribbons streaming from her straw hat. Horner and Thorton had a glimpse of brunette curls and a grey dress, then she was gone. They heard her voice, "I have it! You knocked it all the way up into the gallery!"

Noticing their distraction, the ambassador turned and looked out the window. "My daughters. The oldest is the widow of Captain Wadsworth. I believe you knew him. She has grieved a long time. I hope the change of scenery will end her mourning."

"I did. He was captain of the *Kestrel* when it was lost at Cherbourg," Horner replied.

"Indeed he was. You did good work that day, Captain, but God's hand is in everything. Some were saved and some were not. So it ever was and ever will be."

"So it is, sir."

Recalling himself, the baron turned back to the business at hand. "I called you here to question you about the Portuguese situation. I understand you are both acquainted with the Duke of Coimbra. He has a claim to the throne of Portugal."

"We have met him, my lord," Horner replied. Thorton nodded.

"I understand he does not have the support of the Catholic Church, which prefers João. The question is whether he has Protestant leanings, and would therefore be a more reliable friend to England. João seems to be on uncommonly good terms with the Spanish for all that he has raised a revolt against them."

"I don't believe Henrique is a religious man," Horner replied. Feminine laughter drifted in through the open window. Thorton said nothing.

When nothing further was coming from the captain, the ambassador transferred his attention to Thorton. "What do you think, Lieutenant?"

Thorton sat rigidly in his chair with his feet flat on the floor and his hands on the arms. His back did not touch the back of the chair. "I don't know anything about politics, sir," he replied.

"He's invited you both to his wedding. That's an uncommon mark of favor. He must like you. Surely he said something while he was in British care that revealed his feelings."

"His Grace the Duke did not converse much with me," Horner replied. "I assigned Lieutenant Thorton to assist him while he was aboard."

Young women trooped past the window, but stopped to look in when they saw their father seated in his chair. The three of them clustered there a moment, one in pale grey, one in light green, and one in pale yellow. All of them had fair complexions with the natural blush of health upon their cheeks. Framed by the heavy wooden window, they might have been a piece of art, 'English Maidens in Spring.'

Once again Horner was distracted. He stared at the woman in grey until she blushed and ducked her head and the brim of the straw hat covered her eyes. Noticing that he had lost Horner's attention, the baron turned around to see what he was looking at. A smile crossed his face. He waved his hand at them. "Girls! You are interrupting! Off with you. You can meet our guests at dinner. Shoo!" He waggled his hands at them like they were geese.

"We're sorry, Father," the two younger girls piped in their delicate voices. The widow said nothing, but made a curtsy. Her sisters imitated her, then trooped off.

Turning back to his guests the baron brought them back to business. "Yes, I already know that. Come, Lieutenant! Tell me what he said! What were the subjects of his conversation? He must have said something."

Thorton paled. The most obvious topics of interest to the lusty duke were not the sort he could discuss with a complete stranger. He threw his mind back and said, "He was grateful to be rescued. He said he was favorably inclined to anyone who helped him obtain his freedom."

"That's something. Go on." The secretary made a note of it.

"He is to be João's heir, if the king doesn't have any sons of his own."

"We know that. We are not entirely without resources in Lisbon. Tell me about the man. They say he is lascivious and frivolous."

"Aye, he is. But he has a quality about him, an innate nobility, that makes people love him."

"He's a shrewd man," Horner put in. "He has the sense to choose competent officers and listens to their advice. However, he is easily distracted."

The secretary kept making notes.

"This is the sort of thing I want to know. Does he have any mistresses? Any bastards?"

"Not to my knowledge, sir," Thorton replied.

Chippenham had other questions. Thorton answered them in a soft voice, slowly sinking into the chair and growing pale as he tired. He was thin and wan after his illness and Horner was sorry to have dragged him out.

The lieutenant was granted a reprieve. The library door heaved open and the woman in grey entered the room. White lace dangled from her forearms and a white fichu was around her bosom. The straw hat on her head trailed grey ribbons. The only touch of color about her was a pink pocket tied around her waist on a string. Her brunette hair hung down in curls around her shoulders. She was carrying a lawn billiard cue that was shaped something like a spoon with a long handle. It reminded Thorton of a lacrosse stick. All the men in the room rose at her entrance.

"I am sorry to interrupt, Father, but Alder tells me our guest is Captain Horner." She cast a look at the older of the two officers, but her expression revealed nothing.

The baron spoke, "My daughter, Mistress Emily White Wadsworth, the widow of the late Captain Jason Wadsworth of the *Kestrel*. This is Captain Ebenezer Horner and Lieutenant Peter Thorton of the *Amphitrite* frigate."

Horner made a leg. "Your servant, ma'am. Please allow me to express my condolences upon your loss." His always sober demeanor allowed him to make his remarks gracefully.

Thorton bowed but said nothing. He felt a little wobbly and hoped she would go soon so he could sit down before he fell down.

Widow Wadsworth stepped forward and gave Horner her hand. "Thank you, Captain. Your sympathy is appreciated, and I hope I may impose upon your kindness to ask a question. I know Father will forgive me for interrupting." Her voice was a polite contralto.

Horner bowed over her hand but did not kiss it. "If there is any way I may be of service, I am happy to do so." The aloof courtesy they showed each other gave no sign that a few minutes earlier Horner had been staring at her.

"You were at the Battle of Cherbourg, were you not, Captain Horner?"

"I was. I had the privilege of being captain of the *Hermes* at the time."

"The *Kestrel* was sunk at Cherbourg."

"Aye. The *Dauntless*, too."

"My husband's body was not recovered. We held his funeral without it, but it troubles me. I wonder if there is any possibility that it could be retrieved. I have sent inquiries to the Mayor of Cherbourg, but he informs me that the *Kestrel* went down in fifty fathoms of water, and there is no possibility of salvage."

"The water before Cherbourg is very deep, ma'am."

"Is it truly impossible? Is it certain that the *Kestrel* is so very deep?"

"I'm afraid it is, ma'am."

Tears welled up on her eyes. Horner pulled his handkerchief out of his sleeve and offered it to her. She accepted and daubed delicately at her eyes. "We had an empty casket at the funeral. I don't know if you can imagine how hard it is to lose someone but have nothing to bury. I can't quite believe that he's dead. I keep hoping there is some mistake."

"I was at home when my wife died. I found that difficult enough. I cannot imagine how I would have felt if the news had come to me from a distance."

She looked up in surprise. "You're a widower? I'm sorry for your loss! I hope I have not distressed you."

"It has been more than five years since she passed. I don't think I shall ever be reconciled to her death, but time makes all things bearable."

Baron Chippenham came around the end of the desk. "Emily, why don't you ask Captain Horner to walk in the garden? You may talk to him while I finish my interview with Mister Thorton." He made shooing motions with his hand.

The widow and widower gave each other uncomfortable looks, but Horner was in no position to object to anything the ambassador suggested. As for the widow, she knew she had imposed on her father by barging in on his meeting, so she gave a little curtsy and yielded. "If you insist."

"I do. Now go on!"

The two went out.

CHAPTER 24: THE GAMBLING HOUSE

A fortnight later Thorton was entirely recovered and back on duty. It was one of those brilliant spring days where green things were thrusting erect from the ground and nodding agreement to every passing creature. So it was with Thorton. He pinned Perry in his cabin and tried to kiss him, but Perry turned his face aside.

"I'm feeling much better now," Thorton whispered in his ear. "I missed you."

Perry couldn't help but feel flattered; he liked attention. "Did you?"

"Oh yes, a great deal. Let's make up for lost time."

He kissed him again and this time Perry let him. The kiss went on a great deal longer than either of them had intended; it was always that way with Thorton. Once he started something he was loathe to stop. Especially when it was something he liked as much as he liked kissing Perry. His hands wandered below the waist and cupped the muscular fundament through the wool of the coat.

"Stop that. I don't want to be your bugger-boy." Perry kept his voice low even as he complained.

"You like it," Thorton whispered.

Perry squirmed, "I don't want to like it. You have given me a vice I didn't ask for."

Thorton moved his hands to the front, but Perry shoved them away. "It will be the ruin of me and you know it."

Thorton moved his hands to the slightly less dangerous territory of Perry's waist, but he didn't release the other lieutenant, not even though he was cognizant of the Sword of Damocles dangling over his head. "We have to desert. 'Tis the only way."

Perry brooded at him. "Go if you will. I won't. 'Tis your choice, not mine. I want to marry an English lass and retire as a yellow admiral."

His words wounded Thorton. "Are you jilting me?"

"I didn't say that. I just said I won't desert."

Thorton took Perry's hand in his and kissed it. "I'm tired of hiding."

Perry pulled his hand back with a hiss. "You'll ruin both of us if you don't keep the secret!"

Thorton nodded. "I know. They'll hang me for sure. I won't escape a second time."

Perry was in no mood for such talk. He pushed Thorton away. "Damn me, I want a woman! Even Horner wants a woman. He's ashore right now, running after Emily Wadsworth. Did you see the new furniture he bought? All white with rose brocade. Because she liked it. He's as addled as a schoolboy."

It gave Thorton a twinge to think how many invitations Horner had received ashore. He was jealous. "He's lucky," he replied.

Perry leaned against the bulkhead. "I want a plump bosom to lay my head against and a sweet little cunny to welcome me home. That's what I want more than anything in the world right now."

Thorton's broad muscular body was as unlike a woman as it could be. He stood awkwardly next to the man he could not quite call his lover, in spite of what they had done together. He did not know what to do or say.

"Maybe you should visit a brothel," he suggested. He remembered the last time the two of them had gone to hire a whore. Thorton had had the only woman he had ever had in his life, but the skirt-lifters hadn't gotten anything at all. "I still owe you one," he said, feeling sick.

"By God, you do!" Perry's good humor was restored. "Let's go, now, while Old Horny's ashore. We can find one for each of us and be back before he knows."

Thorton chewed his lip and thought about hiring a male whore. Maybe that would be better than arguing with Perry and dealing with his moods. Other men hired whores, why not Peter Thorton? He wasn't sure about it, but he had the horn and Perry wasn't cooperating. "If you say so."

First Lieutenant Forsythe was an easily overcome obstacle and they were soon ashore. An establishment in the older part of the city suited Perry's needs. The first room was a salon done in dark shades of oxblood red, chocolate brown, and gold. It managed to look respectable and decadent all at once. Dark red velvet curtains draped the archway into the next room and only partially obscured the contents. Gaming tables were set up where men and women laid their money on the table and spun the gaudy wheel.

Perry took note of the money riding on the bets and the quality of the clothes worn and elbowed Thorton. "We came to the right place. A pair of lieutenants with money in their pockets ought to do very well here." He led them boldly into the cigar smoke and heat.

A woman with henna hair deigned to notice the new arrivals. She waved her fan in invitation, and Perry immediately answered it. Thorton trailed unhappily in his wake. Up close they had a good view of her extraordinarily generous bosom, pale (although a little sallow), and thrust up to good effect by the action of her corset. The gown was cut as low as it could be without collapsing in an avalanche of pulchritude. A gold chain around her neck supported a pendant that appeared to be rubies but was only paste. The glittering gems dangled at the top of her cleavage. The red dress she wore was made of watered silk, but it had been discreetly mended around the armhole. The lace was not fresh, but most men didn't notice, given that their only concern was whether her bodice might fail entirely and spill the whole cornucopia into their laps.

Perry gave the whore a bow and spoke English to her. "Madame, I am delighted to make your acquaintance. Please allow me to introduce myself. I am Alexander Robbins, and this is my friend, Thomas Peterson."

Thorton startled at the subterfuge, but he was obliged to translate it since the creature knew no English.

"I'm Magdalena La Roja. I'm delighted to meet you," she purred in Portuguese. She gave Perry her hand to kiss.

Perry bowed low over it but his lips did not touch it. "I am enchanted, Miss Roja. I feel that we shall become very good friends." He gazed deeply into her eyes. In response, her lips curved into a smile that was every bit as practiced as Perry's words.

Thorton bowed awkwardly and said, "Your servant, ma'am." He was completely unnecessary in spite of the language difficulties. Perry's cooing needed no translation; his gaze and her breasts spoke a mutually intelligible language. Perry settled on the settee beside her and Thorton wandered away.

The blond lieutenant wedged himself into a corner between a statue of a Greek goddess missing half her clothes and a dainty chair with brocade upholstery that looked as if would break under any normally proportioned adult. The noise and light and warmth washed over him and left him feeling groggy, bored, and lonely. He let his eyes roam over the men present. He did not find them attractive. Some of them were plump with ruddy faces flushed with wine and shining with sweat, while others were badly dressed in rough clothes and badly matched accessories. The better dressed men had the look of grocers and cabinetmakers: solid men who earned enough to disport themselves upon occasion.

A young man at the wheel caught Thorton's attention. Short, no more than nineteen, the black curls gathered around his face were only partly restrained by the red ribbon at his nape. He wore a short black jacket, red breeches that fit snugly, and red woolen stockings fastened under the knees with black garters. His white shirt was ruffled and he had no waistcoat. He had a lively way of moving as he exhorted the wheel. Thorton found the view of his backside agreeable and his mood improved. The short coat was really indecent, especially when the young man bent over the table to scoop up his winnings. At that moment the jacket rode up to show the strings cinching the waistband of his breeches. Thorton had a momentary urge to cut those laces, causing the breeches to drop . . .

No, he ought not think such things. But why not? He was in a den of sin. He was not expected to keep his thoughts pure in a place like this. Over there was a tart putting a grape into her cleavage and her beau was diving in after it. Better to watch a handsome young man gaming.

The victorious gambler turned to get himself a drink from a passing servant. Thorton saw his full face then; it was regular and unmarked, with a straight nose, swarthy complexion, and large lustrous eyes ringed by lashes that would make a woman jealous. The mouth had a twist to it as if he habitually sneered at the world, but his lips were full. He noticed Thorton looking at him, but the lieutenant hastily pulled his eyes away. The youth kept an eye on Thorton while he drank his wine. Thorton peeked, saw himself being observed, and wished he could fade right into the wall. He looked away again but tried to keep track of the young man from the corner of his eye. The object of his gaze drank his wine pensively, then turned back to the table. He put down his next bet. The wheel spun and he lost it. There was laughter and condolences, but he was not daunted. He bet again.

Thorton shifted his position a little further along the wall so he could watch the young man in profile. The gambler's figure was fine and straight, aside from the pleasant bulges that showed him to be male and lightly muscled. The young man bent over the table to place his bet. As he rose he glanced to the side and saw Thorton.

Thorton gave him a weak smile. Having been caught looking a second time, there was no way to pretend it was an accident. He ran a finger inside his stock. The room was too warm and too noisy. He transferred his attention to Perry and his whore then, but the two of them were rising and moving purposefully toward the door. Well then. He was going to be stuck for a while. Fifteen minutes or two hours; it all depended how well the whore liked the brown-haired lieutenant and how deep his purse was. The Englishmen had provided themselves with a goodly supply of cash so that their carousing would not be cut short by a want of funds. Perry could get what he wanted.

The young man was gaming again, gaming and losing. Within twenty minutes he lost everything he had won. His brow furrowed and he gritted his teeth. Then he smiled and attempted to charm the man running the wheel, but his marker was not accepted. He had to stand aside and sulk.

Thorton's heart was in his mouth as he stepped forward. "Good evening. Has your luck turned?" he addressed the young man.

Brown eyes flashed at him. "It has, but bad luck doesn't last. It goes against the rules of nature. If I had another piece of eight, I could make it back, I'm sure." He spoke a lilting Spanish that charmed the lieutenant as much as his appearance.

Thorton pulled out a British guinea and offered it to the handsome youth wordlessly. Brown eyes lit up and the youth flashed a dazzling smile at Thorton. "If I win, I'll split it with you, I promise."

The others at the table were taking note of the newcomer. Some of them had hardbitten faces with scars and pockmarks and Thorton didn't like their looks. Feeling himself to be much older and wiser than his new friend, Thorton decided to stand guard over him. Speaking softly he said, "Be careful if you win, *amigo*. These are some rough men."

A sly smile crept across the youth's face. He looked around at the others, then said meekly to Thorton, "I will count on your protection, *Señor.* I'm Rafael." He offered his hand.

Thorton took it and said, "Peter—" He remembered his alias and added, "—son. Thomas Peterson." Sweat was trickling inside his collar. He gripped the young man's hand but forgot to shake it.

"You are an Englishman? An officer?" Rafael extracted his hand from Thorton's. His eyes roamed over him and took in the quality of his coat and the luster of his lace. He was interested.

"Yes, I am."

"Wonderful."

He would have said more, but the croupier called for the bets. Rafael turned from him and boldly put down his English guinea. It was accepted by the other gamblers without comment; British money was sound. The wheel spun and the ball whirled around the wheel, coming to rest at last. The silver guinea was swept away by the dealer with all the other coins.

Rafael pouted and immediately turned to Thorton. "Another! That one was close, I feel it."

Thorton demurred, "You've already won once tonight. I don't think fortune will favor you a second time."

Rafael's gaze hardened. "Why did you give it to me if you thought I would lose?"

Thorton screwed his courage to the sticking point. "I wanted to meet you. Maybe I could buy you some wine instead."

Rafael's face closed down as he stood looking up at Thorton. His toe tapped, but the croupier called the bets. He turned back to the table, but no one would lend him or give him any money. One of the ruffians said slyly, "Why don't you charm your new friend into being generous?"

Rafael's eyes flashed in anger. Then they narrowed. He weighed the merits of the proposal and swiftly made up his mind. He turned to face Thorton, gave him a sunny smile, and said, "I would be delighted to share a drink with you, Thomas."

Thorton couldn't believe his luck. His heart hammered in his chest as he gingerly took his companion by the arm and went in quest of drinks. They obtained two red wines and retired to Thorton's corner.

"I'm very glad to meet you, Rafael," Thorton said. His blue eyes were eager.

Rafael drank some of his wine before he answered. "I'm glad to meet you, too. Since you're not a gambler, I suppose you came here looking for company?" He looked up at Thorton through lowered lashes.

Thorton nodded eagerly. "I would like to get to know you better."

Rafael looked around at the room. "There are too many people here for that."

Thorton's heart was thudding so hard he couldn't hear anything else. "Do you have a room?" He tried to act nonchalant as if he were used to such assignations.

"I live nearby." He let his fingers walk along Thorton's lapel. "But I have to know if 'tis worth my time."

"I have money," Thorton replied.

"Are you generous, *Señor?*" The young man gave him an encouraging smile. His fingers toyed with the ruffles over Thorton's heart.

Thorton nodded quickly. "I have another guinea. I can take you out to dinner and theater."

Brown eyes lit with avarice, but Rafael pretended to be nettled. "I suppose that will do for tonight."

"I can come back tomorrow."

Sardonic lips smirked. "Let's see how tonight goes. There may not be another night."

Thorton was downcast. "I would like there to be another night. I would like to court you properly."

Rafael couldn't help laughing at that. "Court me? Oh, you are a bumpkin." He took Thorton's arm and whispered in his ear, "Then you must be very good to me tonight, no?"

"Yes," Thorton breathed.

Rafael led him out of the house by the back door. Thorton didn't see it when the young man gave the scar-faced man a nod as they passed.

Chapter 25: The Iron Gate

The night was cloudy and chilly, but the coolness felt good to Thorton after the heat of the gambling house. The alley was dimly lit by light spilling from the rear windows of establishments along its path. The sounds of merriment came from several of the houses, then the retching sound of someone overcome by drink. Rafael set off at a brisk pace in the opposite direction, but Thorton caught up to him and grasped his hand in his. His new friend stiffened and pulled away, but Thorton was stubborn and held onto his hand.

"No one will see us here," he assured the other man. He wanted to hold much more than his new friend's hand. The youth made a moue, but he let Thorton keep his hand.

Emboldened, Thorton kissed his cheek. "You're cold," he said. He himself was plenty warm in his long wool coat and simmering blood. He put an arm around the smaller man to warm him up.

Rafael suffered his embrace. "Soon," he promised Thorton. "'Tisn't far."

The lieutenant smiled and hugged him closer to his side. It felt so very good! His hand began to wander a bit as he investigated his new friend's shape. Rafael quickened his pace.

The alley intersected with a narrow lane and Rafael turned right, bringing Thorton with him. The area was very dark and quiet and their footsteps crunched loudly on the frozen dirt of the alley. They were passing between the high blank wall of a warehouse and a stone wall that surrounded a cemetery when they came to a wrought iron gate. Rafael let go of him and stepped forward to fiddle with the lock until it clicked. He opened the gate, stepped through, and motioned for Thorton to follow him.

Thorton hesitated. Rafael gave him a warm and inviting smile. "A short cut. 'Tis an awfully long way to walk around." His breath was a cloud in the evening chill.

The British lieutenant stepped into the cemetery. Rafael shut the gate behind him.

Thorton paused to look around. Mausoleums and headstones were crowded very close together. No trees grew in the cemetery; it was a necropolis of stone. His guide caught his sleeve and pulled him between some of the tallest markers.

"Here," Rafael whispered. His eyes were luminous and black as he looked up Thorton.

The tall stones afforded a modicum of privacy, but Thorton felt bad. Surely it was sacrilegious to do what he hoped they would do in a cemetery. He had known his lust was a sin, but until now he had not felt it to be abominable; yet what could be more hideous than fornicating with a whore on the tomb of somebody's mother or father? He felt sick to his stomach.

"Not here."

Rafael's eyes flashed. "'Tis better than my room. I can't wait." He reached up, grabbed Thorton's head, and pulled it down so that he could kiss his mouth.

Thorton gave a soft groan and kissed him back, hands going to the slim waist. The lad was warm as he pulled him against him, but the caliginous place with its bone white markers dampened his ardor. He broke the kiss. "Rafael, I'm sorry, but I can't do it. Not here."

"You can't buy me in front of everyone, then change your mind and send me back with nothing to show for it! I only did it for the money." A quick hand dipped into his jacket pocket and came up with a flash of metal.

Too late Thorton saw the switchblade aimed for his ribs. He tried to dodge, but the blade sliced into his coat and he felt fire along his ribs. Then somebody struck him in the back. He lurched forward and the knife cut again. A cudgel struck him in the back of the head and another in the legs. He stumbled and his vision went blurry; the left eye that had been imperfect ever since the Battle of Alborán showed him a fuzzy set of strangers as he turned.

"Help!" he called out. "Rafael, don't!"

"Beat him," the youth replied coldly.

Much later Thorton woke in a bloody heap on the ground. Weeds and headstones surrounded him. The night was cold. He lifted his head gingerly, then let it fall. His nose was broken and hurting while his head rung and the world spun. He groped his ribs and found the cuts; his shirt and waistcoat were a mess, but the blade had slid along the ribs instead of between them. He ached between the legs where they had kicked him to show their contempt for what he was. His mouth was bloody where Rafael had punched him to wipe away the taste of his foul kiss. With an aching hand he felt his pockets. He had been robbed of his purse, watch, and hat, but that was nothing. He was lucky he wasn't murdered. How long he had lain on the ground, he didn't know, but the cold had seeped into his bones and made them ache.

He didn't want to get up, but he had to. Nobody was going to find him lying there in the cemetery. Even if they did, they might not be friends. Rafael and his thugs were not the only criminals in the world. He rolled onto his stomach. That was a major exertion, so he lay on the ground and rested while the cold settled deeper in his body. Slowly he pushed up with his aching arms. He cried out in pain as his pinky finger sent a bolt of pain shooting up his wrist all the way the shoulder. He pushed himself to a sitting position and cradled the broken hand. The left pinky stuck out at an unnatural angle. He pulled it, yelped in pain, and let it go. The finger was straighter, but it wasn't right. He huddled with his arms around himself.

He wanted to pray, but he was a Muslim sodomite beaten and abandoned in a Christian graveyard. He was ashamed, but he felt the need to pray anyhow. He began to whisper the Arabic words, "Come to prayer, come to success," but they sounded hollow. His voice faded away.

With a groan he braced against an obelisk and heaved himself onto his knees, then crawled up the monument with his arms around it. He kept leaning against the stone because the world was swaying. Eventually he propped himself up and staggered forward. He tripped over a footstone lost in the shadows. Falling jolted his wounds and forced a cry from his lips. Fresh blood broke out and spread warmth along his ribs.

Uncertain of his ability to walk, he crawled slowly amid the graves on his hands and knees. That proved as painful as walking, so he found an open patch of ground and slowly got to his feet. He looked around.

The gate where Rafael had let them in was not far away. He made his way over to it. When he got there, he found it locked. He had no lock pick nor art to use one if he did; he could not open the gate. He leaned against the wall for a bit, then began a slow perambulation of the grounds. He staggered with every step, aching worse and worse, but he plodded on. He tripped over something he couldn't see in the dark, rested on the cold ground for a while, then dragged himself up again.

Eventually he came to the front gate, which was also locked. He couldn't open it, so he kept walking. Every step hurt, but he had no choice. He paced the wall with a hanging head and aching flesh, but found no other gates. Walking warmed him and the stiffness in his joints eased a trifle, but it made him bleed and his head pound. He kept a hand pressed to his side and his breath came in shallow pants. He walked gingerly as if a sudden move might pull him apart. His crotch hurt abominably. Eventually he came full circuit back to the side gate. With a whimper he sank to his knees and leaned against the unforgiving stone.

He didn't know what to do. If he were unhurt he could have scaled the wall and escaped, but he wasn't able. He shifted to a more comfortable position and huddled in his coat. All he could do was to wait for dawn and hope somebody came and let him out. At least during the day there would be traffic and he could call out to someone. Who would hopefully help him. Then he would have to explain why he was stuck in the cemetery. That jolted him into action.

The iron gate was made up of vertical bars held in place at the top, bottom, and middle by cross bars. Three hinges secured it to the wall on one side and the lock on the other. He put his foot on the bottom cross bar and hung onto the metal as he lifted his other foot and got his knee onto the middle cross bar. His broken hand did not want to hold on; pain shot up his arm. He hung there like that, trying to figure out how to rearrange himself so he could haul himself up and over the gate. Climbing a gate should not be difficult for a man who had been a foretop hand before he became an officer, but he couldn't do it. Every time he tried to heave himself up his hand and groin and ribs screamed in pain.

He let himself down from the gate. He laced his arms through it and leaned against it in despair. It must be possible. Somehow, he must do it. He was still hanging onto the gate when someone came along the alley.

"Peter?" Perry's voice came from the darkness.

Thorton raised his head. "Roger?"

Perry broke into a run. "There you are! What in the hell have you been doing? Do you have any idea how worried I've been? Why didn't you tell me you were leaving? Don't you know 'tis rude to run off?"

Thorton could only raise his battered face and whisper, "Help me."

Perry stopped dead in his tracks as he saw Thorton's cut mouth, bloody nose, black eye, and bruised face. "My God, Peter. What happened?"

"I was robbed and beaten."

Perry hastily tried to open the gate, but the lock held. "How did you get in?"

"Rafael picked the lock."

"How much do you want to bet his name isn't Rafael, anymore than you are Thomas Peterson?" Perry was no burglar. He had no lock pick. "Can you climb it?"

"I tried, but it hurts too much."

"I'll help you."

Perry easily leaped up the gate. Straddling the top, he perched there, locked his ankles in the bars, and reached down to grab Thorton's collar. "Come on, give it a try. I'll help."

With Perry hauling on his collar Thorton was able to pull himself up. He threw a leg over the top, yelped, and held tight as he perched next to Roger. His weight on the metal bar was hurting a very sensitive portion of his already abused anatomy. Perry held his shoulders to steady him. "Let me get down first so I can catch you."

Thorton was panting too much to answer, but he nodded.

"You're not going to fall if I do?"

Thorton shook his head.

Perry unlocked his legs and lightly dropped to the ground. He reached up to pat Thorton's hip. "Handsomely, lad. Down easy."

Thorton lay his stomach on the top of the iron gate, got the other leg over with some help from Perry, found a foothold on the middle bar, and lowered himself. He put his toes onto the lower bar and started to ease his weight onto it, whimpered, and froze. He hung in that awkward position, but Perry wrapped his arms around his waist and braced his legs to take his weight. The bigger lieutenant put his foot down, lost his grip, fell, and knocked Perry down with him. They sprawled in the dirt of the alley.

Perry popped up immediately and knelt over him. "Peter?"

Thorton gave a groan.

"You've had an adventure. Come on, we're taking you back to the ship." He got an arm under Thorton's shoulders and helped him to sit up. With Perry to prop him up Thorton made it to his feet. He tottered along the alley with his arm over Perry's shoulder. It was a long walk back to the waterfront.

CHAPTER 26: ABSENT WITHOUT LEAVE

Horner did not have much sympathy when he heard Thorton howl; Ferncastle had pulled his broken nose to straighten it. The sound came up from the wardroom through the planks of the deck and into the captain's cabin. Later, when Thorton had recovered, he would be glad to have his nose properly located in the middle of his face, but just at that moment he was a man who felt very much put upon. Ferncastle followed up by setting and splinting his hand. That didn't hurt nearly as much as his nose had. He gritted his teeth while having his ribs stitched up, and listened to Ferncastle's homily about how lucky he was to be alive. A few drops of laudanum numbed his pain and left him lightheaded, and in that condition he and Perry presented themselves to the captain.

The Widow Wadsworth sat on the sofa. It was a dainty thing with curved narrow legs and scallops carved into the woodwork. The upholstery was white brocade with red roses and green leaves. Although the lieutenants had accepted the arrival of the sofa without comment when it had come aboard, to discover Mistress Wadsworth sitting on it in the middle of the night made them gawk. Thorton's head hurt so much he couldn't figure out why she was there, but Perry was a worldly man and thought he knew.

She smiled tightly at them as she sat with her hands tucked into her white fur muff. The portable stove in the captain's cabin had been lit and placed at her feet. She was dressed in a black jacket and bonnet and black and white hound's-tooth skirt. Her appearance was entirely proper. She could have been having her portrait painted so perfectly was she dressed, but it was after midnight.

Horner gave her a little bow. "I regret the necessity of introducing you to Lieutenants Roger Perry and Peter Thorton under these circumstances, Madame."

Perry was holding his hat over his heart; he quickly swept it down and showed a good leg as he bowed. "Your servant, ma'am."

Thorton was hatless, his hand and ribs bandaged, and could barely see out of the blackened eye. He wobbled a few inches, decided that was enough to qualify as a bow, and said nothing. He braced his legs to keep himself in an upright position. Thanks to the drubbing, the opium, and the rocking of the ship, he was not on a good footing.

"I have the pleasure to present Mistress Emily White Wadsworth, the widow of Captain Wadsworth of the *Kestrel*. I believe you gentlemen were acquainted with him."

Perry had met the man, but Thorton had been a mere midshipman at the time and never encountered him. Still, he knew who he was.

"Allow me to offer my condolences upon the loss of your husband. He was a gallant officer," Perry immediately replied.

Thorton nodded. He had no idea what to say in such circumstances at the best of times, and he was in no fit state to exercise his intellect now.

"Thank you, Lieutenant," she replied.

Horner was properly dressed in a navy blue frock coat buttoned across his chest for the sake of warmth. His wig was neat and tidy and he had his dentures in. He was wide awake; he did not have the appearance of a man who had been roused from bed. Three lamps were lit; his three shadows wavered against the walls.

"You were absent without leave, gentlemen, and when you return, Mister Thorton is in a deplorable state. I hope you have an adequate explanation."

"Peter was robbed, sir," Perry immediately replied.

"Mister Thorton would not have been robbed if he were on the ship where he belonged. Just whose idea was it that he should go ashore this evening?" He knew perfectly well whose idea it was.

Perry eyed the lady, then turned his gaze on Horner. "It was business of a personal nature that compelled us to go ashore, sir," he replied with the utmost delicacy.

Horner's eyes narrowed. "Lieutenants do not grant themselves shore leave to satisfy personal whims!" He did not raise his voice, but his wrath was plain.

"Please accept my apologies, sir."

"You have not answered my question, Lieutenant. Where were you and what happened?"

"While I was visiting an acquaintance, Peter was robbed."

Perry was the veteran of many an amorous scrape; he knew how to defend himself. Horner turned his attention to the weaker link. "Mister Thorton. I require a full and complete account of your and Mister Perry's activities this evening."

"We went to a gambling house and tried to buy harlots." Thorton was never any good at dissembling, even when he had his wits about him. Perry kicked his ankle. "Ow!"

"Mister Perry, please refrain from assaulting Mister Thorton. He's battered enough already."

"Aye aye, sir."

"Madame, please forgive me for exposing you to this unpleasant matter," Horner said.

She withdrew a white-gloved hand from the muff and waved it gently. "Please, Evan. I know I have inconvenienced you. Do not refrain from doing your duty out of concern for me. I am aware of the vices to which our young officers sometimes succumb. Perhaps a woman's presence will help to impress upon them the importance of correct behavior at all times." To them she said, "You never know when you will meet a lady, and you should always conduct yourselves in such as way that you are in a fit condition to receive her."

"Well spoken, ma'am." Horner turned back to the two of them. "Thorton, carry on with due respect for the lesson Mistress Wadsworth has shared with you."

Thorton felt the black pit of despair welling up beneath his feet. It would have been difficult enough to tell Horner that he had been duped by a man pretending to be a male prostitute, but how he was to tell the tale without violating the bounds of propriety with a woman present he had no idea. His head ached and the laudanum made him feel like his skull was stuffed with wool fleece. He was tired and in pain. He decided fainting was his best option.

His legs crumpled and his aching body hit the floor. Pain exploded through him and made him moan. Somewhere in the dim and fuzzy recesses of his brain was the awareness that this was one of the most ignoble decisions he had ever made, but he didn't repent, even though he was sorry he had a new knot on his skull as a result.

Perry dropped to his knees. He shook Thorton's shoulder. "Peter! Are you all right? Can you hear me? Peter!"

Thorton lolled on the floor with glazed eyes. He was stunned, thanks to smacking his head on the floor, but he gave a groan.

Emily Wadsworth's hand flew to her mouth and covered a little cry. Horner knelt by Thorton's other side and examined his eyes. Thorton blinked dully, but showed no sign of recognizing him. None of them doubted he had swooned; he'd been pale and glassy when he entered the cabin.

Mrs. Wadsworth came and knelt besides the prostrate lieutenant. She dipped into her reticule, sorted through the items there, and produced a set of smelling salts which she waved under Thorton's nose.

His eyes snapped opened and he asked, "What happened?

"You swooned," Perry replied.

"I did?" Thorton was not inventing now; he really was addled.

Horner and Perry grabbed his arms and helped him sit up, then heaved him up. Perry kept an arm around his waist when Thorton proved unsteady on his feet.

"Doctor Ferncastle tells me that you have a broken hand, a broken nose, contusions, and lacerations. He did not say you were concussed." Horner was peering into Thorton's eyes trying to decide for himself if Ferncastle had overlooked something important. Thorton said nothing. "Put him on the sofa."

Perry supported Thorton over to the seat that Mrs. Wadsworth had formerly occupied. Thorton sank down gratefully. Having a seat beneath him helped restore his sense of equilibrium. "Thank you." He propped himself on the arm of the sofa and stretched his feet to the warmth of the portable stove. The heat was so delicious that it was almost worth being bawled out by Horner.

Mrs. Wadsworth sat on the sofa beside him and patted his arm. "You rest, Lieutenant. You have had an unfortunate experience and I know Evan will not press you too hard about it." She turned a stern look on Horner. "Will you?"

Horner opened his mouth, then shut it with a click.

It gave Perry great pleasure to see that Horner was as helpless before the female sex as any other man. He smiled at nothing and kept his gaze fixed on the green and white curtains.

"Stop smirking, Mister Perry. Tell us what happened to Mister Thorton."

Perry bit his lips to stop his smile, then turned sober as he looked at Thorton. Seeing him by lamplight with the bruises marking his face and his eyes wandering around inside their orbits, he was worried that Thorton was worse off than he had thought. Thorton's coat and waist coat were open and stained with blood. In the dark Perry had not known Thorton had been cut. It sank in on him that he could have been killed.

"He met a gambler who pretended to be a friend to him. They went off together. Later the gambler and his friends came back with English money, which they lost at the tables. When I returned and didn't find Peter, I asked for him. Nobody knew where he was, but they told me what I just told you. They said they went out the back door, so I went up and down the alley and through all the side passages. I found him half out of his wits and brought him back to the ship. I'm very sorry for what happened to him, but he shouldn't have gone off with a stranger he met in a place like that."

The corners of Horner's mouth turned down and the lines beside his nose were deep in the lamplight. "You led Mister Thorton astray. None of this would have happened if you had not enticed him into being absent without leave. You shall reimburse the ship for the cost of his care, and you will also make up his loss to the thieves. How much did he lose?"

"Two guineas and my watch," Thorton said. His head was clear enough when it came to numbers. He had forgotten his missing hat, though.

"Mister Perry, you shall make good Mister Thorton's loss of two guineas. You shall also stand the evening watch every night for a week in addition to your regular duties. If you are kept occupied, perhaps you will be too tired to run ashore."

"Aye aye, sir." The brunet lieutenant looked glum.

"Mister Thorton. You were absent without leave."

"Aye, sir. I'm sorry."

"This is not the first time you have fallen into folly at Mister Perry's instigation. A wise man would learn to discount advice from such a source. You shall bear the loss of the watch yourself so that you may learn the value of wisdom."

Thorton was too unwell to understand. "Huh?"

"I mean, Mister Thorton, that you should have known better than to let Mister Perry talk you into this escapade. Therefore I fine you two guineas for being absent without leave. The money shall be paid into the ship's charitable fund. You are relieved of duty until noon tomorrow. That will be all."

Perry would have fled, but he had to take Thorton in tow and help him out of the cabin. He helped him down the ladder to the wardroom and into his berth.

"What on earth were you thinking, Peter? Why did you go off with that rogue?"

"I was lonely. I wanted to get laid just like you."

Perry made an exasperated noise as he peeled Thorton out of his coat. "I picked a woman in the trade on purpose; we both knew what the business was. You picked a complete stranger who was in the business of robbing foolish men."

"I'm sorry. I didn't know."

Perry was gazing at the bloody mess of Thorton's waistcoat. "I'm sorry for you, Peter. I shouldn't have left you alone. I know you're an idiot."

"Don't say such things. If you had made love to me, this wouldn't have happened."

Perry helped him to get undressed. "I don't want to be your lover."

Thorton crawled into his hammock with a sigh. "I know."

Perry stood looking down at him. "You're going to ruin yourself. I don't want to be part of it."

"You're already part of it."

"Not any more." He walked out and shut the door firmly behind him.

CHAPTER 27: INDEPENDENCE

Bells clamored from every tower throughout the city. Children ran shrieking through the streets and maidens kissed each other and laughed. Portugal was free! That very morning the treaty had been signed granting independence and ending the war. Everywhere wine was flowing and people were dancing in the streets. The girls picked up their skirts and whirled around with their petticoats flashing. Boys did handsprings and dog barked themselves silly. Daisies were everywhere in commemoration of Captain Souza rescuing the Duke of Coimbra from the Isle of Alborán; Souza was with the duke even now.

The British officers, not being Catholic, were obliged to wait on the stone steps outside the cathedral as the royal party, the nobility of Portugal, officers of state, and heroes of the revolution, entered to give thanks for their deliverance. The thanksgiving mass was long and grand and the people waiting outside had plenty of time to get bored and restless. Horner and Thorton had been among the duke's rescuers, but the man most responsible for saving the duke from the Spanish, Shakil bin Nakih, was not present. The Salletine delegation had not yet arrived.

The British officers were not alone on the steps; Captain Alan Abby was splendid in his Portuguese uniform. To him fell the privilege of leading the honor guard of Henrique's naval officers. No marines were on the steps; Henrique had not won his battle to have the green uniforms of the Portuguese marines changed to something that would not clash with the sky blue uniforms of the navy. Horner and Thorton were at the bottom of the steps along with other men who had earned the privilege of waiting for the king outside the cathedral door. A line of soldiers in green coats kept the street open so that the carriages would be able to come and pick up the dignitaries. The crowd continued to grow. A juggler and a contortionist entertained the crowd, and the pickpockets were at work. Sellers of daisies, Portuguese flags, and cheap wine wended their ways among the people.

At last the mass ended. The trumpets flourished and the cathedral doors opened. The Portuguese officers drew their swords and raised them high. Thorton and Horner and the smattering of officers at the foot of the stairs drew and presented their swords as well. Flower girls preceded the royal party to strew petals in their path. From up in the belfries baskets of petals were poured down on the king and his suite in a pink fluttering rain.

King João, dressed in an ermine cloak but not yet crowned (that would follow in a month), descended the steps. He was a portly man well past fifty with a long black curly wig. His black velvet suit was decorated with medals and ribbons. His silk stockings were white and the heels of his black shoes were gilded. The ugliness of his face was smoothed into a smug expression. His eyes were small and set too close together, but that could not be seen by the crowd who was kept away by the solders. His wife was equally plump, very pale of complexion, and never a beauty, but she had great dignity, her hair having gone silver at an early age. She was also soberly dressed all in black with an ermine wrap around her shoulders. She wore a diamond tiara in token of her position as a duchess, a duchess that would soon be elevated to queen.

The crowd surged and screamed, shouted and cheered. The church bells tolled madly. Men threw their hats and women waved their handkerchiefs. Flowers were thrown and sometimes crucifixes were held up, as if the king were a saint that could bless them. João stopped about midway down the steps and nodded graciously to all and sundry. Behind him the nobles and officers of state and other great personages filled the porch and waited patiently. The king held up his hand for silence. Slowly the crowd quieted.

"Good people of Portugal. Today we celebrate our independence, a day as great as the day upon which we drove the Moors from our lands."

Thorton discovered that his arm was suddenly very tired and his sword drooped a bit. He gritted his teeth to keep holding the sword up as the king spoke to the people.

"In one month I shall return to the cathedral with my lady wife by my side," he gave her a little bow and she gave him a little curtsy, "To be crowned in all the pomp and splendor of our noble and ancient country." The crowd roared and a boy did handsprings in the road. João wanted to say quite a bit more, but the crowd was cheering and cheering. He spoke to his attendant, "Bring the carriage. They're already drunk." He descended the last few steps. The carriage rattled up, and the king and queen got in and drove away.

Nobody could hear Abby give the order to sheathe swords amid the tumult, but they saw him bring the hilt to his lips and kiss it, and did the same. The blades rattled home and the officers stood at attention as Duke Henrique and the Princess Antónia descended the steps.

Henrique was splendid in his naval uniform, ostrich-plume laden hat, and diamond earrings. Princess Antónia was dressed very soberly in a dark blue dress with a white veil over her hair. A gold crucifix lay on the bodice of a dress that went all the way up to her neck without the slightest bit of cleavage. She looked like a governess rather than a princess. She shrank to Henrique's side as she confronted the crowd and was cheered in her turn.

"Wave and smile," Henrique hissed at her. He doffed his hat and gave the crowd a gallant bow. Timidly she raised a lace-gloved hand. With her other hand she clung to his elbow. She didn't even come up to his shoulder. Where he was unnaturally tall, she was unnaturally short. She had the close-set eyes of her father, a double chin, and a small piggy nose. Henrique was every bit as ugly, but nobody noticed because he carried himself with dash. He smiled at the screaming blur that was all he could see of the crowd through his crossed eyes.

The next carriage rolled up. The footman descended and opened the door and unfolded the step. The princess' confessor was inside, a friar in a long brown robe and hood. Henrique escorted her down the remaining steps. Happy to see a familiar face, she cried, "Bless me, Father!" and held out her hand.

"Your immortal soul is my lasting concern, child," he said as he untucked his hands from the opposite sleeves. He pointed his pistol straight at Henrique and pulled the trigger.

Princess Antónia screamed.

The hammer clicked down, but the gun did not fire.

Henrique stood frozen in shock. He could not believe that an assassin had fired upon him; neither could he believe he had survived a pointblank shot.

Meanwhile, everyone else was a flurry of action. Thorton, who was only a few feet away, hurled himself forward to tackle the friar as the man was re-cocking the pistol to try again. They crashed to the floor of the carriage and the pistol went off; a flash in the pan spewed sparks and gunsmoke. The princess screamed at the top of her lungs. The horses spooked and took off at a gallop before the horrified driver could regain his wits. Horner leaped for the boot and grabbed onto the footman's rails; he clung to the back of the coach as it careened along the street.

Thorton was better accustomed to gunsmoke than the friar; the man coughed and his eyes teared up. Thorton seized the pistol and took it away from him, then reeled as he was punched in the face and his nose broke for the second time in a week. He dropped the pistol and caught himself on the door frame. The friar kicked him, but Thorton held on even as the door flapped and clattered against the side of the coach.

Years of devoting himself to prayer and self-flagellation had not given the friar a physique that was equal to an angry quarterblood Shawnah Indian. Thorton kicked him hard, knocking him back against the opposite side, then tackled him and dragged him down onto the floor of the coach. The man struggled, but Thorton had learned to wrestle from his Indian relatives and he was in no mood to be merciful. If he had had a tomahawk at that moment, he would have buried it between the man's eyes. Instead he had a naval sword that was entirely too long to be any use to him in the confines of the carriage. Having only one good hand, he opted for a head butt instead. The friar's nose broke and bled. He was an easy target for a good thrashing, and Thorton let him have it.

Meanwhile Horner was doing his part. Shouting at the driver did not bring the coach to a stop, so he crawled up over the top of the carriage. Balancing on the roof and presuming the driver to be the assassin's accomplice, he throttled him from behind.

"Stop the coach," Horner shouted at him in Spanish. He kept his bony hands around the man's neck and squeezed as hard as he could. The man clawed desperately at Horner's hands and the reins slipped down.

"Damn you!" Horner roared and threw the man off the box. He scrambled onto the driver's seat to stare down at the leather reins out of reach among the traces. "I hate horses," he muttered.

The street was full of merrymakers who shrieked and fled as the white horses careened past. A child cried and the sound invigorated Horner. Like it or not, he must retrieve the reins. Laying down on the driver's step, he reached a long arm down and fished for them. His fingertips brushed the leather and he eased himself a little further over the edge of the step. He was well aware what would happen to him should he fall under the wheels of the carriage. He caught one of the reins and pulled it up in to his hands. He looked for the other rein, but it was out of his reach. Using what he had, he pulled slowly on the one rein.

Not a horseman, he marveled to see that the reins were rigged across one another. The left rein from each horse ran together into a single tail that he held in his hand so that when he pulled it, both horses received the signal to turn left. This drove them across the street and onto the sidewalk—the leftmost horse, seeing the danger suddenly appear before his eyes—veered sharply right, crashing into his mate and shouldering him aside.

Inside Thorton was thrown sideways against the seat. He paused, bloody knuckles poised to land another blow on the incapacitated assassin. He looked up as he became sensible to his danger as a passenger in a runaway coach. The flapping door had already shattered its window glass as it banged along the wild ride.

Horner got himself upright on the seat and eased the rein. The horses straightened and crossed the street at angle again, pedestrians scattering and swearing at him. He pulled a little, and the horses came to the middle of the street. He eased up. It was not entirely different from hauling or easing the sheet of a fore-and-aft sail. Little by little the horses slowed and the coach rolled to a stop.

Thorton jumped out, only to be confronted by a clatter of horse's hooves and a cavalry saber held by a green-clad hussar. The lieutenant raised his hands in surrender. The hussar officer wore a scandalously short green dolman with gold braid laddered down the front and a tall cap to match. His green trousers were skintight and buttoned down the outside of the leg with brass buttons. They disappeared into black Hessian boots that came up to his knees. Yellow tassels dangled at the front of the boots. The man shouted at him in a language Thorton would later learn was Magyar, the language of the Hungarian horse lords.

At the moment all the lieutenant could do was to keep his hands up and tell them in excellent Spanish, "The assassin is in the coach. I have beaten him unconscious." The blood splattered on his white lapels confirmed his story, but did not dispose the hussars to regard him well.

The cavalry officer snarled something else he didn't understand, but the blade motioned him away from the coach. He sidled sideways. The other hussars searched the carriage, found Horner and brought him at sword's point to stand next to Thorton with his hands up. They also found the unconscious friar in the coach and dragged him out to dump him on the ground. The pistol was procured and presented to the officer. He sheathed his sword and sniffed the pistol. He continued speaking in Magyar. His troop continued to hold the three captives under their swords.

A minute later the Portuguese cavalry thundered up. They were dressed all in green, but while they had considered themselves to be ornamental enough, they paled by comparison with the hussars. They wore ordinary cocked hats, long coats, and breeches that didn't show off their physiques nearly as well. Neither were their horses as fine as the black beasts the Hungarians rode.

The Portuguese officer addressed the hussar in Spanish, and the man replied in the same language, although with a heavy accent. "I am Colonel Baron Jan Karolyi, commander of the bodyguards for His Excellency Count Orsini, Ambassador from the Kingdom of Hungary. I have apprehended the suspects."

"God's balls! I know who you are. You should have let us go first. I'm Captain Lopes and this is the Royal Bodyguard!"

Karolyi gave the man a supercilious look. "Then you should have ridden better. Hussars do not give ground to lesser men."

The captain of the Royal Bodyguard fumed. "That is an insult I will not tolerate!"

"I will be pleased to meet you in a mounted duel with sabers," Karolyi replied. "You can show me your skill then." His bass voice dripped contempt.

"Enough of you!" The Portuguese officer rounded on the Englishmen. "Who are you? You'll hang for this!" He pointed his sword at the three captives.

Horner lowered his hands and said in good but accented Spanish, "I am Captain Horner of His Britannic Majesty's frigate *Amphitrite*. Lieutenant Thorton and I had the privilege of capturing the assassin." He pointed at the friar groaning on the ground. The assassin's face was bloody and so were Thorton's knuckles.

Karolyi tapped his heel against the black steed and turned to regard them, but his attention was on Thorton. The blond lieutenant was all scuffed up. Old bruises marred his face with a sickly green, his white waistcoat and lapels were splattered with blood, tendrils of blond hair were sticking out in all directions, and his hat was missing. He looked a rogue.

Thorton saw a man who was six foot tall and sat his horse like a centaur. The skintight trousers revealed every muscular curve of Karolyi's legs, including his rump and groin. The Hungarian wore his fur-lined pelisse as a coat because of the chilly weather, but the recent action had brought a flush of color to his face. His jaw was square and strong, he had green eyes, and a long black mustache. His hair was braided into a queue on either side of his face beneath the tall black shako secured to his head by a chin strap. Gold braid laddered across the front of his dolman and pelisse, and Austrian knots decorated the front of his trousers and the back of his pelisse. A heavy gold knot hung from the hilt of his saber, the scabbard of which plain and glossy black, aside from the gilded fittings. All his troop were equally fit and fabulously attired. Not one of them was less than six foot tall. Thorton had never seen such a gorgeous and imposing uniform before and had heard only vaguely about hussars.

The Portuguese officer said, "Give me your swords."

Horner asked coolly, "If you are attempting to arrest me, I decline. Now, if you will pardon me, I must return to my duties." He walked past the Portuguese officers. Thorton jumped to follow after him.

"You there, *Capitán!* Stand and deliver your sword!" Lopes demanded.

Horner kept walking sedately along the street and never looked back. Thorton glanced over his shoulder at the enraged Portuguese. Karolyi smiled beneath his mustache.

"Stand, I said!" Lopes shouted.

Karolyi, not bothering with the reins, tapped his horse's flanks with his heels and guided his horse to walk along next to Horner. Horner looked up at him, back at the enraged Portuguese, and understood that Karolyi had appointed himself as bodyguard to the Englishmen. He gave a brief nod of acknowledgment and received the slightest tip of the chin in answer. Karolyi ambled along beside them like the most amiable of companions.

"*Sois picarones*!" Lopes bellowed after them, shaking his sword.

The hussars fell in behind their commander while the royal bodyguard rounded up the coach and put a driver on it. They tied up the friar and threw him into the coach. In this manner they returned to the ducal party.

CHAPTER 28: THE PORTUGUESE CAPTAIN

The palace belonging to Princess Antónia sat on a hill overlooking the river. A sweeping greensward, paved horseshoe driveway, fruit trees, and gardens reached from the palace down to the road that ran long the river. The palace itself was brand new with the distinctive white facade that had become popular after the infamous earthquake. It was intended for João, but that worthy had never gotten over his claustrophobia contracted during the earthquake, tidal wave, and fire that had wiped out much of Lisbon years before. He had given the palace to his daughter in honor of her betrothal while he continued to live in his palatial pavilion beyond the city limits.

The quay below the palace was reserved for the docking of Henrique's yacht, dispatch boats, and other vessels engaged in business with or on behalf of the palace. Therefore the *Amphitrite's* gig was able to tie up at the pier and deliver Captain Horner, Lieutenants Forsythe, Perry, and Thorton, and the marine Lieutenant Barnes. Horner mounted the ladder to the dock with his usual dignity and looked very fine in his best uniform. His cocked hat was new with a bit of black ostrich feather, a crisp black naval cockade, and a tasteful band of gold lace. The new hat led the lieutenants to speculate that Horner expected to see Emily Wadsworth at the ball.

Naturally the naval officers congregated to inspect the ducal yacht up close. From their position on the dock they were able to look down at her weather deck. It was varnished to a mellow golden color. She was low and sleek with a vermilion hull and red and white striped lateen sails. Good brass guns were secured on deck, six to a broadside. That left plenty of room for more sociable activities. A black and white pinwheel awning covered the aft portion of the deck. Beneath it were dainty white chairs and chaises, the curved legs and oval backs all carved and gilded.

"The *Gitano!*" Thorton exclaimed.

So it was. The former Spanish royal yacht retained her gilded lion because the arms of Coimbra also bore a lion, but the gunwale paint and other decorative devices had been redone. Now she sported a band of black and white gyronny interspersed with suitable figures, such as gilded wyverns and lions. A portrait of Princess Antónia in sculpture was centered on the tafferel above the great cabin's windows. The sculpture was not true to life; it was beautiful. The British would have assumed it to be a cameo of a goddess had not a ribbon with the name been carved and painted below the bust. The vessel had been renamed *Infanta Antónia* in her honor.

Just then a figure emerged from under the break of the quarterdeck. The Portuguese cry of "Captain on deck!" rang out. Officers snapped to attention as the captain in his sky blue uniform mounted to the quarterdeck. He wore a matching sky blue cocked hat trimmed with gold braid. A black and white pinwheel cockade and a yellow panache jutted up from it. Smoked glasses perched on his nose even though it was dusk. His blond hair was pulled back into a pigtail and bound with a yellow ribbon.

"Abby!" Thorton exclaimed.

The blind man had paid no attention to the shadowy figures on the dock, but he recognized Thorton's voice. He turned and pulled the glasses down to peer over them. "Peter?" he asked.

"'Tis I!" Thorton replied. "Are you captain of this vessel?" he asked in wonder.

Alan Abby broke out in a broad grin. "I am! I'm captain of the *Princess Antónia,* the ducal yacht. I have a secretary and a clerk, and half a dozen servants to do my bidding, every one of whom is far more satisfactory than the worthless boy who abandoned me in Gibraltar."

"Congratulations on your commission," Horner said.

Perry, Forsythe, and Barnes crowded the edge of the dock to stare down enviously.

"Damme, Alan, you've got a fine berth now!" Perry exclaimed.

Captain Abby grinned happily. "I do! You're all invited to dinner as soon as I can get clear of the duke. He doesn't have a house of his own in the city, and his *novia* won't let him sleep under the same roof until they're married, so he lives on the yacht."

"We would be delighted to join you. Is His Grace aboard?" Horner replied.

"No, he went up this morning. He's been fussing over preparations all day. Bide a moment while I give orders, then I'll join you for the walk."

"Certainly, Captain," Horner replied.

Abby came ashore with all the pomp due a captain in the good graces of his admiral. He had a pair of midshipmen as servants and a marine guard. They were all handsome men. He took one of the midshipmen by the elbow and the young gentleman guided him over to the Englishmen. Captain Abby bowed politely to them. His velveteen coat was well cut with a tasteful amount of gold braid. On him the Portuguese uniform was elegant.

After introductions were conducted all around, he hooked his arm companionably in Thorton's as they strolled along. "You must tell me how you've been."

"I had the small pox." He didn't mentioned getting robbed and beaten.

Abby peered at him in alarm. "Are you well?"

"I am. Only one scar shows," Thorton assured him.

"Where is it, if you don't mind my asking? I can't see any." He couldn't see much more than a blur for Thorton's face, dark spots for eyes, and a moving shape that was his mouth.

"On my cheek, near the corner of my left eye."

Perry and Barnes fell in behind the two. Barnes muttered under his breath, "The sods are back together again, damn them both."

Perry, who had followed in Abby's wake, regarded the two blond men with a sour expression. "He knows how to kiss up to his betters, doesn't he?"

"I'd like to see them both in the pillory. They wouldn't be so pretty when the crowd got through with them."

The venom in his voice made Perry uneasy. "As long as they don't bother the rest of us, I suppose it doesn't matter."

"'Tis unnatural and against the will of God."

"You're a fine one to speak of God with your wenching, drinking, and swearing," Perry snapped.

Barnes drew himself up. "Who can blame me? 'Tis red blood that runs in my veins. Thorton got what he deserved."

Perry treated Barnes to an icy silence for the rest of the walk.

Meanwhile Horner and Forsythe led the way to the palace. Carriages rattled along the road, but not many; the Portuguese had the Mediterranean habit of tardiness. Although one might have expected the naval officers to be on time, not many were, the Admiral Duke Henrique do Coimbra having set them a poor example in that regard. However, the Princess Antónia, regardless of her lack of personal charms, had one virtue: she was punctual. Being of a pious disposition, she had become accustomed to keeping a schedule in order to perform her daily devotions and expected those around her to be equally devout. Her ladies were there on time.

At the entrance, the naval officers stood aside for the Count of Oeiras, the Prime Minister, a man who had distinguished himself in the rebuilding of the city and had become head of the new royal government. He felt it incumbent to show himself willing and eager to assume the responsibilities placed upon him and arrived promptly. The naval officers fell in behind his party.

The palace was as grand inside as out. Great banks of windows stretched up from the floor almost to the ceiling. Ornaments ran up the corners of the rooms to the ceilings to create sinuous lines of foliage that formed asymmetrical ornaments at their peaks. Marble window sills, tile floors, and slender elegant furniture in pale woods and pastel brocades added to the luster of the place. The interior color scheme was white, rose, and powder blue with a liberal application of gilding.

"'Tis like being inside a wedding cake," Perry whispered.

Barnes laughed. Horner turned and glared over his shoulder at him. "Your pardon, sir."

"'Tis the height of fashion, borrowed from the French," Abby informed them. "Very elegant, but it can be overdone."

The Princess Antónia was wearing a rose colored split-skirt gown over a white petticoat. It had no collar and showed her collarbones, but she could not be persuaded to let the neckline plunge any lower. She wore a white wig of sensible proportions, and indeed, everything about her dress was restrained to the point of plainness. The materials were of very fine silk or she would have been dowdy. Her diamond tiara and earrings sparkled and she had a plain gold crucifix on a chain around her neck. Jesus rested safely on the watered silk over her breastbone.

Henrique, macaroni that he was, was not in uniform. He wore a powder blue suit with rose-colored facings to match his betrothed, plenty of gold lace, white silk stockings, shoes with gilded heels, and a white wig with long curls. His hand rested on the gold head of his cane and showed his diamond rings to good effect. His face was powdered and he had even affected an artificial black mole in the shape of an anchor near the corner of his mouth. His white waistcoat was of the shorter style that was coming into fashion for younger men, and heavily embroidered in rose and blue. The fabric would have done well as a cover for a lady's toilette cushion. Below it he wore pristine white breeches with diamond-studded buttons at the knee.

The dandy duke took great pleasure in booming out, "Ah, here are my British heroes! Do them honor, dear, do them honor. If it were not for them, you would not have me." He proceeded to kiss every one of them on each cheek.

The princess gave them an obligatory smile, but her expression was somewhat pained. She extended her hand first to Horner, who bowed deeply over it, and said, "Congratulations on your impending nuptials, Your Highness," in accented Spanish.

She did not extend her hand to Abby and turned her head away quite pointedly. Captain Abby made her a deep and gracious bow, and said in accented Portuguese, "My felicitations to you and your future husband." His voice was cool. He did not wait for her to answer, but turned on his heel and walked away.

Henrique elbowed her sharply in the side. "Say hello to Captain Abby, my dear," he said in a smooth voice. Abby stopped and turned back. He gave Henrique a look that said he did not care for this scene, but Henrique continued smiling genially.

The princess looked a little sick. She stared at Abby in distaste. Henrique said lowly to her, "If you dislike someone, at least be well-bred enough not to show it in public. You may expend your venom on me as much as you wish in private, but by God, you'll be a gracious hostess to those you have invited."

She bit her lip and tears welled in the corners of her eyes. She abruptly stuck out her hand. "I didn't want to invite him!" she whispered back. "I only did because you insisted!"

Abby stalked back to her. Not a tall man, he still loomed over the diminutive princess. He pulled down the smoked glasses to try to find her hand, then took it and bowed over it. Through gritted teeth he said, "I would not have come if the duke had not assured me I would be welcome," he replied. "I shall leave immediately, if you desire it."

"No, no, you're here now. You're . . . um . . ." she groped for something to say that was a compliment to him, but not dishonest to her own feelings. "Punctual."

"Thank you," he said drily. "I'm pleased to discover I have at least one virtue that pleases you. I shall endeavor to never fail you on the point."

The princess had found a safe topic to rant upon. She smacked Henrique in the arm with her fan. "Where is everyone? Why are they late?"

"'Tis only a few minutes after the hour, my dear," Henrique replied unperturbed. He was a giant being flagellated by a gnat. He barely noticed. "I told you there was no point in being early. We could have made a stately entrance an hour from now when everyone was here."

The princess' silk-clad bosom heaved in indignation. "They're rude, and you encourage it! No one who is more than fifteen minutes late tonight shall ever be invited again."

"My dear, you will be confined to hosting nothing bigger than a card game if you adopt such a draconian policy."

"I mean it. *Senhor* Neves, take down the names of everyone and what time they arrive. I will not tolerate such rudeness!"

The secretary, who had the duty of checking names against the list of guests, bowed and replied, "As you wish, Your Highness." He checked his watch and made a note of all the arrivals thus far.

The British lieutenants were presented in order. The princess smiled to each of them and nodded to their bows, but deemed it beneath her rank to offer her hand to mere lieutenants. They murmured their felicitations for her upcoming nuptials, and she replied, "Thank you for being on time."

That chore completed, they entered the ballroom.

CHAPTER 29: NIGHT WALTZ

The ballroom was a suite of five rooms consisting of four smaller rooms gathered around a central oval. Tall doors separated by ormolu caryatids held up the ceiling so that the room had no 'walls' at all, but a series of pilasters separating double doors. So distorted was the shape of the pilaster ornaments that they could be mistaken for golden vines or serpents, and it was not until the capital that the heads and shoulders, with arms uplifted to support the headdresses of the figures, emerged. The ceiling was formed of two ovals, one within the other, each subdivided into areas of interest, presenting scantily clad, draped figures of allegory, all pastel and gilt. Three magnificent crystal chandeliers hung from the ceiling, and each chandelier's value would have fed five thousand Brazilian Indians for a year.

The rooms that opened around the ballroom extended it so that dancers could flow freely from one to another. Perry found one of the smaller rooms to contain a punch table and he swiftly imbibed. Captain Horner spotted Emily White Wadsworth the moment she arrived and presented himself to her. As for Thorton, he was hopelessly lost in the splendid frippery. He backed up to a pilaster near a corner and contented himself with watching. Uniforms from a dozen nations mixed among the periwigs and ball gowns; he guessed there must be three hundred guests in attendance.

He drank *sangría* and watched the dancers. There were hussars in indecently short green jackets and skintight breeches tucked into tall Hessian boots, Portuguese naval officers in long, sky blue coats, Portuguese army officers in green coats, French and Italian officers in various shades of blue, English officers in navy blue, and civilians dressed like peacocks in bright colors, except for the churchmen dressed in black, and the women under their sway who dressed in equally sober colors. A hussar danced past and he caught a glimpse of muscular haunches flexing, then the man was gone. He was left with a warm tingle suffusing his middle. He couldn't approve of such scandalous apparel, but he enjoyed watching it all the same. He had been nervous about the lofty social venue, but as long as he was left alone in his corner, he was happy. He could enjoy the sights without feeling awkward.

When the set ended, the musicians adjusted their music stands and checked their instruments. They drank their own wine and rested a bit. Thorton had an excellent view of a hussar's backside as the Hungarian gave some ladies a bow. The pelisse draped down so that a fur-trimmed sleeve covered one taut buttock, but the other was revealed in its sculpted perfection. The black wool breeches buttoned down the outside with a row of brass buttons from waist to boot, and gold braid around them formed a scalloped pattern that drew attention to the long line of the leg and the tightness of the trousers. Thorton could see every bulge of the muscular thigh as plain as if the man had been carved of marble. Raising his eyes he discovered Colonel Karolyi looking over his shoulder at him.

Thorton flushed bright red and turned away. He walked into the next room and opened a casement window to let in the cool breeze.

"Good evening, Lieutenant. It is 'Lieutenant,' yes?" The bass voice with its heavy Hungarian accent was right behind him.

Thorton startled, then turned around and nodded wordlessly. He was trapped in the window embrasure; to make his escape he would have to push pass the hussar, but he didn't feel equal to the challenge. Still, he had to say something. "Good evening, sir."

Karolyi's expression was amused, and his lip curled into a sardonic grin. "I remember you, the man who caught Henrique's assassin, yes?" He put one hand up to lean on the pilaster, effectively cutting off any attempt at escape.

Thorton did not want to offend the temperamental hussar; even so, his eyes could not help straying down that muscular body. The legs were exceptionally well-developed even for a cavalry officer, and the torso above it was powerfully built with excellent arms. The Hungarian was a magnificent specimen of physical manhood. As attractive as Thorton found it, he forced himself to look the man in his face. He was afraid that if he gave offense the hussar would offer to trounce him with swords or pistols. He was certain that even in a wrestling match— where he was well-qualified and usually victorious—he would come off the worse. The momentary thought of the hussar's muscular body grappling with him made him flush. He fumbled for words to cover his tumult.

"Lieutenant Peter Thorton of His Britannic Majesty's frigate *Amphitrite,* at your service, sir." He stepped back so that he could give the man a short bow. It was a relief to put some distance between himself and the handsome Hungarian.

"Oh, I do hope so," the colonel purred. His green eyes sparkled with lascivious mischief. "I am delighted to meet the famous renegade at last. I have heard so many stories, but I confess, I didn't realize the brawling fellow I met in the street was the famous corsair. I am Baron Jan Karolyi, colonel of the First Regiment of Hussars." He offered his hand to Thorton.

Thorton was always uneasy when his reputation was mentioned, but he took the hand and gave it a determined shake. "I am not a renegade any more, sir. I am in British service. Besides, most of the stories aren't true."

The baron's eyebrows arched up. He didn't let go of Thorton's hand. "Not true? How disappointing. But some of them are true, aren't they, Lieutenant?" Again that sardonic, knowing smile.

Thorton flushed and tugged in a vain attempt to free his hand. "I don't know what you mean, sir."

Karolyi grinned at him. "I think you do. You're blushing, Lieutenant. How charming. I had not expected to find the bold corsair so shy in close quarters." He stepped into the window embrasure.

Thorton was mortified even as his body flushed with heat. Karolyi's bold advances unnerved him—he was at the pious princess' party! He had no intention of getting into any more trouble, but the Hungarian had him trapped. His only hope of escape was to jump out the window, and he turned to do it.

Karolyi seized him by the pigtail and Thorton jerked up short. His heart hammered in his chest and his eyes went wide. "What do you want, Colonel?"

Karolyi stepped behind him so that his groin brushed Thorton's backside. He didn't let go of the lieutenant's pigtail as he leaned in close. "Many things," he breathed, lips brushing ever so lightly against the blond man's ear as he spoke.

Thorton shivered and his own breath came more quickly. "I'm not at liberty to give you things, sir," he replied desperately. He gave the open window a longing look.

Karolyi's lips brushed the rim of his ear as he grinned, "Not even a waltz? Don't be churlish, Lieutenant. I have not said anything indecent."

Thorton was pretty sure that throwing himself out the window was his best course of action. He might ruin his stockings in the flowerbed below, but stockings could be replaced. Unfortunately, Karolyi had a firm grip his hair.

"I don't know what a 'waltz' is, sir, but it wouldn't be proper for me to give you one even if I had it!"

Karolyi convulsed with laughter. He tried to swallow it for the sake of the lieutenant's dignity, but he couldn't. He let go of Thorton's hair and held his sides as he rumbled in amusement, "'Tis a dance, Lieutenant. Nothing more. A common, ordinary dance. Our peasants do it all the time."

Thorton grew wroth. He turned around to face the hussar and his gunmetal blue eyes snapped. "I don't know how to 'waltz,' sir, so stand aside!"

Karolyi's lips quirked into a smile. "I'll teach you. It begins with an embrace, like this." He took Thorton's right hand in his left and put his other hand on Thorton's hip. "Now you put your hand on my shoulder."

Thorton's eyes grew wide. "Do you really expect me—"

"Yes, I do," Karolyi cut in. He picked up Thorton's hand and put it on his shoulder.

Thorton's hand rested as light as a butterfly on the fancy shoulder. "What if someone sees us?"

"Then I'll teach them to waltz, too. Someone must."

"But—"

"We'll begin slowly, so you can learn the steps. They're simple. Follow me." He gently pulled Thorton out of the window embrasure and into the room.

The hapless lieutenant followed. His blue eyes were fixed on Karolyi's emerald ones as the man glided around the room in three-quarter time that only he could hear. The dance was slow and easy. Not knowing anything about it, Thorton had to let the pressure of Karolyi's hand on his hip tell him which way to move. Other people were in the room and they turned to watch. Thorton suddenly became aware of them, flushed, and broke the embrace by stepping backwards. He did not know what to say to excuse himself for having been caught in another man's arms.

Karolyi was unflappable. He smiled to the other guests and said, "'Tis a popular dance in my country called the 'waltz.' Do you know it? I am attempting to teach it to the lieutenant."

The others shook their heads.

"Come, I'll teach it to you, but you require a partner. Lieutenant, please." He held out his hand to Thorton.

Thorton hesitated. He gave the others a worried look, but a man in a fawn-colored suit was offering his arm to a lady in a yellow dress. Before the lieutenant could make up his mind, Karolyi had taken charge, gripped his hand firmly in his, and lifted his other hand onto his shoulder. He spoke easily as he did it. "The gentleman takes the lady's right hand in his left, and places his right hand on her waist. The lady places her hand on his shoulder like this."

Thorton wanted to fall through the floor when everybody looked at them to check the pose. He stood as far back as possible from the hussar. His face was quite pink.

"Three-quarter time. The gentleman steps off with the left foot, his partner with the right." The baron demonstrated. Thorton followed. The two glided slowly about the room. Thorton tightened his grip on the man's shoulder. In spite of himself he was creeping closer. Karolyi smiled warmly at him.

"Now we must have music," the Hungarian announced. Keeping Thorton's hand tight in his, he pulled him into the main room. The other dancers followed. Karolyi had to release Thorton to dig into the interior pocket of his pelisse to produce his purse. His breeches were much too tight to have any room for pockets. Taking out a silver coin, he handed it to the maestro. "A lively tune in three-quarter time, if you please. We are going to waltz."

The maestro didn't know what a 'waltz' was either, but he knew 'three-quarter time.' He took the coin, flipped through his music, and spoke to the others. Sheet music rustled and Karolyi put his purse away. The three couples that had learned the basic steps were with them when the music began. Karolyi whirled Thorton along. The English lieutenant knew he ought not be dancing with a man in public, but he didn't stop. He didn't want to stop. He had a reputation for doing far worse with men, how could it matter if they saw him dancing? It was only dancing, he told himself. But it was more than dancing because he was dancing with a man. His color was high and he avoided looking at the room by staring into Karolyi's dazzling eyes.

Duke Henrique was surprised by the new dance but excited too. He liked novel things, and he liked scandalizing those who had appointed themselves his keepers. Lame though he was, he would not be left out. "May I have this dance?" he asked the princess.

"I will not dance such an indecent dance!" Antónia snapped back.

Coolly Henrique replied, "If you will not, I will find someone that will." He turned his back on her and approached Captain Abby.

The princess gave a little shriek and fled the ballroom when her husband-to-be and his male paramour glided onto the floor. Her ladies and others who wished to curry favor with her followed her out. Others stood gawking on the sidelines, thoroughly affronted, but taking in every detail to enliven their future gossip.

The duke's guests were pleased to put their high-heeled shoes in the Church's face, so more couples glided out onto the floor. They were not alone; the hussars were all hand-picked men and shared their commander's taste. They had no trouble finding obliging men among Henrique's associates. A pair of Portuguese ladies, delighted by the scandal, danced with each other. Couples of every sort laughed and whirled, spun in delight, and exalted in the freedom of the foreign dance. For one giddy night, everyone danced with their secret lovers as the bishops looked on with impotent rage.

Captain Horner glided by with Emily Wadsworth in his arms. Barnes galloped past with a plump Portuguese girl in his. Abby whirled past in Henrique's arms. Perry stood sulking on the sidelines, but Thorton never noticed him. He was too intent on the Hungarian horse officer.

Karolyi pulled him closer. "Do you like this dance, Lieutenant?"

Thorton realized how close they were dancing and his heart pounded in his throat. He tried to pull back, but Karolyi held him tight. "You're too close, sir," he whispered.

Karolyi laughed. "On the contrary, I am not close enough!"

He pulled Thorton in again in until their legs and groins brushed together. Thorton resisted and tried to widen the distance, but Karolyi wouldn't let him go. The lieutenant was bright red, but he didn't want to make a scene either.

"'Tis a scandalous dance that has no place in the ballroom!" he protested.

"If you like, we can transfer it to the bedroom," the bold hussar replied.

Thorton gaped at him in astonishment. Karolyi chose to take that as consent. The colonel didn't know his way around the palace, but he was not one to let minor obstacles balk him. He danced Thorton into one of the side rooms and from there into the library. He let go of Thorton to shut the doors and set the latch. Then he turned and stalked towards the Englishman.

CHAPTER 30: WHEN THE EARTH TREMBLED

Thorton backed up until his backside collided with a bookcase. The room around him was painted a muted mustard color, the bookcases were a light-colored wood, and a thick wool carpet of gold and cream was on the floor. A single lamp burned on the desk. He felt like he was floating liquid gold. He stared at the hussar's green eyes and his heart hammered in his chest. What would happen? What would the Hungarian do? What would Thorton do? This couldn't be happening. He had only meant to dance. No, not even that. He had meant to jump out the window and run like a coward.

Karolyi stalked up to him with a hunter's grace. His mouth was smiling beneath his long mustache. Thorton licked suddenly dry lips. Then the cavalryman was pressing against him. Mouth met mouth in a hot kiss. Thorton groaned softly. The man was hard against him and he felt the answering heat in his own veins. He turned his face away, "I don't even know you."

Karolyi kissed his neck and ear above the shirt collar. "But I want to get to know you very, very well."

Thorton's head tilted back as the hussar kissed his throat. Then his stock was being unfastened and removed. His blue eyes went wide. He tried to say something, but the words stuck in his throat. The stock was stuffed into one of his pockets, then the buttons of the white waistcoat yielded one by one to the hussar's fingers.

A year ago Thorton would have been horrified by such advances. Now he was aching with lust. Other men took their pleasures where they could find them; why not him? He trembled with indecision and his hands acted on their own: they grabbed the baron's hands and held them still when he attempted to undo Thorton's fly. He shook his head frantically. "We shouldn't do this."

Karolyi wrapped his arms around the Englishman's waist and pulled him close. "'Tis a little late to change your mind. Everyone thinks we are doing it anyhow."

"I haven't made up my mind," Thorton protested. His arms were going around the man's shoulders.

Amused green eyes looked into his. "You haven't?" He rubbed his groin against Thorton's where two erections were trapped by woolen breeches.

Thorton tried to push the hussar away, but his arms were weak and his push was feeble.

Karolyi didn't budge. He bent to whisper in Thorton's ears, "You're not a virgin, are you?"

"No," Thorton admitted. His resolve crumbled. What did he have left to save? Not virginity, not reputation, not love. He wasn't in love with Roger Perry. He wasn't in love Alan Abby or Shakil bin Nakih or even Captain Tangle. Only lust. Trembling, he put his arms around Karolyi's neck. "I want you."

The earth beneath his feet seemed to shake as he made his decision, but it was only his knees knocking. He pressed himself against the hussar for support as much as for pleasure. Karolyi was in no mood for dalliance; he swiftly undid Thorton's breeches and pushed them down. The blond lieutenant trembled again as he turned and braced against the bookcase. He held on for dear life as the cavalryman mounted up. A book on the top shelf toppled over as the rocking transmitted itself to the furniture. Thorton found himself eyeball-to-spine with the *Apologia* of Saint Augustine. He felt a bit embarrassed about committing a cardinal sin with a saint's book for witness, but the impetuous hussar wasn't a reader and didn't spare the spurs.

Thorton moaned into the books. It was all he could do to avoid being crushed betwixt the hussar and the saint. It was sex for no other reason than that he wanted it and had a handsome companion willing to give it to him. He ought to feel guilty, but he didn't; he felt a wicked pleasure for enjoying it in the pious princess' library—if she thought the waltz was scandalous, she would have a fit if she knew what else he was up to!

Music came faintly through the walls, something soothing and respectable in the wake of the wild waltz. Out there order had returned and the laughing couples were refreshing themselves with wine. The wayward lieutenant found himself purged of something that had festered a long time; he was what he was, and there was no point in having remorse over what could never change. Everyone who knew him knew what he was; he had nothing left to lose. He stopped worrying about whether it was right or wrong and surrendered to the most intense pleasure of his life.

After it was all done, he was quite worn out and his trembling legs would scarcely hold him up. The hussar leaned heavily against him as they caught their breath. Neither spoke, yet the trembling grew and communicated through the bookcase and into the walls. One of the paintings dropped a corner.

Karolyi jerked away. "Earthquake!" he exclaimed, swiftly stuffing himself back into his britches.

Thorton had never experienced an earthquake. He looked up in wonder because Karolyi was looking up, but he understood nothing. He tucked his shirt into his breeches and buttoned up. "Are you sure?"

A low rumble like thunder groaned through the earth beneath the palace. A crack ran through the plaster ceiling. There was no music now, just a strange unearthly silence split by the sound of falling plaster. Their paralysis was shattered by a woman's scream.

Karolyi sprang into action. He seized Thorton's arm and dragged him to the window. He threw up the sash and commanded, "Jump!"

Thorton climbed onto the window sill, looked down, realized it was at least ten feet to the lawn level, and hesitated. Karolyi shoved him between the shoulder blades and he plummeted from the window with a yell.

He landed in flowerbeds six inches deep with straw and soft earth. His shoes filled with dirt as he tumbled over and onto the lawn. Karolyi dropped into the dirt next to him, rolled, and leaped up. "Get away from the building!"

Women screamed in chorus. The earth rumbled louder. Dogs barked in the distance. Horses trumpeted in the stables. A swath of roof tiles came crashing down twenty feet away. Bits of broken tile bounced like shrapnel and Thorton was stung in the calf. Blood and dirt stained his white silk stocking. He and Karolyi ran. He was used to a pitching deck and kept his knees bent to change his balance in an instant. Karolyi, accustomed sitting his mount, was not so sure-footed on the heaving turf. He sprawled with a Magyar curse. Thorton paused to help him up.

A cornice piece detached from one of the windows and plummeted down; another scream sounded. Dancers were running out the French doors onto the terrace at the rear of the palace. Lamps fell and shattered and flames licked through the dust and debris of fallen plaster and exposed lathes.

Thorton and Karolyi dashed down a grassy aisle past scented lilacs and evergreens. Reaching a rose garden with its sundial, they turned around to look. Flames were filling a third floor window above the library. The garden was full of weeping women and their men. The churchmen got down on their knees and prayed aloud. Thorton and Karolyi grabbed each other to keep from being knocked down by the pitching of the earth. A chandelier in the ballroom plummeted past the tall windows and shattered, flinging fire into the window draperies. Orange light filled the window embrasure where a cavalryman had cornered a navy officer not so long ago.

A stallion trumpeted close at hand. "The horses!" Karolyi exclaimed. He ran in the direction of the stables.

Thorton called, "Wait!" but Karolyi didn't stop.

Thorton lost his feet, got up, and made his way through the garden until he spotted Captain Horner. He hurried to present himself to his commander.

"Mister Thorton! Praise God, you're alive. Are you alone?"

"I was with Colonel Karolyi, but he's gone to the stable." The hussars made their careers on the backs of fine-blooded horses—the rest of them were running for the stable, too.

Duke Henrique stared at the fiery palace. He was a paralyzed, hunchbacked, ungainly figure in an expensive wig limned against the light of the burning palace.

Abby touched his sleeve. "Shall we form a bucket brigade, Your Grace?"

The duke shook himself, then shouted, "Form a bucket brigade!"

Nobody moved. A Portuguese gentleman in a fawn colored coat said, "We are gentlemen. We do not do menial labor. Send the servants to do it."

"You'll do what I tell you!" Henrique roared, but they didn't move.

Horner barked, "*Amphitrite,* form bucket brigade! Let's show them what British gentlemen can do!"

"Aye aye, sir!" the British lieutenants replied, startled into sudden motion.

"I'll go to the stable for buckets," Thorton said.

"Barnes, you and I get the winch at the well," Perry suggested.

"Forsythe, help Thorton with buckets," Horner barked. "We need everything you can find that will hold water!"

Abby called out in Portuguese, "Fire stations!" The other Portuguese naval officers rallied to him.

The Count of Oeiras came up. "With your permission, Your Grace, I will lead the bucket brigade myself."

Henrique shot him a grateful look. "With pleasure, sir. With pleasure."

Oeiras called out to his own coterie and started the line. There was only one bucket at the well head, but Barnes cranked and Perry pulled it over the stone rim, untied it from the winch, and handed it to the nearest gentleman. The bucket went down the line and the man who was Portugal's head of government braved the heat to throw it into the fire. The water was gone in a flash and hiss of steam, but his example was not lost on other gentlemen who had thought themselves too good to stand side by side with servants in fighting the fire.

Meanwhile Thorton arrived at the stable. He fell back as hussars he didn't know led horses out by their halters. The sound of fire crackling was loud in his ears, but he ducked in and searched frantically, snatching all the feed buckets and pails he could find. He tossed them outside where Forsythe, who was not brave enough to front the fire, gathered up as many as he could carry and ran back to the bucket brigade. Thorton felt the oppressive heat and leaned into it to reach more feed buckets off a shelf. A horse trumpeted, then a panicked stallion with Karolyi clinging to its bare back shot from the depths of the stable, passed the column of fire around the fallen lantern, and bolted out the door. Thorton ran out with the rest of the buckets.

Karolyi grabbed the horse's mane, and with one leg hooked over the horse's back, leaned down to scoop up a bucket. His men also collected buckets, and putting heels to hide, loped across the lawn to deliver them. Thorton came running along in their wake.

Princess Antónia was on her knees crying and praying with her ladies around her. They held each other and shrieked each time something else fell—a roof tile, a bit of plaster, a painting. Henrique was issuing orders in Portuguese; some of the men braved the kitchen of the burning palace to fetch out tubs, jugs, pans, pails, and anything else that would hold water.

Then a casement was flung open on the third floor and a girl no more than fourteen shrieked, "Help me, please! Mama's sick!"

All eyes went to the pathetic figure.

The fire was eating up the middle of the palace and the far wing, but the girl was not yet trapped. "Come down, girl!" Henrique bellowed.

"I can't! Mama won't wake up!"

Abby marched up to Henrique. "Permission to lead a rescue party, sir?"

"Permission granted. Take whomever you need," the duke replied.

Abby called names and his midshipmen and two marines formed up. They marched across the lawn, up the steps to the terrace, and disappeared into the fiery ballroom. Their figures could be seen silhouetted against the glass windows as they worked their way around the edge of the fire. The crowd watched in silence.

"Water!" bellowed Henrique. Everyone began moving again.

Princess Antónia clasped her hands and prayed fervently aloud. Henrique's temper snapped, "God will help if you help yourself! If you want to save your palace, grab a bucket!"

She stared at him in white-faced horror. Then her eyes went to the great palace with its blazing windows. Somewhere in there her betrothed's *namorado* was risking his life to save a child while she sat and wailed on the lawn. Silently she got up, put herself in line, and received an empty bucket returning to the well. She ran a few steps to carry it to the next man and received from him a full and heavy bucket that made her shoulders feel as if they would come apart. She ran back the other way to hand it off to the next man in line.

"Princess!" her ladies protested.

"Don't just stand there! Do something useful! Grab a bucket!" she shouted at them.

Bewildered but obedient, they stood up and joined her in line. They wept as they worked, but they worked. Gentlemen who had been reluctant to sully their hands before were ashamed to see ladies doing what they would not and joined the line. A few snobs remained standing, but the princess shouted, "Work, or never show your face at court again!"

The last holdouts joined the line.

Captain Souza ran up to Henrique and saluted. "Permission to mount a salvage operation, sir?"

Henrique shook his head. "I am a frivolous man, but I will not risk your lives in the pursuit of baubles. There is no material thing in that palace that cannot be replaced."

Souza replied, "You are a prince among men, Your Grace. God bless and watch over you." He returned to his place in the bucket brigade.

They labored on. There was no hope for the bucket brigade to save the palace; they concentrated their efforts on keeping a path open through the ballroom for the escape of Captain Abby and his party. Minutes ticked by. Everyone worked; nobody could stand by and watch the princess with her makeup running down her face and remain idle. Very soon the princess was gasping for breath.

"My stays," she panted. "Somebody loosen my stays. I can't breathe."

Henrique came over immediately and said kindly, "Step down, my dear. You've done your part."

"I won't. They aren't back," she panted. "Loose my stays, *Senhor*. I can't breathe."

Henrique untied the laces that bound up the back of her gown, then untied the laces of her corset. He had to hop around to keep up with her as she reached and worked and wouldn't even stop even to have her stays undone. In frustration, he took out his pocket knife and cut the laces. Freed from the corset, the princess heaved in great gasps of air. "That's so much better!"

Her dress slid down one arm as she carried the bucket in both hands. The white shift she wore underneath was revealed. Henrique remonstrated with her again.

"You have done your part. It is enough, Antónia."

She kept working. "Don't just stand there, do something useful!" she snapped at him.

"*Sim, senhora*," he replied. He stepped into line next to her and started passing buckets.

"There they are!" someone cried.

Everyone craned their necks to look. They saw nothing, then figures dashed across a window filled with amber light. They ran out one of the French doors and onto the terrace. Four officers were carrying the corners of a blanket with an inert figure in the middle. Captain Abby had the girl by the hand to lead the party. When they emerged, more hands came to help and the insensible woman was carried a safe distance away from the palace.

The ladies gathered around the prostrate figure. "What's wrong with her?" they asked.

Antónia knelt by the unconscious woman, and getting a whiff of her, exclaimed, "She's drunk! I did this for a drunk chambermaid?"

The girl, a little thing no more than fourteen years old, got on her knees, held up her hands, and begged, "Please forgive her, Princess! Please forgive mama!"

Never an attractive woman, Antónia's face contorted with rage. She raised her hand to strike the girl.

Henrique caught the upraised wrist in his hand. He laid his other hand on her shoulder and said quietly, "No. You did it for all of us." He leaned down and whispered, "Grace is not grace if it is given only to those deemed worthy, *querida*. 'Tis the unfortunate who are most in need of your mercy. You may have lost a palace, but you are still rich; this girl has nothing but her mother. Stay your hand."

The princess looked up at the crowd of ladies and gentlemen who were watching her. She looked over at Abby and then at Henrique. Although her own face was contorted with dismay and displeasure, she took hold of Henrique's arm and he helped her up. Then he removed his coat and wrapped it around her dishabille.

Reaching deep inside herself, the woman who would be queen said, "Thank you all for your assistance. We are grateful for your help and will remember it." The crowd of men and women bowed and curtsied deeply to her. "Your Highness," they murmured.

Henrique spoke, "Thanks be to God, no one was killed. The palace is nothing. Our kingdom is Portugal, and Portugal is eternal."

A cry erupted from the throats of all present, "Eternal Portugal!" and for a moment the roar of the fire was drowned out.

"Eternal Portugal!" shouted the princess. Then she buried her face in her Henrique's chest.

The duke wrapped her in his arms, patted her back, and murmured, "There there, it will be all right."

Alan Abby stood off to the side. Although he was blind, he could see the general shapes of the various people lit by the flickering orange light. His coat was scorched and holed where embers had landed on it. Thorton went over to him. "Are you all right?"

Abby gave him a bitter look. "Does anyone care? I'm Henrique's catamite. *She* is everything."

"I care."

Abby was silent for a while, then asked, "Aren't you angry with me for running off with the duke?"

"Not anymore."

Abby smiled. "You forgive too easily, Peter, but I'm glad of it."

"You're my friend. I don't have many friends, so I don't want to lose any of them."

Abby kissed him on the cheek. "You're a dear boy, and I hope you never change."

"Thank you," Thorton replied in bewilderment. "What did I do?"

Abby patted his shoulder. "Just go on being you, Peter."

CHAPTER 31: THE BOLD LIGHT HORSEMAN

It had become Horner's habit to attend church ashore because it enabled him to encounter Emily White Wadsworth as she attended the English Church with her family. Sometimes he was even invited to dinner, followed by lawn billiards, quadrille, or other entertainments, which he was usually delighted to accept. The Sunday after the earthquake the service was a solemn one, and although Horner was invited to join them for dinner, he declined, pleading a previous engagement.

Horner and Thorton got into a hired chariot and rolled through the city. Fortunately, the city had suffered only minor damage in the recent quake; the Great Earthquake had leveled anything that would fall years before. The remaining construction was solid, and the new construction was of the modern style built to resist earthquakes. The river palace was the only major loss. Although there had been several fires, they had not spread. The reconstructed city had been laid out with wide avenues and spacious squares. The light damage and minor injuries were accepted as proof of the Count of Oeiras' wisdom in regulating the new construction, and he was very popular as a result. The king elevated him to the rank of Marquis of Pombal; his position as Prime Minister was secure from all challenges after that.

The chariot arrived in a village in the suburbs along the river shortly after noon. The British officers alighted from the carriage, paid the man, and told him to wait. Content to have such an easy day of it, the driver did as he was bid, and headed into the tavern opposite the church. The village was old and small with modest houses and shops surrounding the square. Behind the church was an open pasture. Sheep grazed, watched over by a shaggy hound and a skinny boy.

Horner and Thorton surveyed the place, but not seeing any sign of their appointment, entered the tavern as well. The place was small with a low ceiling, a fireplace over which the tavernkeeper's wife cooked, and eight or ten rough wooden tables with half a dozen local men sitting at them, and a hard-packed, earthern floor. They chose a table in a corner away from them. The mutton stew they were served was hearty and they sopped up the broth with good brown bread.

Captain Lopes and his party arrived as the Englishmen were finishing their meals. He banged into the tavern with a scowl and his brown eyes swept the room, but not seeing whom he expected, gave the British a stiff nod. Horner gave him a slight bow. The Portuguese bodyguard and his friends settled around one of the tables in the middle of the room and called for wine and food. The locals moved aside, finished their meals quickly, and slipped out. They smelled trouble brewing and wanted no part of it.

Half an hour later the hussars arrived. They traveled in a troop. Since most of them didn't speak Spanish or Portuguese, they needed to stick together. They numbered eight, including the colonel.

Thorton's heart leaped in his mouth when he saw Colonel Karolyi silhouetted in the door. The horseman's pelisse hung from his shoulder and his black cloth shako was tall on his head. He filled the doorframe with his broad shoulders as he paused to let his eyes adjust to the dim interior, and Thorton couldn't help staring at the powerful legs limned against the bright light. He flushed to remember just how well the colonel could ride.

Seeing who was present, Karolyi swaggered into the tavern, and taking the other table in the center of the room, called for the tavernkeeper. His men crowded around the table with him. He made no acknowledgment of Lopes' presence. Lopes said nothing, but began to simmer at the sight of Karolyi's back.

The tavernkeeper hurried forward as the hungry Hungarians settled around the table. Their sabers rattled against their chairs and their spurs jingled. They were all big men, not one under five foot ten, and all of them young and muscular. They were a handpicked elite and their swagger said they knew it. The tavernkeeper was a small man, round and short-haired. He wore a plain brown smock and canvas breeches. His woolen stockings were darned and his shoes well-worn and in need of polish. He hastened to present himself.

"I'm sorry, sirs, but there is nothing left to eat. I had no idea how many visitors would arrive today. These gentlemen have already eaten all the stew."

Karolyi glared at him. "We're hungry. You will feed us." He slapped some silver coins on the table.

"I'm sorry, sir. I can boil some vegetables and serve you bread, but that's all I have. Do you want some wine?"

"I do. And chicken. I saw chickens in the street. Boil four chickens."

"They are not my chickens, begging your pardon, sir."

Karolyi rose from his seat and loomed over the man. The tavernkeeper shrank back. "I don't care whose chickens they are! We're hungry."

The tavernkeeper retreated quickly and sent his son, a small man of some two and twenty years, to serve wine to the foreigners to placate them. He consulted with his wife. Their conversation was a hurried one with worried looks cast over their shoulders at the light horsemen.

Lopes was pleased by the Hungarians' discomfort. He leaned back in his seat, propped a booted heel on the next chair, and tipped back on two legs. "If you'd been on time, you wouldn't have missed your mess," he observed. "I should have known you'd be late to the field of honor. You're going to keep us waiting while you boil your chickens, aren't you? Maybe you think if you stall long enough, we'll get bored and leave. Then you get away with your skin."

Horner pinched the bridge of his nose and muttered to Thorton, "There's no avoiding it now. They will fight."

Karolyi had his wine cup halfway to his mouth. He didn't move. It took a moment for him to master himself.

Thorton had to do something. He rose abruptly from his seat and walked over to the man. He addressed him in Spanish. "Good afternoon, Colonel. Did you have a good ride?"

Karolyi looked up at Thorton, grinned wolfishly at him, and said, "I had a very good ride, Lieutenant. I enjoyed it immensely." His bass voice was thick with insinuation. Thorton flushed and the other light horsemen grinned at him. With a sick feeling, he realized that the colonel must have bragged about his conquest.

"Sit, join us," Karolyi was saying. He reached over to the Portuguese table, grabbed the chair that Lopes using to prop up his boot, and said, "Pardon me, the lieutenant needs a seat." He yanked the chair out from under Lopes' boot. Lopes' foot crashed to the floor with a jangle of the spur.

Thorton sank into the chair. He kept his back to the Portuguese and also Horner. He could not bear to see their faces as he sat with the man who had been his knave for an evening.

"More wine!" Karolyi roared. "Bring a cup for my friend, the English rover!" The waiter hurried to obey.

Karolyi let his arm rest casually along the back of Thorton's chair as he introduced him to the other Hungarians. Thorton smiled and nodded to the men, who smiled warmly at him, and let their eyes run over his body as they examined him. Thorton was very careful to sit with his knees together, feet flat on the floor, and his back not touching the back of the chair. His hands were folded primly in his lap.

Lopes glared at Karolyi's back. His friends were restive and talked lowly among themselves. The Hungarians didn't bother to remove their shako caps indoors, but the Portuguese had removed their cocked hats.

"They act like they're in a stable. They were probably born in one," remarked one of the Portuguese officers. He said it loudly so it carried to the other table. It was fortunate most of the hussars couldn't speak

Portuguese, or his remark would have provoked a brawl right then and there.

Horner decided it was his turn to act. "Captain Lopes. I am glad to see you under better circumstances. Has the assassin talked?" He crossed to the Portuguese table.

"He talked when the thumbscrews were put to him. He implicated the Bishop of Coimbra. The Church doesn't support Henrique." His tone was cool.

"I'm glad to hear he has confessed. Reflecting on the matter, it seems to me that we were all rather hot that afternoon, and for good reason to be sure. I suggest we all reflect on the evil the assassin has wrought among us, and that we overcome it by apologizing for words spoken in haste. If this business comes to a fatal end, the assassin will have accomplished his goal. He will have diminished the number of honest men, who, regardless of their country, adhere to the laws of the king, and stand against the rebellion of malcontents. Let us make peace and be friends."

Lopes unraveled the diplomatic speech. "Do you mean to say that if I rid the world of the arrogant Hungarian, it will be taken as a victory by forces who oppose the king?"

Karolyi turned right around then with a scraping of his chair. His green eyes were flashing, but Horner held up a placating hand. "I cannot know God's will, but surely if two valiant gentlemen have at each other today, one will fall, and that cannot please any man who loves righteousness and opposes rebellion."

Lopes rocked back in his chair and sucked his teeth as he considered Horner's point of view. "There is no reason for it to come to blood. He can apologize and be done with it."

Karolyi's chair tipped over as he jumped to his feet. "I never apologize for telling the truth. You were slow then, and you're slack now."

Lopes leaped to his feet. "I will cut those words out of your mouth!" He threw himself at Karolyi.

Hampered by the confines of the table and chairs, Karolyi could not dodge. He caught the full brunt of Lopes' rush, staggered back, and collided with Thorton who was jumping to his feet in a vain attempt to get out of the way. The three crashed down with Thorton on the bottom. He grunted as the wind was knocked out of him, then the two cavalry men were rolling and wrestling on top of him so that he could scarcely breathe. Karolyi's shako hit him in the eye and somebody stepped on his foot. He wanted to cry out, "Get off me!" but he couldn't breathe.

The rest of the hussars leaped up and flung chairs aside to come to their commander's aid, but the Portuguese would not stand idly by to see their captain overwhelmed by the Hungarians. They waded in. Being fewer in number, they did not scruple to spare the furniture, but beat the Hungarians with chairs and anything else that came to hand.

Horner cried, "Gentlemen! Please! No brawling!" but was ignored.

Karolyi rolled off Thorton and Lopes crashed into the legs of the Hungarians' table, but before Thorton could get up, somebody was tackling Karolyi's legs and that meant he was pinning Thorton's legs down, too. The British lieutenant kicked and swore. "Get off me, you vile slubberdegullion!"

The lieutenant received a blow to the face with no idea who threw it. He punched back and his fist made a satisfying smack. Somebody grabbed his fist, but somebody else stepped on his chest. Karolyi lunged up but a Portuguese officer leaped on his back. He staggered, tripped over Thorton, and fell on him again. A pewter mug flew and its contents splattered the Portuguese officer and left a great stain on the back of his coat. The tavernkeeper's wife shrieked, then did something useful. She ran to the fireplace, grabbed the bucket full of water standing by, and dashed it on the writhing mass of men as if they were mad dogs. The Portuguese who was on the top of the heap surged up in reaction, but Karolyi grabbed him by the throat and pulled him down again.

Lopes was under the Hungarians' table and managed to crawl out through the maze of chairs and gain his feet again, but found himself jumped by one of the other hussars. He crashed onto the table on his back. Being a sturdy plank table, it did not collapse, so he was able to roll off, dealing a mighty kick to his assailant's face. The Hungarian hit the floor with Lopes on top. Two more hussars grabbed the Portuguese captain, hauled him off, and threw him against the wall so hard his eyes rolled up inside his head, and he slid down the wall to land in a heap. Thereafter the greater numbers of the Hungarians prevailed. They beat the Portuguese bloody, then threw them into the street.

Karolyi got to his feet, dusted himself off, and nursing a split lip, black eye, and various contusions, surveyed the scene. His pelisse had been torn from his body and stained with wine, he was covered in dirt, and his shako was gone. His black hair was disheveled and his face flushed red. He loomed over the shambles like a bull over a defeated matador. Finding himself in possession of the field, he tucked his shirt back into his trousers, and ordered, "Wine!"

Horner came over and gave Thorton a hand up. The lieutenant groaned as he got to his feet. The British captain began to methodically brush the blond man's coat to try and knock the dust off. "You look a fright, Lieutenant. Are you hurt?"

Thorton rubbed his chest where getting stepped on had ground a button into his breastbone. "Ow. Not seriously. You, sir?"

"I stayed out of it."

Victory put Karolyi in an excellent mood. He gave the Englishmen a grin. "That was a fine afternoon's sport. It can only be followed by an equally fine evening. Join me for a cup of wine." He picked up an unbroken chair and offered it to Thorton.

Thorton hesitated. He looked back and forth between the unruly hussar and the modest captain. Karolyi glowed with an animal vitality that he found exciting. He was dismayed by the brawl, but he could not help finding the horse officer attractive. Lopes had provoked the Hungarians; any red-blooded man would have taken offense. Horner was thin, prim, and reticent. In a word, dull. Unbidden a third image came to mind: the dark good looks of Isam Rais Tangueli, *kapitan pasha* of the Sallee rovers. He combined the animal magnetism of the hussar with the coolness of the British captain. Tangle would not have let hot words provoke him into a tavern brawl.

Thorton straightened up and shook his head. "Thank you, sir, but I only came because I hoped I could talk you out of the duel."

Karolyi's smile hardened. "The only reason? You had no other reason for coming, just a staunch dedication to the public peace?"

Thorton flushed. "I did hope to spend an agreeable afternoon in your company, sir." He could feel Horner's eyes on him and it made him nervous.

Karolyi sauntered up to Thorton. He flicked his gaze over to Horner, and said, "I'll send him back to you this evening."

"That won't be necessary. We have a carriage waiting. Come, Mister Thorton. We must return to the ship."

Karolyi put his arm around Thorton's shoulders and drew him away. He said coldly, "I said I'd send him back to you. You don't need to wait."

Thorton's pulse was hammering in his temples and his blood was singing in his veins. He took a step under the pressure of Karolyi's arm. He had waltzed with him just so, the bold light horseman leading him step by step in a dance, having made up his mind what Thorton's answer would be long before Thorton even knew what the question was. He saw it now, and it made him stubborn. He planted his feet. "I'm sorry, sir, but I must go with my captain."

Karolyi's voice was warm and knowing. "You don't want to go, do you."

The lieutenant's breath caught in his throat and he licked his lips. "I would like to see you again, Colonel, but my captain hasn't given me leave."

"I can arrange it." Karolyi wrapped the younger man in an embrace and kissed him full on the mouth.

CHAPTER 32: SABER RATTLING

Thorton was shocked Karolyi took such liberties in front of so many people. Shocked, but also titillated. The sinfulness of the display made him want to flaunt himself for what he was to spite them all. He wanted to get away with it, just like Karolyi did. His legs grew weak and wobbly. He wanted desperately to give up all pretense of propriety and go with the bold hussar. He was tired of hiding what he was, tired of pretending he didn't notice handsome men, and tired of pretending to be chaste. The hussars not only tolerated the colonel's proclivities, but actively supported him.

The colonel broke the kiss and smiled sardonically down at him. "Now you can't go back."

Thorton tried to slap him across the face, but Karolyi caught his wrist and held it tight. "Unhand me, sir! You presume too much!" Thorton cried.

"I presume nothing. On the contrary, I'm doing you a favor."

"Ruining my reputation is no favor!" Thorton shouted.

Karolyi cocked a sardonic eyebrow at him. "Me? 'Tis you who likes kissing men and isn't brave enough to admit it. You make your own reputation, Lieutenant."

"I demand satisfaction for that remark!" Thorton snarled in fury.

The hussar's lip curled. "Very well. I shall give it to you. On horseback. With sabers."

Horner stepped up, "Lieutenant Thorton, you do not have leave to duel. It is against my express orders."

"I can't let him get away with this!" Thorton cried.

"I came prepared to fight a duel this afternoon, and I shall fight," Karolyi replied.

"Mister Thorton, come to your senses! You will be slaughtered. You are no horseman."

"If I must die to defend mine honor, I will, sir. How could I live knowing I must suffer the caprice of any man that cares to make sport of me?"

Horner put his hand on the younger man's shoulder. "Peter, your friends love you. Any man who would treat you so is not worthy of your blood. Walk away."

"I can't!"

Karolyi snorted and stepped back. He began swinging his arms to limber up. "You have a sword. We will lend you a horse."

Not getting anywhere with Thorton, Horner addressed Karolyi. "For God's sake, Colonel. Apologize. You have done him wrong. Admit it and make amends. I beg you. 'Tis murder to go forward. Peter is not your equal at arms and you know it."

"You want to save his life? Give him to me. Twenty-four hours leave. We'll settle this matter privately."

Horner stopped as if he had been struck. "That is a dishonorable proposition."

Karolyi smirked. "If your objection is strenuous, then I will be happy to give you satisfaction after I have finished with Lieutenant Thorton."

Horner's jaw set. "No leave."

"Very well. A second horse." He spoke Magyar to his men. Two of them went out to get the horses ready.

"I have not accepted your terms, Colonel. As the challenged party, I assert my right to select the manner of duel, and as captain, I assert the right of precedence to duel you before Lieutenant Thorton."

Karolyi looked Horner up and down, saw a thin man not as tall nor bulky as himself, and nowhere near the specimen needed to give him real sport in any physical exertion. "With all due respect, Captain, I think Lieutenant Thorton would have a better chance than you, but I will hear your terms."

"If I am victorious, you will apologize to Lieutenant Thorton."

Karolyi was amused and an insouciant grin grew beneath his mustache. "Very well. If you are victorious, I will apologize."

Horner turned to Thorton. "You must accept it. I am not going to duel the man so that you can be stubborn and get yourself killed."

Thorton was relieved to have an honorable way out for himself, but worried for Horner. His brow wrinkled in concern, but he said, "I will, sir."

Karolyi spoke. "Very well, name your weapon. Pistols? Swords? Mounted? On foot?"

"Swimming," Horner replied.

Karolyi blinked. "I beg your pardon? My Spanish is imperfect. I don't think I understand you."

"Swimming." Horner mimed it.

Karolyi replied testily, "I don't know how to swim."

"Thorton doesn't know how to ride, but you were willing to take unfair advantage of him. I am following your example."

"Swimming and what? Penknives?" the colonel scoffed.

"Just swimming. I feel no need to shed your bled, Colonel. Given the advantage I have in swimming, 'twould be murder to use a weapon."

The other hussar who could speak Spanish was translating for the rest. The Hungarians huddled together in puzzlement. Thorton was grinning from ear to ear. In that moment he loved Horner with the pure and unadulterated hero worship of a young man for a wise and honorable officer.

Karolyi looked at his men who grinned back at him. He was their commander and they were loyal to him, so they would gladly participate in any sort of mischief in which he led, but they also appreciated the British captain's cleverness.

"Drowning is not my idea of a duel," the hussar snapped.

"Then apologize to Lieutenant Thorton."

"I hate you," Karolyi informed Horner.

"That is neither here nor there. If you will not swim, you must apologize."

Karolyi stared at Thorton. "I cannot kill where I have kissed. I didn't plan to do you any harm, but neither could I back away from your challenge."

"That isn't an apology," Thorton retorted.

Karolyi gave him a crooked smile. "I have never apologized to anyone in my life. You are the very first, and there will not be a second. Please forgive me for offending you. I underestimated your captain."

Thorton was uncertain if that was a suitable apology. He looked at Horner. "Sir? Is that sufficient?"

"I think it is as much of an apology as you are going to get from Colonel Karolyi. I advise you to accept it."

"I accept your apology, sir." Thorton put out his hand to shake.

Karolyi studied him a while before he accepted Thorton's hand. "No hard feelings then. Will you join me for dinner?"

Thorton looked at Horner for guidance.

"We have already dined, but we will keep you company, sir. Then we must return to the ship," Horner replied.

Karolyi was very gracious during dinner, especially when the roasted chickens appeared. He chatted and told stories, poured their glasses full of wine, and urged them to drink. The hussars were cheerful fellows, and they talked and laughed as they killed the bottles, and even dared to twit their colonel about the afternoon's events. Thorton was getting tipsy when Horner put his hand over his cup to prevent Karolyi from filling it again. He rose.

"Time to return to the ship, Lieutenant. We thank you for your hospitality, Colonel." He gave a little bow.

"'Tis early," the Hungarian protested.

"The sun is over the yardarm," Horner replied, which meant nothing to the equestrian. "Come along, Lieutenant."

Standing up made Thorton's head spin and Horner had to help him into the chariot. It was a long ride back to the quay, and Thorton fell asleep with his head on Horner's shoulder. The captain sat still and did not disturb him. After a while a jolt of the carriage woke the lieutenant. He lifted his head and said, "I beg your pardon, sir."

"'Tis quite all right, Peter."

Thorton yawned and sat up. He could not forget what had happened at the tavern and sat brooding over it.

"You're pensive."

Thorton flushed. "I was thinking about Karolyi."

"I wouldn't get too friendly with that one if I were you."

Thorton winced. "Too late. I already was."

"That was unwise."

"I'm tired of being lonely. I want a lover."

"He's no lover. He only wants sport."

"I know that now. I didn't at first."

"You must be patient, Peter. Eventually you will find someone suitable. If you accept the advances of whatever man turns your head, you will only get into trouble. You should see that by now."

Thorton sighed. "As long as I'm in the Service, any man will get me into trouble."

"If you are discreet, the trouble will not come from me."

"Thank you, sir."

"Chasing after gamblers and hussars is not discreet."

Thorton cringed. "No, sir."

"Shakil was a good man, sober and respectable."

"He jilted me."

Horner sighed. "I'm sorry for that. I liked him."

"I did too."

They were silent for a while, then Horner spoke again. "I thought I would never find someone to love. My marriage was not entirely satisfactory. Upon reflection, I should not have married because I didn't have the deep feelings that a man ought have for his wife. We were both miserable. Now I have met someone I admire very much. I feel no rush, just a joyful delight in her company and a keen anticipation for when I will see her again. Time will tell if we are suited for marriage. There is no reason to rush it. I value her friendship, so I am content. So you see, Peter, it may not happen soon, but it will eventually happen. You must conduct yourself as a gentleman so that you will be worthy when you find him."

"Aye aye, sir." The younger man was glum. As much as he appreciated Horner kindness, he had little hope of finding a suitable match. Any single woman was a potential match for Ebenezer Horner, and yet, it had taken him a long time to find Emily Wadsworth. The number of potential matches for Thorton was much smaller. He didn't have much hope of finding 'the one.' He slumped in his seat and didn't speak for the rest of the ride.

CHAPTER 33: THE PURPLE ADMIRAL

Midshipman Bettancourt stuck his head in the open door of Thorton's berth. "You're wanted on deck, sir."

"I'm coming." The blond lieutenant unfolded his legs, threw off the blanket in which he had been wrapped, thrust his book into his pocket and his feet into his shoes. He strapped his sword belt around his waist, clapped his cocked hat on his head, and pulled on his gloves as he hurried up two flights of ladders to the quarterdeck. When he arrived, Horner was gazing through his spyglass.

"Sir," Thorton said, standing to attention.

"At ease, Mister Thorton. Have a look and tell me if you know that ship."

Thorton's own spyglass was in his sea chest. He rarely needed it while at anchor. "May I borrow your glass, sir?" Horner handed it over to him and Thorton put it to his good eye.

A line of lateen sail was coming into port from the southwest. Their flagship sported purple and white striped lateen sails and three masts. Thorton lowered the glass and said, "I'm sorry, sir. I never heard of a ship with purple-striped sails before."

Horner ruminated, "Purple, so I suppose it is the Salletines. Could it be the Dey himself, do you think? Who else would imagine himself to be on a par with the King of Spain or the Captain-General of the Knights of Malta?"

"I don't know, sir. I can't imagine a corsair carrying striped sails. How would they deceive their prey if they could be so easily recognized?"

The line was wending up the Tagus towards the anchorage. The fleet numbered thirteen including the flagship. They came in perfect formation with an exact distance between them.

"They keep space well enough," Horner allowed. "Sound general quarters. Idlers on deck."

"General quarters, all hands on deck," Forsythe bawled. The boatswain's pipe shrilled and hands boiled up from below decks.

"Prepare to render honors. Mister Thorton, bide a moment."

"Render honors, aye," the lieutenants answered. Perry, Chambers, and Bettancourt descended to the gundeck calling, "Gun stations!" as they went. Thorton's men, who had been idle off watch, descended to take their places.

Over the course of the next half hour the Salletine fleet grew large as they approached. "Swallow tail pennant, sir," Thorton reported.

The Portuguese squadron anchored in the west began their salute: seventeen guns.

"An admiral then. Very well, we shall deliver a seventeen gun salute. Make ready."

"Seventeen gun salute, aye," Thorton replied. He went below.

"Salute, seventeen guns," he called to Perry as he went to his own spot.

"We'll take 'em in order, one, two, three," Lieutenant Perry informed him. The *Amphitrite* normally fired her salute from one broadside, but she didn't have that many guns to a side. She was a small vessel—a battleship could have fired such a salute from a single deck's broadside.

"Run in the guns! Two, six, heave!" The iron tires rumbled across the deck as men heaved at the iron behemoths. Tampions were removed from the muzzles and lead aprons removed from the vents. Thorton went to the tub of sand, and striking flint and steel, struck a spark into a bit of trash on the first try. He regarded it as a good omen, and used the trash to light the slow matches in their linstocks. The powder monkeys came up with their charges and the familiar ritual of ramming and loading was carried out.

"Are you ready, Mister Thorton?" Perry called.

"Ready, sir!"

"Steady there. Wait for my command."

They waited. Thorton stuck his head out a gun port. The *Amphitrite* was at anchor near the west end of the harbor with other foreign warships in a line outside the merchant ships. He could see the lines of the Salletine flagship; she was very near.

"The *Sea Leopard!*" he exclaimed.

He knew her even though her hull had been painted purple. As he watched she put out her sweeps and began to row. The Salletines were in perfect cadence and the yellow-painted oars flashed like gold against the purple hull. Her gun ports were all open and her guns run out; guns alternated with sweeps on the weather deck. Marines in short brown jackets and purple pantaloons were lined up on the foredeck. Their white turbans were spotless and neat. Officers in long purple coats were lined up at the quarterdeck rail. Among them was a very tall man with a white-streaked black beard.

"Tangle!" Thorton exclaimed.

"Run out your guns!" Perry commanded.

Thorton pulled his head in and repeated, "Run out your guns, you lollygagging whoresons!"

One after another the Portuguese squadron boomed out their welcome to the Salletine admiral. In the moment of silence afterwards, Midshipman Bettancourt careened down the ladder. "Fire!" he shouted.

"Fire!" bellowed Perry. The first gun on the starboard side roared out.

Thorton counted seconds, and shouted, "Number two, present fire!"

All the crew made certain they were well clear of the gun as the gun captain approached with the linstock in his hand. "Fire!" he called loud and clear. He touched the slow match to the powder in the vent. A hiss of flame flew through the primer and the gun thundered, sending up a spray of sparks from the vent hole. The deckhead above was scalded yet again, adding to the dark stain overhead.

Perry watched the second hand sweeping round his watch face and bellowed, "Number three, present fire!"

The second gun's captain presented fire and the gun roared with a satisfying billow of grey smoke.

Thorton counted off the seconds and shouted, "Number four, present fire!"

Again the dance of fire and flame was performed with a hiss of sparks and a throaty roar.

"Number five!" Perry shouted.

Orange sparks flung themselves from the vent and the gun roared. A pall of gunsmoke was beginning to gather in and around the ship.

"Number six, fire!" The noise rocked Thorton in his bones and left him nearly deaf.

"Seven!"

The stately barrage continued at a walking pace with Lieutenants Thorton and Perry moving from gun to gun. They fired by the numbers and each one was as satisfying as the one before it. Gunsmoke grew thick below decks and Thorton waved his hand through it.

"Thirteen!" Perry shouted.

With no shot there was no recoil and the men had to sweat and curse to run the guns in after firing. The iron growl of trucks on deck was added to the din.

"Fourteen!" Thorton shouted.

The vent sparked and sizzled, then hung fire. Nothing happened. Thorton burst out, "God damn it. 'Tis the offspring of a French whore!" He whirled to the next gun. "Number sixteen, fire! Number eighteen, stand by, you slack-jawed idiots!" An extra gun was always loaded for salutes in case of misfires.

The gun captain presented fire in haste and number sixteen roared. The crew had forgotten to run the gun out, and the orange blast from the muzzle scorched the paint of the gun port and added a charred, burning smell to the brimstone of the discharge.

"Son-of-a-bitch!" Thorton bellowed. "Douse it!" A man seized the gun bucket and threw the contents against the side and doused the sparks.

Meanwhile Perry was busy on the other side. "Fifteen!" he shouted. The gun answered him. "What the hell is wrong over there?"

"Hung gun!" Thorton called back, watch in his hand. He did not call 'misfire,' that could be too easily misunderstood in the clamor. "Number eighteen, fire!"

The last blast left them a little stunned, but the rumble of the trucks reminded them of their business. Up above the crew gave three cheers, "Hip hip, huzzah! Hip hip, huzzah! Hip hip, huzzah!" and waved their hats.

The salute finished, the gun captain held his linstock over his head in warning, and announced, "Ware the gun, she's still hung." He was a man of about thirty, experienced, steady, and knowledgeable. Careless men did not live to become gun captains.

"Still foul, Lieutenant Perry," Thorton replied. "With your permission, we'll take care of it."

"Carry on, Mister Thorton." Perry supervised the remainder of the gun crew in sponging out and running in their guns.

"Messenger! Inform Captain Horner we have a hung gun. We shall attempt to fire it again in a few minutes." Thorton stood by with his watch in his hand to time the gun until he thought all reasonable chance of a slow burn had passed.

Midshipman Bettancourt replied, "Hung gun, aye," and ran up the ladder.

Meanwhile the foreign warships started their salutes and the reverberations rolled back from the hills along the river. Merchants, who knew nothing about the proper method of giving salutes, fired whatever they had whenever they pleased, adding to the din. Some small arms were also heard, along with the ringing of bells, banging of pots and pans, and other improper noises from the fishboats and merchantmen. The noise went on and on, and in the city, crowds came to the quay to see what the fuss was about. The *Sea Leopard* swept past like a queen with all her maids in train, the lateen-rigged fleet rowing precisely in her wake. When the salutes were all finished, she replied with thirteen of her own, and then her crew cheered their strange ululating cry, *"Allahu akbar! Allahu akbar! Allahu akbar! Allahu akbar!"* The shrill sound rang in the Portuguese air and chilled the hearts of Christians.

The sound pierced Thorton clean through. "God is great," he whispered to himself. How he wished he were on that deck, wearing purple, not blue, with friends from whom he need keep no secrets, serving a navy he need not fear.

"Time," Perry told him. Thorton, caught up in the noise and his own thoughts, didn't hear him. Perry gave him a sharp elbow.

Thorton said, "I'm sorry, sir, I didn't hear you come up."

"Commence clearing the misfire."

"Aye aye, sir. Number fourteen, prick the piece!"

"Prick the piece, aye!" The gun captain advanced, drove the iron prick into the vent with his left hand, and jabbed it well. "Charge is seated and pricked."

"Seated and pricked, aye," Thorton acknowledged. "Carry on."

The gun captain re-primed the gun with a twist of paper from his cartouche. "Gun primed." He looked to Thorton.

"Everyone stand clear." Thorton took several steps back and the men shuffled away from the fouled gun. "Present fire."

"Present fire!" called the gun captain. He advanced grimly on the gun, and standing to the side, extended the linstock with his left hand. The primer caught with a sizzle and orange sparks scattered from the vent hole. Nothing further happened.

"God damn me if she'd not fucked and good," the gun captain said. Then he held the linstock horizontally over his head and cried out in a voice that carried, "Ware the gun!"

Thorton watched the minutes sweep by. "Prick her again."

The gun captain replied, "Aye aye, sir."

Once more he pricked and primed the gun. They all stood clear as he presented fire. Once more the gun didn't fire.

"Damn it all to hell," said Thorton.

"Bollocks," the gun captain agreed.

"Drown the gun," said Thorton.

"Aye aye, sir." He cleared the vent again, then received one of the gun's buckets and poured it into the vent. "Run 'er in!"

The gun crew heaved the tackle and drew the gun far enough inboard they could work at the muzzle.

"Flood the bore!" the gun captain cried.

A bucket of salt water was presented and poured into the barrel, the man pouring careful to keep his body and hands out of the way.

"More water!" Another wooden bucket was handed to the man, and he poured it in.

"Worm the piece!" The gun captain called.

The wormer advanced reluctantly. Using his off hand and keeping his back to the piece to minimize the damage should the gun fire, he inserted the worm into the barrel and twisted it.

"Harder!" Thorton snapped. "You can't draw it if you fiddle around like that."

The man gritted his teeth, wiped sweat from his face with his free hand, and twisted the worm violently. Everyone held their breaths.

"Got it!" he crowed.

"Draw it," the gun captain commanded.

One hand at a time the wormer pulled the shaft out of the piece. The cartridge appeared, impaled on the corkscrew end of the shaft. The wormer carefully untwisted it from the tool and handed it to the powder monkey. They boy received it in his leather case and brought it to show Thorton and the gun captain. A little gunpowder spilled from the hole the wormer had made, but there were no other holes in the canvas.

"I pricked her hard though, sir," the man replied.

"The vent must be stopped by corrosion. You never pricked her at all," Thorton said after he had examined the cartridge. "Get Carson. He'll fix it."

"Pass the word for Carson!" was echoed from man to man.

The gunner and his mate came up the powder magazine and took over the gun. It had to be drained and cleaned and an examination made to discover the cause of the misfire.

Thorton reported to Perry, "Gun is clear. The gunner is cleaning it now, sir. We suspect corrosion of the vent."

"Thank you, Mister Thorton. Messenger! Inform Captain Horner that the misfire has been cleared and Mister Carson is cleaning the gun."

"Misfire clear and Carson cleaning the gun, aye," Bettancourt repeated. He ran up the ladder again.

"Gun crews may stand down," Perry said.

Thorton was free at last to run on deck. He joined the other officers as they watched the splendid sight of the Salletine navy sweeping past to take up their positions. Each vessel came on in the wake of the one before it with a precise half-cable's length between them. The ordinary vessels of the Salletine fleet had plain white sails, but the purple hulls were very handsome. The paint was a dark, deep grape color that had a certain dignity. A more barbaric and imposing sight few men had ever seen.

The *Sea Leopard* held water and so did the vessels behind her. One by one they came to a stop. The *Sea Leopard* made signals, then a musket fired. At the sound, every vessel in the fleet backed water on the port and pulled on the starboard, rotating in stately unison like dancers in a minuet. After turning ninety degrees, they held water, received further signals, and at a musket shot, advanced a cable's length towards the shore where they all backed water and dropped their anchors. The *Sea Leopard* brailed up her striped sails, and the moment she did, so did the rest of the line. Thorton, who knew how heavy the great lateen sails were, knew they were hauling like mad and had the backs to do it.

"My God. They are seamen," Perry said in admiration.

"Indeed they are," replied Thorton.

CHAPTER 34: THE RETURN OF THE CAPTIVES

A boat landed Moorish sailors on the pier, then the *Sea Leopard* herself rowed up with yellow oars flashing and neatly placed her lading board against the end of the wharf. The turbaned sailors scampered along the dock and caught the heaving lines which they used to haul the heavier lines ashore and make fast around the pilings. Next the gangway was run out and the end settled on the wooden surface of the pier. The tide was high, so the galley rode with her rail above the pier.

The admiral himself, resplendent in a long purple coat heavily laddered across the chest with gold lace and a fine pair of epaulettes, walked up a gun as easily as if it were a stair and stood balanced upon the railing. A large white turban wrapped around a black fez was on his head, gold hoops in his ears, and gold rings on his hands. His black boots were highly polished. Little of the buff pantaloons could be seen beneath the full purple skirts of the coat, but a scimitar was thrust through the golden sash on his right hip. His panoply was completed by a leopard skin worn as a cloak, the paws secured under the epaulettes to hang down his chest. The costume would have been remarkable on any man, but the admiral was a Sallee Turk, over six feet high, with broad shoulders, powerful chest, and narrow hips. He was so swarthy he might have been thought a native of the wilds of Africa rather than a Turk. His brown eyes were hawk-like beside the long nose, slightly humped at the bridge where it had been broken long ago, and his lower face was covered by a short neat black beard and mustache. A grizzled streak ran down the middle of the beard.

Baron Chippenham leaned over and asked Thorton in a whisper, "Who's that?"

Thorton leaned back and whispered, "Admiral Isam al-Tangueli. You have heard of him as 'Captain Tangle.'"

"What a splendid savage."

"He is an honorable gentleman and quick to duel if insulted," Thorton cautioned him.

They were part of the dignitaries lined up to receive the Salletine admiral. Thorton had been borrowed to serve as an interpreter and advisor, he being the only man among the English who knew any Arabic. They flanked the Portuguese party, made up of the Marquis of Pombal, officers of state, bishops, and His Grace, the Admiral Duke Henrique do Coimbra. A boy's choir, retainers, and honor guard with flags flying completed the Portuguese presence. On the other side was the Count Orsini, ambassador from Hungary, whose hussar bodyguards cut a dashing figure even on foot. Behind them were various coteries of Portuguese aristocrats, clergy, visiting dignitaries, and behind the barricades on the street, the common folk. Portuguese soldiers in green coats lined the streets to preserve order.

The Salletine admiral himself had nothing to do but supervise and look regal; practical matters were in the hands of his first lieutenant, a renegade Englishman with red hair and grizzled whiskers. When everything was arranged to his satisfaction, the lieutenant bowed to the admiral with his hand pressed to his brow. A squad of Salletine marines in brown coats and purple pantaloons went ashore and lined up. The banner carrier came next, proudly holding aloft the purple flag of the Sallee Republic with its silver crescent moons and stars. The staff and yardarms of the pennant were adorned with three long black horse tails: the highest honor accorded to any military man in the Ottoman Empire. Even the General of the Janissaries carried only two horsetails. Next the musicians marched ashore and formed up. Reedy clarinets wailed, brass cymbals flashed and clashed in the sunlight, and the drums, both snare and kettle, thundered and sent quivers through the planking of the pier.

The Portuguese did not have a military band. The custom was slowly spreading from Istanbul throughout Europe, but had not yet reached Portugal at the western extremity. They goggled in amazement.

"Damn me, those Turks know how to make a rousing entrance! They have outdone us for splendor. Our choir can't compete. We must rectify the disparity immediately," Henrique exclaimed.

The Archbishop of Lisbon hushed him. "'Tis an infernal noise and affronts the ear of God."

"I'll bet our boys tremble when they hear it on the battlefield," Henrique agreed, which was not at all what the Archbishop meant.

The Salletine admiral walked along the rail to the head of the gangplank, waited for his officer escorts to catch up, then descended to the pier with a swinging stride.

"Arrogant bastard, isn't he?" Chippenham murmured out of the corner of his mouth.

"He earned it," Thorton replied.

The Salletine herald, a barrel-chested black man, announced in a great bass voice and tolerably good Portuguese, "His Excellency, Admiral Isam bin Hamet al-Tangueli, Admiral of the Salletine Fleet and Envoy to Portugal."

The Portuguese herald responded with, "His Excellency, the Marquis of Pombal and Prime Minister of Portugal!"

Tangle advanced and gave the assembled Christians a forty-five degree bow. The Minister stepped forward and gave Tangle a bow that was not quite as deep as the one he had received.

Admiral Tangueli addressed the Marquis in flowery Arabic.

"What's he saying?" Chippenham asked Thorton in a whisper.

Thorton whispered back, "I can't understand all of it, but 'tis the usual courtesies. Peace be upon you and all within this land, a bright future, perpetual amity, that sort of thing."

"I thought you were fluent in Arabic," the baron hissed.

"Not this fancy diplomatic talk. I can order a ship and say my prayers."

Chippenham gave him a glare. "We'll discuss your deficiencies as a translator later."

Thorton sighed and kept translating, "Now he is saying that it is his pleasure to return one hundred Portuguese captives that were taken while they were in Spanish service, before the independence of Portugal. He is . . ." He paused as the Arabic got away from him, "The gist is that there are more Portuguese captives, and he is authorized to treat for their release."

The British and other foreign dignitaries had no role in the formalities except to stand by and smile politely. After a certain amount of discussion, the admiral turned aside and sent a midshipman back to the xebec. Shortly thereafter the hatches were opened and the captives came scrambling on deck. They were dressed in white shirts and pantaloons with round white caps on their heads, but bare foot. Thorton had seen their ilk laboring in the streets of Zokhara to repair the paving, or else carrying heavy loads as porters. When at work the fellows were ragged, thin, and sunburnt, but this lot were in good health, clean, and neat. Sharp orders were given to restrain them, but they could not help praising God in their own tongue and raising their hands to Heaven.

Ashore the sight of the captives excited the pity of the throng. Although soldiers kept the public away from the wharf, the arrival of the Salletine fleet had caused a stir and the news of a hundred Portuguese captives being returned had caused thousands to come to the waterfront. Many of them were families and friends crying in hopes of discovering a loved one.

Salletine marines in short brown jackets, white turbans, and purple pantaloons kept order with the butt of their muskets as the captives came running down the gangplank. They shouted at them in Arabic, Turkish, Spanish, Italian, and Portuguese, but the captives paid them no heed and rushed on. They ran to the bishops, threw themselves on their knees, and kissed their rings. More of them flung themselves at the feet of the Marquis of Pombal. Tears streaked down their cheeks as they thanked the Portuguese lords and bishops for their deliverance.

"Feh. The Portuguese didn't have anything to do with it. 'Tis the pleasure of the Dey of Zokhara to send them back," Chippenham observed. "We've been scrambling all day to get ready."

Thorton knew as much. He had been summoned to assist the ambassador. "Still, 'tis a magnanimous gesture," he replied.

The Portuguese lords and bishops withdrew. They marched along the street with the captives in their wake with soldiers for escort. Families who recognized a loved one wanted to be reunited, but were not allowed. Not yet. The cavalcade went up to the Cathedral of Santa Maria Maior de Lisboa to observe mass first. Not until after they had thanked God for their deliverance would they be permitted to rejoin their families.

Protestants and foreigners were not invited to the mass. That left the Hungarians and British and the rest of the foreigners on the pier. Admiral Tangueli, his marines, and band held their places without moving or speaking. The Portuguese had simply walked off and left them. The British and Hungarians were mere spectators and did not expect to be invited, but the snub to the Muslims was obvious to all.

"Marines, form up! Two ranks." The sharp Arabic commands issued by their admiral caused the Salletine marines to swiftly form up. "Marines, present arms!" The marines drew their scimitars and held them vertically before their bodies. The sun shone on the bright edges. "Honors and band, form up!" As neatly and quickly as folding a piece of paper, the band and banner fell into marching formation. "Mark time, march!" The drums began to roll and the clarinets to wail in a marching cadence. The marines began to tramp in place. "Forward, march!"

Startled Europeans had no way to get out of their way; Tangle was deliberately taking up the entire breadth of the pier. He had a sufficient body of marines to sweep all before him and sweep them he did. The Europeans scrambled and ran to stay ahead of the steadily advancing line. Not one of the brown and purple clad marines hesitated or stumbled even when they ran over a man who failed to get out of the way. They simply marched him down and trod him under foot. He curled into a ball and covered his head with his hands. His hat went cartwheeling over the side to be lost in the waters beneath the pier.

The Portuguese worthies, hearing the piercing cry of the clarinets and rumble of the drums, looked back over their shoulders as they got into their carriages. They did not plan to walk all the way to the church; walking was for commoners. They would lead in their carriages.

A Portuguese captain on horseback dashed back to intercept the Salletine party as it reached the end of the wharf but before it could set foot on shore.

"Mark time!" Tangle ordered in a loud voice.

The marines marched in place. Their boots thundered on the wooden planks and the band continued playing the cadence.

"What the hell are you doing?" the captain demanded.

"Accompanying the party to the steps of the cathedral, as agreed," Tangle replied. "Stand aside. We won't be late."

"You can't do that!"

"Stand aside or we'll run you over," Tangle replied.

The Portuguese captain put spurs to his white horse and flashed back to the line of carriages. With the obstacle removed, Tangle ordered, "Quick time, march!" He drew his sword with his left hand and pointed forward, then lifted the hilt to his lips, swung it down, and sheathed it. The Salletine marines did the same and followed after him. The tromp of boot heels rang on the pavement and echoed off the fronts of buildings. The rattle of the snares and rumble of the kettle drums—carried by one man and played by another walking backwards—reverberated. The Salletine party came up to the rear of the rather disorderly Portuguese party and marked time again.

The Archbishop of Lisbon came to the door of the Marquis of Pombal's carriage to remonstrate with him. He had to be shout to be heard of over the noise. "Get rid of him! Why is he here?"

The Marquis replied, "Apparently he's accompanying us. How are you going to stop him? Shall I order the troops to fire on him? That would be a sad way to treat the envoy who has delivered our brothers to us."

"'Tis unseemly and unchristian! They are making too much noise! 'Tis the Devil's music!"

"Then ask him to march quietly."

When the messenger delivered the message, a smile turned up one corner of Tangle's mouth. "Agreed."

Thereafter the Salletines marched with nothing but the rattling of drumsticks against the rims to keep time, but the heavy tramp of their boots on pavement was percussion enough. It drowned out the choirboys singing. Eventually they arrived at the cathedral. The great bronze doors swung open and the Portuguese lords, churchmen, and captives disappeared inside.

Tangle called a halt. The Salletine ranks stood in perfect order and silence as the organ began to swell; the majestic tones carried even through the stone of the facade. The crowd that had followed stared at the Salletines, and children peeked out from behind their mothers skirts. Thereafter when the mothers of Lisbon threatened the Sallee rovers would get them when they were bad, not all of them thought it was a terrible fate.

Tangle ordered, "About face!" His baritone voice rang clear and true through street, carrying even over the muffled sound of the organ and the restless noises of the crowd. The Salletines took two steps in unison to pivot back the way they had come. Tangle strode along the side to take his place at the head of the purple cavalcade. Turning to face them, he called, "Quick time, march! Loud as you like!"

The Salletines swaggered back to the waterfront in good order. The clarinets shrieked, the drums banged and rolled, and the marines trod heavily to make the ground shake as they passed. Little children cried and hid their faces in their mothers' bosoms, but young boys stood in slack-jawed awe. A crowd followed in their wake, Peter Thorton among them. The British ambassador had no further use for him (or the Salletines) and was going home. Thorton was not the only follower; Count Orsini followed in his chariot. His hussars in their green uniforms mounted on black horses were nearly as extraordinary as the Salletines. There was a similarity in the ladders of gold braid that decorated the front of their coats and the perfection of male forms that wore such effulgent uniforms.

Portuguese women waved their handkerchiefs to the foreigners, which vexed their husbands sorely. Nine months later the offspring born of such infatuations would arrive in the world with a good deal less admiration than their long gone fathers had received.

The Salletine procession marched to the end of the pier and halted, but Tangle marched up the gangway to the rail. He smiled in satisfaction. His men pleased him, the crowd amused him, and the Portuguese annoyed him, but he had come off splendidly. He folded his arms over his chest and surveyed the crowd. Spotting a blue uniform at the front of the throng, he locked gazes with Peter Thorton.

Thorton stood transfixed. There was no doubt Tangle was staring at him. This magnificent man had been his captor, his lover, his friend, his captain, his mentor, his everything. No man had taught him more, loved him better, or proven himself more loyal. His feet moved of their own volition. With a horrified thrill he felt them carry him up the gangplank. Tangle stalked along the rail to meet him.

Thorton said, "I'm not going back."

Tangle's teeth flashed in a ferocious grin. Pulling Thorton into his arms, he kissed him full on the mouth. Thorton turned bright red, but it was too late. He had decided. He put his arms around the admiral's neck and kissed him passionately. He had made his choice.

CHAPTER 35: THE LEOPARD'S PAW

Tangle shut the door of the great cabin behind him. Sunlight slanted warm and golden through the two small sternlights and made the ivory walls glow with color. The purple and white checked canvas that screened the sleeping chamber from the day room was bright but considerably tamer than the gaudy paint job Kasim Rais had inflicted upon the *Sea Leopard's* cabin when he had had her. A kilim rug in tan and cream covered the bare planks of the deck, and another was thrown over the divan and supported cream colored sheepskins, as well as cushions of purple, tan, and cream. A French writing desk and chair were the only European furniture in the room. Moorish lamps of intricate bronze hung in sconces to gently sway as the ship bobbed on the placid waters of the harbor.

"I thought blue was your favorite color," Thorton said. He was unable to address the weighty matters that pressed upon him just yet.

"It is, but I am an admiral now and entitled to an admiral's purple checked cloths for my boat and bulkheads. I will not forgo the privileges of my rank."

"We do not used checked or striped sails in the north," Thorton replied.

"I know. I've been to England." He stepped closer to Thorton and his brown eyes blazed with the intensity of his feelings. "Stop chattering, Peter. Tell me you mean to stay with us, no matter what. Prove it to me."

Thorton's eyes were grey steel and his jaw set in a stubborn line. He tossed his three-cornered hat onto the divan, reached into his pocket and pulled out his penknife and unfolded it. Reaching behind his head, he caught the long blond braid in its queue of black ribbon and severed the hair. He held the long lock of black-bound hair up before him.

"I have not cut it since I ran away to sea when I was sixteen. This is the length of my service to Christian kings. It ends today." He spoke flatly.

Tangle couldn't speak and his brown eyes were wide. He stared at the short hair that hung around Thorton's ears. It was uneven and ragged, but the locks falling beside Thorton's cheeks struck him as powerfully attractive even as he silently lamented the loss of the beautiful long hair. His own hair was kept short as was the Muslim custom.

"May I use your desk? I am going to tender my resignation for a third and final time. I shall not wait for an answer, either." Thorton tossed the braid onto the desk as he spoke.

Tangle found his voice. "Of course. You will find paper in the lower right drawer."

Thorton sat in the scallop-backed chair and opened drawers. He worked methodically to calm his racing mind, then sat a moment chewing on the end of the reed pen. Finally he dipped it in ink. Tangle held his breath as the pen scratched across the paper. Thorton paused and thought again, then wrote some more. Finally he finished and waved his hand over it to speed the drying.

"They didn't accept my previous resignations, so I doubt they will accept this one," he remarked. "Still I will go through the formality."

"It makes no sense. There are plenty of men they can call upon, and any of them would be glad to serve under Horner. He's a good captain. They are punishing you because you took the turban."

Thorton reread his letter, then set it aside. "May I send a letter to Captain Horner? I want to ask him to send my dunnage and Ra'uf. He promised that Ra'uf would only be held as long as I was in the ship; he did not press him."

"Of course you may."

The second letter was much longer and harder to write. It was interrupted with frequent pauses for thought, and several lines were scratched out to draft over.

"Peter, please do not chew on the end of the pen," Tangle said gently.

Thorton pulled the end out of his mouth guiltily. "Sorry." After much labor, he finally had a draft that made him happy. He set about making a fair copy.

My Dearest Captain,

Enclosed you will find my third resignation from the Service. I will not return. I have made every attempt to depart the Service in honor but have been denied. Therefore I will not await an answer from the Admiralty but will remain under Admiral Tangueli's protection. You are free to consider me a Deserter if you must. I am enclosing my Braid of Hair as proof that I am serious. I am tired of living under the Sword of Damocles. I can never guess when Destruction will fall upon me and ruin what little love and honor I have enjoyed while wearing the King's coat.

Please understand that I hold you and Mister Forsythe in the greatest esteem. It is not through any defect on your part

*that I have left the Ship. You have been kind and honorable to
me and faithful to your duty and the customs of the Service.
You are virtuous men and I love you for it, therefore it causes
me great pain to disappoint you. I am ashamed you will think I
have repaid your interest with Ingratitude. Please understand
that I am sensible of the great debt of courtesy I owe you and I
pray God will grant me some way to return your favor. It is
because you are Gentlemen of rectitude and compassion that I
was able to bear up as long as I did, but I can bear it no
longer. My heart has been seeking safety for a long time, and
today, when chance put me in the path to Freedom, I took it.*

*Please forgive me for the trouble I have caused you. I will
remember you in my prayers.*

Your friend,
Peter Thorton

He handed it over to Tangle. The admiral's English was imperfect,
but he understood the gist of it. "I am sorry to separate you from your
friends, Peter. Horner treated you well. I am grateful to him for that. He
has tempered my ire against the British."

They traded places and Tangle wrote his own note in Spanish,
requesting the return of Ra'uf and Thorton's dunnage. Then he bound
them all in a packet together and tied it with purple string. Thorton's
hair made a coil within like a piece of rope. The Turk summoned
Midshipman Kaashifa and gave him particular orders.

"You are to deliver this to the British frigate *Amphitrite* and wait
for an answer, but under no condition are you or any man to set foot on
board that vessel. Once the parcel is delivered, you are to shove off and
keep a distance. I would not put it past Horner to snatch you or any
other man to have a pawn to bargain with. Do you understand me?"

"I do, *effendi*." The young midshipman wore a short purple jacket
and buff pantaloons. He was still in dress uniform from the parade.

"Hopefully Horner will give you Peter Rais' dunnage and his
servant Ra'uf. Insist upon it, but if he will not, return to me. No blame
will attach to you for Horner's intransigence."

"Thank you, *effendi*."

"Take the *Leopard's Whelp*. You're on the admiral's business."

"Aye aye, sir." The midshipman made his exit and called for the
boat and crew. Soon the boat with purple and white checked sails was
skimming over the water. Every bumboat and wherry gave way for her;
only flag officers had boats with checked sails.

When he was gone, Tangle cleaned the reed pen and put it and the
ink away. His eyes were hooded as he brooded over the developments

and their importance to himself. When he rose at last, he looked Thorton in the eye and said, "I have missed you, Peter."

Peter stepped up to him and tilted his head back to look into his face. "I missed you, too, Isam."

Tangle wrapped his arms around the blond and pulled him hard against his chest. His mouth came down full on Thorton's and pressed him with all the feelings he had kept to himself for the past year. Thorton gasped, grabbed onto the powerful body, and kissed him back with equal ardor. The kiss went on for a very long time and led straight to bed. Thorton's navy blue coat and breeches tumbled on the floor with Tangle's purple coat and buff pantaloons. Swords and shoes and boots and shirts fell willy nilly with them. Across it all lay the tawny skin of the leopard. A single paw rested possessively on top of what had once been a British lieutenant's uniform, but was no longer.

Some time later the two rested. Thorton lay on his side and studied his lover's body. Black hair swirled across Tangle's chest to nearly hide two small brown nipples. Black hair covered his forearms and legs, but his groin and armpits were shaved. Thorton had once thought him too fastidious, but he had come to appreciate the better hygiene of Muslim gentlemen.

He touched Tangle's shaved head lightly. The man had a topknot that was five or six inches long, but the rest of his head was bald and smooth. "What's this?"

Tangle grimaced. "I am not happy about growing older. I told the barber to pluck the grey hairs out, but it took so long I told him to shave it instead and leave the topknot."

"You look like a djinn from the Arabian Nights," Thorton told him. A children's storybook was one of the books he had used to help himself learn Arabic.

Tangle smiled crookedly and rubbed his head. "Other corsairs wear their hair so. Shaving is the easiest way to take care of it while at sea."

"Why not shave it all?"

The Admiral took hold of his queue and showed it to be a good handle. "So that if a man is drowning his friends may reach down and haul him up again."

Thorton had seen the style before, but not on Tangle. "I miss your pigtail."

After a moment, Tangle said quietly, "That's what my wife says. I am under orders to grow it out again." He gave Thorton a wry smile and watched him carefully.

Thorton's eyes grew distant as he stared at Tangle's shoulder. In the extremity of his need he had forgotten that the man was married with children. His eyes were troubled when he said, "If you love her, then you must do as she says."

Tangle smiled ruefully. "When you put it like that, I have no choice."

Thorton wrapped his arm across the other man's chest. "I'm jealous. You really love her."

Tangle cradled him in his arms and kissed his short hair. He said quietly, "I do. The children too."

"Then why me?"

"I love you too." He ran his fingers through the loose golden locks.

"I don't see how."

"That's because you're not a father. When a man has children, he discovers that his heart grows larger and he can love as many children as he has, not to mention, his good friends and relatives. I love Shakil, you know."

"You don't sleep with him or your children," Thorton pointed out.

"You're jealous! Very well. I'd sleep with Shakil if he'd have me." He smirked at Thorton.

Thorton thumped him with his fist. "Now you're teasing me!"

Tangle grinned. "Yes, I am. What of it? I love you, I love my wife, I love my children, I love my friends. You deserve it. She deserves it. They deserve it. What is so strange about giving people the affection they deserve?"

"I think you're making excuses for being a libertine," Thorton muttered.

Tangle laughed again. "I am very fond of sex, but I am not quite the animal they make me out to be."

"Have you had a lover since me?" Thorton asked curiously. He had had several himself.

"Sex yes, lovers no. I've been waiting for you."

Thorton stared at him in astonishment. "Waiting?"

"Aye, waiting. You tried my patience, but I waited anyhow."

Thorton propped up on his elbows and gazed into the corsair's face. Many thoughts went through his head. First, that Shakil had not waited for him, even though they had pledged themselves to each other. Second, that he had trusted Tangle's loyalty all this time, and his trust had not been wrong.

"You amaze me," the younger man said softly.

Tangle smiled and crow's feet appeared at the corners of his eyes. "Am I not the most notorious corsair of the age? I amaze everyone."

Thorton thumped him again and Tangle laughed. The renegade pushed him and the corsair rolled onto his back. "You're the vainest corsair of the age!" Thorton retorted.

Tangle laughed again. "That's 'Admiral Corsair' to you, mister!"

Thorton sobered. "Congratulations on your promotion. How did it happen?"

"I thumped a Spanish fleet and seized the royal yacht. Who better? Let Murad Rais be the captain of the corsairs; I'm the Admiral of the Navy. However, they want the Portuguese money, so I am also made envoy and sent to get it. The Portuguese still owe us for Eel Buff, not to mention, various prizes. I am also to spy upon them to find out how powerful their navy is."

"Oh, I know all that. We gathered the intelligence for His Excellency, Baron Chippenham, His Britannic Majesty's ambassador to Portugal."

Tangle sat up in bed. "Then we have work to do! Put your pants on. I need that information. I meet with the Prime Minister in the morning."

CHAPTER 36: AFTERSHOCK

Thorton was getting his hair cut by Tangle's new steward, a wiry little Frenchman with strawberry blond hair who waved his scissors as he spoke. Thorton's French was imperfect, so he was helpless to participate in the spate of gossip that poured from the man's mouth. That suited the barber fine because he was able to supply both sides of the conversation himself.

"Pierre, be quiet. I can't hear myself think," Tangle said. He wore a sleeveless shirt and short pantaloons as he lounged on the divan. He was smoking his pipe to help himself concentrate.

"*Oui, m'sieur.*"

Thorton was facing the barber as he sat cross-legged on the sort of stool the Europeans called an 'ottoman,' having mistaken the furniture for the man who sat on it. It was a small divan the right size for one man. It lifted him up sufficiently for the steward to work. A white linen cloth was around his neck to catch the falls of hair as the Frenchman trimmed Thorton's hack job into something presentable.

"I wonder how soon we'll hear from Horner," Thorton said.

"Soon, I expect. Horner's not the kind to dilly-dally. The man has a brain and he uses it." There was a grudging admiration in the corsair's voice.

"How long will we be in Lisbon?"

Tangle puffed out scented smoke. "A month at least. Longer, I expect. Two or three months likely. I must buy a house for the consul, assuming they agree to accept our consul, as well as collecting the debt."

Thorton made a noise of frustration. "I wish we were going immediately."

"I have to attend João's coronation. As much as I wish to take you away from here, I'm positive my own country would think poorly of me if I failed to secure our national interests because I was distracted by my paramour."

"I know. I didn't mean it that way."

Tangle sighed and leaned against the wall behind him. Thorton stared at the lean, muscular physique displayed before him. It felt good to be able to stare openly at a handsome man. He couldn't help smiling. With the weight of his fear gone, he felt like he was floating.

Tangle was still thinking pragmatically. "I regret I can't offer you a commission. Zahid Amir has instituted an Admiralty board and wants to test officer candidates before granting them commissions. He is keen to modernize the navy. As admiral I must submit to his authority. Although I am sure he will be pleased to grant you a commission once you return to Zokhara."

"I can't wear my purple coat?" Thorton was crestfallen.

Tangle shook his head. "I'm sorry," he said gently. "Were I still a corsair, you could."

"What if I am a gentleman volunteer?"

Tangle tilted his head as he thought about it, then he smiled. "Yes. I shall carry you as a supernumerary. You won't stand watches. You'll be my assistant. Allah knows I have enough to do. You're fluent in Spanish and friends with some of the Portuguese. You'll be a help to me."

"I need clothes. Everything."

"We'll fit you out. I don't want you to go ashore. Horner might snatch you. You're safe as long as you stay aboard the *Sea Leopard*. Promise me you won't do anything rash. You're not going back to them." Tangle pointed his pipe at Thorton.

Thorton smiled. "I promise. I won't go back. I don't want to go back. I want to stay with you. Speaking of which, where shall I bunk?"

"Right here," Tangle grinned at him. "We are packed to the deckhead, Peter. I will not put out another officer when I can accommodate you myself."

Thorton colored. "Everyone will know we're lovers."

"If you talk like that they will. If you keep your mouth shut they will merely suspect it. What of it? I'm the Kapitan Pasha of the Sallee Republic. If they insult you, they insult me, and I won't put up with it."

Pierre had stopped cutting hair to listen avidly to this bit of gossip. Tangle glared at him. "If you betray the confidences of the great cabin, you won't be my servant for long."

Pierre jumped back and resumed trimming Thorton's hair. *"Oui, m'sieur.* I shall be quiet as a mouse." He shook his head for emphasis and waved his scissors. Just then the voice of the muezzin rang out from the quarterdeck overhead, "Come to Allah! Come to success!" Thus were the faithful called to prayer.

Thorton jumped up, tossed off the barber's sheet, and with his hair half cut, exclaimed, "I am impure! I need to wash!"

Pierre had a basin of water which he had planned to use in shaving Thorton, but he surrendered it. Thorton took it, set it on the ottoman for a table, and swiftly washed his face and hands. Tangle, who was equally impure and for the same reason, joined him. He performed the ablution with graceful concentration. "Don't hurry, Peter. Do a good job or the prayer won't count."

Thorton steadied himself, and imitating the other man, performed his washing more carefully. They were a little late and joined the prayer in one of the last rows, which placed them near the foredeck. Thorton pulled out his handkerchief and tied it over his hair so that his head would be respectfully covered. No more of the three-cornered hat that smacked of the Trinity! He was still in his British uniform; it was all he had to wear. Everyone but the watch attended. It was much more orderly than the band of freed galleyslaves who had been Thorton's first congregation.

During the prayer the waves grew choppier and the xebec bobbed at her anchor. The anchor watch hung over the bow to inspect as the vessel rode toward her anchor, then sent word to Lieutenant Aruj. Thorton and Tangle moved aside as Aruj came climbing through the praying men to inspect the line, peg leg thumping on the deck. The boy lieutenant quietly gave orders to the watch to take up the scope and the cable was pulled in and laid out in long bights on the deck. As the worshippers rose for the standing part of the prayer, he ducked underneath their elbows to adjust the line. Long blond curls tumbled about his shoulders; he had not cut his hair when he converted. Satisfied, he returned to the quarterdeck. The xebec then drifted back to where she had started and the scope ran out again, leaving a wet streak across the deck. The meandering of the ship meant that the direction of Mecca kept shifting, too, but Allah would forgive them for being inexact.

The waters of the bay grew more agitated as the prayer continued. The stiff breeze blowing up the Tagus caused the *Sea Leopard* to drift upstream, and still more scope paid out. Aruj came thumping down from the quarterdeck to inspect again. Tangle popped up from his prostration to survey the scene, but since he was kneeling on the deck he couldn't see over the gunwale.

"All's well," Aruj told him quietly. "You're praying. I have it."

The xebec began to ride back towards her anchor. Once again the men on watch took up the slack and laid the scope across the deck in long wet bights. Tangle bowed down again. During the next standing part of the prayer he was looking everywhere but to God. Thorton noticed and elbowed him sharply. "Stop that! Whatever it is, it will wait!" he hissed. Another man hissed at both of them to be quiet.

Tangle tried to turn his attention to the prayers, but his eyes kept straying. He looked aloft and over the side. The vessel pitched in short choppy motions and footing became unsteady. Men sometimes had to put their hands on each other to keep from tumbling. Dogs began to howl in the city, and in the chicken coop on the quarterdeck, the hens began to cluck and fret. A low rumbling that was felt more than heard pervaded the ship. Up front the black imam continued leading the prayer in a sonorous bass voice. A few voices followed him, but most of the men were distracted. Tangle broke ranks.

"General quarters! All hands! Storm stations! Seal the bulkheads!" His baritone rang loud and clear across the deck. The men made haste to do as he ordered. Belowdecks came the slam of bulkhead doors, then the noise of hammering as they were dogged shut.

On shore the buildings trembled and shook. The ships in the harbor were tossed and the *Sea Leopard* ran out her scope again. Tangle ran for the quarterdeck with Thorton close on his heels. The Salletine admiral swiftly surveyed the scene. With the wind blowing up the Tagus, they could not sail out, although some of the merchantmen and fishboats were trying. He could try to row out, but he was at the rear of a line of thirteen Salletine ships that would have to row out ahead of him. "Make a signal, 'Set storm anchors.' We must ride it out. Set ours."

"Aye aye, sir," Lieutenant Aruj replied. The curly haired boy officer bawled his orders in Arabic.

Thorton started to move, then realized as a gentleman volunteer he had no assigned position. "What shall I do, rais?" he asked.

"Stay here. Watch the river. Tell me if the water starts to run out."

"Aye aye, sir." Thorton marked the waterline on the docks and shore, then took his bearings on the Castle of São Jorge to the northeast and Point Calcihas to the south.

Ashore church bells rang in alarm and the city's watchmen ran through the streets with their noisemakers. Some people ran out into the streets while others ran into the churches to cry and pray. The horror of the Great Quake was in everyone's mind. What if the recent earthquake had only been the prelude for worse to come?

The *Infanta Antónia* cast off her lines and rowed away from her dock. She was immediately buffeted by the contrary waters and gusty breezes. The wind blew her up river, but when the gust abated, the current sent her seaward. The choppiness of the water made her course even more irregular.

"Xebec coming, broad on the starboard quarter, sir!" Thorton reported crisply. With her erratic course it was impossible to judge whether she would cross their hawse or their stern.

Tangle swore. "Damn it, the pier was the safer spot. He should have stayed put. Hands stand by fore and aft to fend off!"

The mizzen crew fetched boathooks and stood at the rail and on the lazyboard.

The *Antónia* turned upstream and began to row away from them. The tide was against them, but the wind was helping. They put their backs into it and rowed as hard as they could. Even so, they made scant progress against the force of the current.

"They won't make it," Tangle said. "They're going to run on us. We must hold our ground and take the blow because if we don't, we shall run onto our own line. Set every anchor we've got."

Aruj shouted, "Set all anchors! *Now!*"

The *Antónia's* crew as not as large as a warship's; she was only a yacht and a very pretty one with her vermillion hull and striped sails. When the breeze blew and her sails filled she made progress, but when the breeze abated, the tide pressed hard against her. Thorton eyed the froth boiling around the upstream side of the pier and said, "Sir, the river is running out."

Tangle took a look at the pier as well. "Eight knots. Human muscle can't row out of that."

Somewhere inland the shock of the earthquake was sending the river charging to the sea. The same force was driving the tide out. The two together sent a racing current roaring through the harbor. The *Antónia* was in it and she couldn't escape. She was driving at them stern first. On her quarterdeck a figure in a sky blue uniform waved and shouted in English, "Make way!" The command was repeated in Portuguese and French.

The *Sea Leopard* was anchored with her head to sea and her stern to the river. Being a light vessel, the wind governed how she rode more than the tide, but as the current increased she began to sheer off and that put her further into the yacht's way. The *Infanta Antónia* was sliding helplessly backwards, her stern slowly closing with them as her crew strained against the oars.

"All hands on deck except the carpenter and his gang," Tangle said. "On the quarterdeck, anyone not manning a boathook, go to the weather deck. She's going to hit us. Are the bulkheads sealed?"

"Aye, sir. Bulkheads are sealed," Aruj confirmed. Turning forward, he bellowed in his cracking boy voice, "All hands on deck! Carpenter and mates stand by! Brace for collision!"

Elsewhere the visiting warships set extra anchors. Lacking oars they couldn't row and didn't try. The Portuguese fleet, knowing the local conditions better than the visitors, cut their anchors and let the tide carry them to sea. Having been anchored to the west, they were able to get clear before the hapless flood of small craft and panicking merchants bore down upon them. Aboard the *Amphitrite,* Horner, who had never had to deal with an earthquake before, assessed the actions of the Portuguese and the Salletines and found them divided. He decided to hold his ground. Many collisions fouled vessels against each other and the *Amphitrite* wound up with a fishboat tangled in her hawse.

The rumbling ceased and the buildings stopped shaking, but the Tagus was still running hard and fast.

"We're sheering hard now!" Thorton sang out. He had been watching his sightings and noticed the acceleration in their shift. They had swung so far the *Antónia* was now bearing down on their port quarter.

Tangle whirled and looked over the tafferel. He checked his sightings ashore. He swore in Turkish, then in Arabic. The *Sea Leopard* was swinging broadside to the current at the same time she was running over her anchors.

No time. The *Infanta Antónia's* stern struck them amidships. The shock sent every standing man toppling to the deck. The boathooks were useless; mere human strength could not hold off a vessel of four hundred tons. First the *Antónia's* lazyboard and boomkin came over their gunwale without much damage, then the stern slammed into them. The sound of shattering glass and snapping timbers was loud as the *Antónia's* stern stove in. The *Sea Leopard's* side cracked and the deck sagged. The guns on either side slid sideways on their trucks but were caught up by their tackle. Water roared into the *Sea Leopard's* berth deck. She would have listed further, but the great mass of the *Infanta Antónia* was propping her up. The two vessels rotated with slow majesty in the stream.

"Damage report!" Tangle bellowed. "Where's my sheet anchor?"

"Dragging," reported the black boatswain. His shaved head was gleaming in the sun; he had lost his turban and was soaking wet. "The bowers will cross if this keeps up, sir."

The agitation of the waves and drifting of the *Sea Leopard* would provide every opportunity for a bight of cable to wrap around a fluke, and then, as the xebec rolled downstream from the anchor, pull it right out of the seabed. Worse, if the bower cables crossed, they would pull and chafe at each other, and perhaps cause one of them to part. If the bowers didn't hold, the entangled wrecks would drift onto the next Salletine vessel. With the current running so hard, it was all the anchored vessels could do to hold their own places; if the mass of wreckage caught against them they couldn't possibly hold. The current would carry the wrecks into still more anchored vessels. It was a disaster in slow motion and precious little they could do about it.

"Put out your bower anchors!" Tangle shouted in Spanish at Captain Abby.

Thorton translated for him, and added, "We're drifting! Our anchors aren't holding! We need yours!"

The blind captain could not see all that was happening, but he could hear. He shouted to his crew in bad Portuguese, and they made haste to uncat their anchors.

Tangle snapped, "Make a signal, 'All vessels, reverse order, slip anchors, put to sea.'" Their only hope was take their chances amid the swarm of smaller vessels carried away by the turbulent waters.

Normally the vessels followed the flagship, but since she was furthest inland she must be last. The tail of the Salletine fleet must go first. The command was passed along the line of anchored ships as quick as could be, but each relay took precious time and it was several minutes before the first of the Sallee fleet buoyed her anchor cable, cut it, and ran for the sea.

CHAPTER 37: SHIPWRECKS

The *Infanta Antónia* put out her bower anchors and the mass of wreckage halted its seaward drift. On the quarterdeck of the *Sea Leopard* Tangle snapped, "Carpenter report!"

Thorton checked himself, but aside from having bruised his elbow when he fell, he was fine. He waited in tense silence as the report was brought by Midshipman Kaashifa. She was stove in amidships and filling fast. Thorton prayed for her watertight compartments to hold. The *Antónia* was settling by the stern and pressing the *Sea Leopard* down with her. The lazyboard was a lightweight construction consisting of a grated platform, but the strakes that supported it were integral to the hull. Wood bent and creaked ominously, but the *Antónia* held fast to their side.

"We have to get her off us," Tangle said. "Mister Thorton, axes to clear debris. Hack off her lazyboard. Take her boomkin off, too."

Thorton raced to the weather deck, paused to fetch an axe from its locker in the coach, and gathered a work gang. They climbed up on the rail and from there Thorton clambered onto the *Antónia's* lazyboard and so reached the quarterdeck of the ducal yacht. He walked up to Captain Abby and saluted.

"Lieutenant Peter Thorton of the *Sea Leopard,* sir. We must cut you loose. Please haul in your boomkin."

"Peter?" Abby asked in surprise. He peered at the navy blue blur of Thorton's coat. "You're back in Sallee service?"

"I am. Please, Captain, Admiral Tangueli has ordered me to cut you lose."

"We'll sink! You're the only thing holding us up!"

"Have you sealed your watertight bulkheads?"

"What watertight bulkheads?"

"Good God. Permission to go below?"

"Granted. Do what you can!"

On the *Sea Leopard* Tangle's voice rang out loud and clear, "Man the pumps!"

Thorton hastened down the ladders of the *Infanta Antónia.* Belowdecks she was not at all like the *Sea Leopard;* she had been built as a yacht in a Spanish shipyard. To his horror he discovered her bulkheads were of the usual European model—not tight and with no way to seal them. Where the wardroom was in the *Sea Leopard* was a saloon lined by luxurious berths for the yacht's guests. The officers' quarters were forward of that. Crimson velvet drapes screened the entrances. No expense had been spared in the construction and furnishing of the vessel. Her lamps were crystal chandeliers, her mirrors (mirrors!) had gilt frames. Thick carpets lay on the floor of the private staterooms. And yet, eschewing lessons they could have learned from the Muslims, no watertight bulkheads. There was no way at all to shut up the damage and confine the water to one portion vessel. She was doomed.

A pale-faced Portuguese marine pointed a gun at him as he walked through the gilded interior of the yacht. "Halt!"

Thorton put the axe behind his back. "Get on deck. You're sinking," he told the man in perfect Castilian Spanish. The man wavered, looked at the water welling up through the floorboards to soak the expensive carpets, and bolted up the mahogany ladder. Thorton ran after him.

Returning to the quarterdeck, Thorton reported, "You haven't got watertight bulkheads! She's a European vessel. I'm sorry, sir, but I can't save her."

Abby took off the smoked glasses and rubbed his eyes. "Please ask Admiral Tangueli if we may board him. I am abandoning ship."

"How big's your crew?"

"Fifty. The rest have shore leave right now."

"Of course. Dismantle your boomkin first, please. You're dragging us down with you."

Thorton ran back onto the lazyboard, halted, and watched his step. His work gang had already hacked partway through it. Behind him Abby bawled orders in bad Portuguese and his crew began to hack away at the base of the boomkin where it was affixed to the mizzen mast.

Thorton picked his way through the wreckage hanging over the gunwale and made his way up to the quarterdeck. "Captain Abby and crew request permission to come aboard."

"Granted." Tangle was watching the progress of the debris and keeping an eye out for other vessels. A second shock agitated the waters of the bay. He held his breath, hoped the anchors would hold, and they did.

Thorton went to the gunwale and climbed up on it. "Permission granted. Bring your portable salvage with you."

The decision made, Abby was crisply efficient. Teams went below to seize what portable valuables they could—paintings, small pieces of furniture, mirrors, and Duke Henrique's personal effects. The officers' sea chests were hauled out. Part of the Portuguese crew went across to the *Sea Leopard.* Thorton rigged the arm tackle himself to haul the chests aboard—he left the paintings and gilded chairs for last. He had hauled only two chests to the *Sea Leopard* when the last of the debris snapped with a mighty crack. The broken ends scraped down the *Sea Leopard's* side with a wooden scream, scarring the paint with marks like giant fingernails. The *Sea Leopard* rose a little, but the *Infanta Antónia* started sinking rapidly by the stern.

Captain Abby and several men were still on the *Infanta Antónia's* quarterdeck. "Jump, lads! We'll pick you up!" Thorton shouted. To his own crew he shouted, "Send lines over the side!"

The Portuguese lieutenant leaped into the sea, followed by the midshipman and sailor. Captain Abby remained on his quarterdeck.

"Alan, jump!" Thorton shouted.

Tangle was calling orders, "Man overboard! Launch boats!"

The space between the *Infanta Antónia* and *Sea Leopard* was narrow but full of fast water; only two of the men were able to thrash their way to the *Sea Leopard's* side and grab onto the lifelines. Willing hands leaned over the side (with the *Sea Leopard* settling so badly, her already low freeboard was lower still) and hauled them aboard. One of the ship's boats went into the water in pursuit of the missing man.

Abby watched through his smoked glasses. He could discern shapes in the water but was unable to recognize them. He called across, "Is everyone accounted for?" as the water washed over the tafferel.

"All but one! For the love of God, Alan, jump!" Thorton screamed.

"Good bye, Peter," he replied. He turned his back to them.

A new danger loomed. As the *Infanta Antónia's* bow rose, her stern sank, and her mizzen mast, which raked aft anyhow, overshadowed the *Sea Leopard.*

With a quick glance to make certain the Salletine vessel next to them had cleared out, Tangle roared, "Let slip the anchors!"

Sailors set their knives against the cables, then brought the blunt side of the axehead down on the spine of the knife. Several blows drove the blade through the cable with minimal damage to the deck. The cables shot out the hawseholes and the *Sea Leopard* drifted free. She was listing towards the *Infanta Antónia* and her own spars threatened to snarl with the sinking ship. "Send down the main!"

It was too late. The mizzen mast of the *Infanta Antónia* fouled in their mainsail and tore a great rent in it, then clattered against their deck and hung up. The quarterdeck of the yacht was underwater with her bow high in the air, but she hung on the *Sea Leopard.*

"Cut it loose!" Tangle was shouting, but men were already at work with their axes to cut it off at the gunwale. The mizzen mast was a thick timber and it took time to hack through it; time during which the

Infanta Antónia continued to sink and drag the wounded *Sea Leopard* with her.

In the chasm of debris, Thorton saw a blond head as Abby went under. The blind captain thrashed in the water; he didn't know how to swim. He had expected the *Infanta Antónia* to go down fast and take him with her, but she and he were now tangled in an agonized predicament as their death throes were extended by accident.

Thorton threw off his coat and sword and kicked off his shoes. Down to his waistcoat, breeches, and stockings, he peered into the green waters of the bay. Seeing a manlike shape below the surface, he jumped. The icy shock nearly drove the air from his lungs, but he kept going.

A green eternity passed. Sun shone bright and clear above, but the waters of the bay were murky. Roiled by the earthquake, all manner of debris and sediment filled the waters. Timbers from the *Infanta Antónia* and *Sea Leopard* littered the water. A gilt-framed mirror sank past him. Seeing a human shape reflected at him, he reached out, but his fingers knocked against the smooth surface of the glass. He swam deeper, holding his breath until the fire in his lungs threatened to burst. There! His fingers brushed something that felt like wool. He was out of air. He had to surface, but he wouldn't give up. He kicked his feet and his hand brushed the wool coat again, but he couldn't get a hold of it. His lungs were failing; he couldn't hold his breath any longer. He inhaled.

He nearly swooned from the agony of the sea invading his lungs. Darkness crowded his vision. Instinctively he knew that when his vision went entirely black, he would be dead. He was drowning. Terrified, he looked up toward the shimmering light of the surface and kicked up. He was coughing and thrashing, but he forced his arms to simulate swimming and his feet to kick. Crying and coughing, he burst the surface of the water.

"We've got you, sir," a kindly Moorish voice told him. He was seized by the collar and waistband and hauled aboard the *Leopard's Whelp*. The sailors pumped his back and made him vomit the sea out of his body. He was trembling and cold, mewling, weeping, and coughing in the bottom of the boat.

A voice hailed them in English, "Ahoy the boat! Do you need help?" Other ships had sent their boats to help the *Sea Leopard* and *Infanta Antónia* once they were sure of their own survival.

Thorton dragged himself up to drape over the side of the boat. He puked into the sea until all that was left was bile. He coughed and hacked some more.

"Peter! Are you all right? Recognizing Perry's voice, Thorton lifted his face and saw the *Amphitrite's* boat rowing towards them.

"They're offering help," Thorton explained to the *Whelp's* crew. He was the only one of the Salletines who could speak English, although he was in no condition to act as translator.

The cockswain, a coffee-skinned African, shook his head. "The *Sea Leopard* is still afloat. We'll stand by."

The *Amphitrite's* boat drew abreast of them. "Peter, are you all right?" Perry asked him.

"Alan's dead! He went down with the *Antónia!*" He coughed and retched again.

"Damn me. That's hard news." The two boats drew in their oars and the men put out their hands to fend off so Thorton wasn't hurt when the boats came together. He was incapable of moving. Perry climbed over a thwart to be directly beside Thorton. "Are you all right? What happened?"

"I jumped in after him, but I couldn't get him. I touched his coat, but lost my air and started drowning. I had to come up. I almost had him, but I lost him!" Tears squeezed out of his eyes.

Suddenly Perry seized him by the collar and waistband and dragged him into the English boat. "Fend off! Row like hell! Don't let the Moors get him!" His crew moved swiftly to separate from the Salletine boat and drag Thorton aboard.

Thorton yelped and flailed as he found himself heaved into the bottom of the English boat. Surprised, the men in the *Whelp* rose up— but Thorton was wearing the remains of an English uniform. They didn't know he had joined the crew of the *Sea Leopard*.

Perry grinned at them and spoke French which some of them understood. "Thank you for returning our lieutenant to us!"

The Salletines looked at each other uncertainly as the distance between the two boats widened. Thorton scrambled up. Seeing himself being carried away, he attempted to dive into the sea, but Perry was right beside him and held him back. The two wrestled, but the half-drowned lieutenant was unable to make an effective defense.

"Help!" Thorton shouted in Arabic.

That settled the matter. The Salletines felt themselves honor-bound to aid any man who asked for it in Arabic. They started in pursuit of the English.

On the quarterdeck of the *Sea Leopard* Tangle was busy. He hadn't seen see Thorton jump into the sea, but he saw him hauled into the *Whelp*, and now, a few minutes later, he saw his own boat in pursuit of the British boat. He couldn't see Thorton because the English had knocked him down and Perry was sitting on him.

He shouted, *"Whelp!* Belay that! You're off station!"

"They've got Peter Rais!" came the cry. The rowers hesitated and waited to find out what they were supposed to do. The English boat widened the distance between them.

"What?" The English boat was too far away for Tangle to see into it, but Thorton stuck his arm up in spite of being held down. A white sleeve with gold braid appeared above the gunwale. "Give him back!" Tangle shouted in Arabic, then English.

"Row, you bastards! Don't let the rovers catch us!" Perry continued sitting on Thorton's chest and hanging onto the thwarts as the renegade struggled to throw him off. Looking down at him, Perry said, "Sorry about this." He put his hand on Thorton's throat and choked him into unconsciousness.

The Salletines rowed like mad in pursuit of the English boat. Smaller and lighter but with fewer rowers, it was an uneven contest. They rowed until they were ready to puke, but they couldn't catch the English boat. She tore down the bay to the British anchorage. They tied a rope under Thorton's arms and hauled him up. He was dumped unceremoniously on the deck at Horner's feet. Limp, cold, wet, barely conscious, and utterly demoralized, he just lay there. He didn't look up. He stared at the shoes in front of his face. He recognized them, but he didn't want to acknowledge the man who was wearing them.

Horner knelt and peered into his face. "Peter, are you drowned?" he asked in concern.

"No, sir," Thorton replied. "Alan's dead. He went down with the *Antónia.* I tried to save him." He would have said more, but he was exhausted.

They put Thorton to bed in his own hammock and called the doctor. Ferncastle arrived, examined him, and pronounced him to be suffering from a shock to the nerves and warned that he might catch pneumonia. He was ordered to keep to his bed until told otherwise. Horner sent his portable stove to warm up the room and dry out the patient.

Meanwhile the *Leopard's Whelp* arrived, demanded the return of the renegade lieutenant, and was refused. They remonstrated angrily in Arabic, but there was nothing they could do against a British frigate. They were forced to go back empty-handed when a British sailor heaved up a twelve pound cannon ball in his hand and threatened to let it fall into their boat. A few of those would incapacitate the crew, the boat, or both. Horner remained on his quarterdeck to watch the Salletine admiral's flagship, but satisfied that the xebec was too badly wounded and Tangle too busy dealing with her to get up to any mischief, went below to visit the turncoat lieutenant. Once clear of wreck, the *Sea Leopard's* last anchor was holding.

Thorton was curled up in a miserable ball in the familiar discomfort of his own berth. His wet hair was cold and his drenched clothes were hanging on pegs. He huddled in his blanket in his hammock. Ra'uf had toweled him off, put a nightshirt on him, then gone in search of portable soup.

Horner knocked, and receiving no answer, stuck his head in, "Mister Thorton?" he asked with his usual crispness.

Thorton didn't answer.

Horner let himself into the tiny room and shut the louvered door behind him. He crossed to the hammock and peered into it. Thorton's eyes were open, but he was staring at something invisible.

When Horner appeared in his line of vision, the younger man blinked and looked up. "I'm sorry, sir. I wish I could have been a better officer for you."

"You're a fine officer. I have added my endorsement to your request to depart the Service. I don't think they will deny you again. If they do, I will give you my own discharge and argue it with them."

"Thank you, sir. But I deserted. I didn't want to wait."

"Have you taken a Salletine commission?"

"No, sir. Admiral Tangueli tells me I must wait until we—they—get back to Zokhara. There's an examination now."

Horner nodded. "That's well then. In the general confusion of the afternoon, we can overlook your absence. As far as the log needs know, you went to Baron Chippenham, were caught in the earthquake, and came back on your own."

"I can't serve. I promised Admiral Tangueli I wouldn't go back. I can't bear to disappoint both of you. I'd rather die."

"You've had a shock and you're on medical leave until Ferncastle clears you. You'll feel better after some rest."

"I'll kill myself if you make me stay."

"Peter, suicide is self-murder, and murder is a mortal sin. We worship the same God, so I'm sure that's true for Mohammedans as well as Christians. Don't say such desperate things."

"I'm a sodomite. I'm going to Hell anyhow. I might as well go sooner than later. If it stops me from sinning, 'tis justified. Besides, I'll see Alan there."

Horner stared at the distraught officer. He had never heard such wildness from Thorton before. He knew that the wayward lieutenant, whatever his faults, was earnest in all that he said and did. He was afraid he truly meant it. "I'm sorry about Alan. He was a gallant officer."

"I wish I was dead!"

"That's drastic and unwarranted. You have to give the mail enough time. If you killed yourself, only to be granted an honorable release from the Service, it would be too tragic. You have my word, if they deny you, I will take up your case."

"I won't work. I can't work."

"That is insubordination. However, I will chalk it up to exhaustion. I trust you will feel better tomorrow." He was afraid to leave Thorton alone and remained in the berth until Ra'uf returned. He spoke softly to the little Arab.

"Watch over him. He's saying desperate things and I'm afraid he might do himself harm."

Ra'uf nodded and touched his forelock. "Aye aye, sir. I'll look after him. He'll be all right. You'll see."

CHAPTER 38: SICK LEAVE

Thorton developed pneumonia. Although he had survived drowning, human lungs were not meant to breathe muddy water, and he was soon coughing up bloody phlegm. He was put ashore at Ferncastle's insistence. The doctor prescribed a hot dry climate to dry out his damp lungs. Baron Chippenham received the invalid into his own house; there were few facilities for British subjects in the city and the ambassador felt duty bound to look after a British officer. True to his word, Horner had kept his desertion quiet, but the story of how he had attempted to save Alan Abby's life and nearly lost his own was well known.

Thorton spent part of his days sitting wrapped in red flannel in a sunny spot in the garden. It was not a very large yard and he had to share it with the young ladies of the house. They were in great sympathy with him, and one or two would have fallen in love with the invalid if they had been allowed to nurse him, but Mistress Wadsworth, perceiving the danger, chased them away and told them not to pester the sick man. She attended him herself. Which is to say, she sat in a wicker chair next to his and read edifying material aloud until he fell asleep in his chair, at which point she took up her embroidery. She performed the more genteel aspects of nursing, such as wiping his chin when he coughed and giving him sips of water, but it was the faithful Ra'uf, delivered along with invalid's sea chest, that changed his linens when he threw up in them, bathed his master, and spoon fed him when he was too tired to hold up his head.

One afternoon Mrs. Wadsworth came to him and said, "A Colonel Karolyi is here to call upon you. I sent him away, but he insists that I bring his name to you. He says you will receive him."

Thorton brightened. "I will."

The handsome hussar limped into the courtyard. Three buttons of the skintight trousers were undone along his thigh to make room for the bandage underneath. A bit of the linen showed in the gap. He leaned on a cane for support.

"What happened to you?" Thorton asked in surprise.

Colonel Karolyi's smile was a little strained. He gave a nod to Mrs. Wadsworth and said, "*Señora*, if you please," in Spanish.

She withdrew so that he could speak privately with Thorton. The hussar eased himself into the chair she usually occupied.

223

"A comedy of errors. I lifted a wench's skirt and her angry father came seeking revenge. He pounced upon Antal, who had no idea what he was talking about since he's never lifted a skirt in his life. Antal was affronted and beat the man on the bare buttocks with the flat of his sword and sent him away. Next his son accosted us in the street and tried to assassinate me, thinking I had humiliated his father, but he was cut down by Farkas. The boy's gun went off and shot Török's horse, causing him to stumble, and it was Török's sword that ran me through the thigh when he toppled. So it appears I have paid with my body for what I did to the girl after all. God works in mysterious ways." His tone was amused.

Thorton stared at him, not sure if he believed the story or not.

"What about you, Peter? I hear you are an invalid."

"I am. I nearly drowned. I was trying to save Alan Abby when he went down with the *Antónia*."

"Captain Abby? I heard about that. Did you know him?"

Thorton was wan and sad. "He was my friend and lover before he went off with Duke Henrique."

Karolyi stretched out his wounded leg with a grimace. "I'm sorry to hear that. I've buried a lot of friends. Some of them were even lovers."

"How do you do it? How can you live so openly, loving where you please?"

"Simple. If anyone insults me, I challenge him to a duel. They're afraid of me, so they keep their mouths shut. If they don't, they pay for it in blood."

Thorton looked glum. "I don't want to go around challenging people all the time. It isn't practical. I'm not that good a swordsman."

"Then you need a lover who will challenge them for you."

Thorton remembered Tangle dueling Captain Bishop and Admiral Walters; his heart grew tight. Tangle had been wounded once. "I don't want my lover to risk his life. What if he dies?"

Karolyi shrugged. "We all die sooner or later. Me, I would have rather been shot by the youngster avenging his sister's honor than be run through by accident by one of my own men. It would have been an embarrassing death."

"I think it is better to be a peaceable man. Live and let live, I say."

Karolyi snorted. "Run right at 'em, I say. At them, over them, through them, and never slow down."

"I'm a sailor. That doesn't work with ships."

Karolyi laughed at that. "Ships! Like being in prison, but with a chance of drowning."

"To each his own," Thorton replied. Then he was taken with a fit of coughing.

Mistress Wadsworth bore down on him like a frigate under full sail and made the hussar sheer off. "You've tired yourself, Mister Thorton. You need to go back to bed." Turning to Colonel Karolyi, she said, "I'm sorry, Colonel, but Mister Thorton needs his rest. You, too, sir. You should not have come out until you were well." She clucked at him in passable Spanish.

Karolyi heaved himself up out of the chair and said, "By your leave, *Señora*. Good day, Peter. Come see me when you're better."

"I will, sir."

Mrs. Wadsworth escorted the colonel out. Thorton was sorry to see him go, but he did like watching those tight trousers walk away. His mood brightened—until he coughed again. His illness reasserted itself and Ra'uf appeared to help him back into the house.

Thorton slept the rest of the afternoon. The solarium on the ground floor had been turned into his bedroom so he didn't need to go up and down the stairs to reach the sunny garden. The room had a brick floor, windows to the south and east, and small fireplace in the corner. It was quite warm, and with the door shut, the noise and aromas of the kitchen did not penetrate. He woke in time for dinner and was told by Ra'uf that Admiral Tangueli had stopped by, but had been sent away because he was sleeping. Thorton was glum to have missed the rover's visit.

Ra'uf brown eyes sparkled in his narrow face. "He said he'll come tonight. We are to listen for the Sallee private signal."

Thorton was sitting up in bed with a lap tray for his supper. He had soup and toast for dinner again. He brightened. "When?"

"After the house is asleep."

Thorton's eyes widened. "He's sneaking in?"

Ra'uf grinned at him and ducked his head. He didn't explain any further. "Do you want a bath, rais?" he asked.

"Yes, I do!" After his long nap he felt better. "See if you can fetch me some cheese and fruit from the kitchen. I feel better this evening." Then he coughed, putting the lie to his claim.

Thorton had been laying in bed for a week. He washed himself and Ra'uf trimmed his hair so that he was no longer lopsided. His hair was very short now—easier to care for a sick man that way. A clean nightshirt, and a change of linens, too. The chambermaid grumbled that the linens weren't supposed to be changed until Monday, but Thorton insisted. The windows to the room were opened and aired out, but as the evening deepened, the evening grew chill and he started shivering. Ra'uf shut them without asking. At last there was nothing to do but wait.

Thorton dozed off, but the rattle at the window woke him. He lay there drowsing in the dark and the sound came again. Rat-a-tat-tat, pause, tat.

Ra'uf sat up on the truckle bed. "Rais, 'tis the Sallee private signal."

"Answer it!" Thorton replied, pushing himself up in bed.

Again the rattle on the window pane. Ra'uf crossed the room silently in bare feet, looked out, but saw nothing but the night. He opened the window, stuck his head out and called softly in Arabic, "Ahoy the garden!"

A soft Turkish baritone replied, "Ahoy the house!"

Thorton grinned and said, "Let him in, Ra'uf! Go stand guard in the hallway. Don't let them surprise us."

Tangle climbed in through the window. He was dressed in dark clothes like a second story man. He wore a black fez but no turban, and his short jacket was navy blue and open over a black tunic. He had on black and blue striped pantaloons stuffed into tall black boots. A black sash wrapped several times around his waist. He had even blackened the white streak in his beard so it wouldn't give him away. Only the whites of his eyes and flashing grin showed in the darkness. He crossed swiftly to Thorton's bed, stretched out on it, and kissed him passionately. Thorton kissed him back and hugged him tight, then coughed, breaking the kiss.

"You're too heavy," he wheezed.

Tangle shifted to lie beside him. "Peter? Are you truly sick? I thought they were just saying that to make me leave."

"I've got pneumonia," the invalid replied. "I inhaled water when I tried to rescue Alan, but I failed! He's dead!" Then he started crying. He was sick, he was lonely, and he was grieving. Crying became coughing and he had to roll over to spit blood into the chamber pot. Tangle held his shoulders as he hacked and shuddered. When the fit was over, Thorton slumped against him and tried to breathe. The corsair's shoulders were broad and strong, and the swarthy hand that stroked his arm was gentle. Soft lips pressed an equally soft kiss against his hair.

"I was going to carry you off tonight, Peter, but I don't think I should. I thought they were trying to keep us apart, but you're not well. Are they taking good care of you?"

"Aye, they are. I sit in the garden half an hour every day, and Mistress Wadsworth makes certain people don't pester me. They made this room into a bedroom so I don't have to go up and down stairs. Doctor Ferncastle and Captain Horner come to see me. Sometimes I get other visitors. Colonel Karolyi came today."

"Who's Karolyi?"

Thorton told him the story and Tangle laughed at the swimming duel. "Damn it, Horner's sly! I'm glad I'm not the only one to be outfoxed by him. Still, I begrudge him carrying you off when you'd tendered your resignation."

"That was Roger being zealous again. He saw his chance and hauled me back. However, Horner has added his endorsement to my resignation, so I am hoping they will let me go this time."

Tangle's jaw set. Thorton could feel his body tense. "I'm tired," Thorton whispered. He didn't want to argue with the corsair about his English friends.

Tangle murmured, "You're getting cold, too. You need your rest."

The sick lieutenant lay down and Tangle tucked him in. Then he took off his hat, jacket, and boots, and laid his dagger in easy reach on the nightstand. He slipped under the covers next to Thorton and wrapped his arms around him. The corsair was a veritable furnace next to the shivering lieutenant. Thorton nestled gratefully against him and soaked up the heat. He dozed off.

Tangle was unwilling to disturb the sleeping man. He lay quietly until he himself fell asleep. He had been busy all week. He had had the *Sea Leopard* towed into the shipyard to be repaired, which meant arguing with the Portuguese about who would pay for the damage. That had to wait for the court martial over the sinking of the *Antónia*. There was Abby's funeral to attend, the slipped anchors to salvage, plus all the official duties of an admiral and envoy, which were numerous and complex, thanks to the Portuguese captives and debt. Not to mention, foreign dignitaries to meet and greet to discover which ones would be of use to him. Politics, the most wearying profession of them all.

Faithful Ra'uf stood guard the whole time, but when he wasn't called, he curled up in front of the door and made a pillow of his arms. It wasn't until he got very cold on the bricks about five in the morning that he woke stiff and sore. The scullery maid came down the stairs to light the kitchen fire. Ra'uf let himself into the solarium and was appalled to see Tangle asleep in bed even as the fingers of dawn were starting to poke through the windows.

Tangle snapped awake when Ra'uf shook his shoulder and spoke urgently to him. He slid out of bed and swiftly pulled on his boots. While he was dressing, the back door to the garden rattled and the dogs barked in their kennel as the servant went out to feed them. They were let out to romp in the garden while the man came back inside with an armload of wood.

Tangle swore softly in Turkish. "Why didn't you wake me?"

"I did wake you, sir. Why didn't you tell me what hour you wanted to be roused?" Ra'uf replied.

"I didn't mean to sleep! How am I going to get out of here?"

"How did you get in?"

"A rope over the wall. I brought it with me."

Footsteps sounded overhead as some of the other occupants of the house woke and began moving around. The cook came downstairs and pans clattered in the kitchen.

Thorton yawned and rolled over. He blinked into the room. "Ra'uf?" he asked.

"Good morning, Peter," Tangle replied.

Thorton smiled up at him, then froze as he heard the door bang as the manservant went out for another load of wood. "What time is it?"

"Morning. We all fell asleep," Ra'uf replied.

"I'm going to use the chamber pot as long as I'm here. Whatever I have to do will be easier with an empty bladder." Tangle suited words to action.

Someone rapped on the door. Tangle tried to button his fly while he dove under the bed. It was dusty under there and he held his nose to keep from sneezing. Thorton looked desperately around the room, "Tell them I'm sleeping!" He pulled the covers over his head.

Ra'uf went to the door and cracked it. "Mister Thorton is still sleeping," he told the chambermaid.

"I'm here for the chamber pot," the maid said.

"Come back later." He shut the door. She shrugged and went away.

Ra'uf made up the truckle bed and rolled it under Thorton's bed. Tangle stayed under the bed, a little squeezed now that the truckle was put away. A little while later the maid returned with a tray of breakfast for Thorton. Ra'uf took it and shut the door on her again.

"Lock the door, Ra'uf," Thorton said.

The little Arab did. He put the tray on Thorton's lap. The smell of porridge and tea wafted through the air, but Thorton wasn't hungry. Tangle crawled out from under the bed with a mighty sneeze. He beat the dust off himself, but his stomach rumbled in discontent. He was not the sort of cad who would ask a sick man to share his breakfast though.

It was Ra'uf who noticed. "I'll tell them you're hungry this morning, Peter."

He slipped out and Tangle shut and locked the door behind him. When the Arab knocked the Sallee private signal, the admiral let him in. Once again the door was locked. This time Ra'uf had a tray with one poached egg in an eggcup and a single piece of toast. It was accompanied by a glass of milk. "They won't let him have anything more unless the doctor orders it," he said apologetically.

"I'll take it." Tangle sat on the edge of Thorton's bed and ate the egg like a famished man. Thorton pushed his porridge over to him. He had only eaten half of it. "You need to eat," Tangle objected.

"I'm not hungry. Besides, I'll ask for a piece of fruit later. They'll think my appetite is improving and give it to me."

Tangle took the leftover porridge and ate it. He scraped the sides with the toast, too. "How do I get out?

"After they put the dogs in the kennel I'll let you out the back gate," Ra'uf replied. "I'll be back shortly."

The little Arab went and joined the servants for breakfast in the kitchen; when he returned he had a pair of oranges in his pockets. He gave one to Tangle and kept the other for himself. Meanwhile the manservant went out to put the dogs back in their kennel. The scullery maids started cleaning up the kitchen and the ladies' maids went upstairs. Ra'uf slipped out to reconnoiter. Returning, he gave Tangle the nod.

The admiral went out the window, stayed close to the house, then started nonchalantly across the yard. The dogs started barking when they saw him. He immediately pressed himself back against the wall of the house. The dogs could still see him and kept barking. Ra'uf ran over to the kennel and let himself in. He started petting and wrestling with the dogs. Tangle slid along the house to the wall on the south side. He uncoiled the rope from beneath his sash, tied a bowline in it, and expertly threw it over a spike. The loop settled around the haft below the blade, so he shinnied up the rope and carefully maneuvered his lanky body over the points. The dogs barked wildly when they saw him. Baron Chippenham stepped out onto the gallery, took a look at Ra'uf roughhousing with the dogs, and called, "Leave the dogs be!"

Ra'uf looked back, saw Tangle on top of the wall, and put his hand to his ear and looked a question at the baron. The baron shouted louder, "Leave the dogs alone!"

Tangle had frozen when the baron came out, but the level of the wall was about three feet lower than the floor of the gallery. If Chippenham didn't walk his way, he was hidden below the gallery. However, he was also exposed to anyone that happened to walk along the street. Deciding to take his chances, he dropped with a thud to the pavement, picked himself up, and limped off, taking care to walk where the house itself would screen him from the baron.

Seeing the corsair make his escape but leave his rope, Ra'uf stopped playing with the dogs and let himself out of the kennel. "Sorry, sir," he called back to the baron. With Tangle and their playmate gone, the dogs quieted.

Ra'uf walked toward the house and Chippenham went back inside. As soon as the wily Arab was under the gallery, he darted to the wall and tried to fetch Tangle's rope down, but he was too short. He solved the problem by shinnying up, hanging onto the haft of a spear point below its blade, loosing the rope, and dropping down again. He crawled in Thorton's open window and hid it under the bed.

Just then Mrs. Wadsworth walked in. "Why is this window open? 'Twill chill the patient," she chided Ra'uf.

"I want it open," Thorton interjected.

"Shush. You don't know what's good for you," she replied.

Ra'uf rose from where he was and said, "Sorry, ma'am." He hurried to shut the window.

"What were you doing under the bed?" she asked him.

"Inspecting. The maid hasn't swept under the bed at all."

"What?"

Lifting the bed skirt well away from where he'd hidden the rope, he reached under and scooped out a handful of dust bunnies. "See?"

"These Portuguese girls are no good. I catch them sweeping dirt under the rug all the time! I'll see to it." She flounced out.

Ra'uf retrieved the rope and hid it under the mattress of his truckle bed while she was gone. He made the bed up neatly and shoved it under the master bed so that she would have no call to investigate further. He plopped onto the side of Thorton's bed and wiped his brow. "That was a near thing."

Thorton smiled at him. "So it was. But I was glad of his visit. I have missed him."

Ra'uf said, "I'll be glad when we can go home, sir." He took it for granted that the Sallee Republic was 'home' for Thorton, too.

The renegade settled down in his sheets and closed his eyes. Memories of the Sallee Republic and a certain rover filled his mind. "Me too."

CHAPTER 39: THE LIEUTENANT'S DEATHBED

Thorton continued to decline. He coughed more and more. He was always cold and shook with chills. They put hot bricks at his feet and under his hands, they gave him spicy cider so hot it scalded his tongue, and they rubbed invigorating oils along his spine and on his chest, but he didn't rally. The Portuguese doctor could do nothing but advise prayer and repentance. Emily Wadsworth dipped a cloth in a basin of tepid water and wiped the sick man's face. She was his usual nurse.

The house was very grim. Sometimes Captain Horner and Doctor Ferncastle came, but they drew no comfort from their visits. Thorton was slowly turning blue. As for the invalid, he felt he was drowning all over again. His lungs filled with fluid so that he could scarcely breathe. His breath came in shallow, painful pants, and he was stabbed with excruciating pain whenever he was taken with a coughing fit.

On one particular afternoon he had a caller. The housekeeper came and spoke softly to the mistress of the sickroom, "Admiral Tangueli is here to call on Lieutenant Thorton."

Mistress Wadsworth was sitting at an embroidery frame working a chain of daisies along the edge of a pillow case. She shook her head firmly. "Send him away. Mister Thorton is too ill for curiosity-seekers."

Thorton's eyes opened when he heard the name and he croaked a protest as the housekeeper went out.

"Ra'uf, go fetch him! I want to see him!" He started coughing. Ra'uf hesitated, but Mrs. Wadsworth was bearing down on the invalid. Ra'uf ran upstairs and overtook the housekeeper.

Thorton coughed up blood again, and Mrs. Wadsworth wiped his face again. "Lie down, Mister Thorton. If you excite yourself, you'll make yourself worse."

"I want to see my friend!" he rasped out and coughed again.

She held the cloth to his face, then folded it over the blood and wiped his mouth. Her mouth set in a disapproving line. "That one is no friend to you. You must trust in God, Mister Thorton. I will pray with you."

She got down on her knees and folded her hands on the edge of his bed. "The Lord is my shepherd; I shall not want. He maketh me to lie down in green pastures: he leadeth me beside the still waters. He restoreth my soul: he leadeth me in the paths of righteousness for his name's sake."

The most famous prayer in Christendom gave him no comfort. "I testify there is no god worthy of worship but Allah and Mohammed is his prophet." He gasped out the testament amid a flurry of coughs.

"Mister Thorton, give up your apostasy and save your immortal soul! You are on the verge of death; make peace with your Creator. You may not save your body, but you still can save your soul!"

He could hardly speak. "God knows what I do. How can I be apostate when I still believe in God?"

"Do you accept the Lord Jesus as your Savior?"

"No," he answered in a broken voice. "Jesus was mortal like you and I. He was the messenger, not the message." He pressed the bloody cloth to his mouth to stifle more coughing.

"Mister Thorton, confess your error and repent! You will be cradled in the bosom of your friends."

"You're not my friend. A friend would not torment me on my deathbed."

His words struck her with horror, but before she could form a response, Admiral Tangueli strode into the room. Mrs. Alder, the housekeeper, was dancing around him and remonstrating. "You can't go in there!"

"Isam!" Thorton rasped in delight.

Tangle threw himself on his knees beside Thorton's bed, clasped his hand, and kissed it. "Peter! By Allah, you look terrible!"

The petite Mistress Wadsworth got to her feet in order to loom over the kneeling corsair. "You cannot barge in here!" she remonstrated.

"I didn't barge in. Mister Thorton invited me."

"You have to go!"

"Why? So he will die shut up and alone? I will not abandon him. Sit down, woman!" he snarled at her.

The Turk's fury frightened her. The bright morning lit up his face so that the hard brown eyes glittered and she could see the wicked scar that ran down the right side of his face in spite of the black beard that covered it. The gold epaulettes and purple coat loaded with ladders of gold lace were a horrid sight to her. She wrung her hands and turned to the housekeeper, "Send a message to my father. He's meeting with Duke Henrique right now. Tell him what has happened here!"

Mrs. Alder hastened from the room and called for a manservant.

Thorton held Tangle's hand with a weak grip. He begged, "Pray for me. I'm too sick."

Tangle settled his weight on his heels, closed his eyes, and opened up his throat. The sonorous baritone rang through the house with the majestic syllables of the Arabic call to prayer. It pierced the walls, it pierced the bones, it pierced the soul. Everyone in the house heard it and no one who heard it would forget it. Tangle's grief rolled through the undulating syllables. Ra'uf came and knelt beside his master's bed, and when Tangle began the congregational prayer, he answered him in a clear and solemn tenor. Thorton was so weak he couldn't pray. He sighed and settled on the mattress, closed his eyes, and let the sound wash over him.

Tangle continued to hold onto his hand with both of his. He did not perform the required bows and prostrations; Allah knew what was in his heart. Tangle's voice filled the room like a palpable thing, and Mrs. Wadsworth retreated from it, found her chair at the embroidery stand, and fell into it, but she could not tear her eyes from the sight of the Salletine admiral praying. His faith was alien to her, but she could not deny it was faith; the power of his belief was unmistakeable. Although it horrified her, it soothed Thorton, and he fell into a sleep or swoon.

Tangle prayed the entire prayer to the end. There was no sign of consciousness in the sick lieutenant, no rise and fall of the chest, no rattle in the watery lungs. He pressed his hand against Thorton's chest and felt nothing, although the chest was still warm.

"Is he dead?" Mrs. Wadsworth whispered. She pressed her hands to her face.

Tangle put his fingers against Thorton's throat. He had to try several times before he found a pulse. "He's still alive, but he won't be for long."

She wept into her hands then. Her sisters ran to her and knelt and embraced her waist and cried aloud. The maids and menservants milled about the door and the Baroness Chippenham eased her petite plumpness into the other chair. "We must send word to his captain," she said.

Messengers went hither and yon. Over the course of the afternoon Horner, Ferncastle, Forsythe, and Perry showed up in a body. Colonel Karolyi limped in and squeezed himself into a corner. Soto showed up wearing a green Portuguese coat and slunk around the back of the crowd. Baron Chippenham arrived home, and with him, Admiral Duke Henrique do Coimbra.

When the baron saw the admiral's purple coat and turban, he barreled forward. "What's the meaning of this? You're not welcome here! Leave this instant." He turned on his servants. "Who let him in?" he roared.

Tangle rose from his spot by Thorton's bedside and loomed over the baron. He was so angry that what came out of his mouth was Turkish, which was just as well, because the baron understood that the admiral was angry without being able to take offense at his choice of words.

"Do not take that tone with me, sirrah!" Chippenham shouted.

Henrique's cane thudded down on the bricks, "Baron Chippenham!" he roared. "How dare you address the Salletine envoy and my good friend that way! How dare you keep my friend, Mister Thorton, the savior of Portugal, in a cellar!" He had to switch to Spanish because his scant supply of English failed him. He was able to barrel along full speed in the more familiar language. "If it weren't for Mister Thorton and Mister Shakil, I'd still be a prisoner of the Spanish, and Portugal would be groaning under the heel of the Spanish tyrant! How dare you address our ally, Admiral Tangueli, in such a tone! How dare you show so little regard for Mister Thorton! This is an insult for which there is no excuse!" That was just the beginning of his rant.

Chippenham paled before the wrath of the intended son-in-law of the King of Portugal. When Henrique paused to draw breath, he swiftly interjected, "Doctor's orders! He was kept in the solarium because it was warm and convenient to the garden!"

Henrique looked around the sunny room. It was quite warm (especially with so many people in it), but the walls were whitewashed brick and nothing more. The iron bedstead was piled with red flannel sheets, wool blankets and a coverlet, but the furnishings of the room were minimal: a washstand, a pair of chairs, a lamp, the embroidery hoop. The smell of bread baking was wafting in from the kitchen, also located on the ground floor.

"It looks like a cell!" Henrique burst out.

Tangle had recovered his temper and put in his oar. "Baron Chippenham has refused to respond to my notes, and his staff have tried to prevent me from seeing Mister Thorton. I was able to sneak over the wall once without his knowledge, but if Mister Thorton hadn't called me in today, I'd still be standing on the doorstep, begging to see my dying friend."

Chippenham was quite startled and offended to learn Tangle had come over his wall, but before he could say anything, Thorton groaned. Everyone turned to the dying lieutenant. Tangle threw himself on his knees beside the bed as Thorton's eyes flickered open.

Startled to see so many people in the room, the sick man asked, "Who are all these people?"

Horner advanced to the side of the bed and knelt. He clasped his hands in an attitude of prayer and rested them on the edge of the bed. Forsythe, Perry, and Ferncastle knelt around the bed and did the same. Horner spoke gently. "Your friends have come to bid you good bye, Peter."

Thorton was confused. "What? Why?"

Ra'uf was a little man, but he pushed his way to the foot of the bed. "You saved my life, Peter Rais. You saved Isam Rais' life too. You saved all of us in the galley that day. You didn't have to do it. You risked your own life even though we were strangers to you. You're dying now because you risked your life to try and save Captain Abby. We love and admire you, sir."

Tangle spoke up. "You saved me and I loved you for it, Peter. Not just me, and not just one galley. Nearly eight hundred men lived and went home to their families because of you. You nursed me with your own hands and you treated everyone one of us like he was a human being. It didn't matter to you what color or religion we were. Of course we love you."

Henrique pushed forward. "You and Shakil bin Nakih rescued me from the Spanish, and that started the Portuguese Revolt which has lead to the independence of our country. All of Portugal is beholden to you, Mister Thorton."

Horner spoke up. "You rescued me from the bottom of a bottle of brandy and saved the *Resolute* from mutiny with the help of Mister Perry."

Forsythe continued the story. "It was your warning that woke Mahon. We had time to get the *Ajax* off the stocks, thanks to you."

Perry spoke with great emotion. "I owe you my personal thanks. I got the dispatch last night. They have restored my seniority and given me a command. After your funeral—" his voice broke. "I go home to England to take command of the *Otter.* She's an advice boat on the Gibraltar run. Horner tells me it was your doing."

"Mine?"

Horner spoke up. "Marcus Wolfe sent me a letter before he died. He told me you asked for his help in restoring Roger's seniority. They shot Wolfe on the deck of the *Resolute,* but they granted his last request."

Thorton looked at him in wonder. "He's dead?"

Horner nodded. "Aye. The newspapers came along with the dispatches."

"Is there a letter for me?"

"No. Not yet."

Thorton started coughing. Tangle slipped an arm under his shoulders and supported him as he leaned over the side of the bed and spit up blood. Ra'uf came over with a cloth and wiped up. Thorton's breath was harsh and his color worse. "I feel like I'm drowning," he whispered.

Mrs. Wadsworth bowed her head and wrapped her arms around her younger sisters as the girls cried again. The young ladies had never seen a dying man before, and the horror of watching him slowly drowning in his own lungs was something they couldn't bear.

Tangle held him cradled against his own breast and stroked the short blond hair as he remembered the long blond strands he had loved to run his hands through.

Thorton's breath rattled in his chest. "I love you, *habibi,*" he whispered in Arabic. He was sorry to die, but was glad if he must die, he was in the corsair's arms. "You were always a friend to me."

He closed his eyes and sank down. His strength was gone. He was limp in Tangle's arms. The rover held him in his arms and tried to blink back the tears that threatened to spill over. His arm was getting tired, but he wouldn't lay him down. The lieutenant had been a strong and healthy young man before the injury to his lungs; it would take him a long time to die. Ferncastle got off his knees and came around the bed.

"May I?" he asked softly.

Tangle nodded. He eased the lieutenant onto the mattress. Thorton didn't stir. Ferncastle put his ear to Thorton's chest, held his cheek to the slack mouth, and felt for his pulse in his wrist and then his neck. "Very weak. He won't last the night."

There was nothing to do but wait. Mrs. Wadsworth rose and lead her sisters out. "Go supervise the food," she told them.

The servants had started baking once it was understood Thorton was in his death throes; they would need to furnish a funeral feast. The sweet smell of cinnamon and yeast wafted through the house. Teacakes and tea were put out in the salon on the first floor and the visitors trooped upstairs to devour them. Everyone was subdued. Karoyli, Soto, Forsythe, Perry, and Horner trooped past the foot of the bed to take one last look at the dying man, then they too went upstairs. At last no one was left but Tangle and Ra'uf.

Tangle stared at the supine man, then he got up and began to pace. He yearned to do something, anything, but there was nothing. All he could do was wait for nature to take its course. His movements were wooden and his eyes stared blankly. Ra'uf was very tired and he knew that he would have to attend the deathbed through the night, so he pulled out the truckle bed from beneath the big bed, curled up on it, and slept. He had a sailor's ability to sleep any time he had the chance. Tangle smiled wanly at him. He was an admiral and an envoy. He had much business to take to attend, but he ignored it. His best friend was dying.

CHAPTER 40: THE SALLETINE DOCTORS

The afternoon wore into evening. Thorton did not regain consciousness. His color worsened, but a faint pulse could still be found in his throat. Henrique stayed and so did the officers from the *Amphitrite*, but everyone else left at last. Baron Chippenham invited those who remained to dine with him, even Tangle, but the rover would not come up. He sat on the side of the bed and stared at Thorton's face and willed him to get better. When he got tired of that, he paced. After dinner Ferncastle came down to check on the patient again.

"What do they do for pneumonia in Sallee?" he asked the corsair.

"Keep him warm. I don't know what else. I'm not a doctor."

Ferncastle sighed. "I wish I could study at the Charity Hospital in Zokhara. Such a marvelous facility! I am forced to admit, it is better than the hospitals we have in England."

"I sent to Zahid Amir as soon as I knew Thorton was ill and begged him for help, but it takes time to go between here and there. I'm hoping he will send some medicine, or some advice. Anything. I thought about kidnapping Peter and taking him home to Zokhara, but I was afraid the voyage would kill him."

Ferncastle shook his head, "That would have been unwise. We've done what we can for him. 'Tis in God's hands now."

"I know you've been here. I've had my men watching the house and getting what news they can. I knew you wouldn't let the Portuguese doctor do him any harm."

"I think that's a compliment, but 'tis a little difficult to tell," Ferncastle said ruefully.

Tangle gave him a sheepish look. "So it is. Let me be more gracious. If you come to Zokhara to study, please accept my hospitality. You may stay with my family as long as you need."

"That is a generous offer," said Ferncastle. He knew very well how helpful the patronage and financial support of a Salletine officer like Tangle would be. "I will be happy to accept if I get the opportunity."

The bell rang. Ferncastle said, "More well-wishers, no doubt. I shall go up and give my report."

The commotion on the first floor grew loud and descended the steps to the ground floor. Tangle was getting up to rebuke the invaders when a tall, trim, erect Salletine man with a white turban and purple coat walked into the room.

"Zahid Amir!" Tangle exclaimed in joy. He crossed immediately to kiss the man on each cheek and received the same in return.

"Isam Rais," the doctor replied warmly.

The Moorish doctor was followed by a small woman dressed all in white. Her white hair was covered by a veil and she wore a loose fitting, broad-sleeved cloak over her pantaloons and shirt. A dark-skinned blackamoor, also dressed in white, followed her. He had a brown leather case in either hand but set them down when the party came to a halt.

Zahid smiled and said. "I have brought help. Allow me to introduce Doctor Afrah Umm Mutee, the celebrated pulmonologist."

The rest of the English were gathered around the door to peep in. They had no idea what a 'pulmonologist' was; he had used the Arabic word. "A lung doctor," he explained to the eavesdroppers.

"This is Isam Kapitan Pasha," he introduced Tangle to her.

Tangle put his hand on his forehead and bowed very deeply. "If you can help my friend, I will be grateful to you, doctor."

She returned his bow. "If Allah wills it," she replied in a grave voice. She advanced to the bed and addressed Zahid in Arabic. He took Thorton's pulse and reported it to her. She spoke to the black, who opened one of the cases and brought a small brass trumpet to her. She put the bell against Thorton's chest, and leaning carefully so that her robes did not brush him, put her ear to the end and listened to his chest. She moved the bell to several locations, then rose up. "Turn him over."

Tangle and Ra'uf pulled down the covers and rolled Thorton onto his stomach. The sick man gave a low groan, but didn't rouse. She listened to his back.

"What's she doing?" Mrs. Wadsworth asked Captain Horner softly. She was holding to his arm as they stood in a corner of the room. The curious English had trickled into the room behind the doctor.

Zahid explained, "Listening to the heart and lungs. 'Tis an ordinary ear trumpet. Just as it magnifies the sound of speech, so it magnifies the sounds of the body."

"Oh," she said, her blue eyes growing large.

Chippenham asked, "What does that signify? Why a woman?"

"Because she's the best pulmonologist in all of Barbary," Zahid replied in his crisp Cambridge accent.

"A female doctor!" the baron exclaimed incredulously.

"Of course. It would be improper for a male doctor to treat female patients," Zahid replied patiently.

"Sh!" she said. She didn't speak English, but she didn't like the noise. She spoke rapid Arabic to Zahid who nodded and translated.

"We need a barrel and two strong men. Admiral, you'll do. And you." He pointed at Forsythe because he was young and sturdy-looking. "We need the barrel first. We are going to pump Mister Thorton's lungs manually. If that doesn't clear them, we will operate. 'Tis a dangerous operation, but he is sick enough that if pumping doesn't clear his lungs, surgery is warranted. He's dying. Surgery might save him." He clapped his hands together. "A barrel, if you please!"

People jumped. A flour barrel was emptied out, the lid nailed back on, then rolled into the room.

"Chocks, please," Zahid said. The manservant went and found pieces of firewood and the barrel was chocked. He pointed at Forsythe again. "Your job is to make certain the barrel doesn't move."

Then the orderly and Tangle carried Thorton to the barrel. The patient roused enough to mumble a complaint, but they ignored it. They put him on his stomach over the barrel. His head hung down. He immediately started coughing and blood and phlegm splattered from his mouth. Ra'uf darted forward with a cloth to wipe his face and mop the floor. Zahid continued giving instructions in English and Arabic. It was Tangle's job to hold Thorton's ankles to make certain he didn't roll off the barrel. The orderly stepped up.

The orderly was not a tall man, but he was powerfully built. His head was shaved and he wore a simple white turban, a short white jacket and pantaloons, and sandals on his feet. He was at least forty and well accustomed to assisting the doctors. He was stronger than Zahid and more experienced in pulmonary pumping. Doctor Afrah knelt down so she could watch the patient's face. Zahid knelt across from her so he could be her hands and do whatever she directed. When she gave the order, the orderly put his hands on Thorton's back and compressed Thorton's chest against the barrel, but at the same time gave it a downward thrust.

Thorton coughed and hacked violently. He was awake but incapable of communicating except to kick and flail. Tangle held his ankles tight. Forsythe put his hands on the barrel to hold it steady. The orderly pumped Thorton's back in swift repeated motions. Thorton threw up as well as spitting up and coughing up. He braced his hands against the brick floor and kept spitting and drooling and coughing and vomiting. Ra'uf darted in with the cloth to wipe his face and Zahid held his head up so he was puking on the floor instead of up his nose.

Doctor Afrah gave a command and the orderly stopped. She examined the quantity of bodily fluids that Thorton had expelled, rose, then listened to his back with the ear trumpet. Thorton continued coughing and mewling. She resumed her kneeling position, the orderly moved into position, and at her command, pumped his back again.

Thorton moaned and hacked up more bodily fluids, but he didn't puke again, even if he did retch. He was in agony, but too weak to do anything but suffer it. Zahid kept his head up to keep him from aspirating the mess up into his sinuses.

The doctor repeated her examination. Thorton was left hanging over the barrel while Zahid translated.

"Do you have any bolster pillows about this thick?" He mimed a size with his hands.

The Baroness said, "We don't have any bolsters at all."

"I'll take a stack of pillows then. Mister Thorton must be propped in a position that will allow gravity to drain his lungs instead of keeping the fluid trapped inside."

Mrs. Wadsworth and her sisters went to find all the pillows in the house. When they returned, the orderly took them and stacked them very precisely on the bed. Only then did the orderly and Doctor Zahid lift him up and put him face down on the bed with his middle supported by the pillows. It was an undignified position with his butt in the air, and drafty too, until Tangle pulled the bedclothes up over him.

Doctor Afrah listened to him again once he was settled in the new position, nodded, and discussed his case in Arabic. Thorton was to ill to understand. Tangle understood only half of it; the medical terminology was beyond him.

Thorton sucked in a great breath, "I can breathe!"

Zahid broke off his conversation with Afrah to step over and smile at him. "Your color is improving. So far manual pumping is working. As long as it does, you will be able to breathe and will eventually recover."

"I'm going to live?"

"God willing. The immediate danger is averted. However, the fluid will continue to flow, so you must stay like this to drain it."

"How long?"

"Several days at least."

Thorton gave a groan at that, then started coughing again. "Ow," he whispered. He hugged his chest to try and keep it from moving. The pumping had squashed him hard and his chest was bruised and sore.

Tangle gave his butt a light swat. "I always liked you this way," he said jovially.

Thorton wanted to be angry, but only had enough energy for petulance. "You're wicked to abuse a sick man." Even that small exertion set off another fit of coughing.

"Don't molest the patient, Admiral. He needs his rest," Zahid rebuked him in Arabic.

Tangle was contrite. "I'm sorry. I'm just glad to see him better."

Thorton privately thought that if the current situation was 'better,' he must have been bad indeed.

Ra'uf wiped Thorton's face and put a towel under it to protect the bedclothes. Mrs. Wadsworth dispatched a maid to fetch more towels.

Doctor Afrah made shooing motions with her hand and spoke to them in Arabic. They all left the room except for the medical staff, Tangle, and Ra'uf. Tangle collapsed into Mistress Wadsworth's chair. He was very tired now that the crisis was over. "I'm glad you came," he told Zahid.

"I was seasick all the way. The weather was rough, but we made good time." Zahid broke off as Doctor Afrah spoke again. He listened, then said, "I need to make arrangements for us. We came straight from the ship. We'll return later to check on the patient, but Belial will remain. He'll pump Thorton's lungs again if it is needed." With that he and Doctor Afrah departed.

Tangle removed his turban, baldric, sword, coat, and boots, and crawled into bed next to Thorton. "Make certain no one but the doctors come in," he told Ra'uf. He snuggled up as close to Thorton as he could get. "If anyone asks, I'm trying to warm him up."

Thorton was tired of his position. It hurt his chest even if it did drain his lungs. He was cold, too, and the corsair's body was warm. He eased off the pillows and pressed his back against the corsair's front. Tangle's arm went around his waist.

The orderly protested. "Sir! You must remain where the doctors put you!"

"I need a rest. My chest hurts. I'll go back in a little bit."

"Your lungs will fill again!"

"Just a few minutes," Thorton said. Then he started coughing. When the fit subsided, Tangle prodded his back. The sick man grumbled, but crawled on top of the stack pillows again. "Ow. It really does hurt," he complained.

"It won't hurt when you're dead!" the orderly replied in exasperation.

Tangle winced and stroked Thorton's back gently. Thorton had felt quite a bit better once he could breathe, but the sense of wellbeing was fading. He was tired and sore. He inhaled cautiously and coughed up more blood. He moved the towel so that he could lay his face in a dry spot. His survival was not at all certain.

CHAPTER 41: GOING HOME

A fortnight later the three doctors, Ferncastle, Zahid, and Afrah, arrived in Thorton's bed chamber. Once again the invalid was thrown over the barrel and pumped, but with little result.

"There's nothing in me, I swear it!" This time the invalid was strong enough to push up with his hands and give the trio of physicians a hot glare.

The doctors conferred, then Zahid said, "You may sit up for half an hour this morning and have some soft food. If all goes well, we will leave off the pumping and let you eat. You're on the mend, but we must not be hastily and precipitate a relapse."

Thorton was very pleased to be allowed to sit propped up with the pillows behind him. His room was no longer a Spartan domicile. Since the *Sea Leopard* had gone into the royal shipyard for repairs and Henrique had set the baron straight about the courtesies he expected his friends to receive, Tangle had pulled a great many things out of his own cabin and sent them to the invalid. Thorton now had an African rug on the floor and a kilim made of tan and cream on his bed. A Moorish lamp of bronze and yellow glass hung nearby. Cushions from the admiral's divan in purple, tan, and cream equipped his bed. The inhabitants of the house were glad to have their pillows back, although Mrs. Wadsworth and her sisters had made a bolster exactly calculated to meet the invalid's needs. A small Moorish table had appeared and supported a bowl of fruit and pitcher of mint water. A whole row of chairs was lined up along one wall for the comfort of his numerous visitors. At any given time they might be filled with half a dozen Portuguese doctors who wanted to see the famous female physician at work, various aristocrats who were curious about the whole business, and gentlemen of the city who had no interest in Thorton but wanted to importune the famous doctors about their own ailments. For the latter Doctor Afrah generally prescribed emetics and purges. That kept them home for several days, although one particular case sent his servants to pester the doctor with an exact account of the nature and frequency of his stools. She prescribed a water fast for him.

On this particular morning, when Thorton was happy to sit up and listen to the birds singing outside his window, he received Captain Horner.

"I have brought you a letter from the Admiralty, Mister Thorton." The corners of the captain's eyes crinkled in pleasure, although no other change in his expression betrayed his feeling. Never a clever man when it came to perceiving the feelings of others, illness had not improved Thorton's perspicacity. The sick man received the letter with trepidation.

He stared at the envelope a while, then broke the Admiralty seal with trembling hands. He dropped it, picked it up, and extracted the letter. A glad cry started from him and Horner allowed himself to smile. The older man sat on the edge of the bed. "They have accepted your resignation at last. You're a free man."

Thorton fell back against his pillows and for a moment Horner thought he had fainted. His complexion was sallow and he had lost a great deal of weight. Horner laid a hand on his brow and found him feverish but conscious.

Thorton picked up his letter and read it again. It was short and to the point; they had received his letter of resignation and approved it. That was all. "You knew?"

"Naturally they referred to the matter in their dispatch to me. I have lost you and Perry both. The new lieutenants arrived with the dispatches."

"What sort of men are they?"

"I shall find out. I already know they have will have a hard time filling your shoes. I have grown fond of you, Peter." The last was spoken a bit gruffly.

Thorton turned pink and ducked his head. "Thank you, sir. I'm fond of you, too."

Horner continued on briskly. "I also have instructions. Since you are no longer in the Service as of your receipt of this letter, you are no longer my responsibility and your care cannot be charged to the ship." He raised a hand to forestall Thorton's response. "Admiral Tangueli has been covering your medical expenses since the Salletine doctors arrived. However, Doctor Ferncastle, I must withdraw you to the ship. Mister Thorton is no longer our responsibility. He is on the mend and will do fine without us."

Ferncastle came forward. "But I have learned so much by attending these great physicians! I beg you for leave to continue attending Mister Thorton and further my education. Everything I learn here makes me a better doctor and an asset to the Service."

"After Henrique's wedding we return to England. I give you leave until then. Please attend the ship at least twice a week, or oftener if the men require it."

"Thank you, sir! I will!"

Doctor Zahid was also Lord Zahid, Marine Minister of the Sallee Republic. Upon hearing the news he stepped forward and asked,

"Mister Thorton, do you wish to take the examination for a Salletine commission?"

"Aye, sir. I do!" Thorton perked up immediately.

"Not now. When you are well," the doctor said in a soothing voice.

Thorton was all smiles, but he was also tired. He lay back on the pillows. "How long?"

"If you continue as you have, I expect you will be over the pneumonia within the fortnight. It will take longer to regain your strength."

"I am grateful to you, sir." Then he spoke Arabic and addressed Doctor Afrah, "Thank you for saving my life. If I can ever do anything for you, please let me know."

She smiled and came to the bedside. "All success belongs to Allah. It is He who gives a cure for every disease."

"Thank you from the bottom of my heart."

"It has been a pleasure to attend you, Peter Rais. God willing, you will recover fully."

The Salletine doctors collected their things and left, then Horner gave the invalid's hand a squeeze. "Good bye, Peter. I wish you well." He gave Thorton a swift peck on the cheek and rose.

Thorton kept hold of his hand. "Good bye! Will I see you again?"

"Only God knows. You have departed the Service, but I must continue my duty."

Thorton wouldn't let go of him. "Farewell, sir." It was a prayer.

"And you, my friend." He gave Thorton's hand a last squeeze and pulled lose.

"Write to me!" the invalid begged.

Horner paused at the door and smiled. "I will. You must write also."

"I will!"

Horner gave him a salute and smile, then vanished through the door.

Ferncastle sat on the side of the bed and patted the younger man's hand. He gave him a reassuring look. "I'm glad for you, Peter. I know how unhappy you were, for all you did your duty."

"Thank you, sir."

"Call me Joshua. We're friends now, aren't we?"

Thorton gave him an uncertain smile. "Are we?"

"Do you have any doubt about it?" Ferncastle's plain and ordinary face was smiling warmly.

Thorton wavered. "Well, there are some matters . . ."

"Tell me."

Thorton didn't know how to broach it. He hugged his knees and knit his brow. Finally he said, "I am very fond of Admiral Tangueli."

"He is fond of you, too. More than fond. He loves you, Peter."

Thorton continued to hug his knees, but he blushed with pleasure to hear it. "I return the feeling," he whispered.

"Good for you. He's a splendid man."

Thorton began to smile. "Do you think so?"

"I do."

"I guess we are friends then. Thank you, Joshua." He gave him his hand.

Ferncastle took it and gave it a squeeze. "I wish you joy. You're a remarkable man, Peter."

Such a smile stretched across the younger man's face that Ferncastle could not help smiling himself. However, he was a doctor as well as a friend, so he said, "You must not overexert yourself. Lie down and rest so that you can sit up when Admiral Tangueli calls on you tonight."

Thorton obediently scrunched down in the bed, but he couldn't sleep or lie still. "I can't wait. I wish he were here."

Ferncastle watched him fidget, then said, "Ra'uf. Go find Admiral Tangueli. Tell him that Mister Thorton has been released from British service and is well enough to move, if he wishes."

The little man leaped up, gave the doctor a flashing white grin, and ran out.

After he was gone, Ferncastle spoke. "I wonder if I might ask you for a favor, Peter."

"If I can I will."

"I have made up my mind. I want to study at the Charity Hospital in Zokhara. Will you intercede on my behalf with Doctor Zahid?"

"Of course!"

"I want to study ophthalmology. Surely there is no greater thing a physician can do than restore sight to the blind."

"You must study Arabic. I'll help you."

"Thank you." They passed the next half hour in elementary Arabic lessons. Ferncastle found it difficult to pronounce, but being fluent in Latin and French, he found it easy enough to pick up the grammar and vocabulary.

Tangle arrived while they were thus occupied. The tall Turk was dressed in his undress purple coat with a modest amount of gold braid, no epaulettes, and no pelisse. It was a practical coat for getting work done; he had been in the shipyard overseeing repairs to the *Sea Leopard.*

Ferncastle withdrew to take a smoke in the garden. Ra'uf stood guard outside Thorton's door to make certain no one interrupted the them. Quite alone, with no fear of King or God, the two stared at each other for a long moment.

"Is it true?" Tangle asked. "Are you free at last?"

Thorton's grin split his face from ear to ear. "I am."

Tangle threw himself on Thorton and kissed him passionately. "Finally! Peter, I have never waited for a man as long as I waited for you. Then you went and got pneumonia and I had to wait again!"

Thorton laughed. "I'll be better in a week or two. I'll make it up to you."

Tangle kissed his cheek and felt the roughness of the beard sprouting on him. "You need a shave." Then he sniffed and said, "And a bath. I'll bathe you myself."

"That will scandalize the house! Won't you take me to your place to do that?"

Tangle grinned. "Are you well enough to move? Ra'uf said you were, but will Ferncastle let you go?"

"He will. He suggested it. Also Isam, he wants to study at the hospital in Zokhara. Can we take him with us?"

"If he can get the leave, yes."

"Good. I like him. He knows about us and doesn't mind."

"Then I like him, too." Tangle grinned at him, then touched his forehead to the recuperating invalid's. "Can you move today? I bought a house for the consul and moved in. I'm staying there while they work on the *Sea Leopard.*"

"Have the Portuguese paid up?"

"They have accepted financial responsibility for her repair, but we are still wrangling over Eel Buff. They have also told me that if I wait until after the coronation next week, they will redeem the letters of credit for the prizes at face value. So I am waiting."

"But you and I don't have to wait any longer."

Tangle's brown eyes were as hot and liquid as coffee. "No. Never again. You're mine, Peter."

Thorton threw his arms around his neck. "I can finally go home! I miss Zokhara."

Tangle held him tight. "Your friends have missed you, too." He kissed his face and brow. "Let's get you packed. I'll send Ra'uf to hire a cart and carriage."

Thorton dressed slowly and carefully and Tangle wrapped the turban for him. He donned the purple coat he had worn in the Salletine service. Carefully, hanging on Tangle's arm for support, he emerged from the sickroom to say his goodbyes. With Ferncastle dancing attendance and worrying about him, he tottered into the street. The radiant sun warmed them even as the breeze fluttered the skirts of their coats around them. The two lovers walked arm and arm to the carriage and didn't care what anyone thought. Tangle lifted Thorton into the carriage, climbed in beside him, and shut the door.

"I love you, Isam," Thorton whispered in the dimness of the carriage.

"I love you, too," Tangle replied.

The carriage rocked on its springs as it pulled away, leaving the Royal navy far behind.

THE END

.